# FIRST TIME
## (Penny's Story)

Abigail Barnette

FIRST TIME (PENNY'S STORY)
Abigail Barnette

## CHAPTER ONE

*Get your mind set. Confidence will lead you.*

That's what the fortune cookie that had come with my Thai lunch had said. And yes, I knew that fortune cookie fortunes weren't supposed to be real, and also that it didn't make any sense for one to come with Thai food. But fortune cookies aren't really Chinese. They were just made up in America and sold with Americanized Chinese food. So, if it didn't make any sense that they should come with Thai food, but they did, anyway, then what was to say the fortunes couldn't be real, even if they weren't supposed to be?

Standing on the sidewalk outside the wide white stone arch and tall double doors of One If By Land, Two If By Sea, I tried to get my mind set. Waiting inside the restaurant—hopefully still waiting, since I was about ten minutes late—was a guy who was supposed to be "perfect" for me. Or so said my boss.

"Trust me, he's perfect for you." Sophie had barely looked up from her phone as she'd texted him. She had a way of saying things that made her sound like the expert in whatever she was talking about, so I'd gone along with it.

Then she'd paused, squinted up at me and asked, "Maybe perfect? How do you feel about older guys?"

How *did* I feel about them? Sophie was married to a guy twice her age, and she seemed happy. If it was no big deal for her, why did it have to be a big deal for me?

The problem was the guy I was meeting wasn't just twice my age. He was thirty years older. He was a year younger than my dad, and two years older than my mom. And he was divorced. I'd never dated a divorced guy before. What was he going to expect?

This whole situation felt way too adult for me. I was an adult, but you know. Not a *real* adult. I was only twenty-two. Give me a 401K option, and I was on the phone to my dad quicker than you could say, well, "401K option". I had no idea what I wanted to do with my life, aside from the vague "I'd like to have a husband and kids someday" that Sophie had found so compatible with her half-century-old friend.

Everything since the day I'd graduated college had been a confusing mess, and this wasn't an exception. Was I really cut out for this?

Plus, there was my virginity, that one teensy complication I wasn't sure Sophie had accounted for. I had a hard enough time finding guys my age who were cool with not having sex; a guy who'd been thirty when I'd been born would probably be long past his days of patiently waiting for silly girls to sleep with him.

I fished the scrap of fortune cookie paper from my pocket. *Get your mind set. Confidence will lead you.* Maybe making up my mind would give me confidence?

I squared my shoulders, took a deep breath, and stepped toward the entrance. The doorman rolled his eyes as he held the door open. I didn't blame him; this was my fourth attempt to come in. I lifted my chin and pretended not to notice him. Oh! There was that confidence I was supposed to be getting! The worst that could happen, I reasoned as I stepped inside, was that I would meet this guy and not like him.

The restaurant was super dressy. Sophie had advised me of that beforehand, thank god. I'd worn my "Fête to Print" dress from ModCloth, because the subtle sequins and deep teal color made my eyes sparkle. I'd also worn about sixty pairs of Spanx to smooth everything down. I remembered my mother's motto: *Definite jiggle calls for decisive measures.*

I walked in like a person who could breathe and smiled at the maître d' as though I knew exactly what I was doing. "I'm here to meet someone. The reservation is under...um...Pratchett?"

"Of course. This way."

I followed along behind, my gaze darting nervously around the candlelit dining room. Shining silver chandeliers hung from the ceiling in front of a leaded glass rose window. Paintings of colonial figures hung on the walls, and diners sat at round tables with more candles. I was surprised it wasn't seven hundred degrees in the room from all the fire. This was exactly the kind of restaurant I'd been forced to go to for my father's work occasions or my mother's social functions. That didn't make it very easy to relax.

As we wound through the tables, I saw a guy near the corner who looked like he could be fifty-two, but he was with a woman who looked like she could be, as well. Another man sat at a table alone and looked very pissed off. I hoped that wasn't my date.

"Mr. Pratchett? Your guest has arrived."

I nearly collided with the maître d's back; I'd been too busy staring at the mean-looking man and corner dude. I stopped short and teetered in my matte black heels before I looked at the guy sitting at the table we'd stopped by, the guy I was actually there to meet.

The first thing I noticed was his eyes. They were very green and looked…concerned, I suppose would be a nice word for it. Terrified would be more apt but less kind. I wondered how bad I looked that he made the expression he did. It was hard to remember to assign myself blame for his reaction when it was so easy to focus on his intense gaze.

He stood. He was impressively tall. Sophie hadn't mentioned that, or the fact his black hair had a very hot going-gray thing happening. She also hadn't warned me that he had a weird, magnetic sort of charisma that would shock me to my toes.

His smile crinkled the corners of his eyes and drew lines around his mouth. "Penelope?"

"Penny," I corrected him, then regretted it. This restaurant was not a place were a Penny would go. This was a place for a Penelope if ever there was one.

"Ian." He put his hand out. I gave him mine, afraid he might try to kiss it. I hated it when guys tried to do that. Instead, he gave me a very firm, very awkward shake.

Okay. That was one way to start a date, I guessed. Maybe I should have brought my résumé.

The maître d' pulled my chair back, but Ian waved him off. "Let me. I'm trying to impress the lady."

That was cute. I'd give him that. He helped me scoot my chair in, and his fingers accidentally brushed my back. Tingles shot straight up my spine. So, clearly I'd gotten over my fear that I might not find him attractive.

When he took his own seat, he didn't say anything for a moment, and I worried that I had a tell, some twitch about me that clued him in to my thoughts. It was difficult to hold up under that scrutiny without cracking. I giggled and covered my mouth with one hand to hide it. "What are you looking at?"

"You," he said with an answering laugh. "You're... Well, I wasn't expecting you."

"Oh? What about me is so unexpected?" I flashed him a big smile, as though I were sure he'd say something overwhelmingly positive. Because no matter how he responded, I would just react as though it was complimentary. It was one of my ways of coping with extreme embarrassment. Just ignore whatever happened and move on. Since I found myself routinely embarrassed, I'd gotten really good at that technique.

"Well, maybe I should have assumed, because you're Sophie's friend..." He sat back in his chair and cleared his throat. "But I didn't expect you to be so young."

That was not even slightly what I'd thought he was going to say. "I assumed Sophie had told you that our ages were...way different. She told me."

"She probably figured you needed more preparation." He reached up and brushed the side of his nose with his thumb.

"H-how so?" I asked, my gaze following tha
until it disappeared under the table. *Oh, wow, So,
right, he really does have attractive hands.* But m.
importantly, Sophie hadn't told Ian that I was you
him? That was so rude!

He leaned forward slightly, as though he were te
some huge secret. "Imagine if you came in here, exp
some young, handsome guy, and here was a slightly
gray-haired old man. The fact that you showed up at ι
reassuring."

"Wait a minute, are you comparing me to a young,
handsome guy? That's kind of a weird compliment, but
take it." Usually, I hated when people made self-depreca
comments. It was hard to form a response to them, and it
made me uncomfortable. Of course, a year ago I'd been
making them nonstop; Sophie and Deja's confidence had
rubbed off on me.

But when Ian described himself so candidly, it made him
seem genuine. Like he didn't care if his flaws were on
display, and it didn't matter who brought them up first.

"When you put it that way, it does sound like a strange
way of flattering you." His smile was a bit goofy and
lopsided. Boyish, even, though I wasn't sure if that was
supposed to be a good thing.

I liked it, anyway.

"But you are not fat," I corrected him seriously.

He made a face. "You haven't seen what's under here."
He gestured to his chest with an open palm, as if to
encompass the whole of his body. "This is all a gory wreck,
courtesy of the ravages of age."

"Oh, shut up." My laugh startled me with the revelation
that I had actually relaxed some.

A waiter came over and offered us a wine list. Why do
they always show up right when things are getting
interesting? I listened to the man as he rattled off a lot of
words I didn't understand. To my horror, Ian was looking

xpectantly to me.

"Oh, um. You pick?" I looked from the waiter to Ian, my nails digging into my palms before I realized I was clenching my fists below the table. It wasn't as though I'd never been to a restaurant that had a wine list. I was just used to my parents ordering without consulting me.

"We probably don't want to order the wine until we've decided what we want from the menu. These are just suggestions to keep in mind," Ian said, and I instantly knew I'd made a gaffe. The waiter had probably been pointing out something of interest, not asking for our choices. Still, Ian played it off like it was no big deal and took the list. When the waiter walked away, Ian said, "Pardon my curious expression, I was just trying to figure out if you were of legal drinking age."

He winked at me, and my stomach took me by surprise with a giddy flutter. I felt the color rising in my cheeks. "Yes. I'm old enough. I'm twenty-two."

He made a low whistle. "That is…young."

Back to the crux of the issue. Why did I get the feeling that if Sophie *had* told him, he would have turned down the date? Which was all the more reason for her to have been honest. Now I was here, feeling foolish and unwanted, going through the motions of a date with someone who'd changed his mind.

I plucked up my courage and said, "Look, I'll understand if you're not cool with the age gap. I'm not going to be offended."

"Oh, neither will I, if you decide it's mad to be on a date with a man who's old enough to be your father," he assured me, still with that oddly endearing bluntness about himself. "But I came to meet a woman with whom my friend thought I would 'work well'. I think it would be short-sighted of me to not at least get to know a little about you."

"And I…" *…know that you're staying here because you feel bad, and everything is going to get a thousand times*

*more awkward*. But he was right. Sophie had matched us up for a reason. It would be silly not to at least try to find out why. So I finished, "…would like to get to know you, too."

"Excellent." He paused. "Although, at the moment, I'd like to get to know the menu. They brought them while I was waiting. I think they were hinting I should do something or surrender the table."

I winced. "Sorry I was late."

He waved a hand. "No, no, don't worry about it. It's New York, for Christ's sake; everybody's late going somewhere." He looked back down at the menu.

Back in olden times, the dude picked up the check at dinner. But this wasn't olden times, and I liked to buy my own food. This place, though, was just slightly out of the price range I was comfortable with. I liked fancy food, but I also liked paying my rent.

The lines of print wobbled in front of my eyes, and I looked up to find Ian tapping my menu. *Shit. He knows I'm broke.*

Somehow, when it came to money, I always felt stupid. Maybe because my parents had drilled into my head, every moment since birth, that I should "behave rich, live cheap". Having someone be able to tell you can't afford something? Just by looking at you? Horrifying.

"I hate to sound old fashioned," he began, and the crushing discomfort of the moment increased ten-fold, "but when it comes to some things, I am. Since I picked this restaurant, dinner is on me."

"Well, thanks."

He tapped the top of my menu. "Just so you know, that's not me angling for sex."

"I didn't think it w-was," I stuttered. *Oh god, get that under control.* The embarrassment train had derailed and spilled toxic embarrassment waste all over the place. I tried to make a joke of it, saying, "That was mortifying," but it didn't land.

I wasn't just embarrassed. I had second-hand embarrassment for *myself*.

Worst of all, he seemed to take my remark personally. "I know, I'm sorry. I heard it as it was coming out, and I couldn't stop it." He paused and muttered, "damn," under his breath. "I haven't done this in a long, long time, and I just didn't want you to get the wrong impression. I tried to look all of this up on the internet and—"

"You researched how to date on the internet?" I interrupted. That was so adorably vulnerable. Under all the weirdness and self-deprecating humor, he seemed like he was probably a very confident guy. I guess you'd have to be, to try and re-enter the dating pool with a complete stranger. I almost suggested he try this over, but with someone he knew well. Then I found myself becoming a little defensive and prickly over his imaginary next date, like she was moving in on my turf.

So…that was strange.

He winced slightly at my question. "I did. I'm not sure how great the advice was…"

"Tell me some of it. I can coach you," I offered. I put my menu down—I think I'd decided on what I wanted, anyway—and leaned my folded arms on the table. And, what the hell, I'd try to flirt a little. "I'm excellent at dating. I do it all the time. Sometimes even twice with the same guy."

*Oh. My god. Who the frick am I, Mae West?*

"Then, you sound like quite the expert." He was still deciding on food, so I couldn't tell what he was thinking. I hoped he didn't think I meant I was going on another date later and wasn't invested in this one. He set the menu aside, sat up straight, and said, "All right. Well, the first suggestion was 'don't talk about your exes'."

"That's definitely good advice. Don't talk about that until… Well, I don't know when. But I don't want to hear about it," I blurted. *How are you still doing this?* I was never this disoriented around a guy. I like guys. And I know I'm cute and fun to be with. I've had enough men tell me that. But my game had totally deserted me the second I'd gotten out of the cab.

"Oh my god, that sounded so rude. I'm so sorry," I apologized. Sophie had even told me he was newly divorced. I'd probably opened up some awful wound.

He started to wave it off, saying, "Don't worry about—" but our waiter came to the table, and he seemed a little impatient.

"Have you made your selections, then?"

*Rude.* I thought they were supposed to be nicer in fancy places like this.

Ian gestured to me. "If the lady is ready."

I'd totally forgotten what I'd wanted. I'd been concentrating on how much I was messing up this date. He was staring at me, probably wondering why I couldn't function like a human being, so I stalled, saying, "Oh, you go first."

"Sir?" the waiter addressed him.

"I'll have the warm octopus eschabeshe, I think."

Of all the characteristics that define me as a person, the one that I truly believe will be mentioned not only in my obituary, but my eulogy and the engraving on my headstone is my unwavering passion for octopods. They're one of the most intelligent, if not *the* most intelligent, invertebrate. They can solve puzzles and navigate mazes. They're incredible escape artists. Of all the creatures in the sea, they are by far my favorite. Actually, of all the creatures on the planet. I'd take a pet octopus over a pet dog, any day.

So, when this previously charming stranger announced his intention to *eat one*, every instinct I had was to flip the table and shout, "No!" at him like he was a puppy who'd gotten into the trash.

Instead, I made a high-pitched noise that was completely out of my control.

11

He raised an eyebrow and leaned slightly forward. "Is there something wrong?"

"No, it's nothing." The smile on my face felt like when you're waiting forever for someone to take a picture. "I just really, um. I really like octopods."

In a split second decision, I made up my mind to walk out of the restaurant if he tried to correct me with "octopi".

Instead, he looked a little impressed and said, "Really?"

"I do this donation thing to conserve the habitat of the giant Pacific octopus. *Enteroctopus dofleini*?" I glanced up at the waiter, whose expression said, quite clearly, *please stop talking.* But I couldn't. Conversational self-preservation is not a skill I possess. "But I love all of them. I even have a tattoo of one."

For a long moment, Ian just stared at me. Probably because he thought I was demented or that I had a little bucket of red paint in my purse to throw over his dinner, right before I ripped my dress in half to reveal a PeTA T-shirt underneath. That might have been why he said, "Then, I revise my selection, and I will have the lobster pappardelle, instead."

"And for you, ma'am?"

I wasn't sure if I should eat dinner since I'd already filled up on butterflies. My hand shook as I gave the waiter my menu. "The frog legs, please."

"Very good. Do we have a wine selection?"

A smile flickered at the edges of Ian's mouth. "What goes with frog legs?"

I wanted to laugh or make my own quip back. I would have settled for just reacting, at all. But I was still stunned that he'd changed his order for me. I tried to imagine Brad ever doing anything like that. He would have probably just made a face and told me to get over it.

That thought had to leave immediately. I wasn't going to compare this perfectly nice guy to Brad. It wasn't fair to compare anyone to your ex on a first date. And in this case, the comparison would have been extra tactless, because Ian…

Ian was starting to seem better and better.

But as he looked at me, his expression fell. He asked the waiter, "Could you give us a moment?" and the guy looked ready to stab both of us.

Oh great. Just when I'd relaxed and realized this guy actually, astoundingly, had potential, he was ready to cut out. I could sense it. I tried to hide my disappointment as he leaned in and motioned for me to do the same.

"This is, quite literally, the worst date I have ever been on," he began, and the butterflies in my stomach dropped dead. But he continued, "And I think you're in the same boat with me. Do you want to start over? Somewhere that we're not so pressured to be on our best behavior, and actually be ourselves?"

Maybe I shouldn't have felt the enormous relief I felt at his offer. Especially when I'd been trying to talk myself out of meeting him less than an hour ago. But Sophie had told me I would like him, and he would like me.

I was going to find out what she meant.

## CHAPTER TWO

A change of venue was exactly what we'd needed. I'd suggested a restaurant near my apartment, not because I thought I'd be taking him home or anything, but because I always got the best guidance from their fortune cookies.

With the way the date was going, I could use all the help I could get. Ian was the trifecta of confusion for me. My heart? Really, really liked him and wanted to get to know him better. My brain? Thought it was a crazy idea and had no problem listing off all the reasons why it was crazy, from our ages to the fact that he would willingly eat an octopus. And my body…

Okay, being a virgin? Doesn't mean I'm not interested in sex. And it definitely doesn't mean I have some iron willpower. The only thing that held me back so far was my stupid family superstition. Every woman in my family had found their true love, and it had always been the man she'd first slept with. Which was great and all, if they stayed together. But my great aunt Aggie had fallen hard for her first, and he'd married someone else. She'd been miserable for the rest of her life. My cousin Ashley had given it up to her high school boyfriend, and while she fully believed that he was her true love, the timing must have been crazy off, because they broke up and she immediately got pregnant with some loser football player's baby. So while I'd been tempted before—and oh man, had I been tempted—it wasn't worth it to risk my future happiness.

That said I'd almost jumped into Ian's lap in the cab. When he talked, he talked with his hands, and I'd somehow gone from innocently appreciating their sexiness to actively imagining them on me. Then I'd thought about how weird it was that I'd even think of him that way when he was so much older than me, which had led down the very dangerous path of reasoning that wisdom comes with experience, and maybe the whole superstition thing had more to do with coincidence than reality.

When we got our food, I ordered guaranteed breath killers: kung pao chicken with extra spice and pork egg rolls stuffed with lots of smelly cabbage. There was no way we were doing *anything* tonight.

Getting out of that stuffy restaurant had been a great idea. Now that we were alone, sitting on a bench in the deserted little park down the street from my apartment, we could really get to know each other. And maybe I was just a tad overeager, because as I paused in my recounting of my wisdom teeth extraction, he asked, "Wait…weren't we talking about Shakespeare in the park, a moment ago?"

I subdued a groan. "I talk too much. Sorry."

"No," he was quick to reassure me. "You talk just enough. Any more than this and you'd be overwhelming. But you're at a good level right here."

My frozen expression thawed with my relief.

He moved for his Styrofoam cup as he said, "Unfortunately, I know the name of the cat you left behind to go to college, and I know that cherry is your favorite flavor of cough syrup. But I think we skipped over some important information."

Ugh. How could I be this tragically awkward?

He went on, "Tell me about your family."

This was one of my least favorite parts of getting to know someone new. They asked about my family, I told them, and they would say things that sounded innocent but felt prying and personal. "Wow, it must have been lonely, being an only child," or "I bet you were really spoiled." The truth was, I'd been incredibly spoiled and unlikeable until I'd arrived at NYU and gotten the world's biggest you're-not-special-at-all slap in the face. Yes, my parents had indulged my every whim, but damn straight I'd been lonely. My father had worked all the time, and my mother had been so involved in her own career and various community activities that I'd spent a lot of days and nights with a babysitter. Of course I'd been lonely and spoiled, but it was humiliating to explain that to my best friends. Telling a stranger on a date? No, thank you.

"Ugh. Okay, please don't tell me this sounds lonely, but I'm an only child, and my parents are not close to their families, so it was kind of just the three of us."

He blinked and shrugged. "I don't think that sounds all that lonely. Honestly, around the time my last little brother was born, I would have been happy to live on my own in a cave somewhere."

My hair was coming dangerously close to getting into my food. I flipped it over my shoulder and hoped the motion didn't look as jerky as it felt. I'd never been able to pull off the smooth, graceful thing with my hair. "Why? What's your family like?"

"I'm the fourth of nine children—" he began, and I tried not to cut him off, but that was beyond out-of-the-ordinary. I'd never met anyone with so many brothers and sisters.

"Nine?" I almost spit half-chewed kung pao everywhere. I couldn't imagine growing up with eight siblings. I'd always wanted at least one, but nine was beyond excessive.

"Four boys, five girls." He seemed amused by my reaction.

I swallowed with a little difficulty and grabbed for my drink. "Wow. And do they all live in… You're from Scotland, right?"

"Yes. I am originally from Scotland." He nodded along as he answered. "And yes, all but one of my siblings still live there."

"So, how long have you lived here? The country. Not New York." I didn't mean to interrogate him, but he was way more interesting than I was. If I kept asking questions, he might not figure that out.

"Oh, about…" he paused, his brow furrowing as he

silently counted it up, "twenty…seven? Yeah, twenty-seven years now."

"Wow, I didn't know they'd let you stay that long." I put my drink down. "So, you were here before I was born."

Why did I have to go and say something like that? Right when we were getting comfortable?

It didn't seem to bother him. "Well, they don't really have much of a choice about letting me in. My dad is American."

"You've got dual citizenship? I've never met anybody who had that before!" I had no idea why that seemed so cool to me. Probably because I'd literally never been out of the country.

He grinned at me. "Well, I'm glad to be your first. I hope it was amazing."

I froze. Just for a second, but enough that he must have noticed, because we both stared at each other with this deer-in-headlights look.

He couldn't have possibly known where my mind went, or why, when he said that; I'd expressly asked Sophie not to mention the virgin thing, and I trusted that she hadn't. So…that could be a sign.

I filed the coincidence away, in case more came up later.

"What about you?" he asked. "Where are you from?"

"Pennsylvania. Harrisburg. Very upper-middle and boring." Nothing like New York. I wished I'd been born and raised in the city, like a "real" New Yorker. "But then, I moved here, gosh, almost five years ago, and it completely changed me."

There was that smile, again, that adorable smile that had made me immediately like him.

Well, sort of immediately. I just hadn't known it at the time.

"You grew a second head?" he joked. "Or you shed the superfluous head you already had?"

"Thank god. That second one was totally ugly." When he

teased me, it didn't feel like something I had to be defensive about. When Brad had done it, it had always felt like a put-down. "I just meant I went from having a personality that had been written for me by all the people around me, to coming to this place where I was a blank slate. I didn't have to fit in with my clique back home anymore—we were so The Plastics—"

He made a confused face. "Plastics?"

Oh, yeah. He hadn't been in middle school when that movie came out. "Yeah, from *Mean Girls*? It's a movie. Anyway, I felt like I had to fit in with them, I had to get perfect grades, make my parents happy. Now, I'm here, and I get to be whoever I want." I couldn't keep a straight face; I knew how silly and idealistic that sounded. "And, someday, I'll figure out who that person is."

He tilted his head and shook it sadly. "I hate to break it to you, but no, you won't. Look at me. I'm fifty-three years old, newly divorced, absolutely none of my life goals accomplished, and I'm out on a blind date."

"I'm on a blind date, too," I pointed out.

"Yeah, well, you're on a blind date, but you're on a blind date thinking you might meet someone new and exciting you can really connect with. I'm just terrified that you're going to start laughing at me."

I did start laughing, but not because I thought he was pathetic. It was because he somehow managed to be confident and vulnerable at the same time. I felt like I was actually getting to know him, in a way that was more honest than first dates usually felt to me.

"See, we're there already," he joked.

"Gosh, is that what I have to look forward to at fifty-three?" My laughter faded into contemplation. I studied him a moment, then turned back to my food. "You know, I like you a lot better here than in some stuffy restaurant," I said, my heart beating in my throat the whole time. I didn't just like him *better*. I *liked* him. Enough that it bummed me out to think this might just be a one-time date due to the age thing.

He cleared his throat. "I find you just unbearable, with your beautiful face and your infectious laughter. I haven't had a fun night like this for a while, and I just hate it."

I looked down, too embarrassed and flattered by his comment. I had to change the subject, or he'd see how giddy I was from his compliments, but my brain went totally blank. I tried to remember any other pre-game intel I'd gotten and thankfully remembered a bit. "Sophie told me you're an artist?"

"Ugh."

*Okay. Ugh. Not great. Thanks, Sophie.*

"Am I not supposed to ask?"

He grimaced uncomfortably. "You can ask."

Since he'd given me the go ahead, and I was curious enough to ignore the part where he'd only reluctantly given me permission, I looked back to my food and asked, "What do you do? Painting, sculpture—"

"Drawing," he interjected. "Portraiture, mostly. Figure drawing."

"So, people." Nope. I was not going to imagine posing for him. That was too *Titanic* a road to go down when I was already seriously attracted to him. "Are you any good?"

"Now, how am I supposed to answer that?" For a second, he sounded like he might be angry with me, and it shocked me. As he went on, it was clear that he was teasing me, again. "Am I any good? If I tell you, 'yeah, I'm fuckin' great,' I sound like I'm bragging. If I say, 'No, I'm shite,' it's like I'm fishing for compliments. Either way, I come off a fucking prick."

I couldn't help my startled burst of giggles. I covered my face with one hand. "That is the most swearing I've ever heard on a first date."

"This is me on my best behavior. I may as well own up to it, now," he said, like he truly didn't give a, well, a *fuck* what

I might think. It was nice to not get treated "like a lady".

I put my food down. I'd only been picking at it, anyway, and not to impress him. I was just too excited to eat. The date had seemed doomed before it even began, but now I saw all kinds of possibilities ahead of us. Possibilities I was even willing to open up a teeny can of hope for.

But it was way too early to get any farther than "gosh, I hope he calls me after this". One of my biggest problems was creating expectations and setting myself up for disappointment.

I reached into the paper bag our takeout came in, feeling for the fortune cookies. "Okay. We have to find out what our future holds."

"Or our lucky numbers and how to say 'pork' in Chinese," he said dryly. The wrapper crinkled in his hand as he opened it.

"I'll have you know, I take these things very seriously." *Like horoscopes and numerology and tarot cards*, I did not say, because I didn't want him to think I was some granola-fed new-age indigo child. I was just a little superstitious, but most people couldn't tell the difference between the two.

"What, fortune cookies?" He sounded surprised, and a little wary.

"A fortune cookie is the reason I walked into that restaurant tonight." I cracked mine apart and fished the paper out. "Aren't you glad I did?"

"I am. Maybe I'll start putting more stock into these, then."

"Mine says, 'Humor usually works at the moment of awkwardness.'" Wow, that summed up, basically, our entire date. That one was going into the jar. It was definitely a sign.

He hadn't said anything, yet, and there couldn't have been that much to read. "What does yours say?" I prompted.

"Nothing, it's stupid." He crumpled it in his hand. "And it's got a typo."

"A lot of them have typos." I reached for the paper, and

he jerked it away. My forward momentum didn't stop, and I caught myself with a hand on his knee.

Hmmm. Innocent, accidental physical contact, and he hadn't recoiled? Under the guise of trying to grab the printed fortune, I leaned across him.

He moved his arm out of my reach. "No! I don't want you to see my lucky numbers and steal the lottery winnings that are rightfully mine."

The side of my boob pressed against his chest, and it was enough of a distraction that he dropped the paper. I caught it and sat back, trying to disguise my rapid breathing. Whether it had been playful or not, being that close to Ian was a surprising turn-on.

I looked down at the red print on the scrap of paper in my hand. *The love of your live will step into your path this summer.* Well, there was the typo. But holy shit, what kind of fortune was that to get on a first date?

Not to mention the fact that that his first lucky number was an eight, and in numerology, my lifepath number was eight.

It was a sign.

Oh my god, it was a total sign.

I had to keep it cool, but the laugh I faked came out like a pig snort, and I sounded so ditzy when I said, "Well, I hope she hurries up. It's already August twenty-first."

When I looked at him, I couldn't keep fake-laughing. I couldn't say or do anything, at all, because I'd never received such clear messages from the universe before, and now even *I* thought I was reading too much into things.

So, maybe Ian wasn't destined to be the love of my life. That seemed like a long shot on a first date. But that didn't mean I couldn't hope for a chance to find out.

We were sitting there, just staring at each other, when the police officer came up the pathway.

"Uh-oh." I knew the park was supposed to be closed after sunset. There was a sign at the gate and everything. We'd broken the law. On our first date. This was going to be a disaster.

"NYPD," the officer identified himself. "Are you two aware that this park is closed from sundown to seven a.m.?"

"No, I can't say as I noticed," Ian said, not even slightly intimidated. And there really wasn't any reason he should have been; as a white, middle-aged taxpayer, he was pretty much safe from the police. I'd learned a lot about that subject from my roommate.

"Terribly sorry. We'll go." Ian stood and tried to shake the officer's hand, but the cop wasn't having it.

In fact, the officer looked suspiciously between the two of us. Did he think we were in the middle of a heist or something? "Miss, how old are you?"

Did he think I was drinking out here? Trespassing, yes, but public intoxication? Absolutely not. "I'm twenty-two. Do you want to see my ID?"

"No, ma'am." The cop wasn't looking at me, he was looking at Ian, like he was trying to figure out something bad he knew we'd been up to. "Are we on a date here?"

"Yeah, a blind date." What kind of a question was that for a police officer to ask? But if he was so interested in personal details, I could give them. "We were set up by a mutual friend."

"A friend? You mind telling me what kind of friend?"

"A work friend." I tried to smile at him and use my feminine charm the way I assumed would be effective with a policeman.

And then I totally understood what he was getting at. *Penny, you idiot.*

I had to fix this. I stood and waved my hands, trying to wipe away the entire notion he'd gotten into his brain. "Oh, no. No, no, no. I am not a prostitute. Not that there's anything wrong with sex work. I mean, besides the illegality of it. I don't know why it's illegal, I mean, if it's ethical and nobody is getting hurt—"

*Shut up, Penny! Shut up now!*

"I'm sorry. I'll stop talking, sir." But I didn't stop talking. I didn't stop at all. "Officer. Is that impolite to call you sir? I've never talked to a police officer before in a disciplinary…Am I getting arrested?"

"Penny works at a magazine," Ian explained. Thank god for him, because if I had kept going, I would have admitted to something, even something I didn't do, out of a guilty conscience. He stepped in at the right moment and prevented me from confessing to the kidnapping of the Lindbergh baby. "I'm old friends with her boss, and she set us up. That's really all that's going on here."

"Trespassing's your idea of romance?" the cop asked, but he seemed like he was starting to believe us.

"No, I took her to a very expensive restaurant where neither one of us were having a good time. This seemed like the better option. So far, I think it's going pretty well." It was possible that Ian had the most charming smile on the planet. But it was also possible that charm wouldn't work on a police officer who'd looked exhausted and pissed off the moment he'd approached us.

"I think it should be going away from the park." The way the officer said it, I didn't think it was a joke, but it seemed like it could have been a very dry one. He pointed his flashlight down the path. "I'm coming back around this way in five minutes, and I don't want to see you here."

I nodded, ready to prove that everything was on the up and up. "And we don't want to see you, either."

The look Ian gave me plainly said, "stop talking."

"We're going," he promised the cop. Then Ian reached for my arm and steered me gently toward the bench. At his touch, my skin prickled all over with need.

One of the worst things about my breakup with Brad was the absence of cuddling. Brad had been a champion cuddler—though in hindsight I suspected he'd never really been all that interested in cuddling for cuddling's sake—and

I liked touching other people. I needed it, like plants need water.

"Are you cold?" Ian asked.

"No." Then I realized that he'd felt the goose bumps on my arm, and possibly the slight shiver that had gone through me when he'd put his hand on my bare skin. I had to cover for myself. I rubbed my arms to feign a chill, even though the city night was like an oven. "Or, um. Yeah? A little bit?"

He took off his suit jacket before I could answer him when he asked, "Would you like my jacket, then?"

The last time a guy had done that for me, it had been at Dunkin' Donuts after senior prom. It had made me melt then, and it made me melt now. "Thanks. That's very chivalrous of you."

He put the jacket over my shoulders—it was warm from his body and smelled like his cologne, and I had to restrain myself from openly sniffing the lapels—and said, "Aye, I learned it in the thirteenth century."

He'd said "Aye." Not "yeah" or "yes." "Aye." Like Jamie from *Outlander*.

An older, less muscular, graying Jamie from *Outlander*, but still. If I could get him to call me *Sassenach* just once, I'd be happy.

He gestured to the cartons and cups on the bench. "Let's get out of here before Officer Friendly comes back."

We grabbed up our stuff and found a garbage can, and I realized too late that I hadn't kept my fortune for the jar. *Crap*. It wasn't like I was going to go back and look for it in the trash. That seemed like the way to assure there would be no second date, and I was really, really hoping there would be one.

We made it to the sidewalk without being arrested. "I assume we're safe here. Try not to solicit sex from me, though."

*Or, you know. Do.*

"I already promised I wouldn't. I'm a man of my word."

I had to get myself under control. I reminded myself—as I often found myself reminding myself—that I'd waited this long for a reason. But damn, it was really hard when everyone around you was having dessert and talking about how good it was while you were on a diet.

Ian reached into his front trouser pocket and pulled out a slip of paper. "Here. Hopefully, this rings true."

It was my fortune. He must have saved it for me when we picked up all our garbage.

I said, "We'll look back on tonight and laugh," because I couldn't think of anything original to say. He'd actually listened when I'd said I believed in fortune cookie messages. That was so sweet it was like sugar poured into the gas tank of my brain, and I couldn't make anything start up again. So I automatically asked, "Did you keep yours?"

I couldn't believe I said that. I might as well have asked him if I was the love of his *live*.

"Nah," he responded, and I could barely look him in the eye.

"Well, won't you be embarrassed when you meet the love of your live tomorrow and you don't have the proper paperwork." *Humor usually works at the point of awkwardness.*

The corners of his mouth lifted, and he said, with obvious reluctance, "Let me walk you home?"

I didn't have to check my phone to know it was getting late. At least tomorrow was a Saturday, and I could sleep in. But the night had gone so fast; I didn't want it to end.

We walked around the corner. My building was the second down the block, with the heavy gray door slashed with lines of a sloppy spray-painted anarchy symbol. As we went, we kept that careful cushion of personal space that exists between people who have been flirting, but weren't ready for purposeful physical contact yet between them. "This is me."

Ian might have thought he'd covered up his horror at my

living arrangement, but he'd failed. I'd challenge him to find rent lower than twelve-hundred a month without going to the other end of the of borough.

I remembered I was wearing his jacket and took it off. When he took it out of my hand, he did that thing guys in suits do, where they hold onto their jacket over their shoulder. Guys doing that? Did something to me physically. Something that involved a lot of throbbing.

"So…thank you. I wasn't joking when I said I was having fun. Even after the cops came," he said.

Then he looked at my mouth. He was going to kiss me. Oh my god, he was going to kiss me. My toes curled in my shoes. He was going to kiss me, a real, actual kiss, not just a peck on the cheek or an awkward first date hug. He leaned down, I took a breath and…

My breath! I jerked backward. "Nope! No. No, sorry, it's not you. It's just that my breath is really, really bad from dinner. I actually did that on purpose. I thought I might be tempted, so I went with spicy and full of cabbage."

"Oh." He felt rejected, that was clear enough from his surprised expression. Usually I wouldn't have felt bad; guys need to learn to live with disappointment. But I actually wanted to kiss him, more than I'd anticipated, and with a clearer head.

I had to learn to trust myself.

But I also had to be honest, right off the bat. If this became anything, I had to prepare him for the fact there wasn't going to be any third date sex. Or fourth or fifth. "It's just that… I like you, Ian. And you know how you said you were old fashioned about paying for dinner? I'm old fashioned about this. I move really, really slow, and I think it's only fair that you know that, if you were thinking about…calling me?"

"I was actually thinking about how much pepper spray was going to hurt," he joked.

The night had had its rough spots, but not *that* rough.

"Why would I pepper spray you?"

He chuckled. "Because this entire date has been a disaster, and I thought going in for the kiss might have been the last straw."

"It wasn't a total disaster."

He cleared his throat. I wondered if it was a nervous tick. "I'm a bit out of practice with dating, and I overstepped my bounds. But slow doesn't bother me. Slow, I can do."

I really wanted to believe that. On the other hand, I wanted to believe that I could manage to be slow with him, too.

"You know, police involvement aside, I had fun tonight, too." I twisted the toe of my shoe on the sidewalk. "Would you want to do it again?"

"Oh, I suppose I could stomach it." How was he so cool and dorky at the same time?

I couldn't be cool, not when I was thrilling to my toes about all the possibility packed into the conversation. "Well, good. I think you should be old fashioned and call me."

"No texts," he swore, and I almost swooned. I hated texting. Everyone else on the planet seemed to love it, so I did it when I had to. It was nice to meet a kindred spirit who would rather talk on the phone.

I didn't want to go inside, but it was perfect to end it right here. "Thanks for a really... Let's go with memorable. A really memorable night."

"It was my pleasure."

I stepped away, but every cell in my body wanted to stay. I turned back and moved fast, grabbing his tie and pulling him down to kiss him on the cheek. There. That was cute, and just the right amount of aggressive. "Have a good night."

My face was burning as I unlocked the door. Actually, it was probably flashing on and off like Rudolph's nose. At least it didn't make that weird noise.

I couldn't resist a look back at him. He was not the kind

of guy I was usually attracted to. But in the flickering glow of the nearly-broken light over my door, everything seemed unusual. This didn't feel like a usual date, at all. It felt like the start of something important, and I couldn't convince myself that it was my overactive imagination telling me that.

It was August twenty-first. I guess I would get my answer in a few weeks.

# CHAPTER THREE

My roommate, Rosa, would be on me the second I came through the door, and she would call me out if I was breathing hard and blushing, so I waited in the tiny vestibule at the bottom of the stairs, leaning against the mailboxes.

There was also no way she was going to miss the fact that my high-beams were definitely on. I had never in my life kissed someone on the cheek and had a physical reaction like the one I was feeling at the moment. The skin on my neck tingled—no, ached—from imagining his mouth there.

Then, there was the fortune. I didn't want to get my hopes up; it would be silly when we'd only gone on a first date. But cookies have never steered me wrong. Was I destined to be the love of Ian's life? Did I want to be? Was fate giving me a choice in the matter?

I climbed the four flights of narrow stairs to my apartment and slipped the key in the door. Our place is so small. Two teensy bedrooms on either side of a cramped living space with a weird, bay window-shaped end, despite the criminally steep rent we paid. I entered through the small kitchenette and saw Rosa had beat me to the dishes, again.

"I told you I would do those when I got home," I said in lieu of a greeting.

Rosa was sitting on the couch, watching *The Mindy Project*. Her dark, curly hair was pulled up in a sock bun. The torn-out neck of her sweatshirt dipped on her shoulder, and no bra strap showed. "Does it look like I had a lot of exciting plans tonight?"

I smiled to myself as I slipped off my heels and padded toward my bedroom. Rosa was too distracted by the television to ask about my date. Thank god for Hulu. Thank god for Mindy Kaling.

Of course I would tell Rosa about my date with Ian, but I

needed to process how I felt about the whole night. The evening really did have disaster written all over it, but it had been funny and exciting. *He* had been funny and exciting.

"No, no," Rosa called after me, pausing her show. "You're not getting off that easy."

"I know. You get the beer. I'll get my PJs."

When I was comfy and changed and Rosa and I each had a Bud Light in hand, I made a "bring it" motion. "Let's do this."

She got straight to what had been her biggest curiosity since the first time I'd mentioned that I was going out with an older guy. "How did he look? Did he look rough fifty? Did he look Brad Pitt fifty? What's up?"

I held out my hand and flipped it back and forth. "Business guy fifty? Is that a thing?"

She considered. "Hot dad fifty?"

I snapped my fingers. "Yes, exactly. But not in bad way. He's handsome."

"I'm going to need more."

I considered a moment. Altogether, he was good-looking, but I couldn't think of one feature that really stood out. Then I realized that it had been his expressions, his face in motion, that had made him so appealing. Without his goofy charm, he would have been average. "He has really nice eyes, and his smile is kind of... I don't know. Like a naughty little boy."

"Hot. Hair?"

"Black. With a lot of gray in it."

"Nose? Ears?"

"Eh. Ears just slightly on the large side."

Rosa nodded, with exactly the same expression Oprah has when she's interviewing Lindsey Lohan. Finally, she said, "Okay. So you think he's good-looking. How about the personality?"

"Really sweet." I snickered, remembering the way he'd said he came off as a "fucking prick" when talking about his artwork. "He swears like no one I've ever met."

"Even me?" Rosa sat up, like she was accepting a call to protect her honor.

"Yeah, unbelievably. But it doesn't even seem crass when he does it. Maybe it's the accent." Ooh, that was gonna make Rosa jealous. She had such a thing for accents.

Her eyes widened. "What kind of accent?"

"Scottish. He grew up in Glasgow." I grinned at her from ear to ear. "Not gonna lie, it's pretty hot."

"So, the date went well, then?" Rosa wriggled on the couch cushion. "You're going to see him, again?"

"Oh, the date was horrible. He took me to this crazy fancy restaurant and ordered *octopus*." It made me sad to even think about that, but he *had* changed his selection to avoid offending me further, rather than telling me I was overreacting. "It was going so not well he suggested we go somewhere else, so we ended up eating Chinese takeout in the park."

"Okay, that's kind of cute and romantic," Rosa insisted.

"Yeah, it would have been." I paused. "Except for the part where we got busted for trespassing and the cop assumed I was a prostitute."

"Nothing wrong with prostitutes," Rosa reminded me.

"I know. But there is something wrong with going to jail on a first date." Still, I couldn't help my giddy smile as I said, "And he tried to kiss me."

Rosa took a sip from her bottle. "Did you?"

I shook my head. "I kissed him on the cheek, though. And he said he wanted to call me."

"So, you're going to go out with him, again." She shook her head. "Okay. If that's your deal."

"What?" Here it was. I'd been expecting this ever since I'd told her I was going on a date with a much older guy.

"Well, I'm just saying. When you're thirty, he'll be sixty—"

"And I might not be dating him." *Oh really, Miss August*

*Twenty-First?* I ignored that snarky part of my brain. "I'm not making a lifetime commitment here. He's just really sweet."

"And you told him…" She raised an eyebrow.

"Ugh, no. I did not tell him." I rolled my eyes at her. "You don't have to say that like I have a terrible secret. You make it sound like I murdered someone."

"I just don't want this to go down like Brad."

My heart was still tender when it came to the subject of Brad. *I've spent two years waiting. Maybe if I'm not the one, I should go find someone who isn't afraid to fuck me.*

I swallowed the lump in my throat. Even though I'd dated Brad for two years, there had always been something about him, something I hadn't been able to put my finger on, that had prevented me from being totally convinced that he was the one. He'd managed to hide it for two years. "Any guy I go out with could end up being a jerk about it."

"That wasn't fair of me. It's not my place to worry about it. Sorry." She took another sip of her beer.

"It was weird, though. When I mentioned it, Ian didn't even react." Most guys either made a huge deal about how unusual it was for someone to be a twenty-two-year-old virgin or tried to joke about how they'd be the first. One guy had described it as "voiding the warranty".

I had *not* called him back.

After my early morning, the date, and now, the beer, I could barely keep my eyes open.

"Maybe it's better that he's an older guy. He won't come with any of the younger guy bullshit." Rosa shrugged. "I need sleep, and you look like you're going to pass out. But I'm glad you had fun tonight."

"Yeah, I really did." I motioned to the bottles. "Leave those, I'll get them in the morning."

I yawned and shuffled the few steps to my bedroom. "You wanna get breakfast?"

She made an apologetic face. "I can't. Transgender

women of color support group brunch."

"Right. Last Saturday of the month." I'm not such a bad friend that I would begrudge Rosa her time with girlfriends who shared the same experiences as her. "Tell Amanda I said hi."

Rosa shook her head. "I would rather stick my face in the blade of a riding lawn mower than talk to Amanda, but for you, I will convey this message of misguided politeness."

"Rosa and Amanda sittin' in a tree—" I didn't even get to the first *s* before she threw her slipper at me, and I shielded myself by closing the bedroom door before she could throw the second one.

As small as it is, my bedroom is like a little oasis for me. The twinkly white Christmas lights were something I should have totally left to my dorm room days, and I could barely fit my full-sized bed and nightstand between the walls. At least I had a shallow closet and two outlets, and there was space at the foot of my bed for a storage cube upon which to perch my teensy little twenty-seven-inch television. In a city of a bajillion people, I would take whatever private space I could get, even if it was tiny.

I decided I'd take off my makeup and brush my teeth in the morning; my feet hurt too much from wearing heels all night. My snuggly bed awaited.

Also, maybe some light research.

I'd held off on Facebook snooping before the date. That had seemed rude. But now that I'd met him, I wanted to know more. If he had a public profile, well…it wasn't really intruding, right?

I pulled up Facebook on my Kindle and tapped in Ian Pratchett. He was fifth down on the list, and his profile was public. *Jackpot.*

His profile picture looked like it had been taken on a boat, off the shore of some Mediterranean country with gleaming white buildings high on the bluff behind him. The water was sparkling blue, and the scenery was truly beautiful, but it wasn't the locale that interested me. Ian was shirtless and smiling, his broad shoulders suntanned. The dark hair on his chest was sprinkled with gray, and I saw no evidence of the "gory wreck" he'd claimed his body was. Sure, he had a little tummy, but seven days out of the month I did, too. It wasn't my place to judge.

Under "relationship status" it said, "single," and I breathed a sigh of relief. Not that people didn't lie about that sort of thing, but Sophie had said Ian was in the process of divorcing his wife. If he hadn't changed his status, I would have questioned that.

His wall was full of birthday wishes from July fifteenth. I flipped through my mental calendar. So, he was a Cancer with a Pisces influence. His cute, considerate manner hadn't been an act. I wished I knew his middle name. Or if Ian was his birth name, at all. I would love to figure out his lifepath number and how compatible it was with mine.

I tapped my way into his photo albums, and immediately wished I hadn't. The first album was titled, "Greece, 2013". The display photo was of Ian and a gorgeous, full-figured redhead in a playful embrace by the Acropolis.

That was his ex-wife. She looked like a 1950's movie star. I looked like a dollar store Barbie knock off.

Nope. I wasn't going to do this. They were divorced, and he seemed like he really liked me. This woman was no competition to me, and there was nothing to compete for. I'd been on one date with the guy.

Well, one date, and there was that fortune cookie.

But I wasn't going to bank on that until after Labor Day.

\* \* \* \*

My favorite part of Sunday is my run. I love to run, and I'm good at it. I ran track in high school, but in college, I'd gotten invested in long distances. The longest race I'd ever done was a half-marathon, and I was super proud of myself. But after college, I somehow had even less time to indulge. I'd thought when I'd broken free of papers and late night study sessions, I'd have a lot of free time, but now I only got a few days a week in, and only three and a half miles most mornings. Sundays, though, I was free to do my long run, and it was epic. I was guessing it was around eight miles; despite all the free apps out there, I'd never wanted to make it that strict. I just ran where I wanted, for as long as I wanted, and if I went too far, I'd get on the subway and go home.

My preferred route took me across the Williamsburg Bridge and back, then east again to run through East River Park, which had awesome pavement. I'd just reached the north end of the park and turned around when I spotted someone I thought I recognized.

Oh, fudgesicle. It was Ian. In a suit and tie, doing that hot over-the-shoulder-jacket thing, again. And I was wearing a running bra and a pair of spandex shorts, both of which were soaked in sweat, and absolutely no makeup. So, basically, the complete opposite of how hot I'd looked on Friday night.

He was walking beside someone else, so I kept my head down and hoped he wouldn't notice me, but I looked up at the last moment, and we made eye contact. His face lit up as he recognized me, and I slowed my steps and popped my earbuds out.

"Penny," Ian said with a big smile. "This is an unexpected surprise."

"All surprises are unexpected," the guy next to him said. "That's why they're surprises."

At first glance, I'd been too focused on Ian to really get a look at the man next to him. Now that I was closer, I could see that it wasn't a guy in a black t-shirt, but a priest in a short-sleeved black button down with a Roman collar.

So, I was now half-naked and sweaty not only in front of the man I had been wanting to go on another date with but his priest friend, as well.

Ian frowned at his friend's remark. "This sarcastic bastard is my nephew, Danny."

"Oh." I reached for the hand Danny offered and shook it. "Nice to meet you."

Ian gestured to a bench and said to his nephew, "Why don't you fuck off over there and give me some privacy?"

"Nice to meet you, too. He's been talking about you all day," Danny said, a hint of retaliation in his statement.

It worked, because Ian turned bright red and told me, "Well, not all day."

I blushed, too, ridiculously pleased with myself. I was glad I was already red-faced, so he wouldn't be able to tell. I gestured to his shirt and tie. "So, do you not have any other clothes? Or is this your park-going suit?"

"What?" He looked down. "Oh. No, I just came from mass. I'm feeling a wee bit overdressed, now."

His nephew was a priest, and they'd just come from mass. That was interesting new information.

I didn't want to make him feel like he had to stand there talking to me, so I pointed to the heart rate monitor on my arm. "Well, I'd better—"

"Yes! Sorry. I didn't mean to imperil your cardiovascular fitness." He put his free hand in his pocket. His sleeves were rolled up, yet another item on my hot list, and the dark hair on his arms was an added turn-on. "But while you're here, uh, I was planning to call you tonight. I thought it would look desperate and uncool if I called you yesterday, but now it's day two and I don't have to look desperate and uncool, because you're here and I can just ask you now." He stopped, made an expression that was more of a wince than a smile, and looked out over the river. "Would you like to go on another date with me? If you aren't busy on Saturday, I was thinking we could go on a picnic. A legal, daytime picnic."

I laughed, because I had to do something about the hysterical elation that swelled up in me. Combined with the endorphins I was already rushing on, my rapidly increasing crush on him was threatening to crack all my ribs from the inside out. "I'm totally free. And I would love to go on a picnic with you."

"Great. I'll call you this week, and we can hash out the details." His look of profound relief made me melt.

"Great," I echoed him. Then I gestured over my shoulder with my thumb. "I'm gonna…"

"Yeah. Have a good one. I'll call you."

As I jogged away, I mentally counted to ten, making a bet with myself that he would still be watching me. I looked over my shoulder. Sure enough, he was watching. I gave him a wave, which he returned with a nod, and when I turned back, I made a triumphant fist that I totally did not throw into the air.

On my run home, I couldn't stop smiling like a doofus. My ponytail swished a little more than usual behind me, and I'm sure people thought I was on a really cheerful brand of cocaine or secretly filming a tampon commercial. A day date? For a second date? He was definitely into me.

It was a general agreement among my friends and I that a day date meant that the other person wasn't trying to set a time limit. A day could turn into an evening, and an evening could turn into a night. If someone wanted to go on a day date with you, they wanted the option of spending a lot of time with you.

Normally, I wouldn't have agreed to a daytime meet up for a second date, but I hadn't wanted Friday night to end. The odds seemed good that we would hit it off that well again.

Unfortunately, it might also mean telling him about my no-sex policy. But I'd found through trial and error that it was better to share stuff like that right at the beginning, so neither of us would be disappointed if it wouldn't work out. But he was Catholic, so maybe he'd be cool with the virginity thing.

They were big into my kind.

## CHAPTER FOUR

As much as I loved my job, I usually dreaded Monday mornings, but I knew Sophie was going to have questions about my date, and Monday was one of the days she was in the office. Tuesday through Thursday she worked from home, which was fine by me because that meant I had only one editor-in-chief to assist.

I arrived at eight and slid Sophie's usual coffee order— small sugar-free vanilla cappuccino—onto her desk in anticipation of her arrival. Then I sat down and opened her schedule and Deja's. Deja was my other boss. She'd founded the magazine with Sophie and was one of those people who were so cool they would be intimidating if not for how nice they are. She has dark skin, with a gorgeous glowing tan, probably from laying in the sun at Sophie's seaside house in the Hamptons. Her hair is always changing; currently she was sporting a short bob that tapered to the back of her head on one side, while the other was shaved super close. She was the first to arrive, coming in with her stylish navy linen jacket already off. She lunged for a hanger on the coat rack.

"That's my job!" I jumped up like I was going to rush her for it, and she held out a hand.

"Get back or so help me god, you'll never hang up a coat in this office again!" she warned. "I will throw this coat rack out!"

"Guys!" Sophie came through the door, balancing a square pink box on her arm. "I got cookies. You don't get cookies for fighting."

Sophie sported a totally weird Marc Jacobs sundress that looked like a wadded up army tent with black shoulder straps. She had paired it with a bright yellow crop top, and pulled her sleek dark hair into a high ponytail. She wore a lot of strange stuff, but she was the editor of a fashion magazine, so she knew better than me what was fashionable.

Deja pulled the tail of her ruched-sided black blouse from the back of her skinny jeans and cracked her neck. She was the only person who could dress like a rock star in dark colors in the summer and pull it off. "All right. What are we doing today?"

"Staff is coming in at nine—you had to cut hours from payroll after last month," I reminded them, tapping the wireless trackpad for the Mac on my desk. "Deja, you have a ten o'clock with a representative from Illamasqua. Sophie, you're interviewing Grace Smith from Barneys for your editorial feature at nine-fifteen, and both of you are supposed to be in the conference room at ten-thirty for the October pitch meeting.

"In the meantime, Sophie has to approve the photos for the tights piece, and you both have calls to return." Before they could ask, I added, "I've forwarded their messages."

"Oh." Deja looked at Sophie and shrugged.

"Yeah, we'd better get to it," Sophie said, and they both headed off to their offices.

I rolled my eyes and waited. They only got a few steps before they dissolved into laughter.

"Okay," Deja said as she turned back. "Obviously we want to know how it went."

"I have seriously been dying." Sophie grabbed a chair from another desk—our office is open floor plan—and practically used it as a scooter to pull up beside me. "How did it go?"

"It went…really well." My smile grew as I once again pored over the evening in my mind. "It started off just horrible. Sophie, why didn't you tell him I was twenty-two?"

"Because I thought he might not show up if I did," she said defensively. "And he would have been missing out on some primo Penny."

"You didn't tell him?" Deja exclaimed in disbelief.

"He totally freaked out. I think he was looking for the *To*

*Catch A Predator* guy to pop out from somewhere." I shot Sophie a pointed look. "But we ditched the restaurant, got some takeout, and ate it in a park."

"See?" Sophie said triumphantly. "I bet it was really romantic."

"It was!" I agreed. "Until the cops showed up and thought he was trying to buy sex from me."

I watched as the color drained from both of their faces. "He handled it like a pro. Almost too good. Do you think he solicits sex from women in the park a lot?"

"I'm guessing probably not," Sophie assured me.

"Okay, so, how bad are your other dates, if you would describe this one as going well?" Deja asked dryly.

"It was so bad it was funny. And…pretty fun." I sighed and told Sophie, "Yes, I liked him. A lot."

"Are you going out again?" She asked.

I nodded. "We ran into each other yesterday in East River Park. I was out for a run and caught him after church—"

Sophie sat up straight, her eyes wide. "Ian? Goes to church?"

"I guess so." It made me a little bit happy that I knew that and the person who was friends with him didn't. It made our connection independent, somehow. "He said he would call me about going on a picnic on Saturday."

"And he was okay with the whole…" Deja gestured at me like I was wearing a big red V on my chest.

"I didn't tell him. It's not exactly something you tell a guy on a first date." People who knew I was a virgin always seemed to think I started every relationship with a disclosure. The way I saw it, sex was no guarantee for anyone. It wasn't an obligation. If Ian found out that "go slow" might mean "go nowhere", it was up to him if he was willing to walk away. "If a guy can't be happy with me without having sex with me, then I'm never going to be happy with *him*."

"Good for you." Sophie lightly tapped my arm with her

fingers. "And I bet he really liked you."

Hopes I didn't realize I'd had fell a little. Now that I thought about it, maybe I'd been expecting some intel from Sophie regarding how Ian felt about me. "I think he did. He tried to kiss me, but my breath was so bad, I turned him down. I really regretted that."

"I'm sure you'll get your chance," Deja said. "Look, we've got a busy day. Enough gossip. And Penny? You get four minutes today to sigh dreamily and stare into space, but that's it."

"Understood," I swore, crossing my heart.

I would have to set a stopwatch on my phone.

* * * *

Central Park on a Saturday in August was nuts. It was the worst idea in the history of bad ideas for a date, which seemed fitting; Ian's fancy restaurant gig was the mythical dream first date, and it had blown up horribly. So maybe having the second one in a bad location would go really well.

I hopped up the steps from the subway and crossed the street, and pulled the map I'd printed off the internet out of my purse. I'd lived in New York for a few years, now, and I could still get lost in the communal backyard. I couldn't afford to go unintentionally exploring in the shoes I was wearing.

Yes, it was stupid, beyond stupid, to be wearing strappy high-heeled sandals to a date in Central Park. But I didn't care. I wanted to look hot. I wanted Ian to be interested in me.

I just wanted Ian.

Over the week, we'd talked on the phone four times. They were short conversations about the logistics of our picnic, but both of us lingered at the end of them, like we didn't want to hang up.

"This whole thing shouts mid-life crisis," Rosa had

warned me before I'd left the apartment. "And a quarter-life one for you. You're both acting like middle schoolers."

Maybe that's what made it so fun.

My heart was beating like crazy by the time I reached Turtle Pond. I stepped to the side of the path so as not to be run down by cyclists, put away my map and found my phone, all while juggling the handled paper bag full of highly bruise-able fruit over my arm. I dialed up Ian's number, scanning the area. There were so many people around, but my eyes zeroed in on him. Who was I kidding? Everything zeroed in on him. He was wearing jeans—an odd choice, considering how hot it was, but at least they weren't Obama jeans—and a casual white button down with the sleeves rolled up. He was also standing with his back turned to me. I could have just told him I saw him and headed on over, but I had a much better, much sillier idea.

"I have managed to get us the perfect spot," Ian answered, instead of a hello. I noticed he had a habit of just picking up in the middle of a conversation we weren't having. "But you've got to act fast. There are some sinister-looking hipsters nearby, and they've got anti-capitalist literature."

What a dork. But the cute kind of dork. "I am in the general vicinity. Stand up, so I can find you."

I picked my way across the lawn, wobbling a little in my stupid sandals as I passed a guy in a Papa John's delivery uniform napping on the grass.

I'd almost reached Ian by the time he said, "I am standing up. Where are you?"

Just before he could turn, I tapped him on the shoulder. He startled and fumbled his phone as he turned, and his shock and annoyance vanished as I smiled at him. "Fruit and water, as requested."

He pointed to the blanket he'd promised to bring and said, "Something so you don't have to touch the grass." Those were the exact words I used when I'd requested it. He added, "And sandwiches."

His gaze strayed obviously to my bare shoulder. I'd gone out and bought a new sundress for our date, because I got stupid when I came down with a crush. The fabric was pale daisy yellow and light as a breeze, with spaghetti straps that tied at my shoulders. The bodice was blousy and pintucked above the vintage high waist, so it disguised the ruffle on the bandeau I wore to restrain my breasts. I wanted to look good, but there was no way I would have worn an actual strapless bra outside in this sweaty heat.

But I doubted Ian was appreciating the structure of the garment, so much as he was imaging untying the long, loopy bows on my shoulders. I'd spent the entire train ride alternately fearing that a stranger would pull one and fantasizing about Ian doing it. So I recognized the sort of dazed look in his eyes; I'd seen it in my own in my reflection in the train window.

"You look very pretty today," he said, shaking himself from his momentary trance.

I felt my smile becoming too beauty-pageant for words, but I couldn't help it. My brain went one hundred percent goofy, too, because when I tried to compliment him, I ended up insulting him. "Thanks. You look good, too. I like that you ditched the undertaker look."

"Undertaker? That's a bit harsh, isn't it?" He sounded actually hurt a bit.

I quickly added, "Nah. Sometimes the undertaker look is sexy."

It wasn't a lie. Men in suits were hotness catnip. When the guy had a genuinely sweet personality, too? Bingo. But even without the suit, Ian was handsome. Just not in the way I was used to qualifying handsome.

Any offense I'd caused must have been forgiven, because he put his arm around my shoulders and drew me close to his side. I held my breath; the contact of his bare forearm against my shoulder made me hyperaware of my skin in ways I never had been before.

"Let's sit down. It's been a battle not to eat both of these sandwiches myself."

I leaned into him. It felt unreasonably good. Too good. "Well, you wouldn't have had any water, so you would have gotten thirsty."

Ugh, my brain was not working. I blamed the hug. Of all the things I'd expected when I'd agreed to go on a date with a fifty-three-year-old man, the last thing had been that I would find him overwhelmingly sexually attractive.

Better to change the subject. I sat on the blanket and made sure my skirt wouldn't fly up then reached into the bag. Fruit. Fruit was a safe, nonsexual topic. "So, I brought strawberries and peaches." I squinted at the alleged peach as I examined it. "I thought I got peaches. Live and learn."

"In this case, learn the difference between peaches and nectarines." He reached out and playfully snatched it, adding, "I like these better, anyway."

I appreciated the effort at making me feel less stupid. "Show me the goods. You've been bragging up these sandwiches all week."

Before he could make a move, I pulled the picnic basket toward us. The only thing I'd eaten all day was the banana I'd bought at the same market I'd gotten the strawberries and nectarines from, and that was just to ensure that I didn't pass out from low blood sugar on the train over. I'd had nervous stomach all morning. It had all cleared up the moment I'd arrived. I guess I'd just been worried that our plans would fall through and I wouldn't get to see him. But now, those nerves were gone, and the scent wafting from the basket put me just a step below "newly-infected rage zombie" in terms of hunger.

He reached into the basket and pulled out sandwiches wrapped in tinfoil. "Grilled Cubans. You said you liked ham, so here you go."

I do. Oh, I *do* like ham.

Going into raptures over how much I liked ham would have probably been off-putting, so I just lifted the edge of the foil and took a long, greedy inhale. Whatever was in the thing, it was amazing. I spotted roasted pork in addition to the promised ham, some pickles, Swiss cheese and whole-grain mustard.

There was no way I could politely nibble. "I'm going to be rude and dive right into this."

"I don't mind at all," he said, unwrapping his own.

I took a bite—and probably got mustard seeds stuck in my teeth—and my eyes rolled back in my head. I may have even made some not-safe-for-work noises as I savored it. Wiping a little dribble of grease from my lower lip, I forced myself to act like a person and not a wild food scavenger. But I couldn't downplay how awesome this was. "Oh my god. This sandwich is a religious experience."

"I told you," he said, taking his own bite.

"Where did you get these?" I grabbed a bottled water from the bag and gave it to him before I opened my own.

He swallowed and said, "There's a deli not far from my place that makes fantastic grilled sandwiches. They do a portabella panini that's phenomenal."

I mentally added *loves sandwiches* to the list of positive qualities I'd noticed about him. But I needed a more specific location with regards to these, just in case things didn't work out between us. "Where do you live?"

"Brooklyn. Dumbo."

I had no idea where Dumbo was, but I'd heard people say it in reference to the neighborhood before, so I knew he wasn't insulting me.

The most important thing was, I knew what train to ride to get closer to the mythical deli. "Get out! I work in Brooklyn!"

"I know you do," he said with a laugh that slightly embarrassed me. Of course he knew where I worked. I worked for Sophie. He went on, "Do you know the gray building with the clock tower? Used to be a textile factory, but now it's all condos?"

"I wouldn't know what it used to be, but you mean the big square clock tower with the green roof?" Wait, if he lived there, and I worked nearby, did that mean I finally knew were Dumbo was? I'd always been too afraid to ask. "Is that your building?"

"It's my clock tower," he said.

He couldn't mean… "You live in there?" Before he could answer, I jumped the gun and added, "That's so cool!"

He nodded, clearly downplaying the awesomeness of living inside a clock. If *I* lived in a clock tower, I would introduce myself that way. My business cards would say, "Penelope Parker, clock tower dweller." If I had any business cards. No, actually, I would *get* business cards, just to put that on them.

"I would love to see it, sometime," I blurted, before I could remember how rude it was to assume an invitation. "You know…if you're cool with that."

"I think I could be very cool with that." But as he said it, his gaze shifted, like he was seeing something very grim happening just slightly in the future. And it wasn't momentary; it was like he'd completely checked out.

"Ian?" I asked, though I felt like I was somehow intruding by interrupting what appeared to be a thoughtful moment.

He snapped back to himself and looked a little sheepish. "Sorry."

Judging from past experience—our singular past experience—I was pretty sure Ian was tense about our date. And last time, a pretty large portion of that had been caused by the internet. "You seem really tense. You weren't reading a bunch of bad dating advice again, were you?"

He couldn't hide anything with that face of his. "I may have done. You should be impressed. Do you know how difficult it is to find *second* date advice?"

I leaned forward, like I was telling him a secret. "You made it to the second date. That means whatever you did on the first date was fine."

"Was it? I don't know these things. I'm rubbish when it comes to dating." He looked so lost I was starting to feel really sorry for him. But I wanted to laugh at him, too. He had way more life experience—and way more romantic experience—than I had, but he was more nervous than I was. Maybe ignorance really was bliss, then?

I reached into my purse for my phone. "You're doing fine. But where are you getting your advice?" Nah, we needed a more decisive plan of action. "Never mind. I'll look it up. What did you google?"

I hadn't thought he could have looked any more embarrassed, but he went from the color of pink Starburst to the color of a red Solo cup and mumbled, "'Dating don'ts for men.'"

"Don'ts". Not "do's" for how to get a chick in bed with you. Not "how to trick a woman into having sex". At least, not that he was admitting. The results loaded, and I turned the screen out to him. "Which one?"

He hesitated before tapping on the first link. "Why are you so interested in this?"

*Because I'm a genius.* "Because. We are going to break every single one of these rules." I bit my lip as I read the list. Maybe it wasn't the greatest idea. The very first one was about money, and that subject made me more panicky than a cat on a car ride. But it wouldn't be fair if we just went over all of the stuff that made him uncomfortable. "That way, you wouldn't be so nervous anymore."

"Ah, because the worst will have already occurred." He still seemed reluctant, which was good, because then I could pretend to be full of bravado about the whole process.

I stared at "don't talk about money" while I chewed another bite of sandwich and tried to bolster my courage. *Look at me! I'm brave! Fearless! I've got everything figured out!* I lied to myself as I read the first one. "'Don't talk about money.' Okay. Ian, I make thirty thousand dollars a year."

Whether he was surprised by how much or how little that was, I couldn't tell. Maybe he just hadn't expected me to give him my annual salary like that. He responded, "I, uh… I make three hundred."

"Three hundred thousand a year? I thought architects made like eighty or something." *No. No, no, no.* Now he would know I'd researched his salary. Personally, I felt like that should be acceptable for anybody who was agreeing to go on a date with anyone else, but other people hadn't been raised with the money weirdness I had. I probably looked like I was fishing for marital assets. It was better to be upfront about it than try to cover it up and dig a bigger hole. "This sounds so nosy of me, but I looked it up."

"No, it's fine. That's one of the first questions anyone asks me, anyway. After, 'so, uh, do you like, draw buildings and stuff?'" He finished his sentence in a surprisingly good imitation of an American stoner. "I'm a partner at our firm, and we do big ticket commercial work. It's not the average salary."

I wondered if I should try to compliment him about how successful he was, but that seemed tacky. Was it tacky? To people who hadn't been raised with money as a primary focus of their life? "You're doing better than me, at any rate. Okay, next on the list…" Yikes. Whose bright idea had this one been? "It's 'Don't bring up the b-word.' I assume they mean babies and not Beetlejuice?"

"You want them, right?" he asked, and before I could get offended at his wild assumption that, as a woman, *of course* I would want babies, I remembered he'd probably talked to Sophie about that.

"Yup," I confirmed. "And Sophie said you did?"

"I do. In fact, that could lead us into number four. It's why my ex-wife and I divorced." He took another bite, like he could cover up the bitterness in his sentence with the salty, buttery amazingness of the sandwich.

It probably would work.

But the fact that he remembered what number four was, off the top of his head? That made me want to hug him and promise everything was going to be okay for him. Instead, I said, "Yikes," and tried to move us into more cheerful territory. "Well, how many do you want to have?"

"Ex-wives?"

I rolled my eyes. "Kids. How many kids do you want?"

Having heard all about his giant family, I was relieved when he said, "Not as many as my parents had. Three or four, at most. But I'd be happy with just one. You?"

"Three, I think. Any more than that and they can overpower you." Not that I would know.

"Isn't that the truth? About when, do you think, you'd like to have kids?"

The question shocked me with the realization that, hey, I might be talking to the guy I ended up having kids with. And he might be talking to the future mother of his children, too. I managed a squeaky little sigh to let off some of the giddy pressure and tried to come up with an answer that didn't sound too much like *now, right now.* "I'm still really young, and I know that. But I want to have my kids young. Within the next two to three years."

There. That would give us a while to figure it out.

He smiled. "Well, it would never work out between us. I was going to wait another fifteen years."

"Oh, shut up," I said, laughing. But he hadn't answered the question, and he was fifty-three years old. Even if everything worked out perfectly between us, I didn't want to be having my first baby with my seventy-year-old husband. "But seriously, that's a pretty important one. If we ended up..."

"You're right, it is important." Most of the time we'd spent together, Ian had been affable and charming in the way that people were affable and charming when they were first getting to know someone. But now, he turned serious, and I appreciated that; if the topic split up him and his wife, he clearly didn't want to make any future mistakes where this was concerned. "I would say that if something were to work out, and I were to find myself in a committed relationship within the next year or so, and things were just right... I'd be ready to start. I'm not getting any younger. I just turned fifty-three in July, so the clock is ticking."

Within the next year or so didn't seem quite so far away when it was the time frame for a major life change like having kids. And it was weirdly pleasing to know Ian was able to accept that as a possible eventuality for us without running away screaming.

*But speaking of running away screaming...*

There was nothing so disappointing as reaching this part of the getting-to-know-you stage only to have everything fall apart, but it had happened to me more times than not. And while I'd sometimes used my virginity as a handy excuse to ditch dates I wasn't interested in, I *was* interested in Ian. But number five was coming up.

It was now or never.

"Okay, we talked about number four," I said, a sick feeling rising in my stomach and threatening to spoil that lovely sandwich. "So, let's go on to number five. 'Don't talk about sex.'"

"We just did, in a roundabout way. Unless you don't know where babies come from. In which case, I have some shocking news for you," he said, like we were both in on the joke somehow.

Oh, if he thought *he* had shocking news...

"Look, Ian. I have to tell you something, and it might be a deal breaker."

"All right. I suppose if it is, this is only our second date, so it's better to find out, now?" His reasoning was the same as mine. That didn't make it suck any less that chances were high he'd be getting up and walking away.

*Rip it off like a Band-Aid. And it won't even be pathetic if you go home and cry.* I took a deep breath and said, "I'm a virgin."

## CHAPTER FIVE

"I'm sorry, what?"

My face was hot, and not just because it was a sunny day in August. "I've never had sex with anyone."

Ian's "Huh," had to be one of the most infuriatingly obtuse reactions I'd ever experienced.

Huh? What did he mean by *huh?* What was I supposed to think he meant by it?

Then he said the awful thing that so many guys had said, right before they realized I wasn't joking and I could see them becoming visibly uncomfortable: "Well, I hope this isn't a deal breaker, but I'm not."

I knew I shouldn't have gotten my hopes up, but disappointment came crashing down on me hard. I didn't have the grace to be kind when I felt like the wind had been knocked out of me. "You have no idea how often I hear that."

"I'm sorry. I didn't mean to offend you." He did look sorry, and that helped soften the blow a bit. But I'd gotten the I'm-not-a-virgin joke from enough guys that I knew what it meant. The next thing Ian asked would be...

"Do you mind if I ask why?" It was like he had a script.

I summoned up a gentle, Zen-like patience. "No, I don't mind. The why is, I haven't found anyone yet that I wanted to have sex with. I'm not super religious, or waiting for marriage or anything. I'll just know when it's the right guy." And that was that. I couldn't sugar coat it, and I wasn't about to bend or apologize. Or tell him it was because of a family superstition. That would only make me look ditzy as hell. Instead, I shrugged and told him, "If you can't handle that in a relationship, I understand. That's where my ex-boyfriend went. I think he saw himself as being able to conquer my virginity."

It sucked that, because I hadn't felt comfortable or ready to have sex yet, I had to be so defensive about a choice that was mine and mine alone. There had been guys—Ian definitely did not seem like one of them—who felt like my acceptance of a second date, or a third, had been false advertising. Or they wanted me to feel grateful to them, that they would accept such an unreasonable restriction. Brad had been one of those guys.

"He sounds like a shitty boyfriend."

Had Ian read my mind? I froze in place for just a blink.

He must have taken that as a sign of offense, because he said, "I'm sorry, that was uncalled for."

Uncalled for or not, it was nice to hear it verified by an independent party. "No, you're right. He was a shitty boyfriend. It just took me a while to see it."

Was the same thing happening with Ian? Was I seeing some funny, kind of dorky older man as hot because he was new? Eventually, that novelty would wear off, especially if he turned out to be a jerk about this. And I really, really wanted him to not be a jerk.

I held up my hands and let them drop to my lap. "So, now, you know what I mean about 'going slow'. Like I said, there won't be any hard feelings if—"

"Well, I don't know if you noticed last Sunday, but I'm a Catholic. Not having pre-marital sex is something we're supposed to be very good at."

That was…unexpected. Maybe because I wanted so badly for this to go forward, to really get to know each other, I'd figured it was doomed. But he'd answered so easily and quickly. He hadn't asked if he could sleep on it and call me if he decided he could *handle* the situation. He hadn't made some insulting attempt at humor about how he would *cure* me. He'd just accepted my words at face value.

My eyebrows were never going to come down from my hairline. "Oh. I kind of assumed that would be a date-ender. It has been in the past."

"Nah. I said I was fine with slow." He looked out at the pond, the way he'd looked out at the river when he'd asked me to come on this date. I wondered if it was something he did out of nerves. Did talking about sex make him nervous? He reached for his bottled water. "I wasn't expecting to have sex with you any time soon, anyway."

"Good. Glad we're on the same page." I picked up my phone, but I could barely read the words on the screen. Talking about sex with Ian—even though we were talking about *not* having sex—made me imagine having sex with Ian. I'd never wanted so badly to reassure a man that my virginity didn't mean we'd be playing Yahtzee and chastely holding hands. With a surge of horny bravery, I added, "But just so you know, I give great hand jobs, so there's that to look forward to."

He sputtered, water bursting from his mouth in a sloppy spit-take. "Jesus! Give a man some warning."

I laughed to myself and scrolled down the phone screen, because I couldn't look him in the eye at the moment. I couldn't believe I'd said that. "Let's go onto the next one, since you just mentioned it. We're not supposed to bring up religion."

"Technically you brought it up, by running into me in the park on Sunday," he said.

Oh my gosh, did he think I was stalking him or something?

I was about to defend myself when he went on. "So, are you religious? 'Not religious, but spiritual'? Are you a druid?"

"No. I wanted to be a druid, but I just couldn't get past the human sacrifice." I reached for a nectarine. I didn't want to get strawberry seeds in my teeth. "I'm not religious. Or spiritual. I wasn't raised in a religious family, so it never occurred to me to pick up a faith." Well, a faith besides financial success. "I went to bible camp with my best friend when we were in high school, but it didn't change anything.

But I am *very* superstitious."

"That's fair. At least you're not a godless Protestant."

I couldn't tell if he was kidding, or if he was actually *that* Catholic.

"Catholic joke," he clarified.

I knew absolutely nothing about Catholicism, and definitely no jokes about it, but that didn't stop me from trying and failing and embarrassing myself. "Right, because of Henry the Eighth."

I took a bite of nectarine, because it would taste better than my foot.

"Sure, yeah." Ian cleared his throat and asked, "Are there any more items on the list we haven't covered?" and I couldn't tell if he was offended by my remark or not.

There was such a high potential to look like a jerk when I tried too hard, but I could never seem to stop myself. "Pets," I read, grateful for the subject change. "It says guys don't like hearing about our cats on first dates. That's rude. It's not like every woman who has a cat is a cat lady."

His eyebrows rose. "I have a cat, and I'm not a cat lady. Of course, I'm not a woman, either."

"You have a cat? I love cats!" I couldn't remember ever meeting a single guy who owned a cat. Maybe it was his ex-wife's cat, and she didn't take it with her? Either way, Ian considered it his cat, and that was going on the "pro" side of my pros and cons list. But just so my enthusiasm didn't scare him, I added, "Which is probably the exact reaction 'don't talk about pets' was warning you about."

"Ambrose is a great cat. And I'm not just saying that. He's never once peed in my shoes." He paused and picked imaginary lint from his shirt. "Except for the shedding. I could do without all the fucking shedding."

"Hey, you used the f-word!" I blurted. I'd been delighted to hear it; on our first date, he hadn't started swearing until we'd both relaxed and started actually communicating.

"I'm sorry. I do curse a lot. It's something I should work

on."

I hoped that he didn't. I kept a pretty clean vocabulary, myself, unless I got a little alcohol in me, but I enjoyed people who had the confidence to fling obscenities like candy at a parade. It was funny, as long as the situation wasn't inappropriate. Sometimes even when it was.

"No, it's fine! I think it's a sign that you're loosening up. Maybe all the taboo topics did you some good." I dropped my phone and took another bite of my nectarine, noting the way Ian's gaze moved to my mouth. Even though I hadn't had sex yet, I still appreciated feeling sexy. The way he was looking at me, I felt the way Rihanna must feel every single time she looked in a mirror.

There was that flirty bravery again. I slowly dragged the tip of my finger across my bottom lip to wipe away a drop of juice while he watched like he wanted to lick it off himself.

"So. Do you feel any better, now that we've made all the mistakes?"

He shook himself out of his momentary trance. "I do. Honestly, I don't know why they say not to talk about these things on first dates. It would get a lot of out of the way right at the start."

"But imagine if we'd had this conversation on our first date. At the restaurant. Where you wanted to kill an octopus," I teased. It would have been a disaster if we'd tried to talk about any of the things we'd just talked about, because every word out of our mouths had been some sort of misunderstanding at the time.

"The octopus was probably already dead," he defended himself. "I didn't realize you were so passionate about them. I didn't realize anyone was that passionate about them. Speaking of which... I have to know where the tattoo is."

"You don't have to know." I was going to tell him, but the flirting was too fun. "But if you *want* to know..."

He reached for my hand, pulling it away from where I smoothed down my skirt. The moment his skin touched mine, goose bumps stood up on my shoulders. His hands swallowed mine between them. My heart beat out of control. I couldn't remember what we were talking about.

Then he said, very serious, his voice low, "Penny. May I please know where the octopus tattoo is?"

I couldn't tell if I was relieved I hadn't made a fool of myself over his joke or disappointed it had been a joke. With a nervous laugh, I pushed his hands away and said, "Yes, fine. It's on my right hip, in front. And it's about the size of a fifty-cent piece."

He visibly swallowed.

"Do you have any tattoos?" I tilted my head as I considered the possibility. "You seem like the type." Or maybe I just wanted him to be the type. The foul language, the drawing, I kind of wanted to find out he was some reformed bad boy with an artistic soul.

"There's a type?" It sounded like news to him. "No, no tattoos. I've never felt the urge."

*Well, damn.* "Here I was, imagining that under your suits and ties you were hiding some sexy bad boy past." I finished my nectarine and wrapped the pit in a napkin.

"The extent of my sexy bad boy past are some very stupid pranks I pulled in college."

Ah, well. You can't win 'em all.

I leaned back on my hands. The sky was bright, crystal blue and dotted with cumulus clouds. It was exactly the kind of sky you'd expect on a hot summer day. It reminded me of *Up*, and how my friends and I had left the theatre and gone back to my house to lay on the grass and point out shapes in the clouds while we talked about what college was going to be like.

That seemed like such a long time ago, now.

"This was a perfect idea. Even if it's a little crowded." There were women next to us having a competitive-sounding conversation about their babies' weights and percentiles, and two artsy types sketching the castle across the pond. Joggers and cyclists and tourists crammed the paths, but our little blanket felt like a calm, private island in the sea of activity.

"Is it?" Ian looked around us. He was obviously way more used to being constantly surrounded by tons of people than I was.

That was one thing I hadn't gotten used to in New York, and since I'd been living here for four years, I probably never would. Everyone was right on top of each other.

"Yeah, I just noticed, myself. I guess I was so caught up in—" *you*, I finished mentally. I waved at the picnic basket between us. Suddenly, it seemed like a total third wheel. "Here." I moved it then scooted a little closer to him. "We still have room to stretch out. I want to do something I haven't done in a really long time. Since Pennsylvania, actually."

It was a little difficult to lie down on the blanket and get comfortable without my skirt flying up, but I managed, and folded my hands over my stomach because I was far too aware of my body in the moment. "You have to look up," I told him with a nod.

He hesitated but got down on the blanket, too, close enough to me that his arm brushed mine. "I assume we're looking for shapes."

"Yes. And then I'm going to judge whether or not you're a weirdo or a pervert based on the shapes you see." And speaking of weirdos and perverts, there seemed to be a giant set of tits floating in the sky. "Oh my gosh, that one looks like boobs!"

"I was going to say an ice cream sundae, but look who's the pervert, now," he said dryly. "The sky today looks like something out of a cartoon."

"Those are cumulus clouds," I said without thinking. After years of hearing "no one likes a know-it-all, Penny," from my mother and seeing exactly how true that was with guys I'd dated, I should have learned by now. "Sorry. I didn't mean to sound like a know-it-all."

He gave me a strange look. "You don't sound like a know-it-all. But you do apparently know it all. First octopuses, now this?"

"Octopods," I corrected him automatically and cringed. "Sometimes, I can be overbearing, I know."

I couldn't face him. I felt like everyone I met got the same idea: that I was full of myself, that I thought I was a bigger deal than I was or smarter than everyone else. And I didn't feel that way, not one bit. Most of the time, I felt the exact opposite of smarter-than-everyone-else.

"Hey, no. Don't do that," he said softly. He sat up a little, propped on his elbows. "There's nothing wrong with being smart, Penny. Jesus, I'm fifty-three, and I didn't know what that kind of cloud was. I don't remember what any of the clouds are. I would have said cumulonimbus."

"Nimbus is only added if there's precipitation involved," I said, and I bit my lip to stop myself from saying anything else.

His expression shifted, like a barrier had crumbled between us. I'd shown him more than I'd realized. I'd shown him vulnerability, a hole in my super-peppy-positive-Penny armor.

"Penny…can I kiss you?"

My throat closed up. I became dizzy with the ridiculous thought that this didn't feel like just a first kiss, but a first step. And maybe it was too early to think that, but I wanted it, as badly as I wanted to know what his mouth felt like.

I nodded. "Yes, please."

He rolled to his side, rising on his elbow and leaning down. He planted one hand on the blanket beside my waist, so his forearm lay across my ribs. I was sure he could feel how erratic my breathing was.

What the heck was I doing? This was a public park, with people all around, and I didn't care one bit if they saw me kissing a man in broad daylight. Public displays of affection weren't really my thing—at least, this public—but as Ian's mouth touched mine, I couldn't worry about that anymore. Just the smallest contact flushed all shame from my brain. I lifted my head and just went for it, opening my mouth under his, hoping he would follow my lead when I darted my tongue against his lower lip.

He didn't just follow my lead, he took the lead, sweeping his tongue into my mouth, stealing the breath from my lungs.

There's nothing in the world like a first kiss. Tingles zipped from my mouth to the very best place. Ian quickly rose from top five to number one first kiss of my life. It was the most toe-curling, vagina-clenching kiss I'd ever had, first or not. Now I understood how this could have woken Snow White.

I dove my hand into his hair and resisted the temptation to push him down to my neck, my collarbone, my—

"Excuse me!"

The voice was so loud and sharp, I reacted on reflex, jerking away from Ian as he leaned up on his elbow. The women with their babies were staring at us like they'd just seen us slaughter a goat right in front of them. I couldn't look them in the eye, so I pretended to fix my hair.

"Excuse you," Ian replied. "The lady and I were occupied."

"Maybe you shouldn't be occupied with *that* in public."

I snuck a peek at the woman. She was wearing yoga pants and a tank top that said *serenity* on it. She needed to get back to whatever yoga studio that was, pronto, because she had clearly lost her Namaste.

Knowing Ian's love of and proficiency with obscenity, I wondered if he was going to fly off the handle or something. It seemed unlikely, for as chill as he was, but this lady was being super rude. So it surprised me when all he came up with was, "Maybe you should mind your own business."

I chanced a look at the women. They were both packing

up their things.

Then one of them said, "You're old enough to be her father. You should be ashamed of yourself."

I could get objecting to someone making out in front of you—even though there was an entire park full of other people they could have gawked at instead of us. But I didn't understand making such a cruel remark. It had to have embarrassed Ian terribly. And if he was embarrassed…

Would he be too embarrassed to go out with me, again?

And that was it. That's what made me snap, "Take your ugly babies and fuck off."

The moment it came out of my mouth, I hated myself. I recognized the tone of my voice, and it was the immature, stupid girl from Pennsylvania, being cruel just because she could.

If Ian hadn't been embarrassed before, he probably definitely was now.

The women took off fast, while Ian sat there in stunned silence until he managed to choke out a "well".

I covered my face with my hands. "I am…so sorry, that was totally inappropriate and immature."

"Well, you didn't have to insult their babies. That was a bit over the top."

My heart plummeted so fast I imagined it shattering on the ground. But Ian reached out and skimmed the backs of his fingers down my arm, and his touch assured me we were still getting along.

So did his next words. "But if this is something…ah. I know we just met, and this is our second date, but I'm hoping there will be more in the future. And if there are, people are going to comment on the age difference."

His touch gave me goose bumps, so I rubbed my arms. "I know. And I know people will be rude, because people are people. But I like you, Ian. I want to go out with you, again." I laughed. "I want to make out with you again."

"Well, I'm not going to turn you down," he said hoarsely,

and cleared his throat. "And I like you, too. Just so we're even on that score."

I looked down at the blanket and over at the teenagers who were trying to watch us in the wake of our verbal altercation. "Look, I ruined our picnic—"

"They ruined our picnic," he corrected me. "And it's not ruined. We can still have a good time here."

"Yeah, we could do that." I cocked my head. "Or…we could go to my place and do that make-out thing I just mentioned."

His eyebrows went up. Way up. "What happened to going slow?"

"I didn't say you were going to get to round all the bases." I hadn't kissed Brad until our third date. Hot and heavy making out? I hadn't even *wanted* to for a couple months. When I had done it, it had been because I'd felt I'd owed him something. I didn't owe Ian anything. But I really wanted to give something to him.

Not *that*. I still had no idea about *that*.

He scratched the back of his neck and looked away from me. "I'm tempted. I'm sorely tempted. But you said you wanted to go slow. And I want to respect that."

That was sweet. In theory. He was still turning me down, and I couldn't help but worry this was all because I'd lost my temper at those women, and now he was reevaluating me, in general. But that was stupid, because he'd just said he liked me. So what was the problem?

"I've got an idea," he said suddenly. He pointed toward the two teenagers down by the water, drawing the castle. "I'll be right back."

He walked off with purpose, calling out, "Hello there," and crouched down to talk to them. I wasn't sure what he was doing, but he took out his wallet and gave them a bill. Was he buying drugs?

One of them ripped a few pages out of their sketchbook and passed it to Ian, then took a pencil behind their ear and handed it over. Ian stuck out his hand, gave both the people a hearty handshake, stood, and came back like nothing weird had just taken place.

"Um…what was that?" I asked him once he got close enough to hear me.

"Oh, those are my new friends, Nate and Lexi. Lexi was kind enough to sell me her sketchbook." He held up the pencil. "What do you say? May I draw you?"

I took a breath and made a surprised noise I couldn't control. "Wow. Yeah. I can't believe you would pay someone for their sketchbook, just to draw me."

He shrugged. "Money well-spent. It gives me an excuse to stare at you without being creepy or uncool."

I pulled my legs criss-cross applesauce beneath my skirt and sat up straight. "Okay, but if you're going to draw me, you have to make my nose a little shorter."

"Never. Your nose is perfect." He sat across from me and flipped the wire-bound sketchbook open. Then he looked up at me, and I wasn't sure what I was supposed to do. I must have looked nervous, because he smiled and said, "Just relax. You're not sitting for your presidential portrait."

"I've never had anyone draw me before. It's kind of nerve wracking." And sexy. To have someone scrutinize you so closely was exhilarating. I'd never experienced that before, since I'd spent large enough chunks of my life trying to be seen but not looked at. Like a pretty vase or something.

God, that was sad. It was even more sad that it took a virtual stranger being nice enough to just look at me, really look at me instead of letting his eyes pass over me on the way to the next thing to realize how miserable my view of myself had been until that moment.

"It's nerve wracking for you? I'm the one performing here." His gaze darted down to the page, and he made his first marks. I couldn't see, but it seemed like he'd drawn a really fast circle. The pencil jerked around in short, sharp, but very deliberate movements. He kept looking up at me, and his expression was inscrutable. I found myself doubting every part of my face. When he looked too long at my chin, was it because it was too prominent? What did he think of my lips, that his eyebrow twitched up like it did?

I knew what I thought of *his* lips.

The silence was suddenly stifling. The park seemed loud and irritating, when it hadn't been before. I had to distract myself, even if it meant distracting Ian. "I'm trying to not say anything. I don't want to break your concentration."

His brow furrowed as he studied the page. "You're not going to break anything, Doll. I'm almost finished, anyway."

*Doll*? Was that a cute pet name? It was our second date, so I assumed he used it for just any woman he was attracted to. It still gave me warm feelings in my stomach. "Doll?"

His face went beet red, and he kept his gaze trained on his drawing. "It's like honey, or baby. It just slipped out. More creepy second date behavior on my part."

"I'll just interpret it as you being comfortable enough with me that you could accidentally give me a cute nickname." I tried to imagine six months from now, hearing him call me "Doll" every day. I could have melted. "Where did you come up with Doll?"

In hindsight, I shouldn't have asked. What if his answer was "I call all women that" or "It was my pet name for my ex-wife"? I didn't want to know any of that.

"If I tell you, I'm going to sound like a desperately clingy person you'll want to run away from." He erased something on the paper.

Run away. As if I would want to do that. "No you won't, I promise. If I didn't try to run away from you when you tried to murder a defenseless octopus, I won't run away, now."

His mouth bent in a reluctant, close-mouthed smile. Or maybe it was a grimace at what he'd just erased. "My father used to call my mum that. It's very common."

That was a much better answer than I'd feared it would

be.

"So, you're superstitious," he said suddenly, because silence wasn't comfortable for us yet. "What about, besides fortune cookies?"

I used to be ashamed about my silly reliance on signs, until a friend of my mother's started exploring her spirituality when I'd been in high school. My mother hated my insistence on picking through the grass for four-leaf clovers—I'd never found one—and my daily horoscope emails. But then Cheryl told me, "There's no such thing as coincidence," while reading my tarot cards, and I suddenly hadn't cared anymore. I'd learned a universal truth—at least, it had seemed like one to me—and I stopped being shy about sharing it.

Less than a year into her spiritual awakening, Cheryl's presence at my mother's Friday night book club was no more. It had been too late. My belief in red flags from the universe had become non-negotiable by then.

I shrugged and said, "You know, horoscopes. Numerology. I believe in signs. So do you, right? Signs from God? Isn't that a Christian thing?"

Wait, was Catholic and Christian the same thing?

If I'd made a gaffe describing his religion, he seemed unfazed. "It is. I wouldn't say that I listen to them. But yes, I have had times when I've thought maybe I was being pushed in a certain direction. Sometimes, when something illogical is happening, you have to look for a pattern to make sense."

It was something Cheryl could have said, with her wise, no-nonsense tone. And everything clicked into place about Ian.

The fortune cookie had not been wrong. It had not been a coincidence, since they didn't exist. Our star signs were compatible. I hadn't done any serious charting or anything, but I knew that, in general, Cancer and Scorpio were an okay match.

A bubble of elation and delicious anticipation burst inside

me. And even though we were on our second date, even though I knew I was falling too fast, I knew I was falling *right*.

So I just said, "Yeah. I know that feeling," and let a moment of what felt like mutual understanding linger between us.

"So, horoscopes, then," he said, breaking the momentous tension. "I'm a Cancer, and you're a…"

"Scorpio. My birthday is actually October thirty-first. I was crushed when I realized the cause for all the dressing up and candy collecting wasn't a celebration of my birth, but something that had been going on for a really long time." I loved that memory, even though it had been devastating to six-year-old me. Every other person I'd met who shared my weird birthday seemed to have the same story.

He chuckled, tilting his head to examine the drawing. "Well, that explains why you're superstitious. What do the stars have to say about us?"

"What, like, romantic compatibility?" He nodded, and I said, "Scorpios and Cancers work together really well. I mean, you're probably stubborn and opinionated, but I'm stubborn and opinionated, too. But both signs have a lot of energy relating to family and home. Our relationship would probably be pretty intense."

It already seemed intense. Maybe that was just the force of my attraction to him.

"Is that a bad thing?" he asked.

"No, it's not a bad thing." I considered for a blink. "I'm Mars. You're the moon. Your sign is all about the loving and nurturing in a relationship, and mine is about the romance and the passion."

"You can't claim exclusivity there. I'm dead romantic when I put my mind to it."

*Well, duh, Ian.* I smiled at the utter foolishness of his declaration. Of *course* he was romantic. Not many guys sat down and seriously drew a woman's portrait on their second date. Well, maybe art students trying to get laid. But not guys who turned down the possibility. "I can tell. This is probably the most romantic thing anyone has ever done for me."

"I'm not going to take too much credit, because this is really the bare minimum." He handed the sketchbook to me. "Here, all finished."

I'm not sure my heart had ever beat faster than it did at that moment. The drawing he'd done, even in the short amount of time it had taken him to produce it, was the most idealized version of myself I'd ever seen. Was this how he saw me? This gorgeous woman with the wistful expression on the page? "It's incredible. I had no idea I was so pretty."

"Yes, you did," he teased.

I conceded with a nod. "I am really hot." *I just didn't realize how hot you thought I was.* "But this is… this is beautiful. Can I keep it?"

"Of course," he said without hesitation.

I hugged the sketchbook to my chest and kissed him on the cheek. I couldn't help it; it was a kiss on the cheek or a full-on tackle. "I love it. I really do."

And that was the moment I started to fall for Ian Pratchett.

## CHAPTER SIX

The thing with day dates is you can make them last for a really long time. And we definitely had. After the picnic, we'd dropped our stuff at Ian's car—he had a car *in the city*—and took a walk, until he noticed the hell my heels were putting me through. He'd driven us to get drinks at a lovely, almost too-air-conditioned bar. We'd started talking, and before we'd known it, drinks had turned into dinner, and dinner had turned into sitting in his car at the curb in front of my apartment until the sun went down and it was getting dangerously close to being tomorrow.

Ian looked at the clock on the dashboard. "I hate to cut this short, but mass is at ten a.m. And Danny is going to kill me if I don't come to his church tomorrow."

"Cut it short?" I laughed. "Ian. We've been hanging out since two this afternoon. I'm pretty sure we broke a dating rule here."

"Some rules are made to be broken." It was such a cliché thing to say, but coming from him, it sounded kind of dangerous and flirty. He turned off the car—I was surprised it wasn't out of gas by now from running the air conditioner—and gestured to the building. "Come on. I'll walk you to your door."

My door was a whole sidewalk width away, but I let him walk me, anyway, because I was pretty sure I was getting a kiss goodnight. In fact, I'd been anticipating it ever since that fantastic kiss in the park. But between then and now, nothing. He hadn't even tried to hold my hand or put his arm around me. I decided it was because he respected my request that we take it slow, and that it wasn't a comment on my desirability.

I reached into my purse for my keys, distracted. We might be taking it slow, but emotionally, I was already way too into him. Which was so stupid. I knew it was stupid, especially given our situation. Thirty years was one hell of an age gap to have to overcome.

"You look very grim," he said, and though his tone sounded light, there was a nervousness under his words. I thought I was an open book when it came to emotions, and obviously I was, if he'd picked up on my split second of doubt. But he was just as transparent.

"I was just thinking about how much fun we had today." I stopped myself on the edge of revealing too much.

He frowned. "If that was meant to be reassuring…"

"No," I answered quickly, then winced. "I mean, I had a really good time, and—" what the hell— "I hope we keep having fun. I want to know how this story ends."

*Because I'm falling for you, and I'm afraid I'm Cinderella at quarter to midnight.* I didn't want the spell to break. I would be heartbroken; not forever, but even a day or a week would suck. I'd let myself get in way over my head.

He put his hands in his pockets, hunching his shoulders, and looked away. Looking away seemed to be a signal that he was about to say something significant, and it frightened him. That's when he made eye contact with me, again, and I almost dissolved like cotton candy as he said, "Maybe it's better to hope that it doesn't."

He leaned one arm against the building, above my head. I'd forgotten our height difference; beside him, I felt tiny but not threatened. The intent in his expression was clear. I rolled my tongue over my bottom lip as he leaned down, and I tilted my face up.

"This is ill-advised, at the very least," he said, his mouth just millimeters from mine.

"Yeah, I'm way too young for you." But my hands came up between us to rest on his chest, and then we were kissing, my fingers curling in his shirt to pull him closer as the brick wall met my back. His free arm curved around my waist, and our feet tangled. I was pinned. I liked it.

A car door slammed somewhere down the street, and Ian looked up, panting.

"Nobody's going to see. And if they do, they won't care," I said, pleading.

He lowered his head again, the arm on the wall coming down to join the other around my waist. It was a good thing, too. I was breathless and weak-kneed as his tongue swept over mine, and every inch of my skin buzzed, from collarbone to kitty. My ability to stand was imperiled.

Someone, someone very near us, dropped their keys on the sidewalk.

It was my turn to break off our kiss. "Rosa!"

"I'm sorry, I was trying to sneak past." She narrowed her eyes slightly as she looked Ian over. Then to me, she said, "Carry on."

The door closed behind her, and Ian stepped back, laughing as he scratched the back of his neck. "Remember those signs from God you were talking about?"

"Yeah, he is clearly reminding you that you have church in the morning. That's my roommate. You'll have to meet her sometime when you haven't just been feeling me up in front of her."

"I was not feeling you—"

"I'm fucking with you, Ian." I stood on my tiptoes, brushing my lips against his. "Just one more?"

He groaned. Not loudly, just enough that I felt it rumble through his chest as I opened my mouth. The kiss was far too brief.

"I'll call you tomorrow. If that's not too soon," he said softly, stroking the backs of his fingers down my jaw.

He could leave right now and call me in twenty minutes, and it wouldn't be too soon. "Not too soon at all."

"All right. I'll talk to you tomorrow, then." He kissed me again, just a quick peck, and headed to his car.

A strange, crushing feeling swelled in my chest as I unlocked the door, like I missed him already.

*You're not being sensible, Penny. You're going to be let down, and it will be nobody's fault but your own.*

When I got a chance to figure out our numbers, I would have a clearer picture of what was happening between us, and exactly how much I could count on us being a good match. Which reminded me…

"Wait! What's your middle name?" I called after him, not caring how weird the question probably sounded.

He stopped with the car door half opened and turned to me with a bemused expression. "David. Why?"

"Designing our wedding invitations," I said, laughing.

He grinned and slid into the driver's seat. "You're a frightening woman."

I went inside and waited behind the door until I heard his car start and drive away.

"What the fuck was that?" Rosa demanded when I came upstairs.

I shrugged. "That was Ian."

"Yeah, and that was Ian's throat you had your tongue down on your second date." She went to the kitchen, pausing in her scolding as she went about the loud, rattly business of filling the teakettle and setting it on the stove.

When the tea came out, I knew it was therapy time.

"It's not that big a deal." It was a big deal, though. I'd been on two dates with Ian, and I was already falling for him. That was something I never let myself do. "Ugh, you're right. This isn't me. I'm careful—"

"Some would say over-cautious," Rosa interrupted.

I gave her a what-the-hell face. "Is this the conversation where you're telling me to slow down or speed up? Because—"

"I'm just worried that this guy is a rebound for you." She gave me a pitying grimace. "And I'm worried that because he's a rebound, things are going to get too intense, too fast. When that happens… Are you going to be okay, honey?"

"First of all, things *are* too intense, too fast. And yeah, that's on my mind. But this doesn't feel like a rebound. It feels like…destiny." Okay, even *I* thought that sounded overly syrupy.

"Please don't get mad at me, but I have to ask. This guy is…middle-aged," she began, and I knew "old" had formed in her brain first. "What kind of future are you imagining here? A year or two of hanging out and fooling around? Something more permanent?"

"We've both got basically the same five-year plan." Why did I feel so defensive? "He wants to have kids within the next couple of years—"

"Whoa, whoa!" Rosa shook her head in emphatic denial. "You did not talk about kids already."

"We did, but it was under a totally benign set of circumstances. He got all this really bad dating advice from the internet, so we did the opposite, just to get it out of the way." That was reasonable, wasn't it? "And Rosa, he's so nice. He doesn't correct me constantly or cringe like I'm embarrassing him. Even when I did sort of embarrass him today."

I wished I hadn't snapped at those women in the park. At least, I wished I hadn't let their babies take collateral damage.

"And all of that is nice and sweet, but your five-year plan? At the end of that, you're going to be twenty-eight. And he's going to be almost sixty." Her words were an ice-cold bucket of reality splashing in my face.

My heart sank. "I know. But I can't help it. I really like this guy, Rosa."

She nodded in sympathy. "And there are a lot of other guys out there. Guys you can spend the rest of your life with, instead of the rest of their lives. Somebody you can grow old with—"

"Instead of them growing old without me, I get it." When she laid it out like that, it sounded a lot less exciting, and lot more bleak.

But I wanted him. I wanted to talk to him and have breakfast with him and learn what television shows he liked. I wanted to hear him call me "Doll" in a sleepy voice and hate the same grocery store cashier as me. I wanted to pick out paint samples and watch him clean gutters; not on a clock tower, obviously, but that wasn't the point. I just wanted, and wanting sucks.

"I'll run the numbers, see what they have to say," I said weakly.

"Mmhm." She went to the stove and groaned. "It would have helped if I'd turned the damn burner on."

I laughed, but she brought me back to serious town with a pointed look. "Numerology? Astrology? Those things are probably not what you need to make a decision this big. I know, you live by them. But maybe it's time to just sit down and make a cold, logical decision."

My gaze flicked to her phone on counter. The lock screen said it was one-thirty.

Trying not to freak out about the fact that Ian and I had spent almost twelve hours together, I raised an eyebrow at Rosa and turned our conversation sharply around. "So. Who were you out with tonight?"

She folded her arms over her chest, her change of demeanor suspiciously quick. "Of course, you know that, as your friend, I support you in all of your choices."

Now it was my turn to make an incredulous noise. "You were with Amanda."

She turned around and got down teacups, though the water couldn't possibly have boiled yet.

"You're lecturing me about bad relationship choices, and you were out with your ex?" My eyes widened. "You did woo-hoo."

"You have got to stop playing *The Sims*," she said wryly, as if she could change the subject so easily.

"Are you getting back together? Is it revenge sex? What's happening?" I loved gossip, especially if I was the one discovering it. Not that I ever gossiped about Rosa. If I did, she would hold a pillow over my head in my sleep. It was an agreed upon term of our friendship.

"Don't you have some bones to cast?" she asked, and I knew I wasn't going to get any juicy love life details out of her tonight. I'd have to wait about a week, until they were hot and heavy again. Rosa and Amanda were like some wonderful soap opera; they got together and broke up more than Victor and Nikki on *The Young and The Restless.*

I sighed. "Yeah. I'm going to go put his numbers in. See what comes up."

"Good luck. I'll let you know when the water boils," she promised.

My tiny bedroom was just as I'd left it, perfectly rumpled like a comfortable nest. I slid my laptop out from beneath the bed and opened it, then pulled up the bookmarked numerology site I swore by. At the prompt, I entered, "Ian David Pratchett," and his birthday, after a little quick math to deduce the year. Then I plugged in my details and clicked the "calculate" button.

His number came up first. It was a twenty-two. I already knew I was an eight. I watched as the rest of the page loaded, trying to remember the few basic rules I'd learned from the numerology book collecting dust on my nightstand.

"Lifepath numbers twenty-two and eight are naturally compatible lovers, especially when working toward a shared goal." I murmured as I read aloud. "Mutual respect and spiritual harmony can flourish quickly and form lasting bonds. Eight should be mindful of twenty-two's cautious nature, while twenty-two must learn to compromise. If both partners are willing to work together, this couple may expect to spend many happy years together."

It didn't get much more positive than that.

I'd tucked Ian's drawing into my purse, folding it over carefully, though I'd hated to crease it even once. I opened it and smoothed it out gently on my bed. The drawing wasn't sweet just because he'd made me look pretty, but because he'd picked up on emotions that I'd thought only I could see. He'd seen my hope and my fear of rejection, and he'd drawn it in my eyes as plainly as if he'd taken a photograph of my loneliness.

But maybe Rosa was right. She was certainly more objective than I was. And it was true; if things moved at the pace I wanted them to move at, Ian would still be in his mid-fifties before we even started seriously thinking about a family.

In desperation, I opened my nightstand drawer and dug through it, knocking my vibrator aside to find the smooth plastic shell of the magic eight ball in the back of the drawer. I pulled it out and flopped back on my bed, shaking it.

"Okay. Do I keep seeing Ian?" That was the question, whether I wanted to admit it or not.

I turned the black globe over, and the die inside floated to the window. *REPLY HAZY TRY AGAIN.*

I dropped it to the bed beside me. "No shit, Magic Eight Ball."

* * * *

My phone rang at four. I knew there was a strong possibility it would be Ian, but my heart skipped a little when I pulled my phone out of my hoodie pocket and saw his name on the screen. Not wanting to sit up to turn off the television, I waved my arm futilely across the coffee table until I knocked the remote down. Scrabbling for it one-handed, I answered with "Is it too early to give you your own ringtone?" in lieu of a "hello".

There was a brief pause. "Were we having a conversation I don't remember being in the middle of?"

"Seriously?" Did he not realize he did the exact same thing on every call? I hit the mute button on the remote and snuggled back down into the couch. "You do that to me all the time."

"Me? No, I don't." He sounded truly perplexed. "My sister has a habit of doing that, but I don't think I do."

He was such a dork I had to laugh at him. "Trust me, you do. I can't believe no one has ever mentioned it."

"They probably thought it was cool and charming. You just don't appreciate it." Something in his tone changed, and it threw those first few sentences into an odd light. It seemed like he'd relaxed, though I hadn't noticed any tension to begin with.

"Hey, are you okay? You sounded kind of…different," I said, for lack of a better word.

He sighed a tired, rough sound. "It's been a hell of a day already. And it's really good to hear your voice."

Something in my chest squeezed up in that weird feeling that's almost totally emotion and not a physical reaction. "It's good to hear yours, too." I paused. "What are you doing right now?"

"Driving home," he said, that weariness creeping back into his voice. "Where I will probably drink a few beers and nap on the sofa."

It wouldn't have sounded so lonely if *he* hadn't sounded so lonely. Even though I'd planned to spend my afternoon much in the same way—I'd been putting off peeing because the couch was so comfy—now, all I wanted was to cheer him up. I looked down at my scrubby clothes. At least I'd taken a shower after my run. Twisting the end of the string from my hood between two fingers, I asked, "Hey. Do you have a pair of swim trunks?"

"I do… Why?" His suspicion made me giggle.

"Go home, get them, and meet me at my place. We're going to have an adventure." I sat up and brushed the crumbs from my lunch off my shirt.

"And this adventure entails water?"

I smiled to myself. "Yes. It entails water. And taking your shirt off in front of me, so no talking about 'gory wrecks'. Because I looked at your Facebook pictures. You look fine."

"I'm still not thrilled at the prospect of my own partial nudity. However, I assume there will be partial nudity on your part, so you have my attention," he said with a chuckle, and those words did all sorts of things to me.

"Just get here," I said, putting on more confidence than I actually felt. "Trust me, this is going to be perfect."

After we hung up, I went to my bedroom and rumpled all the clothing in my drawers looking for my swimsuit. It was a red gingham print bikini, with thin, tie-up straps at the shoulders and hips. I'd bought it because it was super cute and sexy, and because Brad had told me I dressed like a little girl. Now, I kind of wished I'd kept my vintage one-piece with the wide halter straps and the low-cut legs. It was easy enough to tell Ian to not worry about how he looked, but every little freckle and scar on my body seemed to be magnified by a thousand at the thought of him seeing them. From a logical standpoint, I knew genetics and exercise had given me the kind of shape that got a woman into a men's magazines, but they were airbrushed and pushed up and had tons of makeup on. I couldn't exactly wear a smoky eye look to the pool.

But I assumed Ian wasn't going to be disappointed when I didn't walk out of the locker room looking like a *Maxim* cover model. "Stop being so hard on yourself, Penny," I scolded myself, and stuffed my suit into my purse. Then I changed into pink denim shorts that were just a little too short and a white tank top. If I was going to be in my bathing suit later anyway, might as well put on my hot-girl, hot-weather clothes. That would give me the boost of confidence I so desperately needed, at the moment. I pulled my hair up, put on some waterproof mascara, and waited. About an hour after his call, the buzzer rang.

I hit the button and said, "On my way down," because the apartment was way too trashed to let him come up. As I hopped out the door, I slid my sunglasses on so I wouldn't be all squinty and scrunch-faced in the sunlight.

Ian leaned against his car, wearing navy suit trousers and a white button-down with the sleeves rolled back and collar undone.

*Sunday. Right.* I couldn't imagine how distracting he must be in church to anyone who was attracted to men. Or maybe I was biased, because every time I saw him, he seemed a little hotter.

His gaze flicked down to my legs, then guiltily back up. There was that confidence boost I'd been looking for. He cleared his throat. "So, where is this adventure that requires swim trunks taking us?"

I smiled sweetly and pushed up my sunglass to bat my eyelashes at him. "To trespass."

# CHAPTER SEVEN

I have snuck into the pool at the One UN hotel somewhere around a hundred times. It has a beautiful panoramic view and a canopied ceiling. It was like swimming in an event tent. Not as glamorous as some of the rooftop pools in the city, but there was never an attendant on duty, and in all the times I'd been there, I'd only seen three guests.

We parked on the street. As we walked toward the building, I reiterated the plan we'd gone over in the car. "Walk through the lobby like we're supposed to be there. We're going to go up to the fitness center. We'll split up at the locker rooms, but from there, you can go right to the pool, no hassles."

"You've robbed a bank before, haven't you?" he asked, casting a worried glance up at the edifice of the building.

"It's going to be fine. I do this all the time. I like to break rules if they're ones I know I can't get into actual trouble for." That was true. I would never jump a turnstile or shoplift anything, but I frequently took food and drink into stores with posted signs, just for the thrill I got if no one asked me to throw it out. "My teenage rebellion was really boring."

The air-conditioned lobby cooled the sweat on my neck and cleavage, sweat I hoped Ian wouldn't notice. Luckily, the pool water would wash it off.

The first time I'd visited One UN, the lobby had nearly caused me to run out again. There were so many mirrors and contrasting patterns, it was like a full-on assault on my taste in furnishings. But the more often I came here, the more it grew on me.

"This place is what the Epcot designers probably imagined the future would look like back in the 1970's," Ian mumbled under his breath, and I laughed.

"If you come here often enough, you'll grow fond of it." I led him down the mirrored, vertigo-inducing hallway, to the east tower elevators.

"How often do you come here, exactly?" he asked cautiously.

"Oh, maybe twice a month," I said as I hit the button. "Nobody has ever said anything about it before. I don't know if there are just so many people coming through that they don't recognize me—"

"They, uh…" He cleared his throat. "They might recognize you. They might just think you're *visiting guests*."

It took me a moment to understand what he meant by his inflection. When I did, I laughed. "Oh my gosh, you're probably right. Well, there are definitely worse misconceptions that have been made about me in my life than mixing up what job I have."

"That's true."

We got on the elevator, my mind suddenly blank of any conversational topics.

"What sort of misunderstandings would you say you've run into about yourself?" he asked, saving us from awkward silence purgatory.

The biggest ones all had to do with sex, or my lack of having it. I hated to keep bringing up the virgin thing. There always came a moment, be it in a friendship or a dating situation, when I felt that my virginity started to define me.

"Well, a lot of people assume I'm a total prude when they find out that I'm a virgin. And a few guys have called me a bitch when they realized I wasn't going to sleep with them."

"They called you a bitch because you wouldn't sleep with them? That's fucking terrible." He sounded more offended by it than I'd ever been. Probably because men didn't realize how often women heard that name hurled at them.

"It might sound shocking to you, but trust me, every woman on this planet has been called a bitch enough that it doesn't shock us anymore."

The elevator doors opened onto the twenty-seventh floor, and we stepped out. Ian let me lead the way. "What about you? What are some misconceptions about you?"

"There are some people in my life who think I'm a bit of a playboy. I think I may have earned it." He said it like it was the most horrible thing someone could think of him, and that didn't seem fair. Men were expected to embody that Heffner-esque mystique of the revolving bedroom door.

"Now I'm imagining you in a smoking jacket, surrounded by young, hot blonds," I joked with a sly glance. At least, I hoped it was sly, and not just like I had something in my eye.

It must have worked, because he winked at me and said, "Half-true."

Someday, I would learn to take a compliment without my whole head turning the color of a cooked lobster.

As always, nobody was on guard outside the locker rooms. Rosa said that she'd come here once, and a man had asked for her room key, but she'd just pretended she'd dropped it and made a big deal about having to go all the way back down to the front desk. I think after that she'd gone to the Mondrian and snuck in there. I'd never managed to get into that one.

When you're early-adulthood-poor in New York, you have to make your own fun.

I pointed to the locker rooms. "Here. You go in there, I'll go in there, and we'll meet on the other side."

There was a baby changing table in the largest bathroom stall, so I stuffed my purse, clothes, and shoes in it after I'd slipped on my bikini. I stood in front of the mirror and adjusted my straps, and checked out the rearview to make sure the bottoms weren't saggy. *You've got to start working your lower abs again,* the snotty, critical voice in my head that sounded a lot like my mother said, but I resolutely shook that voice away. I looked fine. Better than fine. I looked amazing.

I would be lying if I said I didn't like it when men paid attention to my appearance. I've been called a tease more times than I could remember, and it used to bother me. Then I grew out of being embarrassed or apologetic for looking good. If a guy could appreciate a car without driving it, he could do the same with me. I took my hair down, because ponytail holders on wet hair are a major no-no. I tried to shake it out to disguise the dent left behind. I would just have to get wet right away to get rid of it.

I grabbed a towel from the stack provided at the pool entrance and strolled out. The flooring had a super weird texture that always took me by surprise. When I looked up from my feet, I saw Ian standing in the water.

"You got in already?" I asked. *No, he materialized there.* I could be so dense, sometimes.

He turned around, and there was no mistaking the fact he was checking me out. It was refreshing he didn't try to hide it. Men usually tried to hide it, and it was always obvious.

His gaze drifted over me from my toes up before he said, "Stop showing off."

How could one person be so dorky but so smooth at the same time? I looked down to hide the goofy smile I couldn't rein in and tucked my hair behind my ear. "Sorry. Somebody has to be the prettiest girl in the room, though."

He looked around. We were totally alone. "Let's go for prettiest in this hotel. Or the city. That would also do."

Yeah, right. "Beyoncé lives in this city. But I appreciate the endorsement."

There were steps into the pool, but Ian was by the ladder, so I used that instead, trying hard not to slip and fall like an idiot as I eased myself down backwards. The water was warm enough I didn't do anything super uncool like shriek or tiptoe once my feet touched down. "Isn't this nice, though?" I asked, sinking down to cover my shoulders with water. It felt uneven to be half-in, half-out. "It's not crowded like those pools you have to pay for."

"And much less Axe body spray, I'm sure."

I dunked my head under. If I were alone, I would reemerge like Ariel breaking the surface in *The Little Mermaid*. That seemed just slightly dramatic, so I came up and pushed my hair back like a normal person. Ian was still just standing there. A sudden realization occurred to me. "Can you swim?"

"That's something you should have asked before you got me into this pool, isn't it?" He pointed at the number on the warning sign on the wall. "It's only five feet deep. I think we'll be fine."

I held my hand up to indicate exactly where the water would hit me, which was somewhere around my eyes. "You'll be fine. I'll be in trouble."

"I promise I won't let you drown," he vowed then plunged under the water himself.

I kicked onto my back and settled into a float, staring at the canopy overhead. When he resurfaced, I mused, "You won't let me drown. That's in my top five must-haves for boyfriends."

He drifted toward the deep end. "One of my top five requirements for girlfriends is buoyancy. How long can you float like that?"

Having your ears underwater is not conducive to conversation. I'd caught his words, but they'd been muffled. I stood, laughing. "For a while. I wouldn't try to do it across the English Channel or anything."

He smirked. "So, you're vetting me as a potential boyfriend?"

That was a weird question. Why else would I have gone out with him in the first place? Even weirder, what was he doing with me if he wasn't interested in being my boyfriend? "Of course I am. That's what dating is about, right? You go on a date with someone to see if you like them enough to have a second date. Then you go out on the second and subsequent dates to find out if you want to see them exclusively. And then, you start seeing them exclusively—"

"And they move in, you spend a few years in that type of domestic bliss, then you get married, grow apart, and finally divorce." The words rolled out of him on a tide of bitterness that made my heart ache for him. He looked immediately remorseful. "I'm sorry, like I said, it's—"

"Been a rough day," I finished for him. Could I ever sympathize. After Brad had dumped me, I'd spent the next few weeks in a constant state of anti-romantic protest. I'd gone along on Sophie's bachelorette weekend in Vegas, and it had been fun, but the whole time, I'd been silently resenting being around three people who were madly in love, two of which were in love with each other. "Believe me, after what I went through with Brad, I was ready to give up on dating and other people in general before Sophie set me up with you. But I don't share your unhappy view of the relationship evolution chain."

"You've been cured of that pessimism?" There was more disbelief than hope in his question.

"I was never really pessimistic to begin with." I smiled, because I wanted badly to convince him, though no one had been able to convince me back then. "I believe that, someday, I'm going to find the person I'm meant to be with. If I didn't believe that, I wouldn't have gone out with you."

"Fair enough," he conceded. "For what it's worth, I'm very glad you did."

"I am, too." And I was. I really was. Even without the numerology report to back it up, even without the fortune cookie that had me counting down the days until the end of the summer, I knew whatever this was, it wasn't inconsequential.

I moved toward him, treading water to stay above the surface. "Isn't this so much better than sitting home alone on our respective couches?"

"The view is definitely better." When he said things like that, I started to wonder how firmly I could stick to my vow of chastity.

"I know you want me to think you're talking about the windows, but I'm on to you," I said, putting my toes down experimentally.

True to his word, he didn't let me drown. He took my hand and pulled me closer to him. Which was just fine by me, because I wanted to touch him. I'd wanted to in the car on the way over. I'd almost taken his hand as we'd walked through the lobby. I just wanted to be nearer to him than casual distance all the time. I slid my hand up his arm to rest on his shoulder. He didn't have Brad's twelve-hours-a-week-at-the-gym arms, but he wasn't as out of shape as he claimed.

I couldn't keep my cool. I started giggling. I needed a way to cover for myself. "When I first started coming here, I was afraid it was actually a part of the UN."

His hands skimmed down my sides, settling around my waist. It was the most contact we'd had so far. His long fingers pushed into my skin just slightly, just enough to hold me and let me know he was there, and he turned us in a circle, like a very slow dance.

"I have to admit I had a moment where I thought that, myself."

*Wait, what did he think?* My short-term memory had fizzled out at the touch of his hands. *Oh, the UN. Right.* "Well, we're safe. I promise. The worst they can do is kick us out." I put my arms around his neck to hang on and lean back, my legs floating up at his side. "But my plan is that we pretend you're a delegate staying here."

"Do I get to pick which country?" he asked.

"Hmm. The obvious choice, and the one you'd be more likely to pull off, would be Scotland. Sorry."

"Scotland doesn't have a delegate in the UN. We're just lumped into the United Kingdom."

I almost defended my joke with a long, rambling explanation about how I'd been in a model UN club in high school and I already knew that, but how seriously geeky could I be without ruining the mood entirely? I was already all over him, apparently to no avail because he hadn't made a move. I doubt he would be turned on hearing about how I'd been Brazil once. Instead, I swam a lazy circle around him. "Well, I'm giving you a seat. You're the delegate from Scotland now."

I pulled him farther into the deep end, so I'd have more of an excuse to cling to him. "And how does the delegate from Scotland feel about the delegate from the United States, at the moment?"

"The delegate from Scotland likes the delegate from the United States very much," he said. It wasn't exactly the declaration of passion I was looking for.

I once again wrapped my arms around his neck, sending totally obvious *kiss me* vibes. It was nice to be face-to-face with him, but I was starting to worry my flirt was broken. I would have to be direct. "The delegate from the United States calls for a resolution to address the fact that Scotland hasn't kissed her, yet, even though the United States is sending out all sorts of signals."

"Are you?" He sounded genuinely shocked.

So, obviously, I hadn't been doing my job. I rolled my eyes at myself. "Yeah, with all my sexy United Nations talk."

Since vibes weren't working, I turned to physical cues. I pulled him down with my hands at his neck and pressed my mouth to his. He got the clue, then.

I'd never thought of kissing as counting for physical intimacy. To me, physical intimacy was when you got down to the serious stuff. And not just intercourse; I'd loved snugging with Brad after I'd gotten him off. Laying against his shoulder, smelling the mix of cheap detergent and cheaper deodorant that clung to his T-shirts, I'd never wanted to be anywhere else.

But kissing Ian? I felt the same thing, multiplied by ten. Our tongues stroking against each other, the way his body felt pressed against mine was so intense, he might as well have been touching me everywhere. My nipples were so hard it hurt, and I knew he could feel them.

I used him for leverage to pull myself up tighter against him, and his arms wrapped around my waist. God, we even fit together right. And we'd never tried to fit together before.

The giddy crush of energy behind my ribs became too much pressure, and I pulled back. I had to, or I wouldn't be able to breathe. Our eyes locked, and adrenaline coursed through me; I could probably use it to lift a car or run a marathon. Instead, I used it to kiss him again and got caught up in the moment. My legs hooked around his hips, and my pelvis bumped against him.

It may have been shortsighted of me to start kissing him when we were both half-naked. His erection was both impressive and obvious.

I jerked away, untangling myself with a gasp. "Oh my gosh, I am so sorry, that was really—" *Awesome.* "—forward of me."

Ugh, how would I have felt if he'd gotten all gropey with me, without asking permission? And in the genital area? I was such a sex offender.

He looked away and scratched his neck, the way he did when he was uncomfortable, and I felt *so* bad. "No, it's fine. A bit embarrassing is all. A good, solid school book would be very helpful right now."

I laughed, because I was nervous, and I covered my face because I was completely mortified. "Okay, I think the water is acting as an aphrodisiac. We may need to get out." *And probably never see each other again because I jumped you.*

"Agreed," he said, and my heart twisted. "Although, I hate to cut our adventure short. Why don't you come to my place and have dinner?"

*Because my years of celibacy will snuff out like a candle in a closed jar.* I raised an eyebrow and stalled with a joke. "Let me guess, you're going to cook dinner to lull me into a false sense of security, then bam, five years from now we're married and you've never cooked since."

"No, I'll be upfront about that right now. Marriage or not, I don't cook. But I'll have something delivered."

He hadn't freaked out about the marriage thing. That was awesome. It was so immature and stupid the way guys would act terrified of marriage, even when it was mentioned in passing. As a divorcee, wasn't Ian supposed to be even more wary? I added the fact he was so chill about it to my list of things I liked about him.

I wasn't sure going to his place was a good idea. I didn't think he was a serial killer or a rapist or anything, despite Rosa's constant warnings that dating was the number one killer of women aged eighteen to sixty-five. But considering how little control I had over myself when we were together, it still might not be the greatest idea.

My body was a hundred percent sure I should be giving it up to Ian, like yesterday, but I resolved I wouldn't even think of the idea until after Labor Day. If I was the love of his life, like the fortune cookie said, and if we were as compatible as our numbers suggested, then we would have plenty of time to get to the physical fun, right? I didn't want to be yet another cautionary tale in my maternal lineage.

I could control myself, I decided. And so far, Ian had proven cautious about respecting my boundaries.

He also lived in a clock. How could I pass the opportunity up?

I agreed after my moment of consideration. "Okay. I'm really curious to see what the inside of that clock tower looks like."

"Oh, it's all gears and pulleys." He had such a great smile. "You'll have to be very careful about where you put your shoes, or they'll rotate off and you'll never see them, again."

I was pretty sure he was kidding. I jerked my thumb over my shoulder. "I'm going to go get changed."

When I got out of the pool, I had the worst wedgie in the world. There was no chance I could pretend to not notice it. I adjusted as much as I could without actually picking my butt and hurried off to the locker rooms.

If he still wanted to have dinner with me after he saw that, he was a keeper.

In the locker room, I did a quick rinse off, combed my hair, and threw on my clothes. Rosa and I had this deal that if we're going out with someone we don't know well, we text each other our whereabouts and what time we plan on returning. I'd broken our agreement by coming to the pool with Ian without thinking about it, and I wasn't going to do it a second time. The problem was, Rosa would probably try to convince me not to go to Ian's place, because Rosa is sensible and knew I wouldn't want to make a stupid choice based on hormones and a dangerous amount of privacy.

Slouched on the bench, I held my phone in front of me and took a deep breath. I typed in, *Having dinner at Ian's house.*

She responded immediately, *ho don't do it.*

*I'm not going to do it. Just dinner.*

A beat later, she replied, again, *ho don't do it.* And this time, she put a thumbs down emoticon.

Okay, I had checked in to let her know my plan. But she wasn't my mother, so I threw my phone in my purse and went to the sink. I'd braided my wet hair, and it fell over my shoulder as I leaned down to splash cold water on my suddenly hot face. When I came up, I met my gaze in the mirror. With my very best determined expression, I said, "Ho. Do it."

\* \* \* \*

On the drive to Ian's apartment, it was clear we were both super nervous. First, he apologized for his apartment not being "very tidy" and kept noncommittally singing along with songs on the radio before he realized what he was doing and stopped himself. But once we were there, in the building, in the elevator, he seemed to relax, and so did I.

"I'm so excited right now." I bounced on the balls of my feet, despite my strict no-jumping-in-elevators policy. I knew it probably wouldn't really send the elevator crashing down, but I never liked to tempt fate.

Speaking of fate, Ian was very tempting. Whatever had brought him down during the day, there was no trace of it, now.

I added, "You have no idea how often I've looked at this place and fantasized about what it might be like inside."

"I hope the fantasy lives up to the reality, but you have to remember, a very single, very depressed man has been living here."

"My mom used to tell people, 'I'm here to see you, not your house,' but then she would bitch about their housekeeping for the entire ride home." I rolled my eyes at the memory. It had seemed like such a hateful thing to do. Especially when I'd seen genuine relief in the expressions of the people she'd said it to. "I promise I won't do that to you. As much as I want to see the inside of your apartment, I really am here to see you."

I hoped he would be kind enough to ignore the fact that my purse sounded like I was smuggling a nest of bees in it. Rosa was having an unholy conniption in our text.

I was already impressed that Ian had an elevator up to his apartment. Not his floor, his apartment. He had to put a key in it and everything. When the doors opened and we stepped into the place…

The room was one big square, broken only by pillars and the raised platform in the center, where we'd entered. The centerpiece of the elevated area that we'd entered onto was another, smaller elevator for the upper floors of the apartment. Some really nerve-wracking floating stairs headed up there, too, arranged in dizzying flights of precisely cut golden wood around the glass elevator shaft.

"Oh my god," I said, hardly believing I was in a place like this, let alone standing with the person who'd dreamed it all up. "You made this."

"I designed it," he corrected me. "Many people who are far more skilled than I am built it."

I approached the living room window, one of the four huge clock faces Ian had described to me on the drive over. From where I stood in front of one, I could see all the others, albeit one of them had to be viewed through the obstruction of the glass elevator shaft. "And they really work?"

"They do. There is a very nice service technician by the name of Andrew who comes by every now and then to inspect the machinery and make sure it's all running properly. There's a room where all of the clock-related equipment is. I don't go into it."

I assumed the clock face and hands were on the outside of the glass, but it was so clean it was hard to tell. For someone who thought he wasn't very tidy, the place looked like a showroom.

Well, except for the pair of jeans over the back of the couch. In the reflection on the glass, I saw Ian hastily shove the garment under the white throw beside it.

The view of Manhattan was as glamorous as if it had come out of a movie. The sun was beginning a late-afternoon descent, taking its time and casting warm golden shadows over the bridges and building faces.

And all I wanted to look at was Ian.

Being with him was easy. All of my senses seemed more alive when we were together. It was like I became some better version of myself, or maybe just the true version of myself. I was certainly at my most authentic when I was with him, because I felt like I had nothing to lose. Whatever happened between us wouldn't hurt me; disappoint me, maybe cause me some pain, but it wouldn't harm me. There was no sense that we were playing a game or that I should be on the defensive. We felt real together, in a way I'd never felt with anyone else.

There were only eight more days until Labor Day.

I turned away from the window. To my left was the longest galley kitchen I'd ever seen, and far wider than the one in my apartment, that was for sure. No walls distinguished it from the dining room beside it, but the placement of the counters and cabinets and the modern, stainless steel hood for the stove—which looked odd all by itself and not installed against a wall and some cupboards—clearly delineated it was its own separate space.

As did the placement of the couch in the living room area. A very modern, very wide circular coffee table in white enamel sat in the center of that, a pleasant contrast with the sharp angles of the room.

"Your decorator really knew what they were doing." I walked around the couch toward him, trailing my fingers along the gray upholstery on the back as I did.

He looked down, his expression darkly humorous. "My—Gena. My ex-wife, Gena, excuse me. She did all of this."

He'd been about to say, *my wife*, I was sure of it. There was a flash of jealousy on my part, but I reeled it back in. He'd probably been married for a long time. I'd known him for two weeks. I didn't really get to be jealous in this situation.

"Did she?" I asked, keeping a neutral expression. "Well, it looks fantastic."

"She's talented. Unfocused, but talented. And I'm not saying that to be bitter, I—" He stopped himself, and I was so glad. I did not want to listen to the guy I was having hopeful dating feelings about describe his ex-wife. He scrubbed a hand over his face. "I'm sorry. I have to confess something."

*He's not really divorced. He's a widower. He's a widower, and he's going to start crying.*

92

"You're the first woman I've had over here, since Gena. Besides her and our female friends at parties and the like. You're actually the first date who's come here." The lines at the corners of his eyes deepened with his pained expression. "I hope I'm not out of line telling you that."

"No, I don't think that's out of line," I assured him. It wasn't necessarily my first choice of conversational topic, but I could roll with it. "Thanks for telling me, instead of being weird all night about it."

He stepped up close to me and reached to tuck an escaped curl behind my ear. "I didn't see the point in being weird. Honesty worked well enough yesterday."

"For what it's worth, I'm glad I'm here."

He cupped my cheek and leaned down to kiss me at the corner of my mouth, and my knees went weak. I was practically swaying from that brief contact when he straightened, put his hands in his pockets, and said, "So. Dinner."

Right. Dinner. That was what we were here for.

He nodded toward the kitchen. "That's where I keep the delivery menus."

I followed him, looking up at the ceiling two floors above our heads. "In the refrigerator?"

"You're going to laugh at me, but I do keep them in the cupboard." He walked around the counter and opened a door.

Ian wasn't kidding when he'd said he didn't have any food in the house. There was a jar of peanut butter, an eighth of a box of macaroni, and a bag of pitted dates. The dates had dust on them.

"Ian…" I didn't want to be rude. I really didn't. But this alarmed me. "What have you been eating?"

"Delivery, mostly," he admitted sheepishly. "And peanut butter."

I looked around the bare counters. "Do you even have any bread?"

"Not as such." He looked guiltily at the floor.

"God, I hope you are using a spoon and not your hand." There. I said it. I couldn't have stopped myself if I'd wanted to.

"Well, of course I'm using a spoon," he said, sounding mildly offended. He pulled a drawer handle, and trash and recycling bins rolled out. One was full of beer bottles, the other was fairly empty but for a clump of peanut butter streaked plastic spoons at the bottom.

He was so unashamedly pathetic that I couldn't hold in my laughter. "You're a mess."

He laughed with me. "Ah, you were going to find out soon, anyway."

"You're right. So, thanks for once again not being weird."

"You're weird enough for the both of us."

We looked through the delivery menus and decided on Italian. While we waited for the order to arrive, Ian showed me around the rest of the apartment. We went up to the second floor, to his studio. It had some amazing square windows that perfectly illuminated the space around the large drafting table. There were some can lights in the ceiling, but I would have expected something more than the adjustable lamp clipped to his desk.

"Why don't you have lights up there, if this is where your table is?" I asked, examining the ceiling before turning my attention to the drawing in progress. I gestured to it. "Can I look?"

"Sure," he said, after a moment's hesitation. "And the reason I don't have lights directly above my desk is because they would be coming right at the back of my head. It's hard to draw in your own shadow."

"Oh. I wouldn't have thought of that." The picture he was working on was a sketch of a young man. Though it was clearly unfinished, I felt as though I were looking at a photograph of a person who looked similar to, but not exactly like, Ian. "Is this a relative?"

"My brother, Robby," he said. "When he was twenty. I'm trying to do it from memory, but I can't quite get it right. I may turn to a photo reference soon."

"Do all of you guys look alike?" I asked. Siblings absolutely fascinated me.

"I take after my dad. Most of us do. My sister, Annie, looks more like Mum," he said, walking slowly beside me as we headed to the door. "The third floor is my bedroom—"

Nope. No way. It wasn't that I thought I would pounce on him or something. Or that I thought he would take advantage of me or anything like that. We'd climbed the stairs to get to the studio, so I said, "No, I'm not used to your creepy stairs yet, and that's way too high."

It was such a bad excuse, with an elevator right there. He could have easily said, "Then we can take the elevator," but he didn't. He said, "We'll take the elevator back down, then."

And that was it. No pressure to get me into his bedroom. He just respected my gentle refusal, even though the reason I'd given him would have been easy to argue with. Despite being some kind of shambling human tragedy, he was unreasonably perfect.

When the food arrived, he said, "Let's bring this with us," and headed for the elevator.

"Where to?" I asked him, following after with silverware and a couple of the beers from his fridge.

He hit the button with his elbow. "Up to the deck."

"The deck?" I'd seen a boxy structure on the peak of the tower on occasions when I'd passed by it, but I hadn't been sure it was a roof access and not just a design feature.

"It's more of a widow's walk, but it has great views," he promised.

As we ascended, I did catch a peek at the third floor, but the doors were closed. A giant, long-haired gray cat was slinking around the loft-style hallway. "Is that Ambrose?" I asked, pointing, but we passed through the ceiling too quickly for Ian to follow my direction.

"If it was a cat, and it was in my apartment, then I very much hope it was."

The doors opened onto what had to be the very best view in Brooklyn. Three-hundred and sixty degrees of pure, purple twilight that stretched over the city like an amethyst blanket.

"This is amazing," I whispered as we stepped out. There was a low-backed black chair with white linen upholstery, and a matching, blocky chaise longue around a square black coffee table that sat at knee level.

"Not an ideal dining arrangement, I know, but I think it's worth it for the atmosphere," he said, depositing our plastic containers of food onto the table.

I took the chair and left the chaise to Ian. "I think it's fantastic. I eat a lot of meals sitting on the floor next to our coffee table at home, anyway."

The bridges were lit up like diamond necklaces strung over the water, and lights from cars winked as they passed through the cross streets. We talked about easier things than we had the day before. I told Ian about what it had been like to move from Pennsylvania to New York, and he talked about the differences he'd found when he'd arrived from Scotland. We were both kind of introverted, in that we didn't have many friends, and the ones we did have were extremely close.

Which made me wonder, "How do you know Sophie?"

He paused with a forkful of spaghetti bolognese hovering just above his plate. Then he said, "I went to university with her husband. Briefly."

That was odd. Why did he hesitate to tell me that? I innocently pressed, "Oh really? Where was that?"

"Exeter. I went for fine art." He took a bite and chewed, never looking up.

"And that turned into…architecture?" Not that I knew

enough about architecture to know if that was an odd development.

He washed his food down with a long swallow of beer. "The two have a lot in common. But some personal circumstances arose that changed my career path, as it were."

"Ah." Something still seemed to be missing, not because his story was suspicious, but because he was acting so suspicious. "So, was Neil a fine arts major?"

I knew he hadn't been. I'd read his Wikipedia article, because it was weird to know someone who was married to somebody famous.

"No, economics," Ian said, and that checked out, so at least I knew he hadn't lied to me. "We met through a club. I'm not sure I want to tell you which."

If he was trying to hide the fact that he'd belonged to a math club or some kind of Star Trek fan club, it was unnecessary. I could already tell he was a nerd. "Well now you have to. You've piqued my interest."

"It may change how you feel about me," he warned.

I laughed. Seriously, whatever he had to say couldn't be that bad. "Ian. I'm pretty much sold on you at this point. Unless you were a Neo-Nazi skinhead, I won't care."

He nodded, looked down at his plate, then looked up and met my gaze directly. "It was a kink club."

"A...oh." Well. That was not the nerdy admission I'd been expecting. Not by half a mile.

"Yeah. It was an experimental time in my youth," he said, looking away.

Ian had belonged to a kink club? I'd heard of them before. I wasn't sure NYU had one, but Columbia did. Rosa's ex, Amanda, had belonged to one. There hadn't been any sex involved in the group, but she'd met people there and fooled around outside of it. Her experience, she'd been quick to inform people, wasn't the norm. Most of them just showed up to talk about their sexuality and learn.

I didn't like the idea of pain or humiliation during sex—it just wasn't a turn on for me—but I didn't want him to think I was judging his choices. "You don't have to apologize. People are into all sorts of things. I might not be—"

"It isn't a relationship requirement," he hurried to assure me. "Besides, we're not sleeping together."

"But that doesn't mean we won't," I reminded him, and I loved the way he visibly swallowed at that. "And it doesn't mean I'd never try something a little risqué. What's your kink?"

He took a breath that sounded like he was resigning himself to something unpleasant. My reaction, probably. "Well, I'm not into whips and chains, if that's what you're thinking. But in the past I've quite enjoyed swinging and group sex."

"So, you like having sex with other people while you're in a relationship?" That didn't seem like something I would ever be comfortable with.

He nodded. "My ex-wife and I did, but together. Never in separate rooms. No individual dates with other people. It wasn't an open relationship. More of a shared sexual experience."

"If we were…together…" I didn't want to phrase it in a way that seemed presumptuous.

"I wouldn't be willing to share you with another boyfriend, no," he said quickly as if that were going to be my concern. That *I* would want to see someone else.

"Ditto. I wouldn't be comfortable in a long-term relationship with you while you were in a relationship with someone else. And I wouldn't be comfortable having sex with someone else with you, or watching you have sex with someone." Oh god, I'd just talked about watching him have sex with someone. I quickly added, "In the interest of full disclosure, is all I'm saying."

His jaw went tight, and a muscle ticked in his neck. "In the interest of full disclosure, then, I should tell you something."

A cold chill, incongruous with the warm August night, skated across my shoulders. "This sounds grim."

"It may well be." He looked me in the eye, again, though it was clear it was difficult for him to. "I've slept with Sophie."

My voice froze in my throat. When I could respond, I had to have some serious clarification. "Sophie…my boss, Sophie."

"Yes. Earlier this spring, before Gena and I split up." He cleared his throat. "It was a—"

"A swinger thing," I finished for him. Holy shit. Sophie had set me up with someone she'd slept with? Without telling me? That was extremely uncool. But at least he hadn't cheated on his wife with her, right?

"Penny?" he prompted gently.

I realized I'd been staring at him, wide-eyed and silent. "Look, I'm not going to say that this doesn't matter to me. It does. I kind of wish I'd known about this sooner."

He nodded. "I wasn't sure what the appropriate time would be to address it."

"I think Sophie should have told me when she set us up."

"Would it have affected your decision to walk into that restaurant last week?" he asked, with a forced smile. "In spite of the fortune cookie?"

Had it only been *one* week? I felt like we'd been doing this for a while. In a good way. And that's what made this harder.

"Honestly? Yes." I knew it would hurt him to say it, but it was the truth. I didn't want to make him feel bad, but I wasn't a liar. "I probably wouldn't have gone out with you."

He twisted his fork on his plate but didn't lift it for a bite. "And now? Does it make a difference?"

Did it? Was I going to think about him and Sophie together every time I spoke to her? That would make my job excruciating. Did I like the idea that someone I knew had, in effect, had something I wanted before I'd gotten there?

The thought stopped me. I wanted Ian, in a way I hadn't wanted any of the handful of boyfriends I'd been with before. It wasn't that I hadn't been attracted to those guys or tempted to sleep with them, but I'd been on two official dates with Ian, and if he'd offered tonight, I might have said yes. And now?

"No," I said after a deep breath. "It doesn't change anything."

It would slow me down, hormone wise, but that wasn't a bad thing.

"Well, that's a relief." His tone shocked me; I'd never heard him sound so serious. "Because I really do like you, Penny. And I would hate to do anything to hurt you."

"I would hate that, too." My ribs ached, pressed from the inside out by the intense jumble of conflicted feelings in my heart. This was so much heavier than third date talk. "Look, I'll talk to Sophie. I want to be on the right page with her. But I don't have any problem with what's happening here."

"Good." He paused. "And I'm certainly not going to be sleeping with Sophie again. That was a particular set of circumstances that occurred one time. And please don't think I'm out sleeping with a new woman every night. This may be too forward, but I'm not interested in seeing anyone else, at the moment."

"You don't have to apologize for your past," I said firmly. There wasn't a reason to feel guilty. It wasn't like he'd known I would be coming along. "The delivery of the news could have been... Well, strike that. Everything happens for a reason."

"That it does." One corner of his mouth lifted in a half-attempt at a smile.

I took a drink from my beer and looked out over the water. Whether it changed anything between us or not, I'd still just gotten some unsettling news. I wanted reassurance somehow, stupid, silly reassurance that he liked me and not

Sophie. Which made no sense; Sophie was obnoxiously in love with her husband and lived like a real-life Cinderella. She wasn't in the market for boyfriend.

But I still wanted to hear it. And there was no way to ask and not sound like the most insecure woman in uncertainty-ville. It sucked.

"Hey, Doll," Ian said softly, and I turned to face him. His expression was caught somewhere between resignation and optimism. He held out his arms a little. "Come here?"

I put my beer on to the table and got up, sliding my hands into my back pockets as I walked to him. I stopped at the end of chaise. "I'm not interested in seeing anyone else right now, either. I'm kind of concentrating on, like, one guy."

Ian looked up at me with tired, glazed eyes but an adorable smirk, and melted me completely. "Well, he's a lucky bastard, isn't he?"

"Yeah," I agreed, leaning down to smile against his mouth. "He is."

## CHAPTER EIGHT

Though I'd been super cool about it at the time, Ian's revelation about Sophie had thrown me for a loop. It genuinely hadn't bothered me when he'd told me, but when I saw Sophie on Monday morning, the knowledge that she'd slept with the guy I liked burrowed under my skin like a horrible parasite you'd see removed from somebody's foot on a gross YouTube video.

I had to do something to stop myself from irrationally hating my boss.

"Hey, Soph?" I asked, leaning around her open door.

She flicked her gaze up from the computer screen she was leaning far too close to. She needed glasses, but Deja and I had decided we weren't going to tell her that. "Yeah?"

"I noticed that you have lunch free today, on your schedule, at least. I was wondering if we could go grab something together. Not as a boss/employee thing, but a people who know each other and have people in common…thing," I rambled. It was hard to stay coherent when all I could think about was the fact that her hands had been all over my soon-to-be boyfriend. I tried very hard not to imagine her smooth, spray-tanned thighs wrapping around his waist.

She frowned a little. "I assume this is about Ian?"

I nodded. "Things are going really well, and I just needed some outside input. If you wouldn't mind?"

I'd been prepared in case of refusal. I wasn't going to be put off about this; if she declined, I would just say I needed to talk to her about the fact that she'd had sex with the guy I wanted to be my boyfriend and potential future husband and father of our three beautiful children.

*Slow down there, Penelope.*

"Um…yeah," she cautiously agreed. "I wouldn't mind

hitting that bistro on Fifth and Prospect."

We took Sophie's car—and driver, because billionaires could pay people to just hang around all day waiting for them—and talked about normal, non-Ian stuff on the way over. The whole time, I kept wondering horrible things, like if she was better at sex than I would be, if Ian would compare us, if he would like her better than me...

It wasn't that I'd already decided I was going to sleep with Ian. Brad and I had dated for two years, and I'd never made up my mind. But the numbers didn't lie, and fortune cookies had never steered me wrong. It felt like destiny had flung us together, when we would have probably never met before.

The restaurant Sophie had picked was a bit pricier than I would have normally eaten at, but ultimately, it wouldn't matter because she always picked up the check and called it a business expense. It was small, dark and pretty much empty, which was a blessing. I didn't necessarily need strangers overhearing our conversation.

"So..." Sophie said, leaning forward slightly after the waiter took our drink orders. Her eyes lit up in clear anticipation of some girl talk. "How are things with Ian?"

I knew she'd been cautiously trying to not pry all morning. "Good. Really fast but good. We've gone out three times, I've had dinner over at his place—"

"Oh my god, isn't it amazing? He had Neil and I over for dinner not too long ago and I got such apartment envy," she gushed, and every jealous hackle I had raised. It wasn't enough that she'd already slept with him, but she'd seen his apartment first, too?

Oh god, what if it had happened *in* his apartment?

It was really difficult to keep talking, because I disliked unpleasant confrontations, and I really disliked the topic. "Yeah. But we're getting way ahead of ourselves, so I'm trying to be cautious about all of this. There are a lot of factors in play here, and it's like we're getting instantly serious. I'm examining a lot of my concerns."

"Which is a totally smart thing to do," she agreed. "When I started falling for Neil, I was a mess. I think we'd only been seeing each other for like a month before I was completely in love with him. It was ridiculous."

"One of my concerns is that Ian has slept with you." There.

She blinked. "Wow. Okay, I have to admit, I'm glad he told you—"

"Why didn't *you* tell me?" I demanded. "You set me up with a guy you'd slept with, and you didn't even bother to mention it in passing?"

"When you put it that way, it does sound really bad." She pressed her fingertips to her forehead and looked down. "I'm sorry. I didn't know if it was my place to tell you, because I assume he told you the whole story?"

"He did," I admitted. "And I'm not going to tell anyone about it, so please don't worry about that. I guess I can see why you wouldn't want to tell me, 'by the way, here's an extremely personal detail about a stranger's sex life.' I just need to get this off my chest, because I'm a really jealous person, and if I started hating you, life would get complicated quick."

"I hope it doesn't complicate our working relationship. Or our personal one." She shook her head. "Is there anything I can do to make it easier? I mean, I have no intention of ever sleeping with him again."

"Would you tell me how it happened? Because, right now, all I can do is imagine you and him together, and it gets more and more… It's bugging the hell out of me." I didn't mean it to sound as harsh as it came out. The amount of hurt that had surged up surprised me.

"When I met Ian," she began, in a tone that suggested she was about to tell me a full story, rather than a simple answer, "it was at Neil's birthday party. Ian's ex-wife was this beautiful redhead—"

Something in my expression must have changed to make her stop short and clear her throat.

She went on, "And Neil has this major thing for redheads, so about a year later, we got together, had dinner, and one thing lead to another. Do you want other details?"

Did I? Sick curiosity drove me to say, "Yes."

"Well, we were all in the same room. There was nothing romantic between us. It was actually more about having the experience with your partner than…well, cheating on them, for lack of a better word." She shrugged. "Neil fucked Gena, I fucked Ian, then Gena and I had sex while Neil and Ian watched."

"Holy…" My jaw dropped. Now that I knew the exact details, I was way more fascinated with Sophie's spirit of adventure than I was concerned about her and Ian.

But then, I wondered if Ian appreciated that spirit of adventure more than he would appreciate boring, cautious me. It was this never-ending cycle of self-doubt that was messing me up, big time.

"I'm worried," I blurted, tears rising to humiliate me at the moment I most wanted to be the strong, confident one in the conversation. "I'm worried that Ian isn't going to be interested in me when I'm not as 'yay, fucking other couples!' as you were and Gena was. I'm afraid I'm not going to be as good as you—"

"Penny, don't do that to yourself. Besides, Ian isn't like that." Sophie's brows drew together in a remorseful frown.

"Can you at least tell me why you thought we'd be good together? I mean, we are. I know it's ridiculously soon to say that, but I was instantly attracted to him. His personality and mine mesh so well. And there was this fortune cookie—"

Sophie raised an eyebrow. I didn't know if she had any superstitions of her own, but I know she thought mine were extremely silly.

I was going to tell her anyway. "Ian got a fortune cookie that said he would meet the love of his life this summer. And

Labor Day is next Monday. Oh, and it was so awkward when he got that, but I got a fortune that said humor would help get through a moment of awkwardness. That's not coincidence, Sophie. There's no such thing as coincidence."

"Well, it definitely sounds like you believe you're the love of Ian's life," she said, stopping just short of "I told you so".

The waiter returned with a seltzer water with two slices of lime for Sophie, a Coke for me. Sophie toyed with her glass as she spoke. "I know you had a really difficult time after you and Brad broke up. So I thought, well, her heart is wounded. Whoever she dates next is going to have to be someone who understands that. Ian and Gena split up… Really, she left him. And I realized that he was going to need someone who understood the need to go slow, too. Plus, you both said similar things about wanting a family. It seemed like the timing was…"

"Fate?" I suggested.

She nodded with a resigned smile. She hated being wrong. "Okay. You got me. I do believe in fate. Because I have to. It's the reason why Neil and I are together. We met six years before we actually started dating. He didn't even give me his real name at the time. We should have never seen each other again, but everything fell into place, and now, here we are."

How was I supposed to argue with her, when she was saying basically the same thing I'd been saying for years? That fate brings people together, that there is someone out there, my true love, just waiting for me.

All the signs were pointing to Ian. And I was okay with that.

Still, what she'd done wasn't right, and I wasn't going to let her slide past that. "Maybe in the future, don't set other people up with people you've slept with."

"Fair enough." She shook her head. "I am really sorry. But I'm not sorry you guys are getting along so well, even if it's super fast."

"I keep feeling like I should pump the brakes, but then, I really don't want to." I'd already heard some of Sophie's embarrassing sex stories when I'd tagged along on her bachelorette weekend, so I didn't feel too weird adding, "And I'm kind of thinking that maybe the whole virginity thing…"

Sophie tilted her head. "Are you thinking about having sex with Ian?"

My face got so hot they could have cooked our meal on it. "Am I considering it? Maybe. Am I *thinking* about it? All the time. But you don't go for years and years being afraid of something, then suddenly go, oh, hey, I've been on two dates with you, let's bone."

"Lots of people think, oh hey, I've been on two dates with you, let's bone," she pointed out. "Look, if my impression of Ian is right—and having discussed this whole setting-you-up situation with Neil, I'm ninety-nine percent sure that it is—then he'll be fine with waiting for you. On the other hand, he would probably be fine with having sex with you if you drove over to his place right now and got on him."

"When you put it that way, it sounds so romantic," I deadpanned.

Sophie pressed her hand over her heart. "My baby snarked me. You're growing up so fast."

* * * *

"Wow, someone's jeans are tight," Rosa said with a low whistle. "I would definitely hit on you, if you weren't… You know. You."

"Thanks, that really works wonders for my confidence." I leaned closer to the mirror in our tiny bathroom to carefully draw on a wing of eyeliner. I had to leave the door open to do my hair and makeup, otherwise the leftover steam from my shower and the heat from my blow dryer would have made the room unbearable. It was so hot I skipped my curling iron in favor of just straightening everything with a round brush.

"Your middle-aged boyfriend is taking you bowling, huh?" she teased. "So, is he on a league?"

"Shut up." I blinked and examined my handiwork. Both sides were nearly symmetrical in appearance. Nerves upped my makeup game like crazy. "I'll have you know that the place we're going looks very hip."

"Of course it's hip. It's in a gentrified neighborhood. Hipsters live to force low-income residents out of the city and ironically appropriate their working class interests." She shook her head.

She had a point there. "I really wish you would reserve judgment of Ian until you actually meet him."

"Sorry," she said, though I knew she wasn't actually sorry about her gentrification comment, and she shouldn't have been, anyway. "But I'm worried about you. Older guys go after younger women all the time, and it never works out."

"He isn't 'going after' me. We were set up on a blind date. And besides, sometimes, it works out. Look at Neil and Sophie." I shouldn't have brought them up as an example; I knew it the moment it came out of my mouth. Rosa had never met either of them, but she knew of them from the occasional mention in a magazine and had formed a pretty definite opinion of what made their marriage work. It involved dollar signs and the faint suggestion of midlife crises.

"I'm just saying, you're planning on deciding on Monday if this guy is the love of your life. Doesn't that strike you as kind of scary?"

"I'm not deciding anything. On Monday, I'm going to find out if *I'm* the love of *Ian's* life. And yes, it's very scary. Everything that I'm feeling about him is scary." I shrugged. "It just makes it seem more...real."

"Okay. It's your life. I'm not going to interfere anymore,"

she said, holding up her hands.

"Yes, you are." I stepped back from the mirror and smoothed down my T-shirt. V-neck with a push-up bra, and I planned to do a lot of leaning over. Rosa was right. My jeans were really tight. With Ian, I felt comfortable looking sexy. Maybe because with Brad, anything I wore got criticized. I'd either been too hot and a "tease", or too buttoned up and "frigid-looking".

It's amazing the kind of personal baggage you shed when you let go of someone super toxic.

"Okay, how do I look?" I asked, turning around and holding my breath.

Rosa considered. "Like Amanda."

Amanda's penchant for tight, low-cut apparel affected Rosa the way the light on a pilot fish attracts other fish. So I took it as a compliment.

I took the subway to Ian's place, but I would lie and tell him I took a cab, because for some reason, men always seem think a woman is destined for rape and murder on the subway. When we'd met for lunch earlier in the week, he'd been appalled I'd braved the same line I took to and from work every day. I understood he cared about me not dying, but I did not like the overprotective vibe.

I rang the buzzer at his place, which, unlike the one at my building didn't not give me a shock, and he met me downstairs. He wore jeans and a black button down with the sleeves rolled up, and I stared at his forearms the way he stared at my chest, so I guess we were even on the objectification front.

He put his arm around my waist briefly to lean in and kiss my cheek. "You look lovely, as ever."

"Thanks. I'm digging this scruffy thing you've got going on," I said, pointing to his hair. Most of the times I'd seen him, with the exception of after our impromptu pool date, his hairstyle had been a very controlled, Cary Grant side part. Now he looked more fourth-date casual, and less like a guy you'd buy a casket from.

He reached up self-consciously and combed his fingers through his hair. "Scruffy?"

"Not in a bad way," I hurried to assure him. "In a perfect-for-bowling way."

"Ah, yes, bowling. About that," he said with a grin. "There's been a change of plans."

I'm always on the fence about whether or not I like surprises, but if Ian had plans to whisk me off somewhere exciting, I was in. "I'm listening."

As we walked to the small parking lot beside his building, he asked, "How do you feel about aquariums?"

"Um. Like they're awesome." I paused. "But also like they're not open at eight o'clock on a Saturday night."

"You're right. They usually aren't. But interestingly enough, I know someone who is a major donor to the New York Aquarium. And they have recently acquired a new Pacific octopus." He let that just hang there, tantalizing me with the suspense.

"And?"

"And I thought you might like to meet him," Ian said with a shrug. "I mean we could always go bowling—"

"No!" I shrieked. This could not be happening to me. I hadn't had any time to prepare. How could I just go and meet an octopus? "I can't... I mean, do I look all right?"

"Do you think an octopus is going to care what you're wearing?" He laughed. Then he put both hands on my upper arms and leaned down to look me in the eye. "If octopods are attracted to people, and who knows, they very well might be, I'm sure he'll find you just as sexy as I do."

Ian thought I was sexy. Not that I hadn't guessed before, after our make-out at the pool. But now my octopus feelings and my Ian feelings were getting all mixed up and combining into one giant ball of endorphins.

"Okay." I rubbed my sweaty palms on my thighs. "Let's do it. Let's go meet the octopus."

On the ride to Coney Island, I managed to maintain an actual conversation with Ian, somehow. I have no memory of what we talked about, so I hoped very much it wasn't important. All I could see in my head was a line of octopus emoticons, stretching into eternity. When we arrived, we didn't go through the front entrance, but a man with a wiry white mustache and a nylon windbreaker emblazoned with the aquarium logo met us at an employees-only door.

"You must be Burt's friend," the man said, thrusting his hand out to Ian. "And this is your—"

"Date," Ian said quickly, probably to avoid the man guessing "daughter". Ian cleared his throat. "Penny Parker. Octopod enthusiast."

"Hi!" I grabbed the man's hand between both of mine and shook it way too vigorously. "It is an honor to meet you."

"I don't actually work with the octopus," he told me, looking as worried as I would have expected someone whose hand was being squeezed to a pulp by a stranger would be.

"This is Jim Bronner," Ian explained to me. "He works on the money side."

"Your friend here knows one of our extremely valued donors," Jim explained. "Why don't you guys come on in."

One time, Rosa had described for me what it had felt like going backstage at an N'Sync concert. This felt exactly how she'd described it.

"He's not in his exhibit, yet. You'll be able to get up close," Jim told us as he led us down a hallway that looked like it could have belonged in a hospital, a far cry from the decorated and themed visitor areas.

"Up close?" I looked nervously to Ian. He just smirked back at me, clearly pleased with himself. As he should have been; this was going to be in my top ten lifelong memories.

"She's a wee bit nervous," he said as we paused for Jim to slide his badge through a card reader.

"Why nervous?" he asked, as though it was just every

day someone could wander up and meet an *enteroctopus dofleini*.

Before I could answer, Ian spoke for me. "She's afraid the octopus is going to be wearing the same outfit, and she'll have to go change."

I laughed the loudest, dorkiest laugh anyone has ever laughed. Ian looked very pleased with himself.

The sign on the door said, "Fish Quarantine," but the room beyond was a surprisingly calm environment. I would have expected a place that had an octopus to be more frantic with science. Instead, various tanks bubbled away against the walls, and two large ones ran down the center of the room. There was a long workstation with a computer and various papers and clipboards, and a coffee maker, the kind you'd see in a roadside diner, with the brown and orange tops on the pots. A gentle, but loud, hum filled the air, like the noise of a fish tank filter combined with the sound inside an airplane.

A middle-aged woman with dark brown skin and salt-and-pepper hair was leaning over one of the tanks, a gloved arm groping for something on the bottom.

"Vivian?" Jim called, and she startled.

"I didn't even hear you come in." She laughed. "The stupid cap fell off my marker, and I can't reach it. And these little jerks are not helping."

As we watched, two very bright yellow fish floated closer to her hand, then darted in to strike it before backing off, again.

"Gimme a hand. Or just your arm, that's all I need." She withdrew her dripping glove, peeled it off, and tossed it into the utility sink behind her. She smiled at Ian and I and said, "You're here to see the new baby?"

"It's a baby?" That was a bit disappointing. Not that babies weren't cool. I was hoping to see a fully-grown one. At least, as fully grown as they get in captivity. But I would take what I could get.

"No, he's about four feet long. But we're as excited over him as a new baby," she said, extending the hand that hadn't just been digging around in a tank. We did our shakes as she introduced herself. "I'm Vivian Jackson, I'm the director of animal care here at the aquarium."

"Wow, and you're the one who's going to be showing us the octopus?" This was so much better than meeting a member of a boy band. "I'm so honored!"

She had the grace to not look totally weirded out by that. "Well, thank you. When I found out Mr. Baker was sending over some guests, I had to be here to meet you."

I had no idea what "Mr. Baker" had done to get Ian and me this kind of access, but I was totally digging it. "Thank you so much, Ms. Jackson—" I began.

She stopped me. "Just call me Vivian. I had to come down to give a tortoise an antibiotic, anyway."

As Vivian led us to the back of the room, I reached for Ian's hand. I don't know why I was so nervous, or why I needed his touch to calm me, but he didn't seem to mind. He threaded his fingers through mine and gave a squeeze, nudging me a little with his elbow.

There was so much I wanted to say to him, about this, about everything I'd been thinking of for the past week, but at least seventy percent of my need to pour emotion everywhere came from the fact that I was about to be overflowing with it.

Vivian took us to a large, square tank, surrounded by PVC pipe and netting. The lid of the tank itself was clamped down and weighted.

"That is a lot of security. Is this the Hannibal Lecter of octopods?" Ian asked, touching the plastic tubing.

"They escape like crazy," I said then realized he was probably asking the actual expert. "Sorry."

"No, you're right. His eventual enclosure will be far more secure, but for right now, we have to prevent prison breaks." She carefully unclipped the net, then unlatched the lid and pulled it back. "Let's see if we can get him back here."

She didn't need to coax him. Though the tank was mostly barren, there was a pile of rocks and some foliage for him to hide in. Slowly, he emerged, detaching himself from the rocks he'd been using as camouflage.

"Here comes Monty," Vivian said, and I grabbed Ian's arm with my free hand. Monty the octopus slid right up to the tank glass then rolled in a vertical surge to slap two tentacles over the rim.

"Jesus Christ!" Ian jumped back, startling me, Vivian, and Monty.

"Ian, you're scaring him!" I turned back to Monty. I came close to the edge of the tank and leaned down. "I am so sorry, sir."

"I don't think you have to call him sir," Ian said with a chuckle.

Poor Ian. He had no idea that the only male capturing my heart tonight was the beautiful, eight-tentacled one hauling himself up for a closer look at us.

Monty was a beautiful reddish brown, with lighter skin on the undersides of his tentacles. The giant Pacific octopus looks kind of like a big, squishy rock someone had painted, and the color had worn off his various protrusions.

"Look at him," I breathed.

I didn't realize my hand was hovering in the air until Vivian said, "You can touch him. It's all right."

I bent over beside the tank and looked into his eye through the glass. Despite their flat pupils, I've always found their eyes to be strangely human. Maybe I was anthropomorphizing Monty a bit, but he seemed as curious about me as I was about him.

That's when I heard the sound of water blowing from his siphon and breaking the surface and felt a tap on my shoulder.

I straightened, and Monty followed, adhering his tentacle to my arm with surprising force. "Wow! They really are strong."

"He's not going to pull her in there, is he?" Ian asked nervously.

"You wouldn't do that to me, would you?" I cooed, like Monty was a baby and not a grown octopus who probably didn't appreciate my condescension.

Vivian shook her head. "He'd just tire himself out. But..." She reached over and gently pried up a few suckers on a section that had wrapped around my arm. "We don't want him to get a real good grip on you, either, or he'll use you as leverage to escape."

Monty's tentacle was like the world's strongest bathmat. Each round protrusion flexed on their own, pulling at my skin. They could taste with their suckers. I wondered if he liked the taste of my body lotion, then I worried that the chemicals in it would hurt him.

"You want to touch him?" Vivian asked Ian.

I turned to find that he'd taken several steps back. He held up his hands and said, "No, I'm fine over here."

"This isn't really his thing," I explained, though I'd had no idea Ian would have been frightened by Monty.

"And he brought you here, anyway?" She looked impressed. "That's devotion. You've got yourself a keeper."

I smiled at Ian, and he smiled back. All the happiness I felt overwhelmed me, and I turned away, tears in my eyes. He was definitely a keeper.

"Are you all right?" Ian laughed softly, genuine concern behind his words.

I nodded and wiped my eyes with my non-octopus hand. "I'm just...a lot happier than I've been in a really long time."

I spent a beautiful twelve minutes with Monty, until he decided to use me as a means of escape, and Vivian had to distract him with some treats. Due to his position against the glass, I got to watch him pull the dismembered fish parts beneath his web. Then he glided away, siphons flaring, his big mantle swaying from side to side.

Vivian took me to a sink where I could wash up—twice, at Ian's insistence, lest I get some "sucker infestation". Then Vivian led us back to the door, and I expressed my thanks again.

"This is one of the top five moments in my life," I told her.

"Well, I'm glad I could be a part of it." She paused. "You know, we take volunteers here. You could be a tour guide."

"Yeah. Maybe some day." Someday when I had the time, and when it wouldn't conflict with my reliable employment. Someday when I didn't have to be practical and carefully guard my limited free time.

Someday when I'd made choices that enabled me to do the things I loved, instead of the things that would make money.

On the walk back to Ian's car, I took his hand, again, then stepped in front of him to stop him. "This was the sweetest thing any guy has ever done for me. I don't know what I did to deserve it—"

"You're you," he said, before I could disparage myself. "And you gave me a chance."

I stood on my tiptoes to kiss him, and he pulled me close. When he released me, he said, "Come on. Let's go get some dinner."

I was octopus obnoxious the whole time. I'm sure he wanted to jump through the plate glass window of the bistro we'd picked, rather than listen to me. I tried to make other conversation, but I talked about Monty the way some people talk about their children.

It didn't stop once we were in the car.

"They're really devoted mothers," I prattled on. Once the trivia started flowing, there was no stemming the tide. "A female giant Pacific octopus will make a den in a nook or a hole, somewhere she can protect, and lay like ten thousand eggs. And she hangs them up on the walls and spends six months just sitting there, cleaning the eggs, moving them around; she doesn't even feed herself. She doesn't sleep. If she's not dead by the time the babies hatch, she's not alive for long."

"Why? Do they eat her?" he asked, his gaze still fixed on the red light.

"No! How dare you!" I exclaimed.

"I'm sorry, I didn't realize it was an offensive question," he said with a laugh. I got the feeling that teasing me into knee-jerk octopus outrage was fun for him.

"No, they don't eat her. You should YouTube octopods sometime. They're fascinating." I leaned back in the seat with a sigh. Ian's car was more comfortable than my couch at home.

"Well, I find *you* fascinating, Penny Parker." He looked over at me and winked.

And that was it. I was in love with him.

## CHAPTER NINE

We pulled up to Ian's building at eleven-thirty. I was still riding the high from meeting the octopus, so I hadn't questioned until that moment why he hadn't headed for my place.

"Well, isn't this presumptuous," I said with a slow smile.

He half-lifted his hand from the steering wheel. "It's Saturday night. There must be something good on television, right?"

"I don't think we're going to watch TV up there." Not that I wasn't okay with that. I'd never felt so alive in my life, and I didn't want the feeling to stop.

"You caught me." He gestured to my arm, still bearing faint marks from Monty. "I was hoping I'd get to put some hickeys on you, as well, since you're being so generous about it tonight."

"Shut up and let's get inside." I laughed.

Once we got into the apartment, Ian headed to the kitchen to open some wine, and I excused myself to go to the bathroom. The half-bath on the main floor was on the other side of the elevator, so I walked through the living room to get there. On my way, the lights dimmed just a touch.

The bathroom, like the rest of the house, was beautiful. It had a big white porcelain vessel sink and a lovely modern-looking toilet. I'd never thought I would find a toilet an attractive furnishing before.

As I washed my hands and checked that my eyeliner hadn't run, music started. I jumped. Ian had a built-in sound system in his apartment? That was so cool. I didn't recognize the song playing, but it was old, and pretty sexy. My nipples tightened against my bra. *This could happen. Tonight, if you wanted to, this could happen.*

Pumping the brakes on my hormones wasn't easy. Yes, I

was a grown woman, free to make my own choices. But so far, that choice had been to not have sex with anyone, and I needed to examine why this thing between Ian and me was my combo breaker. Yes, I was head-over-heels in shiny-new-love with him, but I didn't know how he felt about me, and I only had to wait until Monday to find out if we were destined to be together.

I could wait another week.

But not having sex didn't mean not having dirty fun. I emerged from the bathroom to find Ian setting a bottle and two glasses on the big round coffee table. He handed me a glass. "I hope you like Chardonnay, because it was all I had."

"It's better than a glass of peanut butter." I took a sip. I wasn't as much of a wine girl as I was a beer girl, but there was something sort of magical about wine as a romantic touch that a lager couldn't compete with.

He sat on the couch and patted the spot beside him. "Best living room view in all of New York?"

I sat beside him. He put his arm around me as comfortably as if he'd done it a hundred times, and my heart made a little flutter. I laid my head on his shoulder. "Best seat in all of New York. Best date."

"I'm glad you liked it," he said then sighed. "Of course, now I'll never top it."

"You've set a really high bar for me," I pointed out. "How am I supposed to compete with you providing the culmination of my lifelong dream?"

"I had no idea it would mean that much to you," he said softly. "But I'm honored that it did."

"Can I tell you something?" I asked, even though I'd always thought that was a really stupid phrase, because you were going to tell the person whatever it was you wanted to say, anyway. "Something that might sound...too soon-ish."

His body tensed; I realized he might be interpreting my question as me asking permission to tell him I loved him. I wasn't that foolish. It was way too early to love him, but I did. Telling him that I did? Wouldn't improve the situation.

"Yes?" he said cautiously, as though he weren't sure of that answer.

I turned my head to look him in the eye. "You are a really great guy."

He dropped his head, and he blushed. I loved that.

"You are," I insisted. "You're funny, and you're very good-looking, you've got a sexy accent—"

He made an incredulous noise and slid his wine glass onto the table. "If you like Scrooge McDuck."

"And," I said forcefully, steamrolling over his interruption. "You did something really thoughtful for me, and I know you did it without any expectation of getting something in return."

"How do you know I wasn't trying to get something in return?" he asked, then hastily added, "I wasn't, but how did you know that?"

"Because you're not as good at putting up a front as you think you are." I covered his hand with my own where it rested on my shoulder. "You're a good man, and that shows through. Even if you think you're hiding it under all that self-deprecation."

He looked up, smiling in surrender. "All right. You caught me. I just wanted to make you happy."

"And that's why I'm not scared of how fast things are going." That had been the part I'd feared was too soon, but I was glad I said it.

"Oh?" He looked relieved. "Well, that wasn't as serious as I was expecting."

"I know what you were expecting. And I liked watching you squirm." I wasn't going to lie and tell him that I didn't feel it yet, and I wasn't going to probe around to see if I could get a hint that he felt it, either. If we were meant to be, we'd eventually say the I-love-you words. We didn't have to rush.

"Penny, I have to ask you something." He brushed his thumb over the back of my hand, and my lungs stopped pumping oxygen and started flooding my veins with sparkles, instead.

"Are you ticklish?"

The question was out of left field, and in the moment it took me to process what he'd asked, he attacked with his free hand, burrowing his wriggling fingers into my side. With a glass of wine in one hand and the other firmly in his grip, there was nothing I could do but cackle helplessly and try not to spill.

"The wine! The wine!" I gasped.

"Oh, fuck, I forgot." He relented and reached for his own glass. He took a deep swallow, as I recovered, and he set the drink back on the table. He took my glass and placed it beside his own, and I thought, *this is it. Make out time.* Instead of romancing me, he dove back in to torment me, tickling my sides as I gasped in hysterical laughter. Over the shrieks and squeals involuntarily wrenching from my vocal chords, I managed to hear him tease, "You wanted to watch me squirm, I get to watch you squirm. Fair's fair, isn't it?"

My struggling and his pursuit somehow ended with me on my back, my elbows tucked tight to my sides, and him looming over me with a knee between my legs. Through my helpless laughter, I shouted, "There are better ways of making me squirm!"

I froze as I realized what I'd just said. He froze, too. We probably didn't stare at each other any longer than a heartbeat, but it felt like a long time, with the way the pressure between us built. Then it burst. I lunged up, and he dove down, and our mouths were together, my hands in his hair, his body braced above mine with a forearm on the back of the couch.

Maybe it was the tension we'd been fighting against since our first kiss. It certainly wasn't the few sips of wine. It might have been the octopus, at least, on my part. I didn't really care what was causing this to happen, only that it was happening. He slid an arm under my back and pulled me up, and we clumsily arranged ourselves so that I sat straddling his lap.

This close, I could hear his breathing, and it was an indescribable turn on. I'd imagined what it would be like to have sex with him at least six times a day for the past week, but being this close to him, even just making out, was a little intimidating. He was way more confident than anybody else I'd been with. I didn't feel like he was rushing through perfunctory steps to try to get to the finish line. When he skimmed his fingers down my throat, it was as though he savored just touching me.

He made me feel like a woman. Not a conquest. And no man had ever treated me that way before.

In the intimate position we were in, it wasn't hard to imagine being naked, writhing on top of him. That was a dangerous picture in my mind. *You only have to wait until Monday for your answer. Do you really want to blow it this close to the finish line?*

And at this point, my chastity did seem like a marathon that I was desperately trying to finish. I'd never bought into the whole "your virginity is a gift" mindset that my mother had tried to push on me. If I had sex with Ian, I wasn't giving anything away. It would be celebrating something with him, something I had deemed him worthy of sharing, in a way no other man had been worthy. And I wanted that celebration to be because of love, not horniness. Well, horniness, too. Love and horniness—the two weren't mutually exclusive. But I wanted to know those feelings were returned, or that they would someday be returned.

The surefire way to not have sex tonight would be to tell him I didn't want to have sex tonight. With as cautious and respectful as he was, I couldn't see him letting me change my mind in the heat of the moment if he knew I hadn't planned to go all the way before we'd started. I pressed my hand to his chest. "Just to be clear…tonight is not the night. Do you get my drift?"

He didn't crack a joke or display even the slightest hint of annoyance or disappointment. "I do. We are absolutely clear."

"Good. But…that doesn't mean I don't want to make you feel good." I petted the front of his shirt then thought, *what the hell*, and popped the top button.

"You're making me feel pretty fucking good right now, Doll." He kissed my neck at the intersection of my shoulder and collarbone. I whimpered.

"You know what I mean." Oh god, his lips were so soft and warm, and they felt amazing on my skin. "Can I?"

He shuddered out a long breath. "Jesus, Penny…do you think I could turn you down?"

The hand at my back bunched up my shirt, then slid beneath. He hooked a finger under my bra-strap. "Is this too forward of me?"

"Not at all. I can take it off." My breasts ached in anticipation. I didn't even have to move to get rid of the bra. He popped the closure as easily as snapping his fingers and splayed his palm against my back.

He buried his face in my hair then murmured against my ear, "You smell like flowers."

I leaned into him, tilting my head to the side as he nibbled the shell of my ear. I was so sensitive I swore I got drunk on the feeling. He sucked the lobe into his mouth and grazed it with his teeth, and I moaned.

"I've been wanting to do this," he rasped against my neck as his kisses moved downward, "since we kissed in the park."

"And since the pool?" I added with a breathless laugh.

He chuckled. "Then, too. Giving you that kiss on the cheek after lunch on Wednesday? Was the biggest test of my willpower to date."

"Well, please don't exercise any restraint, now." The

hand on my bare back moved beneath my shirt, then under my unfastened bra to cup my breast, and my ribcage rose on a shuddering inhale.

His lips hovered over my collarbone above the V-neck of my shirt, and his voice rumbled a long, low, "Mmm," against my chest. He lifted his head and met my eyes, his full of naked adoration that seared like a brand across my heart. I bent forward and took his face in my hands. He played his fingers across my skin and gave me the sweetest, deepest kiss of my life, and all the while my head spun with thoughts like, *Is this really happening?* and *Holy shit, this is really happening.*

When I'd walked into the restaurant on our first date, I would have never guessed, never in a million years, that we would ever end up in the situation we were in. I remembered standing on the sidewalk, wondering if I would even be able to force myself to find him physically attractive. Now, all I wanted to do was to rip his shirt off and get my hands on every square inch of him.

"Can I unbutton this?" I gasped against his mouth, tugging on his shirt.

"Be my guest."

My hands fumbled between us, and I opened his shirt enough to slip my hands inside. That was all I needed, to feel the hot skin and crisp hair on his chest, to be able to lean down and kiss his throat, up to his jaw.

If I was going to grade Ian's groping technique, he definitely would have gotten an A-plus. He didn't attack my chest like he was trying to adjust a car's air conditioning, but he stroked me like a painter's brush, the backs of his fingers along the curve of my breast. He drew circles around my nipple, always with a feather light touch. He could have given lessons to all my exes who had manhandled me in the past. He was so slow and careful I lost all sense of time. I lost all sense of everything but him, his mouth, his hands, the way his breath sounded in my ear and the way his stubble scratched my jaw. His skin tasted salty under my tongue, his mouth like the wine.

We were both sweating and gasping when I climbed off his lap. I pressed my hand against his obvious erection, and his penis flexed upward as if it could meet my palm through the denim. "You unzip. I don't want to be held responsible for any accidental maiming."

"Christ, I hope you're not speaking from experience." He laughed nervously.

"No. Caution." I held my breath as his hands moved to his fly. It's odd to see a guy's penis for the first time, because once it's out there, there's really no going back. You see it, and you can't unsee it.

I really hoped he had a nice one.

"This is always a nerve-wracking moment," he said under his breath.

"I promise I won't laugh," I swore.

He rolled his eyes as he pulled down his zipper. "Thank you. Your confidence is very reassuring."

"No, I meant—" My giggle cut me off. I reached down and brushed his hands away, and reached into his open fly.

*He's a boxers man.* I reached for the top of them, and the head of his erection was already poking out, obscured by the tails of his shirt. He took a breath as I curled my fingers around the shaft. He was nice and thick—from my understanding that was very important—and longer than my average experience.

"See, nothing to worry about," I said, pumping my fist back and forth a little. I pushed his shirt up and his boxers down. "Oh my gosh, and you're uncut!"

"And that's a plus, is it?" he asked with a weak laugh.

"Yeah, I've never been with a guy who wasn't circumcised." I slid my hand up experimentally and watched his foreskin roll over the head. "Is there anything I have to do differently?"

I was going to check out some online tutorials as soon as

I got home.

"No, no, that's… What you're doing… Keep doing that." His arm tightened around my back.

It was much easier than with a guy who was cut; I didn't feel like I was churning butter. I could just lay there, in the crook of Ian's arm, my head on his chest, listening to his heartbeat speed up and the changes in his breathing as I touched him. When he started kneading my hip in rhythm with my strokes, I knew I was on the right track.

I sat up, so I could use my other hand, too. I dragged them both up and gave a lazy twist, rubbing his foreskin over the tip and drumming my fingers along the underside.

"How's that?" I asked, but I knew how it was. I'd never had a complaint before, and even with the whole uncut curveball I'd just been pitched, I knew my way around a dick pretty well.

"Jesus." He blew out a long exhale. "You weren't joking at the park, were you?"

"I would never make a promise I couldn't deliver on." I squeezed my thighs together against the ache between them. I was so wet I wondered if I would soak my jeans. What could I say? Getting a guy off made me feel horny and powerful. I was going to change the batteries in my vibrator when I got home and probably come in thirty seconds flat.

"Ah, Penny. That is…" He groaned. "I'm a bit embarrassed, Doll. I don't think I'm going to impress you with my staying power tonight."

Oh god, maybe ten seconds flat. Nothing made me feel sexier than having a guy this helpless in my hands.

"I wouldn't expect you to." I licked my lower lip. "I'm very good."

He closed his eyes, a furrow of concentration forming between his brows. I took that as my cue to speed up a little. I thought about spitting in my hand, just to make it a bit easier. Then I thought, *you could just blow him, you know.*

That was something else I'd never done. And, right now,

watching the way his jaw clenched and the muscles of his forearm flexed as he squeezed his hand into a fist, I wanted to. I wanted to blow his mind.

I licked my lips, leaned over, and sucked the tip of him into my mouth, still pumping him with my hands. In no time at all, he made a strangled noise of surprise, groaned, "Oh fuck," and thrust his hips up, his cock jerking in my mouth as he came.

I didn't really know what to do at that point. This logical conclusion never occurred to me when I'd been conceiving my spur-of-the-moment plan. I was too shocked by the totally weird taste and texture, I made the split second decision to swallow, and he shivered violently.

When I sat back up and pushed my hair away from my face, he stared at me, mortified. "I am so sorry. I didn't have any time to warn you."

I dropped my head and laughed. "I'll take that as praise."

"And fully deserved." He half sat up. "Give me a second. I've got to go clean up a bit."

I reached for my glass of wine. "Okay. I'll just finish this."

"Again," he said as he stood, "I am sorry."

"Don't worry about it." I shrugged. "I guess I'm as good with my mouth as I am with my hands."

He made that strangled noise again, and headed off to the bathroom.

I lay back on the couch with a contented sigh. I was awfully proud of myself for the initiative I'd taken. I deserved two orgasms when I got home.

He came back and sat beside me. "Thank you."

"Any time," I told him with a smirk. It wasn't just to get a reaction; I really meant any time. I could easily get addicted to making Ian come. There was something intimidating about dating a guy who wasn't just charming and funny, but who really had his life together. Logically, I knew it was stupid to compare my life to his. He'd had more time than I'd had to get a great career and his own apartment and pull in enough money to actually live on. Still, being able to have him so completely helpless in my hands gave me a thrill of power. And the fact that he'd been so turned on gave me a sense of pride.

He pulled me into his arms and brushed his lips across my cheek. He kissed the corner of my jawbone. "I apologize for the interruption."

*Interruption?* "I thought we were done."

He stilled, his lips beside my ear. "Do you...want to be?"

"What? No, believe me, I am totally fine with this. I just figured that since you already..."

"But you didn't."

"I usually don't."

"Wait." He leaned up, his brow furrowed. "You've been giving men absolutely splendid hand jobs—"

"Thanks!" I beamed at him.

"Praise well-deserved," he assured me, and went on, "but none of those men ever made you come?"

*No, but listening to that sentence almost made you the first.* "Not because they weren't good at it. They probably were. I didn't let them try."

"Oh," he said, and he didn't press for more details.

So I added, "It was too intimate. O-orgasming in front of someone."

*Orgasming?* How clinical could I possibly sound? And where had all of that sexual confidence gone? I'd already had his dick in my mouth, it wasn't like I could go back to being a shy flower.

His frown changed to one of thoughtfulness. "Fair enough. In that case, forget I mentioned it."

Forget he mentioned it? I wanted him so badly I was almost willing to ignore a family legend and lose my virginity after four dates with him. And he'd just offered to make me come. What would that be like? I mean, I knew what coming was like. But to have someone else, to have

*Ian,* getting me off? That was going to be unbelievable. How could I pass it up?

"I don't want to forget it," I said with a nervous laugh. "I want you to do it."

His eyebrows shot up.

"Let's do it. I'll call it a trial run." I couldn't believe how I was behaving. This was not me. At least, not me in real life. Me in my sexual fantasies would come on this strong. Maybe that was the version of Penny I wanted to be with Ian.

He smiled slowly. "A trial run?"

"In case I ever decide to have sex with you, obviously." I wriggled my hips. My confidence was at an all time high, and I didn't want it to fade. I licked my puffy bottom lip. "So…what do I do?"

He bent his head and kissed me. It didn't matter that my mouth was practically numb from sensation overload; the touch still electrified my whole body. Going home, using my vibrator for thirty seconds, and falling asleep no longer seemed like a satisfactory end to the evening. His hand squeezed my hip, then glided up, under my shirt, to cup my breast again. Chills skated down my arms, and a sharp breath pushed my flesh more fully into his hand.

"What you should do," he murmured against my cheek, "is tell me if I do anything you don't like. And tell me what you do like. I want to learn how to make you come, and it works a lot better with direction than trial and error."

"Oh god." I tipped my head back. Ian's sexy voice alone was enough to make me tingle in every place I could possibly tingle. "Just keep talking like that."

He reached down to slowly pull the zipper of my jeans. Parting my fly with one finger, he stroked up and down the front of my lace panties. "What? Talking about how much I want to make you come?"

"Mhmm," was all I could manage. My knees shook. He hadn't even touched my skin yet.

"I bet it's beautiful when you do," he went on. Two fingers rubbed up and down my slit over my panties. "I can't wait to hear how you sound."

I stifled a moan.

"Don't do that," he said, his voice soft, but his tone firm. "Nobody will hear you but me."

And I wanted him to hear me. I was just so used to not being heard I hadn't remembered that making noise was an option. His hands could conduct a whole symphony of noise from me. "Make me get loud, then."

"Ah, fuck," he groaned. He slipped his hand under my panties, and my breath caught.

My jeans were too tight, that became painfully clear when his hand was trapped in them. My palms got sweaty, and my stomach flipped over on itself. I was going to have to remove some clothing. I pushed my pants down a little. "Do you mind if I take these off?"

"Not at all. It'll definitely make things easier." He withdrew his hand long enough for me to shimmy out of the tight denim. I left my panties on; it was stupid, I knew, but somehow, the thought of him seeing me half-naked made me feel shyer than the thought of him actually touching me.

He didn't ask me to take them off, but he did hook a finger beneath one side and tugged down slightly. "Ah. Now there is the octopus *I* have been wanting to meet."

I laughed and pushed him away from my tattoo. "If you don't get your hand back to where it was, I'm going to cry."

"Well, I don't want that," he said with a smile, and leaned over to kiss me as he slid his hand under my panties again. He cupped my mound and I lifted my hips; this was too much of a tease, when I wanted direct stimulation. I supposed I could have told him that—he wanted to know what I liked, after all—but I liked the anticipation. I opened my legs wider for him. The length of his finger pressed between my labia, and I arched up; he followed my body with this fingertip until he found my clit.

He may as well have shocked me with a taser, for the way I reacted. I felt like I'd been blown apart by lightning. I gripped his shoulder, hard, and my nails sank into his shirt.

"Easy," he said, laughing softly. "I appreciate the compliment, but I also appreciate having skin."

"Sorry." I pulled him closer. I needed him closer. He rubbed slow circles over and over my clit, and my breath stopped with each one. It would be so embarrassing to hyperventilate and need medical attention from this.

It was also embarrassing how close I was getting so fast. Ian may have been worried that he'd come so soon, but was he going to think I was totally hard-up because of this?

"May I go inside?" he asked, gliding his fingers down. His thumb replaced them on my clit, still rubbing those lazy circles.

"Yeah," I breathed. I had to force myself to relax when the excitement pounding through me demanded I tense up. I was blasting through firsts tonight, and the exhilaration was overpowering.

Slowly, he pushed two fingers into me. A shocked exhale rushed out of me. I'd fingered myself before, but his hands were a lot different than mine, slightly rougher and definitely larger. My muscles clenched, and he dropped his head with a low groan. It didn't take a huge leap to figure out what he was imagining, and that made me imagine it, too. I'd thought I couldn't get any wetter, but I'd been wrong.

He swirled his fingertips just inside the opening of my vagina. It was pretty obvious what he was looking for, and he was *almost* there, but I needed it so bad I had to direct him.

"It's just a little deeper," I whimpered.

"Thank God you know where it is," he said with a laugh. "That makes it much easier to find."

He found it. Oh god, he found it. I bucked my hips and gripped the back of the couch. "Oh fuck, oh fuck, oh fuck," I chanted, and heard him murmur something under his breath. I hardly ever swore like that, but at the moment, I couldn't help it. Touching myself felt good. Using my vibrator? Even better. But it felt different when it was someone else doing it. I knew exactly what I liked, and it took me no time at all on my own. Ian had to learn, and his trial and error exploration just made the pleasure last and last, until that unstoppable up-hill rush tightened all my muscles and burst in a shock of ecstasy. My mouth froze open. Maybe I was trying to scream? I couldn't tell, because my mind was blissfully blank, my clit still pulsing under Ian's thumb.

"Do you want to keep going?" he asked, stroking the fingers of his other hand over my belly, under my shirt. The hand in my panties stilled, but stayed where it was, exerting the same pressure over the parts where I still throbbed from my orgasm.

"What?" My voice was hoarse.

"Do you want to come again?" he asked. "Honestly, I could do this all night."

"Yes!" The word burst from my mouth without having to consider the answer. Which was good, because I might have decided it would be polite to tell him no or something absolutely stupid like that. I'd never tried for multiples before, because it always felt too sensitive, but I was being reckless and sexy, and I was totally under his power. It was a good thing I'd told him I didn't want to have sex—well, intercourse—because I would have begged him to fuck me if I'd been able to talk.

I'd come down a little, but not very much, when he started that slow swirl of his thumb again. It was an odd feeling, like I wanted him to stop because it was too much but keep going because it wasn't enough. The fingers inside of me wriggled and rubbed over my g-spot, and I arched up as if pulled by a cord strung right between my hips. His free hand slid beneath my shirt to cup my breast and tease my nipple with his thumb, and the sensation tugged something deep in my pelvis. He leaned down to kiss me, and I held his face in my hands, sucking at his tongue as I rode his fingers and muffled my scream of release with his mouth.

I broke away, panting. "Okay. Okay, that's enough."

He withdrew his hand gently, while my pulse still pounded and my legs still jerked. Before my utterly disbelieving eyes, he lifted his fingers to his mouth and sucked them clean.

No. Fucking. Way.

My thighs trembled. Shock must have showed on my face, because he smirked a little. "Is there anything I can get you?"

"Water," I croaked. I felt like I'd just gone for a brutal run at the hottest part of the day. My muscles hurt, I was impossibly thirsty, yet I was completely satisfied with myself and what my body could do. But the aftermath was so much better than any runner's high.

He kissed my cheek. "I'll be right back."

I closed my eyes and flopped sideways. My everything was too tired to put my pants back on. The white throw was still over the back of the couch, so I pulled it down to cover myself. The jeans he'd stuffed under it last week tumbled across me, belt and all. I laughed.

"What's so funny?" he called from the kitchen.

*How adorably hopeless you are.* I sat up and folded the jeans, then tossed them down the couch. "Nothing. Just tons of endorphins."

"Ah." He came back with a cold bottle of water and handed it to me. "I suppose I've done my job."

"More like charity work," I snorted.

"Then, I'll consider myself a philanthropist, because I'm keenly devoted to the cause." He sat beside me, again, and put his arm around my shoulders. But this time, he held me a little closer than before. The easy intimacy of the gesture warmed me from the inside out, and I stifled a giddy laugh.

I pulled my feet up on the couch and lay back in the

crook of his arm. "Thank you."

"You're more than welcome."

"No, I mean, thank you. For not pushing for more." A rush of emotion overwhelmed me. I knew my voice was going to shake, and I didn't care. "It's really nice to be treated like a person and not a challenge."

He hugged me tight with the arm that lay over my chest. "Penny, I really don't care if you sleep with me. I hope we see each other long enough that we do, but if it never happens, I won't feel like you've deprived me of anything. Being with you has been the best part of the past few weeks."

I frowned at how much his statement managed to echo feelings I hadn't thought to examine.

I took his hand in mine. "You know…you've been the best part for me, too."

\* \* \* \*

The high I'd gotten from my date with Ian was still going strong on Sunday morning. Rosa was tired of hearing the details—the octopus details, not the sexy details—which I think influenced her decision to reschedule our planned Sunday Marvel marathon. We'd been slowly working through all the movies in order, because both of us were woefully behind the trend. She swore she wasn't going to spend the time with Amanda, but I knew she was a liar. And truthfully, I didn't really mind having the day to myself. I felt more positive and upbeat than I had since Brad and I had broken up, and I was ready to run.

I've always wanted to run the Battery Park esplanade, so I threw on my gear and headed out. My plan was to go across town to the Irish Hunger Memorial, then along the river, through Battery Park, and back home. I mentally added it up to about eight miles, but it might have been less.

I started out just before sunset, and the heat was a little more than I had anticipated, but it felt good to get out in the sun and soak up some much needed vitamin D. Also, to have time to just be without thought. My head had been buzzing lately, and so much of it was about Ian. Taking a break from those thoughts was probably the healthiest thing I could do, in terms of keeping a level head about our relationship. I mean, we hadn't committed to exclusivity, even. We'd just said we weren't interested in seeing anyone else. Did that mean for a long time? Or just for now? I needed to get all of those questions out of my head for a little bit.

My brain was fairly empty, my ears full of Kanye's "Stronger," a staple on my running playlist for the past year, when I spotted… Oh god. *Oh no.* Walking along beside a tall, willowy brunette, was Brad. And he was pushing a stroller.

I thought about veering off my route and avoiding him. But something mean inside me, some masochistic part of me, forced me to make eye contact with him. I slowed down some and, popping out my headphones, said, "Hi, Brad."

He looked startled and guilty, and it took me a moment to realize why. My gaze flitted from the baby in the stroller to the fucking enormous ring on the woman's finger.

"Hey, Penny." He tried to smile at me, but it looked as unpleasant and forced as I knew it was for him.

My heart pounded even harder than usual on a run. I thought it might actually burst and kill me. And death by ex-boyfriend was not the way I wanted to go.

"Danielle, this is Penny. Penny, this is my fiancée, Danielle."

*Danielle.* I knew that name. He'd mentioned her in passing every now and then, when she'd texted him about work, or when he'd gone out with a group of office friends. *"About work?" How could you be so stupid, Penny?*

"Penny and I…used to date," Brad said, and he looked at me with such a pleading expression I was sorely tempted to ask her if she knew we'd both been dating him at the same time.

But Danielle's face showed no trace of jealousy or triumph or pity. She smiled wide with perfect, white teeth and put her hand out. "Hi, Penny, it's nice to meet you."

"Wow, fiancée," I repeated, hoping my smile didn't look as fake as his did. "And you have a baby."

"Yeah." She looked at Brad the way I used to look at him, love and adoration forged under the heat of his awe-inspiring charisma. And who could blame her? He was the epitome of tall, dark, and handsome, and he could swing from brooding and romantic to open-hearted and vulnerable with every change of his partner's mood.

And it was all fake. There wasn't anything deep or honest about him. He'd drawn me in the same way he'd obviously drawn Danielle in, and we'd both fallen for it.

I wanted to vomit on his shoes.

I realized that over the sound of the buzzing in my ears, Danielle was still talking. "—even though she was a surprise."

"Aren't surprises just…the best?" I asked, feeling a knot of tears welling in my throat. "How old is she?"

"Four months," Danielle answered, with all the pride of a new mother.

Meanwhile, I was frantically counting backward. Brad and I had broken up in late May. He'd waited. My god, he'd strung us both along, right up until she was ready to give birth? Or maybe even after?

How could he have done this to me? To either of us, really? I wanted to hate her, but I couldn't believe she had any idea. She seemed very nice and enthusiastic to share the details of her romance with *my* boyfriend.

But he wasn't my boyfriend, anymore. And he apparently hadn't been, for god only knew how long.

"Well, congratulations, to both of you." I gestured to my Fitbit. "I don't want to be rude, but I'm trying to keep my heart rate up. Training, you know?"

"Of course," Brad said, as eager to get away from me as I

was to get away from him and his perfect new life with his perfect new fiancée who wasn't me and his perfect baby that wasn't ours. "It was nice to see you, Penny."

I gritted my teeth and replied, "You, too. And it was nice to meet you, Danielle."

I managed to keep running until they were out of sight. Then I doubled over, gasping. I stumbled like a zombie to the nearest train and headed back to my apartment, on the verge of tears the entire time. I hated crying in public. I refused to do it.

By the time I got to the apartment, though, I no longer felt the urge to weep. I was angry. Really angry. But I was numb, too. Numb was the worst thing to be. I showered, replaying every moment of the regrettable meeting in my head. I imagined angrily confronting him, right there in front of his new family. Telling Danielle everything and watching his whole life hopefully crumble. But that would hurt Danielle and whatever the hell the baby was called. I hadn't caught the name. Brad might hurt them, but he might not. Maybe fatherhood would change his spots. But it wasn't my place to destroy another woman's life, just because my ex had acted shitty to me.

I also thought about calling him and screaming at him over the phone. Or going to his work and physically assaulting him. Obviously, I wouldn't act on that. I was embarrassed that I actually thought of it. And I considered, for a brief, wild moment, begging him to take me back. But I didn't want him back. I just wanted to win. Or something. My brain was overwhelmed by a rush of emotion I couldn't control.

And I felt guilty. So, so guilty. Because I had moved on, or I thought I had. I loved Ian, and even though it was a new, fragile love, I felt like a traitor for even considering I might still have feelings for Brad. Or that I would want that snake over a guy who had treated me better in four dates than Brad was ever capable of treating me.

When I got out of the shower, my phone was blinking. I wrapped my towel around myself and reached out with a shaking hand. It was a text from Brad. Had he sent it while he was still out bonding with his fiancée and baby? The thought made my skin crawl with disgust.

*Thank you for your discretion at the park today. I never meant for you to find out this way.*

Bullshit. He had never meant for me to find out.

*How long was this going on?* I texted back. *You owe me an answer.*

It took a minute, a full minute of me staring at the screen before I gave up and moved to drop it. But the familiar chime rang out, and like Pandora opening her stupid box, I looked at his response.

*Since last July. I'm sorry, Penny. But you kind of brought this on yourself. You couldn't really expect me to go on for years waiting for you.*

Waiting for me. Waiting for me to sleep with him. It was somehow *my* fault he hadn't been able to stick to the terms of our relationship, or end things with me before picking up another woman and dating her for almost a year before breaking things off with me.

There were so many things I wanted to say, so many names I wanted to call him, but that would only make him feel smug and right. So I shot back, *Lose my number.* And then, I erased him from my contacts altogether.

I sat on the edge of my bed, my hands shaking. I needed to talk to someone. I needed to not be alone in the apartment, where I was dangerously close to snapping and breaking everything that could be broken.

*This is stupid*, I warned myself as I dressed. *You're being stupid, and you're probably going to ruin everything.* I tried to pretend I didn't know my own intentions as I locked the apartment door behind me. But my heart knew better, and it overrode my brain to direct my feet to the subway, to the familiar route I rode every day. I got off a stop early and kept my head down as I walked, ignoring my usual instinct to stay wary of my surroundings, especially at twilight. I reached Ian's door and pushed the buzzer. There was no answer.

I'd come all this way for nothing. It was clearly a sign that I shouldn't have come at all.

"Penny?"

I turned at Ian's voice. He didn't sound angry, but pleasantly confused. Then he saw my face, and I realized how I must look, standing there with stringy, half-dry hair and no makeup, shivering because I'd worn a tank top and shorts and the night was unusually cool.

I was so embarrassed. "I'm sorry, I should have called—"

"Are you all right?" He was still dressed for church, but he carried his tie and his jacket in one hand. With the other, he reached out and cupped my jaw, looking down with such tender concern that I couldn't hold back my tears anymore.

"I saw… I ran into my ex-boyfriend at the park, and—" It was too difficult to keep talking through the sobs that wracked my shoulders and back, but I managed to sputter out, "With his fiancée and his baby."

"Come here." It wasn't a suggestion, but an order, and one I gladly obeyed. Ian pulled me into his arms and held me tight, as if he could squeeze all the pain out of me. The sound of his breath against the top of my head eased my heart. "Let's get you inside."

## CHAPTER TEN

The only thing I could think of to say as Ian led me to his apartment was, "I'm sorry." I didn't know what I was sorry for. For showing up uninvited? For bringing my past boyfriend problems to my new boyfriend's door? For ever dating Brad in the first place?

I was sorry for it all, but the last one especially. My heart was in my stomach, and my stomach was ready to expel it onto the floor. I let Ian walk me from the elevator to his couch. I was shivering, and he took it to mean I was chilled. "What you need are some warm clothes and a stiff drink."

Was I cold? I was definitely numb. He draped the throw from the back of the couch around my shoulders. "Stay here, I'll be back."

I pulled the blanket tight around me. The air conditioning in the building was an arctic assault that made me long for the humidity outside. My hair felt like it would never get dry. I should have been embarrassed to be seen like this by Ian, but I didn't care about anything.

That scared me. I'd thought I was over Brad, or as over him as I could get after a few months. I hadn't reacted this badly when we'd broken up. I'd done the days of crying thing, then I'd flown to Las Vegas with Deja and Sophie and Holli on an amazing private jet and partied until I couldn't see straight. Maybe that trip, and the feeling that I'd left my cares in the desert, had tricked me into believing I was all better, when I wasn't.

So what was I doing here, with Ian, if I wasn't over my ex? I liked Ian so, so much. I loved him, the new and exciting kind of love, not the kind that destroyed your entire life when you found out the person you loved had basically had a secret family for the last third of your relationship. Now that I'd found out so much of my time with Brad had been a lie, I had to start getting over him, all over again. Did that make the way I felt about Ian a lie, too?

The thought made me even more furious with Brad. It was one thing to dump me, another thing entirely to lie about having some kind of weird double life while he was dating me. But now his actions and my responses to them made me doubt the one really good thing I had going at the moment.

That hit me like a physical punch to the chest. Ian was the one good thing I had going for me? I hadn't realized it, but yeah, I really did think of him that way. And that was depressing, because my life should have been way better than just, "yay, one person!"

Where had I gone wrong?

Ian came back with a dark green merino wool sweater and some gray flannel sleep pants. He handed them to me, and all I could do was stare up at him.

"Go change," he ordered gently. "I'll get you a drink. What's your poison?"

*Crappy boyfriends.* "I have no idea."

"Okay. Well, I'll improvise." He leaned down and kissed my forehead, and my arms tightened around the clothes he'd given me. It was second best to hugging him, which I badly wanted to do, but I was pretty sure would make me cry again.

When I turned on the bathroom light, my reflection scared me. I looked like I'd just shuffled in from the set of a zombie movie. My hair was stringy, and I was pale. My eyes were bloodshot and ringed with dark circles. At least my nose was an attractive shade of raw red. No wonder Ian thought I needed some kind of John Wayne-esque treatment for shock.

I took off my top and shorts and pulled on his sweater. I'd kind of expected it to smell like him, but it just smelled like laundry. I had to cinch up the drawstring waist and roll up the legs to make the pants fit, but there was something comforting about wearing clothes that were way too big, especially when I felt so emotionally small and fragile. It was like armor; hurt would have to penetrate a lot of cloth folds.

All the clothing in the world wouldn't have made me feel less naked on the walk back to the living room. Vulnerability was the worst, because people expected it of me. Especially men. Being little and blond and cute was fun when people were underestimating me and I got to turn the tables. It sucked when I just wanted to have a human moment and not be treated like a kid whose birthday got ruined. I rolled the ends of the sweater over my clenched fists and tried to ignore the pity in Ian's expression as I joined him on the couch. He'd left a glass of something for me on the coffee table, beside another that I assumed was for him. I took mine and tossed it back in one gulp. It burned on the way down, but I carefully composed a blank face. It was embarrassing to look…broken.

My eyes flicked down to the glass in his hand, and he offered it to me. "I'll go get the bottle."

Was I trying to act tough? I didn't know. I did know that I wanted my head to be as numb as my mouth was from the alcohol, which I was pretty sure was whisky. I finished it off as he came back, and he refilled both of our glasses.

"Do you want to talk about it?" he asked. The genuine sympathy in his voice made me ashamed of myself. I was acting so…not the way I wanted to be acting.

I nodded, but I said, "No." Then I launched right in, because it seemed like maybe it would justify why I was there and why I was behaving so oddly. "Brad and I broke up in May. And today I ran into him with his fiancée and their four-month-old baby."

I paused to give him a moment and watched as the realization dawned on him. "Jesus, Penny…"

"I know. And god knows how long it was going on." But I sort of did know, now that I was saying it out loud. "I think they might have been living together. Maybe in January? We

suddenly stopped going to his place then. He said his
roommate was off his meds."

How could I have been so stupid? Why would he have
stayed in that situation if Jeff had been so dangerously
unhinged? Brad hadn't been coming over as often as he had
in the past, and it seemed like he would have wanted to be
out of the apartment as much as possible if he was having so
much roommate difficulty. He hadn't even mentioned
finding a new place, beyond a non-committal, "Uh huh,"
when I'd suggested it.

I was pacing, but I couldn't stop. "I keep going over it in
my mind. I was standing in the shower, trying to think of
every little thing, every way I should have known what was
going on, and none of this came up. I feel like such an idiot."

"You're not an idiot," Ian said, almost before I was
finished saying the word. "Sometimes, we want to love a
person more than they deserve to be loved by us. And we'll
do a lot of rationalizing to fool ourselves into believing that
they deserve it."

He was speaking from experience, I realized. I didn't
really know what had gone down between him and his ex-
wife, aside from what he'd told me at the park. I had a
feeling it went deeper than a few tossed off sentences, or
else she wouldn't be his ex-wife. Maybe he would tell me,
someday.

At the moment, I chose to selfishly wallow in my own
pain. I nodded in agreement with him and took another
drink. I didn't bother to hide my reaction to the taste this
time. The worst part of the entire thing was, I wanted to be
mad at the other woman—I didn't want to think of her name
or admit to myself that I even remembered it, even though it
would be burned into my brain forever—but I just couldn't
muster up the will to hate her. "This girl was so totally into
him. She looked at him like he was every dream come true. I
keep thinking I should have warned her, but why? What if
they're actually meant to be together, and he never does

anything awful or hurts her at all?"

"Then you've ruined their happiness for nothing." From the look on his face, Ian didn't see it the same way I did. Honestly, I didn't see it that way, either, but it was the only thing I had to make me feel better about how things had turned out. If Brad was someone else's destiny, then there was a destiny out there for me, too.

"It's not up to you to help her realize what he is," Ian went on gently. "If you'd told her, do you think she would have believed you?"

"No. I would have been the psycho ex-girlfriend." It smarted, but it was true. Brad would have been able to wriggle out of whatever I might have said. I drank some more of my whisky, but it was almost gone. I held it toward Ian. "This stuff isn't expensive, is it?"

"No." He handed me the bottle. "Just don't get yourself alcohol poisoned."

I knew what that meant. "Or vomit in your apartment?"

"Ah, Penny. There aren't many people I'd let vomit in my home, but you're one of them."

It was an oddly sweet sentiment, and it made me laugh. I tried to pour myself another, and the liquid ended up teetering right on the rim of the glass. I stopped it from spilling just in time. "I shouldn't have run over here to tell you all of my ex-boyfriend problems. That's not fair. You're trying to be the new boyfriend." Oh, shit. Was I so drunk that I was really going to start spilling my feelings everywhere?

Yes. Yes, I was.

"I mean, I think you were," I went on. "I got the impression that you were interested in the position."

"Definitely. I hope I'm still in consideration." He kept a nervous eye on my glass. *Pff.* I wasn't going to spill it.

But I drank about half of it, just to be sure, then put it on the table and wobbled over to sit beside Ian on the couch. "I think it was because I made him wait too long. Two years, you know…"

"So you were supposed to have sex with him to keep him from cheating on you?" Ian sounded outraged at the idea. Oh my gosh, his outrage was so cute. "That wasn't your responsibility. If he wanted to go off and fuck somebody, he should have fucking well broken up with you first."

"You're swearing a bunch." That was so hot. I could barely even get my voice to rise above a whisper. It was nice to have someone swearing on my behalf. Or maybe it was just the whisky. Mostly the whisky. Probably.

"I can stop," he offered.

"No, you can't." And I didn't want him to. I never thought I would really want a guy who would get mad and punch another guy to defend my honor. And Ian wasn't offering to. But he was saying all sorts of angry, offensive words about the guy who hurt me. It made me want to text Brad and tell him, *ha, look! This guy wants me enough to fight for me.*

But Brad wouldn't care. That just made me feel hollow.

Ian sighed. "This prick… He's the kind of man who'll sleep around on you whether you're sleeping with him or not. This other woman was sleeping with him, and he was still seeing you. He was just—"

I knew what he was going to say. Brad had wanted to be the first. He'd wanted to get to the end of the level and defeat the final boss.

All I could do was nod in defeat and say, "I know. I know why he was still with me."

The fact that Ian had figured it out somehow made things ten times worse. It was humiliating. When he put his arms around me, I couldn't hold back my tears. I leaned on his shoulder, taking comfort in the solid warmth of his body. There was also a sort of pain in it, a feeling of intimacy that defied the newness of our connection, making me ache for more.

That was a dangerous line of thinking. It felt too much

like a rebound. I pulled away and reached for my glass, finishing it so I could speak again. "I'm sorry. I'm a mess. I showed up here a mess, and now I'm drunk and a mess."

"If you think this is the only time anyone has gotten drunk on this sofa and cried hard, I have some news for you that will come as a bit of a shock," he said, nudging me with his elbow. "Don't feel sorry for coming here. I'm thrilled to death it was me you wanted."

"Yeah?" Being with someone who was so willing to be open with his feelings, feelings that most people would have tried to play it cool about, was nice but a little intimidating. Probably because it gave me the dangerous sense that I could be just as open and honest with him, and I didn't know how far I should go down that road tonight. I inclined my head toward the bottle. "Can I have some more of whatever that is?"

He considered. "How about a beer, instead? Just to slow down?"

Oh. He thought I was too drunk. That was embarrassing. I gave him a thumbs up and said, "Liquor before beer, in the clear!"

It was pretty obvious from his expression that he didn't think I was in the clear, at all.

I tried to be more sober when he came back. And way less depressing. "Is it weird to feel a little relieved about this, too?"

"How so?" he asked.

"Well, for the last few months that we were dating, Brad was really distant. Now I know why. But, at the time, I had this feeling…" I took a deep breath. Because even though I'd already acknowledged it, it was difficult to say the words out loud. "I had a feeling things were falling apart between us. And that maybe he was with me because he was waiting it out. Like, he wanted to be the winner."

Ian nodded thoughtfully.

"It's nice to have that confirmation. To know that I

wasn't crazy. I mean, it sucks, and it hurts, but it's nice." I shrugged. Maybe it would make it easier to move on, now that I knew it wasn't my fault. Maybe Ian would make it easier to move on. "And I'm glad Brad broke up with me. Because…I got to meet you. You've already been way better to me than he ever was."

"Is it selfish of me to say that I'm glad the two of you broke up, as well?"

My heart fluttered. If Ian could make me feel so special, and so valued, even through the pain and the whisky, then Brad hadn't been the one.

He couldn't have been.

"No, I think you made out like a bandit in the deal." I leaned against Ian, and he let me. We fit so perfectly my chest hurt. It had been months since I'd lain this way with anyone. Even when Brad and I had still been together, he'd felt far away. Ian was present. In the room with me. His aura just clicked with mine, and I felt warm all over.

That could have been the alcohol.

Neither of us said anything. The thrum of his pulse under my ear fell into a slow, steady rhythm, hypnotizing me into a loop of thoughts that went, *am I falling asleep? I think I'm falling asleep. Is he falling asleep? Is it okay if I fall asleep, too?* that circled around and around until he was gently shaking me awake.

"Penny? Open your eyes, Doll. We fell asleep."

He'd called me Doll. I wasn't out of it enough that I didn't recognize the thrill that sent through me every time I heard it. But it was the only word I'd caught, because sleep had made his voice rough and his accent ten times thicker. I said, "I can't understand you when you mumble."

"Do you want me to take you home?" he asked, and I supposed that was my cue to leave.

I didn't want to go home. Everything felt right. Really, really right.

"Can I stay here?"

"Certainly. I don't think the guest bed is made up, but I—"

Seriously? This was the biggest signal in the handbook, and he wasn't getting the hint? "Can I sleep with you? I could really use the snuggles."

*I want to fuck you*, I mentally shouted at him.

"Fine. No funny business, though. I know your type," he said, with his typical dorky humor.

"Come on, before I fall asleep while I'm walking." I yawned to cover up my nerves. I was going to go upstairs and have sex with Ian. He knew that, right? It was why he made that joke, I was sure of it.

I was even more sure when he put his hand on the small of my back as we walked up. The floating staircase took less concentration than I thought it would while drunk.

"You must be desperately tired, if you're willing to brave these stairs," he said as we neared the top.

I laughed. "I was never afraid of the stairs."

"You lied about hating my brilliant stairs?" He pretended to be offended, gasping, "How dare you!"

"At the time, I didn't really know you," I explained, as we walked into the darkened bedroom. "I thought it might have been a trick."

In the dark, I made out the shape of three tall windows that slanted into skylights. The city twinkled beyond them, and from its lights I made out the shape of Ian's bed and the rumpled duvet on top of it. My throat went dry.

"I hope I didn't make you afraid or—"

I stumbled a little and pressed my hand to his chest to steady myself. "If I'd been worried about that, I wouldn't have come here in the first place. And I wouldn't have come back. But I wasn't sure you wouldn't try some clumsy seduction technique."

"Hey. When I'm clumsily seducing you, you'll know it," he said, and stepped away to turn on a light. It was a metal sconce set against the wall above his built-in nightstand. I was dating a guy who could literally make a house. I'd never been able to pull off a decent house in *The Sims*.

I tagged along after him, hoping constant bodily proximity would induce him to touch me. "I just really like you, and I didn't want to give you the chance to disappoint me. I know that's probably not the smartest relationship strategy." When he didn't answer, I changed the subject. I plucked the front of the sweater he'd loaned me. "This is a little hot. Do you have anything more night-shirt-ish?"

*Like a T-shirt I could put on and, whoops, get into bed without anything on underneath it?* God, I was doing all the work here, and I was the drunk one.

Ian went to his dresser and came up with a T-shirt. "I'm going to let you borrow this, but on one condition."

I squinted at him, to keep him in focus.

"You can't look sexier than I do when I'm wearing it," he joked, and tossed it to me. By some miracle, I caught it and probably looked a lot more sober than I was, which would work in my favor. Ian seemed like the kind of guy who would feel bad about sleeping with a drunk girl, even if she was totally in her right mind about wanting it.

I pointed to the door on the other side of the room. "Bathroom, then?"

"Yeah, in there." He went in ahead of me and gathered up contact solution and a case—I hadn't realized he wore contacts, so clearly I needed to look into his eyes more often—and his toothbrush. Yikes, I probably needed one of those. I hadn't thought the plan through.

"I'll use the one downstairs," he said, and closed the door as he left, shutting me in the long room. The ceiling was sloped in there, as well, and three more windows slanted over my head. At the end of the room, on a raised platform, an avocado-shaped black bathtub stood in front of a wall covered in slate tiles. Another window, shorter to accommodate the step-up flooring, lined up for the perfect view during a long soak. Across from that window, behind the tub, was a glassed-front shower.

I looked at my reflection in the mirror over the vanity, above the vessel sink that matched the tub. I did not look great. In fact, I looked a little worse than when I'd arrived, because now my eyes were red from drinking *and* crying. My face wasn't just pale, it was sweaty. I looked like someone who—

Yeah, I looked just like someone who was going to puke.

Thankfully, I got to the toilet in time to heave up everything in my stomach in there, instead of in the sink. It was touch and go for a moment. I prayed with everything in me—which was evidently all just whisky, as I hadn't eaten anything since before my disastrous run—that Ian wouldn't overhear. I clung to the toilet bowl and laid my head on the seat, sweating and shivering and mentally reassuring myself that I could still pull off cute and sexy once I managed to get on my feet.

Eventually, I did get back on my feet, enough to swish water around my mouth and strip out of my loaned clothes and get into his T-shirt. I slipped off my panties but had the presence of mind to rinse them out for the morning—I had to be practical as well as sexually assertive. I hung them on a towel bar and combed my fingers through my hair.

*Are you sure this is what you want to be doing?* My conscience confronted me. It sounded a lot like Rosa. *You might just be drunk and sad, right now.* I was. I was drunk and sad, and my brain had a point. But I didn't want to listen to my brain. I wanted to listen to the desperate landslide of hormones and anger that was burying me. *You could always just wait.*

And I always just couldn't. And I wasn't going to.

I stepped out of the bathroom to see Ian, in his boxers, pulling on a T-shirt. I almost jumped right back and slammed the door. Maybe it was because, besides the day at the pool, he'd always been fully clothed around me, even when we'd been fooling around, but I felt like I was in completely over my head. We were in his bedroom. I had barely any clothes on. And whether he knew it or not, I was just waiting for something to happen.

He didn't say anything. He just went to the bed and got under the blankets quickly, like he was calling shotgun.

"So, that side, then?" I asked, laughing. "You don't have to defend your territory."

"You say that, now. But I know women. I'll wake up on the floor, with you sprawled out like a starfish in here," he said, all grumbly and cute as I got in beside him.

"This is a pretty big first for me." I reached up to click off the light. "I've never slept over before."

"Well, I can see why not," he said as I snuggled against his side, in the crook of his arm. "You look fucking hideous without makeup."

*Rude!* I knew it was a joke, but it didn't do much for my confidence. "Here I am, breaking one of my cardinal relationship rules, and you're being mean to me."

"Never." He kissed my forehead and hugged me close. "I love you, and you know it."

All the brakes screeched. I was suddenly overcome with what could only be described as rigor mortis. "No… I didn't know that."

The silence that followed was more brutal than the final slashing in a graphic horror movie. Then he said, "When I say 'love', I mean—"

"You mean you love me." I hoped the darkness hid my crazy wide smile.

"Well, it's out there." The noise he made could have been a laugh or a cough, I wasn't sure either way. "I would have preferred a more romantic venue to make such a pronouncement, but here we are."

"Here we are…in your bed…and you say you love me." Under any other circumstances, I would have found it extremely sketchy, but Ian seemed to have surprised himself with the revelation as much as he'd surprised me.

"No! No, no. That's isn't why." There was a rustle of sheets as he moved, but I couldn't see what he was doing. "I love you. I'd love you if I was driving you home right now. Or, maybe not as much, since I'm dead tired. But the point I'm trying to make is—"

"Ian? I'm just fucking with you." The rush of excitement I got from hearing that word from him finally couldn't be contained, and I laughed.

"Well, thank you for turning my declaration of love into a heart-stopping anxiety episode."

He loved me. This soon. Was that insane? Was it too fast? Were things careening out of control? Had we just doomed ourselves to a quick flare up and burn out?

In the moment, I couldn't really force myself to care. I just wanted to be swept away from all the other awful stuff I was feeling.

I rolled onto my stomach to lean over him. "I'm glad you said it."

We met each other halfway in a kiss. The touch of his mouth sent darts of electric want through my body. This was it. Now or never. I slipped my hands under his shirt and raked my fingers through his chest hair, digging my nails in. I slid my knee between his legs and sat up, so he could feel that I was absolutely bare, and surprisingly wet. And he did feel it, because his chest hitched beneath my palms.

But he grabbed my hips and groaned, "Wait, wait. No."

"What?" I rocked against his thigh. The heat of his skin sent pulses to my groin, and I clenched hard.

"I can't. Not like this."

His words penetrated the fog around my brain like a knife slicing through me. "You… You don't want to do it?"

"I do. Believe me, I do." He rose up on his elbows. "But I won't."

My heart squeezed in my chest. "But you said you loved me."

"I do. Ah, Doll, I would do just about anything for you.

But having sex with you when you're stoned out of your mind on too much whisky and emotionally rattled... That's not how I want it to be."

I might have been stoned out of my mind on too much whisky, and yes, emotionally rattled, but there was still some piece of me that could recognize his rejection as a good thing. But it sure didn't feel good in the moment. I wasn't proud of myself.

"I'm sure Brad said he loved you, too," Ian went on. "And whoever came before him. You wouldn't have been happy with yourself if you'd slept with them, and you won't be pleased in the morning if you fuck me, now."

"I'm sorry." I swung my leg over him and scooted to the edge of the bed. I should have put on my clothes, apologized, and went home. If I could find home, as drunk as I was.

While I sat there, tears streaming down my face, trying to keep him from noticing the sobs I was holding back, he put his arms around me and pulled me back into bed to lie beside him. In that one gesture, in the strength of his arms around me, my pain and confusion melted into a peace that dulled the sting of the day.

As I drifted into drunken exhaustion, I realized that I hadn't said those three important words back to him. I slipped my hand beneath his shirt and pressed my palm over the beat of his heart, hoping it was enough, for now.

* * * *

I woke with a split second of where-am-I? panic. More accurately, oh-god-there's-a-hole-in-the-ceiling panic. The skylights over Ian's bed were disconcerting.

My head hated me. The daylight hated me. I hated me.

How could I have come on so strong, after pouring my heart out to him about Brad? How could I have... Well, I'd tried to use Ian, plain and simple. He must have hated me, too, because I was alone in his bed. I didn't even know if he was in the apartment.

Then I heard his footsteps in the short hall outside. I combed my fingers through my hair and held my hand in front of my mouth to smell my breath. There was no chance it was just my hand that reeked.

Ian knocked softly on the half-open door. He knocked, in his own house, his own bedroom. What kind of person did that, if not someone who was way, way too good for me?

"I'm awake," I croaked, pushing myself up against the headboard for support.

"Good morning." He came in wearing sleep pants and a T-shirt, his hair wet from a shower, and carrying a glass of water. That was so unfair, when I looked like an extra on *The Walking Dead*.

He sat on the edge of the bed beside me and handed me the glass. "I expect you'll be needing this."

I squinted up at him. "Not to be ungrateful, but do you have any orange juice?"

He raised an eyebrow. "I think you know the answer to that already."

"Right." The thought of drinking water nauseated me, but I knew I needed it. I just hoped I wouldn't throw up in his bed. That would compound the embarrassment.

"You'll need these, as well." He pulled a small bottle of ibuprofen from his pants pocket.

He was being so nice to me I almost burst into tears. I didn't trust my voice, so I just smiled with closed lips and nodded.

"Oh, and one more thing…" He reached into his pocket ,again.

I didn't fully understand what he handed me, even as I set the water on the bedside table and my fingers closed around the slip of paper. Which was weird, because I'd seen enough fortune cookie fortunes in my life. I glanced up at him as I unfolded it. My hands started shaking when I read the words.

*The love of your live will step into your path this summer.*

My head jerked up, and my brain throbbed from the movement. "You said you didn't save this."

"I lied." There wasn't a hint of remorse in his admission. His mouth bent in a small smile. "Happy Labor Day."

Labor Day. The official last day of summer. Well, not official, that was around the twenty-first of September. But I wasn't about to be Pedantic Penny over something like this.

"I…" Crying hurt. Probably because I didn't have a single drop of moisture left in my body. But that didn't stop my chest from heaving and my shoulders from sagging.

"Hey, hey." Ian put his arms around me. "What's that for?"

"Because I ruined everything." I'd gotten drunk and tried to use him to make myself feel better over stupid Brad. Or maybe I'd wanted to sleep with Ian because I was afraid he would walk away? Maybe both.

Either way, I'd messed up, when things had been going so well.

"By trying to have sex with me? I wasn't rejecting you, Doll, I—"

"I know, I know." I pulled back and wiped my eyes. "I wouldn't have wanted to fuck me, either."

The corner of his mouth twitched, ruining his sympathetic expression. "Believe me, it wasn't that I didn't want to fuck you."

"But I was trying to use you to make myself feel better about some other guy. It was so awful of me." I covered my faced and rubbed my forehead, both to hide my stupidity and to try to ease the pounding in my head. Failed on both counts.

"You were in a bad place. It won't be the last time, I promise." He laughed softly. "And you've yet to see how badly I can fuck things up. But I'm ready to be in this with you. All of you."

"I just thought…" I shook my head and finally made eye contact with him again. "I was kind of desperate. After all that stuff we talked about… I didn't want to make you wait."

He took my hands in his and raised them to his mouth to press a few kisses to my knuckles. The soft sounds of his lips on my skin were all I heard, the gentle drift of his breath over my hands the only thing that mattered in the moment. He looked into my eyes, a few strands of hair falling over his forehead. He usually looked so put-together when I saw him that one change in his appearance was enough to make everything around us more vivid and real.

"I'm not them, Penny," he said. "I'm the guy who'll actually wait for you."

I used his grip as leverage to launch myself at him and wrapped my arms around his neck to squeeze him tight. We nearly went over backwards. He caught me with an "oof!" of surprise.

"Careful." He laughed, one hand coming up to push my hair back from my face. "I'm not as shiny and new as you are."

I sat back and wiped at my eyes. "Sorry. I'm overly enthusiastic with expressions of affection. If you're in this with me, you have to get used to that."

"I'll buy protective equipment." He leaned his forehead against mine—oh god, I finally had someone who would do that with me!—and whispered, "Penny?"

"Yeah?"

"I want to kiss you, but your breath is fucking terrible."

I laughed but with my mouth as closed as possible. I shielded it with one hand. "Do you have any mouthwash?"

"I do." He laughed with me. "Go use it."

My pounding headache didn't even seem as bad, anymore. I got out of bed carefully, because the shirt I'd slept in seemed a lot shorter than it had the night before, when my veins had coursed with liquid courage. But I wanted to skip with every step I took toward the bathroom. "I want a kiss when I get back," I called over my shoulder, a hand still in front of my mouth.

"Well, obviously." He grinned, and I hurried into the bathroom. When I shut the door behind me, I had to lean against it to get my bearings.

Ian was right. He wasn't the other guys I'd dated. He was the best guy I'd ever dated.

## CHAPTER ELEVEN

As much as I would have liked to spend the day with Ian, I felt the kind of thoroughly gross that only a shower at home and clean clothes of my own could fix. Instead of asking him to drive me, I made up an excuse about needing to swing by the office for something and took the train.

My phone rang its generic ringtone as I climbed the steps from the subway. My heart dropped into my stomach at the picture of my parents that popped up on the screen.

"Hello?" I answered as I reached the sidewalk.

"I've been trying to reach you all morning," my mother said, sounding put out, as always, that I'd been momentarily unavailable to her. "I saw your Facebook status about Brad. Why didn't you call us?"

*Because it's taken you five months to call me.* The last time we'd spoken had been the week before Brad and I had broken up.

"I guess I've just been really busy. But I'm fine, don't worry about me—"

"How could I not worry about you?" Mother said with a heavy sigh. "You're twenty-two, Penny. Tick-tock."

Sometimes, I felt like my parents thought we were living in an actual Jane Austen novel.

"I know. But I am seeing someone else now. He's an architect." That was going to be my golden ticket, right there. Dating a good guy with a steady income.

"An architect?" I heard the caution in mother's voice. "They don't make very much money, do they?"

"He does," I assured her. "He owns his own company. He's, um, a lot older than me."

"Well, there's nothing wrong with that, if he can give you a secure future. God knows you won't have one working as a secretary. And you certainly weren't having much luck with men your age." Mother laughed. "I'm so relieved. When I read about Brad, I thought, oh, Penny, here we go again."

My stomach always hurt when I talked to my parents.

"Well, I'm calling because your father is speaking at a symposium in the city in two weeks. It's on a Saturday, but we would love to have dinner with you on Friday night." There was no suggestion that maybe I would have plans or anything. Then she said the words I didn't know I'd been dreading: "You could bring your new boyfriend."

"Oh. Um." I reached into my purse for my keys as I neared my building. "You know, it's kind of new—"

"Excellent. I'll tell your father. Will you be able to pick a suitable restaurant? I don't want a disaster like the last time." She chuckled, but the last restaurant we'd gone to had seemed totally suitable to me. I'd have to try harder to find someplace impressive enough.

"Yeah, I'll find someplace." I would ask Ian. He would know better restaurants than I would.

Oh god. I would have to ask Ian. To dinner. With my parents.

Mother and I hung up with our usual sign-off, which consisted of her saying goodbye and ending the call before I could respond. It used to bother me. It didn't anymore.

I trudged up the stairs to the apartment.

My *other* mother was waiting for me on one of the wooden stools at the kitchen pass-through, drumming her fingertips on the counter. "Well, I'm glad you're not dead in a ditch."

"Where would I possibly find a ditch in New York?" I asked with a roll of my eyes.

"At a construction site," Rosa shot back. "Like one an architect might try to bury a body in?"

"Ian isn't going to kill me. Actually, if he hadn't cut me off from drinking last night, I might be dead." My head was still killing me, despite the pills I'd gobbled down at Ian's place. "Can you take Tylenol for a hangover?"

"Only if you want to die." She slid off the stool and walked into the kitchen. "Cake, however…"

"You have cake!" My headache almost entirely disappeared. Then it came pounding back on a wave of suspicion. "Wait. Wasn't it—"

"Yes, it was Amanda's birthday. Yes, I went to her party," Rosa said defensively. "But if you had checked your phone, you would have known the exact location of said party and a reassurance that I hadn't been murdered."

I went for the forks. "Why did you think I was being murdered?"

"Do you know how many people *I* know of who have been murdered?" she snapped back, bending to pull a tinfoil covered paper plate from the oven. "Sorry if that's immediately where my mind goes."

Okay, that chastened me. I had a bad habit of forgetting how dangerous life could be for Rosa and women like her. "Okay. Point. But Ian isn't going to kill me. I don't get what you think is so weird about him."

"Well, he's almost sixty, and he's dating a teenager—"

"He's fifty-three, not sixty. And I'm not a teenager, Miss I'm-So-Twenty-Six-And-Know-Everything." I went to the bar stool and hopped up. Rosa leaned over the counter and snagged a fork from me.

"I know, I know. But haven't you thought about it?" Rosa asked around the bite of cake she put in her mouth. She swallowed and frowned. "You know, like, what's wrong with this guy, that he's into chicks thirty years younger than him?"

"Yeah," I lied. I hadn't really thought about it. At least not deeply enough that it had occurred to me that something might be "wrong" with him. "I mean, he's brought that up, too, a couple of times. We both realize how weird it probably seems to other people. We already get looks."

"Because you look like a sophomore out on a date with

her math teacher." Rosa snorted. "I just don't want this to go badly for you. You really like this guy. I don't want to see you get hurt."

"Well, I'm pretty sure he won't pull a Brad and cheat on me with his future wife," I said, and even buttercream frosting couldn't take the bitterness out of my mouth.

Rosa's eyes flared wide. "No!"

"Yes." I nodded miserably. "I ran into him yesterday. Literally. I mean, literally, I was running, not literally we collided—"

"Focus up."

"He was with his fiancée. And their baby." I swallowed the lump in my throat, which was definitely not cake. "Their four-month-old baby."

Rosa slapped her palm down on the counter. "Motherfucker."

"And then, he had the gall to text me after!" Now, I was less bitter, more angry. It was the mark of a good friendship, that our anger could combine into one giant ball of sheer outrage. "To thank me about being so cool."

"You were *cool* about it? Why? What did you say?" she demanded. She chewed vigorously while I responded.

"I just said it was nice to meet her and congratulations. What else was I going to do?" I shrugged.

"True. You couldn't exactly stomp his foot and knee him in the balls in front of his child." She considered. "Although you did call babies ugly to their faces a couple weeks ago."

I cringed inwardly. "Don't remind me. But I wasn't about to make anymore infant-related missteps."

Rosa tilted her head. "Is that why you went to Ian's all of a sudden?"

"Yeah. Not my finest hour. But he was really sweet and supportive about it." My face flamed, and I couldn't make eye contact with her, because I was pretty sure she was going to go nuclear scold mode when I said what I was going to say. "He, um… He told me he loves me."

When she said nothing, I peeked up at her. She was leaning against the vertical beam of the pass-through. Her expression wasn't critical, as I'd expected, but concerned. "It's only been a few weeks, Penny."

"I know." I don't know why I felt ashamed. Maybe because I knew it was too early, but I didn't care.

"Do you think he meant it?"

That wasn't the question I was expecting. Rosa could be pretty harsh about the guys I went out with. Of course, she'd been one hundred percent right about Brad. I thought about Ian, about how terrified he'd sounded after he'd let slip that he loved me. "I do. The way he said it was kind of accidental. We were in his bed— Wait, listen to the whole thing," I admonished her. "I was super drunk, and he turned me down for sex. And he told me he loved me."

My memory was hazy about the order those events had gone in.

"You were in bed with him, you were drunk, and he didn't sleep with you?" she asked with a skeptically arched brow.

I nodded. "Yeah. I got a little aggressive. A lot aggressive. I kind of...took my panties off and dry-humped his thigh."

"So, you were sending him *subtle* signals, then?" she quipped.

I couldn't help but laugh at how stupid it sounded when I admitted to it. "I was totally wasted. I asked him if I could sleep over, like could I sleep over *in his bed*, and he said yes. I thought we were going to do it."

"And he wouldn't let you, because you were drunk and he..."

"And he loves me. He said he's the guy who's going to wait. And I know they've all said that. Some variation of it. But Rosa...I think he really means it."

"Did you say it back?" she asked, crossing her arms over her chest.

I shook my head. "I did not. I didn't want to say it just because he said it."

"But do you love him?"

The cake suddenly looked very interesting.

"I knew it. Parker, you fall way too fast."

"I do." I couldn't deny that. "But he's really great. And oh my god. Multiple orgasms. I mean, I knew about them. I thought they were a myth, but—"

"Yeah, some of us aren't set up for that, so shut up." She pushed the plate toward me. "Finish this."

I pushed my fork into the last bit of cake left, and paused. "Hey, not to change the subject, but do you ever…"

Rosa waited for me to continue.

I sighed. "Do you ever wonder what your life would be like if you just did what you wanted to do and said to hell with what everybody expected of you?"

"Yes. It was called setting all my old clothes on fire and never speaking to my family again," she said with a wry quirk of her lips.

"Ha ha. I mean, what if you hadn't become an accountant? What if you'd been like, 'you know, I think I would rather be a professional tennis player?' and you didn't let anyone tell you no?"

"You just got your semi-annual call from your parents, didn't you?"

"Yeah," I admitted miserably. "I have to stop answering."

"You have to figure out how to deal with this in your own time, is what you have to do." That was another thing I really liked about Rosa; she might be overprotective, but she wasn't bossy. Not about things that mattered. I'd had plenty of friends in college who'd been more than happy to tell me I needed to cut off my parents and their toxic influence on my life, but it wasn't as easy as they all made it sound. Eventually, I'd stopped sharing my issues and anxiety over my parents, and then, piece by piece, I'd stopped sharing other stuff, too, until none of my friends were actually friends anymore. Rosa would never be like that.

"I thought you liked your job," she reminded me.

"I do." I did. Ish. I liked the people I worked with, and I could definitely stand the pay, compared to what I'd been making working at Subway during college. Deja and Sophie could be kind of demanding, but that was the best part of the job, because most of the time, it wasn't very challenging. "It's just not that interesting."

"Maybe once you work in an actual administration position—" Rosa began.

I stopped her, because that wasn't the issue. "No, I mean…business management? I'm not exactly beating the pavement looking for those jobs. I kind of wish…"

She waited for me to continue, but it was so hard, when I felt like I was saying I wanted to a ballerina or a fireman. *What the hell.* "I wish I would have gone into something more science-y. Marine biology, you know? Or something with bees. Something interesting."

"You know what's cool about colleges?" Rosa asked. "They're all over the place. I heard there are even some here in New York."

"There are also these things called 'student loans'," I reminded her.

"True." She nodded ruefully. "Try not to make any big decisions about running away to study bees until after you've calmed down from your parental phone call, okay?"

"I'm going to dinner with them." My stomach roiled. "And they want me to bring Ian."

"That might not be a bad idea," she said, surprising me. I'd expected more this-is-going-too-fast lecturing from her.

"Yeah?" I asked cautiously.

"You'll have a buffer," she said, dead serious. "And you can gauge Ian's reaction. If he thinks your parents are great and wants to hang with them all the time, that's something you need to find out, right now."

"Oh god, I hadn't even thought about that." Although, it

didn't seem like there would be much of a chance of that happening. Not if he really liked me.

"If Ian is as great as you say he is, he'll pick your side. And he'll listen to you." She came over and hugged me, a warmer, better hug than any my mom had ever given me.

"Thank you, my cool mom," I said with a laugh.

She made a disgusted noise and gave me a shove. "As if I would ever use that kind of alliteration in my daughter's name, Penny Parker."

* * * *

Staying true to our slow down plan was pretty easy once the worst period in the world decided to rain blood and cramps all over me. Ian and I were supposed to go out on Friday night, but I didn't feel like spending the whole time worrying about whether or not I was bleeding through my jeans.

"I hope you didn't have big, big plans," I told him when I called him around dinnertime on Thursday. "I have to cancel on you."

"Exactly what level of disappointed am I allowed to be without appearing needy?"

"You should be totally crushed." I was. Though we'd spoken on the phone twice already during the week, I missed him.

"Oh, I am," he assured me. "May I ask what's come up? This isn't the permanent brush-off, is it?"

"God, no!" I couldn't even laugh, the thought was so horrible. "No, I'm just feeling under the weather."

"Do you need anything? I hear soup is the latest thing for sick people." From anyone else, it might have sounded pushy, like an attempt to get an invite despite my cancellation. It was Ian, though, so I knew he genuinely wanted to help.

Which made me feel really bad about fibbing. "Um. Not that kind of weather. The…monthly kind of under the weather."

There was a pause. Then he said, "Penny? I'm fifty-three. I do know about menstruation. You're not going to shock me."

"Oh, good." That was actually a weird relief. It was tiresome, pretending my period didn't exist just so a man could feel comfortable. "Well, then you understand. I just feel so gross."

"I do understand. But if you need anything, ice cream, hot water bottle, a hormone-fueled argument—"

"Not funny," I snapped. Maybe he did have a point though.

"I'm sorry," he said and I heard the smile in his voice. "But I do mean that. If you need me, I can come over any time this weekend."

"Oh." It hadn't occurred to me that he might want to still see me, knowing that the crimson scourge was bloodying the countryside. "Well, if you wanted to come over." I glanced around my tiny room. "I do have a television in my room. We could watch a movie or something."

"Great, then we're still on for tomorrow?"

It seemed so far away. Unfairly far away. And I had cramps and bloating and tears... "What about tonight?"

"Tonight?" From the tone of his voice, I knew right away that I'd overstepped my bounds.

"Sorry," I said quickly. "You have work tomorrow."

"Don't you?" he asked, as though jogging my memory might lessen the blow of denial.

I should have just said yes and let him off the hook. But I felt like my uterus was trying to destroy me, and I wasn't comfortable whining about that to Rosa. She'd confessed earlier in the week that she'd been struggling with depression more lately, and I didn't want to do anything to trigger feelings of gender dysphoria. Maybe it was over-cautious of me, but I cared about her too much to mess with her mental health because I had five days a month that sucked.

So instead, I said, "No. I called in."

I would have to remember to call in when I got off the phone with him.

When I heard his resigned sigh, I knew I'd won, and I smiled to myself as he said, "All right. Can I sleep there? I'll just go straight to work from your place in the morning."

"Yeah." I brightened up. "I would love it if you would stay over."

"Give me about forty minutes," he said. "Do you want me to bring dinner?"

"How about pizza? I'm buying." My check had just direct deposited, and I had to spend it before it evaporated, anyway. And I was tired of Ian dropping money on our dates all the time.

"You don't—" he began then stopped himself. "That would be lovely. No black olives. Anything else, just no black olives, I beg you."

"One anchovies and pineapple barbecue chicken pizza, then," I said with a laugh.

We hung up, and I floated on my cloud of happy for approximately three seconds before I remembered what a sty the apartment was.

I burst out of my room, probably looking like Medusa, the way all my hair was falling out of my messy bun, and Rosa startled, almost tipping a bowl of cereal into her lap. "Is something on fire?"

"No! Ian is coming over!" I nearly shouted.

"Now?" She jumped up and drank a big mouthful of cereal straight from the bowl before she abandoned it on the coffee table. "You look like shit. Take a shower. I'll clean your room."

I rushed to her and grabbed her shoulders. "I love you so much I want to be buried with you."

"Later! Try to make literally anything about your appearance work." She shooed me off.

I took the fastest shower I'd ever taken in my entire life, brushed my teeth, blow dried my hair and rolled it up in a sock bun, and put on mascara. Just mascara. Otherwise Ian wasn't going to buy my fragile menstrual state.

With regards to that, I abandoned my Diva Cup for a super jumbo industrial strength overnight tampon, threw on black yoga pants and a blue tank top, then dashed off a text to Sophie, apologizing for the late notice and begging forgiveness for calling in. Then I jumped online and ordered a large pepperoni pizza, some breadsticks, some mozzarella sticks, two kinds of soda…

Maybe the person on the first day of her period should not have been in charge of food.

When I'd put in the order, I went to the living room, where Rosa's emergency cleaning spree plan was in major action. She had making the place look and smell presentable in thirty minutes down to a science.

"Do you want me to split?" she asked. "Is tonight the night?"

"No, tonight is not the night. We're just going to eat pizza and watch TV," I promised. "You can stay. You won't be bothering us."

"If you need me to leave, just text me, okay?" she said. "What time is he supposed to be here?"

I checked the clock. "Any minute now?"

It really was "any minute", because no sooner than the words had come out of my mouth, the buzzer sounded. I dashed over and hit the intercom. "Hey! Come on up! We're unit B."

"You are, like, power excited," Rosa said, and I realized I needed to tone it down a little. Because, while I did feel first-day-of-my-period awful, I didn't want Ian to think I was faking to get him over here. I composed my expression into one that looked less like I'd just been ogling Tom Hardy's old MySpace photos and opened the door, waiting and listening to Ian's footsteps coming up the stairs. He looked up as he gained the top step, and though his face was drawn and his eyes bleary, he smiled when he saw me.

"You sounded like you were dying on the phone. I'm glad to see you're not in imminent danger of expiring." He wore broken-in jeans and a T-shirt, which was as casual as I'd ever seen him dressed, and carried a garment bag over his shoulder.

"No. Just generally miserable." I gestured him inside. "This is the place."

"Not a lot of it," Rosa said from the couch. She stood. "I'm Rosa."

"I think we met before," he said, clearing his throat. "Downstairs."

"Right, when you two were making out." Rosa grinned. "We weren't properly introduced."

I turned to Ian. "I was thinking we could watch TV in my room. Keep one foot on the floor so Mom doesn't worry?"

"Sure. Except for the foot thing," he said with wink. Then he looked to Rosa. "Sorry, but I have nothing but lascivious intentions toward your friend."

"Hey, as long as I don't have to listen."

Somehow, having Ian in my apartment made the place feel smaller. Not just because there was a third person in the space; Brad used to come over, and Rosa and I had invited handfuls of friends here plenty of times. But having seen Ian's apartment, with its three stories of amazing open floors and a kitchen larger than my bedroom, I could only imagine how he was seeing things.

I was kind of embarrassed.

It got worse when we stepped into my tiny bedroom. Rosa had stuffed all my dirty laundry somewhere, god bless her, and gotten rid of my tissues and trash, but the space was small and definitely not sophisticated. Ugh, this had been such a terrible idea. I'd just wanted to see him so much—

"Wow," he said, and I cringed. "This reminds me so much of my first apartment in New York."

I turned around, almost afraid to ask. "Because it's so small and shitty?"

"Well, it is small. But this place is better kept than my apartment was. And I shared a bedroom about this size with another guy." He laughed at the memory. "We didn't even have beds."

"I'm sorry. I didn't think about the fact that you probably didn't want to hang out in some dingy twenty-something's crappy apartment." I wanted to crawl into a hole and die of shame.

"Did you not just hear what I said about sleeping on the floor?" he asked, toeing off the battered-looking sneakers he had on. "I didn't expect you to have a million-dollar penthouse. Besides, I'm here to make you feel better, not do a property appraisal."

"Food's here!" Rosa called from the other room.

"Wait right here," I told him, adding, "The remote is on my nightstand."

After I paid the delivery guy, I grabbed a plate and threw some pizza and breadsticks on it for Rosa. I handed it to her as I passed through the living room, and she beamed up at me. "Have fun."

"Nothing's going to happen," I sing-songed back in a low voice.

Ian waited for me on my bed, propped up on the headboard with the remote in his hand. He looked…guilty. Because I had paid for dinner? That was so stupid but also pretty nice, considering the way some of my ex-boyfriends had nickel-and-dimed me. I held up the stack of boxes. "I kind of over-ordered. Owing to my condition."

He sat up and reached for the food while I knelt on the bed beside him. "Are you sure you want to eat in here? Where we're going to get pizza sauce all over your bedding?"

I frowned. "I don't know how *you* eat pizza, but I try not to turn into a yard sprinkler of tomato sauce when I do it.

Besides, you've had roommates before. You know how important space is."

"That's true. It was fairly awkward when I wanted to bring a girl back to my sleeping bag."

I sat beside him cross-legged while we ate. And I did not hold back to be ladylike. When I was on my period, people were lucky they didn't lose body parts while I ate. I let him do most of the talking, nodding and saying, "Uh-huh" a lot while he told me about his day. He asked me about mine, but "I forgot my menstrual cup and had to stuff toilet paper into my panties while I wandered pathetically around the office begging for tampons" wasn't exactly the story I wanted to share, so I said, "Nothing out of the ordinary really happened. Your job seems a lot more exciting than mine."

"Or less frustrating, depending on how you look at it. I'm dreading going in tomorrow." He sounded so tired I felt guilty that he'd hauled his ass all the way out here to sleep in my lumpy bed and eat pizza with me.

I wiped my hands on a napkin, then laid my palm over his knee. "Well, thank you for coming over here, even though you're having a bad week. I've been feeling progressively better since I got off the phone with you."

"Happy to help." He cleared his throat. "Since we're on the subject of work, there is something I need to discuss with you."

"Oh?" I reached for a third breadstick. I was going to have to run thirteen miles on Sunday, but at the moment, the carbs were worth it.

"There's a chance I may have to go away on business for…a while. A temporary relocation."

My heart plunged.

"Nothing permanent. And it's not final, by any means." He must have seen the shock and disappointment in my expression, because his brow crumpled in concern. "It wouldn't be until next summer. But I thought I should let you know the possibility exists."

That calmed me down a little, and I took a bite. Next summer was months away. Although at that point, would he expect me to go with him? I mumbled around a mouthful of garlicky amazingness, "Where would you be going?"

"Nassau. The Bahamas," he clarified. "To work on a resort."

"Oh, wow!" Having a boyfriend in a tropical location wasn't exactly the worst thing anyone had ever faced, for sure. There would be all sorts of snorkeling and scuba opportunities. Swimming with sharks, petting stingrays... That was the least objectionable place to have a long-distance boyfriend. "Would I be able to come visit?"

"I hope you would," he sputtered. "After I came all this way tonight."

I chewed my lip. "Okay. Well, since we're bringing up unpleasant subjects... My parents are coming to town next week."

"And that's unpleasant?" he asked.

I didn't want to get into all the details, at the moment. Rosa was right, it would be a good test, and I didn't want to influence the outcome. "No, but having to ask you this kind of is. They want to meet you."

"They know about me?" He seemed pleased by this, which was a hundred times better than freaking out at being asked to meet my parents after a few weeks of dating.

"Yeah. I mentioned I was seeing someone, and my mom thought this visit would be a good time." I shrugged. "We don't get together often, so I think she wants to check you out before things get serious."

"Are things not?" he asked, and suddenly everything *was*.

"That's not what I meant." I caught my bottom lip between my teeth. "I mean, I didn't want to presume—"

"Neither did I. But I'm quite serious about you, Penny." He reached out to touch my face, and the tender gesture made my chest tight, until I realized he was wiping a smear of marinara off my cheek.

"Oh my gosh, way to ruin the moment with my sloppy eating." I laughed. "Well, I'm serious about you, too. Seriously serious."

"Good." He looked at me for a long time, and I couldn't tell what he was thinking. But I knew it was good, from the small smile that flirted with his mouth. Finally, he looked down, as if breaking himself from a spell, and said, "Of course I'll meet your parents. Just tell me where to be, and when."

"I will." I reached over and took his hand, squeezing it. "Thank you."

"For?"

"Giving me a chance." I looked around my room, still feeling self-conscious about the way I lived. "We don't have much in common. We're in such different places, life-wise."

"You're thanking *me*?" He shook his head. "If you remember correctly, Doll, I was the one who fucked up badly on our first date. And I'm a hundred and thirty years old. So, thank you for giving *me* a chance."

When we finished eating, we got around to turning on the television, and I snuggled down beside him as he stretched out.

"You do the clicking." My full belly made me sleepy; all I wanted to do was lay my head on him and close my eyes. So I did. But they came open again when a thought popped into my head. "You don't have a TV, do you?"

"Of course I do." He almost sounded offended at the suggestion that he wouldn't.

"I didn't see one in your apartment," I countered.

"That's because it's very ingeniously hidden away until I need it." He frowned as he hesitated briefly on what looked like a gardening show then clicked past it.

I half sat up, demanding, "Well, where is it?"

"You know where the couch is? The window in front of it? The television slides up from the floor." He never took his eyes from the screen, and somehow that made him super hot.

I was way too into him if I found being ignored in favor of the television sexy.

"Oh, it does not!" I insisted. "That's like *The Jetsons* or something."

"You're twenty-two, what do you know about *The Jetsons*?" he challenged. Then, he went on, "Remind me the next time you're over, I'll show you."

"Fine. But I won't believe you until you do." I wriggled down closer beside him. My uterus was still trying to destroy me. "Hey, could you reach under the bed? I've got a heating pad under there."

He leaned over the edge and felt around a moment then said, "Aha," and came back up with it. He watched me as I rolled over and plugged it into the outlet. "Do you need any help?"

"No, I'm young, but I'm allowed to plug things in all by myself," I said, wrapping the heating pad low around my waist. It started heating up, and I groaned in anticipation of the relief to come.

"That bad, is it?" he asked with genuine concern, and not one iota of disgust.

"Yeah." I'd heard from some women that their cramps were as bad as contractions during labor. I wouldn't know about that, but I hoped it was the case. Otherwise, labor was going to really suck. "Thank you for not saying, 'it's not that bad.'"

"What idiot would say something like that?" he asked in a tone of horror.

I leaned up and gave him The Look. "Everyone."

"I would never say that. Mostly because I don't know what it feels like, but also because I don't feel like having a woman rip a handful of my intestines out in retaliation." He put his arm around my shoulder.

When I laid my head on his chest, he squeezed me close. "You're the only woman I would eat pizza in bed with. Just so you know."

"You're the only man I wouldn't hide my period from," I mumbled with a yawn.

A laugh rumbled in his chest. "Forgive me for saying so, but I do think you're getting the more pleasant bargain."

I drifted to sleep to the sound of the television and the steady rise and fall of his chest beneath my ear. If being serious meant more nights like this, then I was as serious as a final exam I hadn't studied for.

## CHAPTER TWELVE

"I can't believe you did that," Rosa said, for the thousandth, self-esteem destroying time.

I combed my fingers through my hair. The half of it that was left.

My parents coming to the city made me lose it every single time. My octopus tattoo? Christmas, 2014. In February, when they'd made an unscheduled drop-in for a charity function, I'd seriously flirted with a nose ring, until Sophie had talked me out of it.

"It looks really good, though," Rosa reassured me, walking in a half-circle around me. She could barely get past me in the tiny bathroom. "I just can't believe you did it. For a while I thought you were a part of a religious cult that wouldn't let you cut your hair."

I closed my eyes, trying to block out the sight of my shaggy, chin-length bob. But it haunted me.

"Of all the stupid things I've done, this might be the worst." It was a cute haircut, and it looked fantastic on me. But that wasn't the issue. The issue was the withering conversation it was going to cause at dinner tonight. "I don't know why I do this, every time. It's like I'm baiting them for negative attention."

"That's exactly what you're doing," Rosa agreed. "But I wouldn't consider this a negative. It's a great look on you. Besides, do they really think they can control what you do with your hair?"

I arched a brow at her in the mirror.

"Well, on the bright side, Ian will probably think it's hot."

"Yeah." I smiled to myself and reached for my eyelash curler. I had a half-hour to get ready before I had to leave for the restaurant. Though I was dreading seeing my parents, I

couldn't wait to see Ian. I also didn't want those two worlds
to collide. All of those conflicting emotions, and my hair had
paid the ultimate price.

"So, do they know you're dating Gandalf yet?" Rosa
asked, leaning against the wall with her elbow on the towel
bar.

I made and impatient noise as I released my eyelashes
from the curler's grasp. "Okay, again, not Gandalf. Not
Methuselah. Not Dumbledore."

"Sorry." She held up a hand like I was the one being
unreasonable.

I reached for my mascara. Working at a fashion
magazine, I got all kinds of awesome makeup free from the
beauty editor. I was addicted to Urban Decay. "I'm meeting
them at the hotel and riding with them to the restaurant. I
already told them he was older, but I thought I would save
the specifics until I could tell them in person."

"Are they going to freak?"

I lifted my chin and pointed my eyes down to wiggle the
brush between my lashes. "Nah. They're going to be
psyched that he makes better money than Brad."

"That's a little creepy, don't you think?" She knew what I
thought. Just like I knew what she thought. But if I dwelled
on it, I would just be more rattled than I already was.

"Maybe, but at least it's convenient. If I thought this
would be some huge drama, I would be a wreck."

Rosa snorted. "Well, thank god you're not."

I dressed carefully. Something conservative-ish, but not
too stuffy. I didn't want to get the lecture about dressing
appropriately in public *or* the lecture about never attracting a
man if I looked like a librarian. I chose a black wrap dress
with three-quarter length sleeves and a low neckline that
showed just a little cleavage. Dressing to please my parents
as well as my boyfriend was a land mine of "can't win".

I paid an Uber driver to zip me over to the Pierre, where
my parents always stayed when they were in town. The

Plaza was too predictable, so they told me. As I crossed the checkered floor of the lobby, I touched my hair, straightened my necklace, and hoped for the best.

We were meeting in the bar, an art deco style space that could have come right out of *Mad Men*. Which was basically in keeping with my parents' entire philosophy, really.

"Penny," Mother called from a table near the steps that led down into the room. My father stood, but she didn't; when I came over, I had to lean down to hug her. "Careful of my earrings, dear."

I squeaked out a "sorry" and turned to my father. "Dad."

He stuck out his hand, and I shook it.

I came out a perfect mix of both of my parents. I got my father's eye color, but my mother's eye shape. Her nose, his much fuller, wider mouth. His flawless skin, but her hair color. If a movie director were casting a family, we would be the actors he would pick, if we had better chemistry.

"Oh, darling, what *have* you done with your hair?" Mother had short hair, herself, but it was her opinion that men found longer hair attractive. Since she was already married and "of a certain age", she didn't want to hassle with the upkeep anymore. She wore it in a sort of side-swept, layered cut, suitable for any yacht club wife.

I reached up and self-consciously tucked one side behind my ear. "It's just something I'm trying out."

"It's very…modern." My father rolled the word out like a morgue gurney.

"Thanks, Dad." I mumbled under my breath.

"Your boyfriend didn't come with you?" Mother asked, in a tone that said, *here we go again.*

I took a deep breath. "He's meeting us at the restaurant. I wanted to kind of…prepare you first."

My father paled. "He's not…" he lowered his voice to say the dreaded word, "*urban*?"

Was there time to get a drink? "No, Dad. Ian is white."

"That wasn't what your father was asking," Mother

reassured me with a raised voice. All three of us knew damned well what he'd been asking, but heaven forbid anyone in the immediate vicinity take his racist comment as the racist comment it was.

I knew better than to call them on it and just forged ahead. "Mom, I told you Ian was older than me. But I didn't want it to come as a shock to you when you met him. He's fifty-three."

The outraged pursing of my mother's lips that I had been expecting never came. In fact, it was my father—who never seemed to notice the presence of my boyfriends in the past— who frowned and said, "Kitten…"

"I know. And I know that you probably have some misgivings, and that's totally understandable." I looked my mother pleadingly. "But when you meet him, you'll get it. He's funny and he's sweet, and he really l—" I stopped myself and looked back at my father. "Likes me. He's good for me."

"I'm not sure you know what's good for you," Mother said, lifting her eyebrows. It was then that I noticed the nearly empty martini glass in her hand. Which was a great way to start off the freaking evening. Then she sighed and said, "But finding a man who's interested in you and who has a stable income is a small victory, nonetheless."

My father remained silent.

We rode to the restaurant in a hotel car, and on the way, my mother made passive-aggressive "jokes" about the myriad restaurants in Manhattan that we'd gone to in the past that weren't good enough. I'd always had to walk a fine line between too cheap and too expensive for my bank account. My parents liked places that I couldn't generally afford, but I would rather die than have to tell them I couldn't pay for something. Trying to impress them with hip but frugal restaurants had never worked; they'd seen right through that trick.

I would have to dip into my savings to pay for my meal

tonight.

The place I'd picked was as intimate as it was expensive, which also made it exclusive by reputation. There was no way my parents could object to that. There were a whole twenty-four tables in the place, and they served old world Italian food at modern capitalist prices. The lighting was low, the music soft and instrumental, rather than the old Italian restaurant standby of Sinatra and Bennett, and the gentle murmur of conversation and clinking glasses added a more relaxed ambiance than a traditionally stuffy place.

We'd just reached our table, and I hadn't even sat down yet, when I spotted Ian. He crossed the floor toward us, led by the hostess. My stomach clenched. Usually, when I saw him, another part clenched. Tonight, instead of being excited to see him, I was nervous and braced for disaster.

He did a double take when he saw me. "Penny, I didn't recognize you!" He beamed at me as he reached my side. He put an arm around my waist to pull me in briefly and kissed my cheek. "You got your hair cut. It looks beautiful."

"Thanks." I shouldn't have been able to smile, as riddled with anxiety as I was. But when I was around Ian, I couldn't help it. I remembered that my parents were sitting there. There was a testament to how totally lost I was in Ian that I could forget something *that* unpleasant.

I faced their judgmental expressions, Mother trying to size up Ian's bank account on appearance, Father surprisingly uncomfortable. I'd never realized my father cared enough about me to worry about my boyfriends. He stood, but Mother stayed in her seat.

"Mother, Father, this is Ian Pratchett, my boyfriend," I said, and as Ian reached out to shake my father's hand, I added, "Ian, this is my father, James Parker, and my mother, Deborah Smythe-Parker."

"James, Deborah. Very nice to meet you." Until I'd seen it in contrast with my parents' fake ones, I'd never realized how warm Ian's smile was.

We sat, and Ian said, "Your daughter is one of my favorite people," and winked at me.

Mother laughed, a sharp bark of disbelief that made me cringe. "How kind of you to say."

"Not kind, at all," he insisted, and I sent him a mental *shut up, shut up, or she'll put me down worse* vibe.

"I notice your accent," Father said, as though it were a condemnation. "Where are you from?"

"Scotland."

Silence fell on the conversation, until my mother jumped in with, "How did the two of you meet?"

"My boss fixed us up." It was a relief to be talking again.

"I went to college with her husband," Ian elaborated. "Sophie was adamant that we would like each other."

"And we do," I said, unable to help the smile that wrinkled my nose.

"That we do." Ian returned my smile. And when I looked across the table, my heart fell. My parents weren't happy for me. They were looking for ways to be critical of me, and of Ian, and of the idea of both of us together.

"What do you think of this haircut?" Mother asked, laughing derisively. "Penny is always going through a rebellious stage."

"I said I thought it was beautiful," Ian reminded her. "Are haircuts considered particularly rebellious these days?"

"It is when Penny does it. She's always been a bit of a problem child."

A problem child, for getting my hair cut without consulting them? My face flamed. Why should I be ashamed? I was twenty-two years old, for god's sake.

The worst part was Ian's response to all of this, which was no reaction at all. I couldn't tell if he was oblivious or forcing himself to ignore their pleasant-on-the- surface, yet wholly unfriendly manner, so maybe Rosa's idea of using the evening as a test wasn't going to work out as well as I'd hoped.

The waiter came by with menus and a wine list and suggestions for pairings. When we'd ordered drinks and were left alone again, Ian tried to nudge things along. "So, James, Penny says you're in town for a symposium?"

"Yes, that's correct." Father nodded and didn't say anything else.

"My dad is a surgeon," I told Ian, hoping my parents weren't going to do the monosyllabic conversation thing all night.

"Really?" Ian sat back as the bus boy came to fill our water glasses. "What kind?"

"A hand surgeon." Again, nothing but the most perfunctory answer.

"And you're an architect?" Mother jumped in, raising her eyebrows in interest.

Ian nodded and drummed his fingers on the tabletop. He was so...animated. My parents could have been statues, if you didn't look at them to be sure they were breathing. "Yes. I'm a partner at my firm. Pratchett and Baker. We work on commercial properties, mostly office and medical buildings."

"The occasional hotel, right?" I asked to prompt him to mention the resort thing. World travel would definitely validate him some in my mother's eyes.

"Not too many, but I am looking at a potential project in the Bahamas, soon." He gestured to my mother. "And you, what do you do?"

"I'm an anesthesiologist." She paused for a moment. "So, you're a partner? Does that mean you own the firm?"

"Yes. I founded it with an associate I've worked with for some time." Ian paused. "It's challenging, but I enjoy it."

"It sounds like a lot of work. Long hours?" Mother was tapping away on her mental adding machine.

"I have a strict policy of staying under sixty hours," Ian explained. "There are too many health risks for a man my age if I try to work all the time. Burt, my business partner, he's already had a heart attack. I'd like to avoid that for the rest of my life."

He'd never mentioned any of that to me. While I was alarmed at the reality that it was something he had to worry about, I was grateful that he took care of himself that way. I thought of Deja and Sophie, and how they worked at the office, then went home and worked all night. I wasn't sure I would ever be passionate enough about a job that I would want to work around the clock and have to set limits on myself. I envied Ian that he liked his job that much.

"Working so little, you must be salaried?" Mother asked, only to have my father barrel over the top of her.

"That must be hard on your personal relationships," my father began, and I knew the gloves were coming off. "Have you ever been married?"

"I have," Ian admitted, but he didn't make any apologies for it. "Recently divorced."

"Mm-hmm," Dad grunted. I was strangely conflicted over his sudden protectiveness. My whole life, he'd barely shown any interest in me. Now, he was worried about the guy I was dating? I didn't know if I should be pleased or insulted, so I was a little of both. I didn't like the way it felt.

"I'm sorry to hear that," Mother jumped in. "I've heard spousal support is quite costly in this state."

There was a long silence. Ian's smile no longer reached his eyes. "Why don't you just ask me how much money I have?"

I laughed, like it was a joke, even though I knew it wasn't.

Oh god. He was never going to talk to me ever again after this.

Luckily, the waiter arrived to take our orders. I agonized over the menu. The place was way more than I could force myself to afford, but I couldn't bear the shame if my parents suspected that. They always seemed to be in "gotcha" mode, just looking for things to criticize.

When we were finished ordering, before the waiter left the table, Ian said, "Tonight is on me. As a gesture of gratitude for having such a wonderful daughter."

He looked my mother dead in the eyes as he said it. He was mad. I'd thought he'd been angry over the Brad thing, but I'd never seen Ian like this before. He was controlled and chilly, in contrast to when I got angry and started snapping at everyone and shouting. It was kind of sexy to have him act that way on my behalf, but when we had our first fight, it would be a huge blowup, because our anger styles were not the same.

"Hey, here's something fun," I said, barreling through the awkwardness. "Ian comes from a really large family. Isn't that interesting?"

"Oh? How large?" Mother reached for her water glass.

"I've got two brothers and four sisters," he replied, and my brain screeched to a halt. He'd told me he was from a family of nine. Four boys, five girls. Adding him into the total he'd just given, that would still only add up to seven.

"Do they all live in America?" Father asked.

Ian shook his head. "Just one sister. She and her husband live in Brooklyn, not far from me."

"Such a large family," Mother chuckled.

"Yes, well, we're Catholic, so it's to be expected."

Oh.

Oh no.

*I wish you wouldn't have said that,* I thought as I stared at him in horror.

Mother's face froze. "Really? And are you...religious?"

Ian bristled at the question, or perhaps just the tone it was presented with. "I would say I am, yes. I attend church regularly. And you? Are you religious?"

"No," Mother said, quietly insulted. "I don't have a taste for it."

"A bunch of superstitious nonsense." Father's answer was far more aggressive than anyone ever needed to be about another person's religion.

"Well, I'm pretty superstitious," I reminded him, willing to throw myself on the pyre in Ian's place.

"Against our best efforts." Mother rolled her eyes. "Believe me, darling, we haven't forgotten."

Though I wasn't looking at Ian, I felt him tense beside me, even without touching him.

"You can't really plead innocence yourself," I said, laughing to keep my tone light. "You believe in the family curse."

"The family curse?" Mother frowned. "There isn't any family curse."

"I'm intrigued." Ian turned to me with a small smile. Finally, he looked like he wasn't having the worst time of his life. Probably because I'd caught my mother being hypocritical. "What's the family curse?"

"I'm dying to hear it, myself," Mother said, and I glanced at Father. His brow was crumpled and serious, as though he were trying to remember.

"You know, the curse where if a woman in your family sleeps with a guy, that means he's her true love, and if you do anything to mess it up, you'll...never..." I hadn't spoken it aloud very often, not recently enough it rolled out of my mouth without examination. As I said it, I heard how stupid it was.

"Oh..." Mother made a "tch" sound with her tongue as she remembered. "That story? Darling, that was years ago."

"I know, but—" *Story?*

"We made that all up," Mother said, clearly disappointed that I hadn't figured it out by now.

"After what happened with Ashley, we couldn't be too cautious," Dad chimed in.

"You..." I swallowed a sudden lump in my throat. "You lied?"

"Outright forbidding you from mooning over boys wouldn't have worked." Mother was right; they'd tried, and it hadn't worked. But lying to me, warning me that my life would be ruined by even one sexual experience? They couldn't have actually done that.

Had they?

Panic breached a wall in my heart, flooding me with every painful memory of all the times I'd been called a cocktease, every time a guy had broken up with me because I was "frigid" or "stuck up", every time I'd truly wanted to have sex with a man I had feelings for but didn't because I'd been too afraid…

She went on. "You were so obsessed with tarot cards and horoscopes, so we exploited that a little."

"We didn't think you'd keep on believing it," Father said, taking another sip of his wine. "It was like the Tooth Fairy, or Santa Claus."

"The Tooth Fairy," Ian echoed quietly.

"But for years… You guys, I've been afraid my entire adult life—"

"We told you that you took all that superstitious nonsense too seriously," Mother reminded me.

"But you actively encouraged this superstition, didn't you?" Ian asked, and my already roiling guts cramped harder. Was he actually confronting my parents? Oh god, they would make a scene. And then they would make it my fault.

"Penny…developed early," my father said, clearing his throat uncomfortably. "And she was never the brightest bulb when it came to people. Animals, yes, science…but she didn't exercise the best judgment."

Mother nodded sagely. "We were sure she was going to be an unwed teenage mother, and we did not have the patience for that, at all."

"This has affected Penny her entire adult life, you realize," Ian pressed. "You don't feel even a little guilty about that?"

Mother laughed pleasantly. "Try parenting a

disappointing child, Mr. Pratchett. Then, you'll understand that desperate measures must sometimes be taken."

Hot tears sprang to my eyes. It was one thing to be so thoroughly demoralized by my parents; I was used to that. But to have it happen in front of *Ian*? God, it was so humiliating. It wasn't just that he was finding out about my flaws. He was finding out that I was completely worthless and unlovable. And if my *parents* knew that, how would I hide it from anyone else?

I balled my hands into fists beneath the tabletop and squeezed so hard my nails dug into my palms. I wouldn't let myself start crying in front of all of them.

Ian pushed his chair back so suddenly, my mother and I both jumped.

"I'm sorry," he said, standing. "But I can't sit here and listen to this, anymore."

"Excuse me?" Mother gasped. Her eyes bulged a little. She was going to go nuclear mode, just like she did when a store wouldn't accept a return.

"No, excuse you." Ian pointed a finger at her. Red was creeping up his neck above his collar. "I've never in my life seen a parent treat their own child like this. Look at her. She's beaten down, and you're enjoying it."

"Look here," my father started, but Ian held up a hand.

"I've looked. And I've seen enough. For fuck's sake, you're like a pair of fairy tale monsters." He turned to me. "Penny. I love you. And I'm sorry to make a spectacle. But I can't be here for this. You're welcome to come with me."

I looked from him to my parents and back, my mouth open. I was helpless to say anything. What if I made my parents mad? I'd already disappointed them so much in my life.

He must have surmised an answer in my pleading expression, but I didn't know how, since I hadn't made a decision, myself.

Ian held up one hand and backed away. "Call me when

you're ready to talk about this." He turned to my parents, a muscle ticking in his jaw. "Enjoy your evening torturing your daughter."

Stony silence fell over the table. Both my mother and my father glared at me, their expressions screaming triumphantly that they'd expected this to be a disaster, and it had been. And, while my pain tightened into a hard little ball in my chest, I realized that the only person in this room tonight who truly cared about me at all had just walked out the door.

I stood and knocked my chair over. "Oh, poop!" I bent down and picked it up, grabbing my purse as I righted it.

"Sit down, Penny!" my mother ordered. I didn't listen. I didn't care if they never spoke to me again. Keeping them wasn't worth letting Ian go. I ran toward the door.

My heart pounded but not from exertion. From the fear that he was walking away, and that if I didn't catch him before he got in his car, that would be it. No phone call would ever erase the memory of me choosing those assholes over him. And after he'd defended me.

I plunged out the door. Ian was walking down the sidewalk, fast, but before I could say anything, he turned abruptly and headed back. His eyes were down, so for a second he didn't see me. When he did, anger and apology warred on his face. Apology won out, but as he tried to speak, I cut him off. "No. No, let me say what I want to say first, okay?"

He'd turned around because he'd been coming back for me. That was all that mattered.

I wanted to jump into his arms, but an invisible force field of shame stopped me. "What you did for me tonight... No one in my life has ever stuck up for me the way you just did. No one has made me feel..." Tears filled my eyes. He'd done all that, and I'd seriously almost stayed in my seat there in the restaurant. "No one has ever made me feel so loved and so safe..."

"Hey, hey," he said, taking me in his arms right there, despite the stares of the couple passing us to go into the restaurant. "You don't deserve to be treated the way they treated you in there. And they don't deserve you. You are so much more than a bank account or a job."

He stepped back and put his hands on my shoulders. "You're Penny-Fucking-Parker, all right? A whole person who has thoughts and feelings and ideas that impress me every day. God handed them a gift when he gave you to them, and they're fucking miserable and ungrateful for it? Fuck them. I love you. And I want you to love you as much as I do."

I knew Ian was religious, but he'd never really brought it up strongly. The fact that he would now made me believe him, more so than I might have before. And it was strangely humbling.

"Come on," he said, putting his arm around my shoulder. "We still need dinner, and you need cheering up. I've got an idea."

We walked to his car and drove away in relative silence. I thought of my parents back at that restaurant, what they must be saying.

I bet they were arguing with the waiter about not paying for any of the food we'd ordered. That made me absurdly happy.

After a few blocks, I realized Ian was driving toward my neighborhood. "Are you expecting me to cook for you at my place?" I teased, the anxiety in my chest easing somewhat.

"I thought that you could use some profound spiritual guidance." He didn't say any more, but as soon as we turned onto the street, I knew where he was taking me. It was the little Chinese takeout place where we'd bought our illicit picnic on our first date.

"They do have the best fortune cookies," I said, and I laughed, because if I didn't, I was going to start crying all over again.

We ordered, and I didn't go for the guaranteed breath killers this time. When they gave us our food, Ian suggested, "How about we take this back to my place? I have something I want to show you."

"Okay. But first." I reached in the bag and pulled out our fortune cookies. "Let's see what these say."

We sat in the car with the engine idling, and Ian cracked into his cookie first. He read it and laughed. "You've got to be fucking kidding me."

"What does it say?" I asked, and he handed it to me, a huge grin on his face. I looked down and read aloud, "'An unexpected relationship will become permanent.' You planted this!"

"I swear I didn't. But I'm not complaining about the contents." He nodded toward mine. "Go on."

I opened mine and fished out the paper. "'Stop searching forever. Happiness is just next to you.'"

My heart ached.

"You know, we're going to have to stop doing this," he said. "They're not always going to line up this well."

"I think it's a sign," I said through the lump in my throat.

He put the car in gear. "I think you're right."

I hoped he was right.

\* \* \* \*

Traffic was surprisingly light, but the weight of the mood in the car wasn't. As we drove over the Brooklyn Bridge, I wondered if the heady silence between us would bring the entire roadway crashing into the river. Something had changed between us, and for the better. Which should have been impossible, considering how well things had already gone so far.

"I'm sorry I'm not talkative," Ian said suddenly, quietly. "It feels like I should say something profound."

"I know what you mean." And I did, although I couldn't describe it.

When we got to his apartment, that feeling intensified.

We were solid and real to me, not potential. We'd already happened, and now we just…were. And yet, things seemed fragile, despite the permanence the fortune had promised.

"I want to apologize," I said as we sat across the corner from each other at his dining table. We'd poured our food out onto actual plates this time, which was a nice change from eating off cardboard together.

"For what?" he asked.

Did he not know? "For my parents."

He chewed thoughtfully, and took a swallow of water before he answered. "Why would you apologize for them? You can't control the fact that they're—"

"Assholes?" I finished for him, because I knew he was too considerate to say the word. "I know it's not my fault they act that way. But I'm sorry I exposed you to them and how toxic they are. And I'm sorry I didn't leave with you."

"I shouldn't have put you in that position," he said, looking away, the way he always did when he was uncomfortable. This time, it was out of shame. I could tell by the soft volume of his voice. "It was an ultimatum. You deserve better."

"I do," I agreed. "I deserve you."

After we finished eating, we took the plates to the kitchen. The quiet was killing me.

It must have been making Ian jumpy, too, because when he said, "Hang on a second, and I'll wash these," he was way too loud.

He had a dishwasher, but I supposed he didn't want to run it for two plates and two forks and two glasses we'd only sipped water out of. I thought I should still help, even though there weren't that many. "How about I wash, you dry? You paid for the food, the least I can do is help with the manual labor."

"Sounds like a deal." He jolted, his eyes going wide. "I remembered what it was I wanted to show you."

I'd forgotten he'd mentioned that outside the restaurant.

Now, I really wanted to know what it was. "Show me!"

He reached up and flipped open a cupboard door. Inside, there were things on the shelves. Cans of soup, and boxes of pasta. A loaf of bread. Some quinoa and a packet of sun-dried tomatoes. Oatmeal. Real, actual food.

"You went grocery shopping!" I squealed.

"And look at this." He opened the refrigerator, and inside there were eggs, orange juice, a couple of raw steaks and some leafy greens. "Now the beer won't get lonely."

"I'm so proud of you!" I threw my arms around his neck for a quick hug.

"I thought you might be."

As I turned to the sink and flipped on the tap, he grabbed a dishtowel and threw it over his shoulder in preparation for his duties. I was struck by a vision of him doing the same thing with a burp cloth, juggling a baby—our baby—in his other arm. I wanted that so badly my teeth clenched.

He dropped his phone into the dock on the counter and hit something on the screen, turning away as the music started over the sound system.

"Oh, wow. I haven't heard this in ages." He whistled under his breath. "My iTunes library is too big."

"Stop trying to impress me," I said dryly. The tune was poppy and upbeat, and I couldn't place the era it was from. It sounded like a cross between a sixties song and something out of the eighties. And it was mad repetitive. "What song is this? He sounds like Paul McCartney."

"Close, it is a Beatle. George Harrison. 'I've Got My Mind Set On You.' It's so fucking catchy you'll still be listening to it in your sleep this time next year." He took the dishtowel from his shoulder and slapped it onto the counter. "Come on. Dance with me."

I flicked water from my hands. "In the kitchen?"

"Humor me." He snagged me with an arm around my waist and pulled me into an awkward, fast two-step.

"I always do." I hopped up to kiss his cheek then pushed

myself back with our joined hands. He lifted one arm and spun me, and I stepped on his toes.

He caught me, laughing. "We'll have to take lessons sometime. We can't be a truly chic and sexy couple if we can't dance like we're making love on the floor."

The mental image I had was probably not the one he intended. "That would be some really terrible dancing."

"That's not what I meant, you pervert." He smiled down at me. His smile was perfect.

There was my intrusive imagination, again, creating a scene in my mind so vivid I could almost feel his body above mine, the bite of hard wood at my back.

My chest squeezed, a flutter of nerves. *Stop searching forever. Happiness is just next to you.* My head got light. My throat went dry. I'm sure I looked like I was going to faint, and I might.

He tightened his hold on me. "Did I make you swoon? Because if I did, I need to call some people and brag."

My mouth fell open in a surprised laugh. "No. It's just…you. Being you."

He frowned, his expression changing to something more cautious. I had memorized that transition without realizing it; it was pained distrust, like he thought he could be rejected at any moment.

The big dumb, amazing idiot.

"You're the one, you know," I continued. "You're my forever. I want it to be you."

"I want it to be me, too." he said with a hesitant smile.

I licked my bottom lip, extremely self-conscious of it a heartbeat later. "I mean it. I love you. And I don't really care about some artificial, socially constructed timeline that's supposed to guarantee forever. Even if we broke up two months from now—"

He bowed his back to lean down and take my face in his hands and kissed me, somehow soft and urgent at once. When he raised his head, he still cupped my jaw, holding me like a precious, fragile object. "Never going to happen. So, there's no sense in talking about us ever breaking up. As long as we're discussing artificial, socially constructed timelines, I've known for a while that we belonged together. It just wasn't the sort of thing I felt like I could say without it sounding like... Jesus, I just didn't want to sound like I was trying to get into your knickers."

This was heavy stuff. This was terrifying, exhilarating, joyful, heavy stuff. No wonder people described love as being swept away.

I stepped up to kiss him again, and threaded my arms around his neck. "I have to tell you something, just so we can be totally clear."

"Mmhm," he murmured against my lips.

I pushed my fingers through the hair at the back of his head and tightened my hold just a touch. My heart swam mermaid flips in my stomach, and my thighs squeezed together. "I want to. Tonight."

"Want to what?" Realization washed over his features in an almost comical wave. He cleared his throat and asked, "What, now?"

There was that darn squeeze again, but this time, it was in an *entirely* different location. "Yeah. We could wait until after we do the dishes, but—"

"Fuck the dishes." He boosted me up on the counter and stood between my legs.

I remembered horsing around in the hotel pool, the way his bare skin felt against my thighs. Even the water had been too much of a barrier then, and we had way too many clothes on now. I grabbed the undone collar of his shirt and gave it an impatient tug.

"Wait, wait." He placed his hands over mine and held them to his chest. His heartbeat was a rapid, powerful throb against my palms. "You're sure you don't want to wait for something more romantic?"

"I've been waiting for something 'more romantic' since I

was thirteen years old," I said, the pain of my parents' lie crushing my heart all over. "Can't it just be enough that I love you?"

"It's everything." He covered my mouth with his, and I held onto him, rumpling the fabric of his shirt beneath my fingers. When he lifted his head, his gaze lingered on my mouth, almost dreamily. "Should we go up to the bedroom?"

My head swam. My heart pounded. His eyes flicked up to mine, and I breathed, "Yes."

## CHAPTER THIRTEEN

Stopping in the middle of the buildup was weird. It would have been easier to have just jumped right into sex from making out, with no sharp transition. Now that I knew the night wouldn't stop shy of defloration, my mind went totally blank, and I had no idea how to get back into that sexy mindset.

I went up the stairs ahead of Ian, and he held onto my hand as we went. I looked back to see him popping the remaining buttons on his shirt with one hand, and I turned before he saw me watching.

This was happening. Oh my god, it was actually going to happen.

When we got to his bedroom, he let go of my hand. "I'm going to go get a condom. Just so we have one within reach."

He was so matter of fact about it. Like, *my penis is going to be in your vagina later, better get the equipment.* He threw his shirt across the end of the bed as he walked to the bathroom.

*Get your head together. You want this to be perfect? Make it be perfect.* I slipped my dress down and kicked it aside. I went to the shirt, weighing my idea in my mind. Guys thought it was sexy when women wore their clothes, but it did seem a little weird to put it on right before I was going to have to take it off, again. On the other hand, I wanted to be sexy, and while he'd practically seen everything before, he hadn't seen it all at once. The thought made me suddenly shy.

I shed my bra and reached down to straighten my navy blue lace panties over my butt. Then I snatched up the shirt and pulled it on. The bathroom light snapped off, and Ian stepped out. I moved into the long slant of moonlight on the floor. He froze.

"I didn't know how naked I should be." I pulled the shirt closed at my waist. "I thought I would surprise you, but then I got nervous and—" God, didn't he know when to rescue me from myself? I shifted to my other foot. "Say something."

He started toward me, and with each step he took, my pulse sped up. There was a raw possessiveness his expression, almost too intense as he wrapped an arm around my waist and pulled me against his body. Our skin touched everywhere the shirt was open. The thrill of it raced through me. He tossed the condom on the bed and boosted me up to put my legs around him—I'd never considered that he might actually be strong—and carried me to the bed. I dug my fingers into his shoulders, not to hold on because he couldn't support me, but because they were so damn broad, it was totally hot to hang onto them.

He set me on my feet, letting me slide down him until I hit the floor. He knelt before me, his warm palms closing over my backs of my thighs to support me. I definitely needed support when he nuzzled the shirt open and scraped over my belly with his slightly prickly chin. I sucked in a breath on a sound like a tiny, panicked dog yipping in alarm.

"You know, that makes me nervous. If this takes your breath away, what will happen when I do this?" He kissed my stomach, just under my belly button, and my hips jerked. Before I noticed I was sinking my fingers into it, I had two handfuls of his hair. His hands smoothed up my thighs, his fingertips brushing my ass.

"Take the shirt off," he said softly, kissing lower, his mouth half on my skin, half on the scalloped lace edge of my panties. "Let me see you."

My breasts tingled, goose bumps jumping out all over. I practically tore off the shirt to stand in front of him in nothing but my underwear. He looked up at me as if in worship; I'd never seen so much open adoration aimed at me before. He reached up, bracketing my ribs to pull me down to sit on the bed in front of him.

"You know we can stop if you're not ready, or you don't like it. Just tell me," he reassured me.

"Okay. I'll remember that." I took a deep breath. "But right now, can you please fuck me?"

"Happy to oblige. But can I do one thing first?" He beckoned me with a finger, and I leaned down so we were eye to eye.

"Um. Okay." I had no idea what that thing would be, but I probably wanted to do it.

He brushed my hair back from my ear, his breath teasing my cheek as he sucked my earlobe into his mouth. Then he released it and whispered, "I want to get my head between your thighs and taste you. What do you say, Doll? Are you up for it?"

"Oh god. Y-yes." The answer broke from me as a whimper. I lay back, orienting myself correctly on the bed rather than laying across it, so Ian had room to lie between my legs. He leaned down to kiss me, and I lifted my pelvis up to bump against his.

"You have no patience," he teased, grinding against me and kissing the pulse point in my throat. He kissed a trail over my breasts and down my stomach, but he wasn't leisurely about it. He wasn't out for a Sunday drive, he was on his way to work, and he wasn't going to be late.

Thank god, because by the time he got down there, I wasn't in the mood to be kept waiting. He grasped both sides of my panties with two fingers and ran his tongue along the seam between the fabric and my skin. He didn't pull them down. Instead, he leaned in and ran his nose up and down the wet crotch.

My breath caught. What if I smelled gross? What if I was too wet and it was, like, abnormal?

"You smell good enough to eat," he groaned, kissing my bare inner thigh and smashing the last of my reservations.

Ian wouldn't make me feel bad or act disgusted by me. All he wanted was to make me feel good.

I wasn't going to stop him.

He pulled my panties down my legs, and I helped by bending my knee and bringing one foot out. He didn't bother pulling the other side off. Instead, he leaned in close to my pussy and parted me with his thumbs. My eyes squeezed closed, but I forced myself to keep them open, so I could see his face between my thighs. He kissed me, a soft, sucking kiss right at the tip of my clit, and I let out a shuddering moan.

With an arm hooked beneath each of my knees, he grasped my hips and pulled me down to meet a slow lick that started at my already wet opening and ended with a swirl around my clit. Then his mouth closed over me and I curled up from the bed, grabbing his hair and pushing him harder against me. His tongue was like the ultimate sex toy, moving from firm and pointed to soft and flat, circling or flicking at any given moment. When he found the motion that made me shout, "Oh god!"—a rapid side-to-side slide that felt like he was touching every nerve in my lower body—he stuck with it until I was thrashing and almost crying, the sensation so overwhelmed me. My hands fisted in the duvet, and he grabbed them, lacing our fingers together. With my legs over his shoulders and my hands captured, I was locked against his mouth in a sweet trap I didn't want to escape.

"I'm coming," I gasped, because it was all I could say. In fact, I repeated it several times, my throat becoming more hoarse with each one; all the wetness in my body was concentrated below his lips. I was probably making a spot on his bedspread. I lifted my hips against his face, imitating the speed and rhythm of the sucking pulse of his mouth, and I finally broke, my body bucking.

He lifted his head, breathing heavy, like he'd been submerged under water. He disentangled our hands to wipe his mouth. "Do you want me to keep going?"

It was tempting. Very tempting. But I needed him. I'd never felt so physically empty as I did at the moment. "No. I need you to fuck me right now. I need you inside me."

"Fuck," he breathed, scrubbing his hand down his face. "I'm going to remember that, the way you said it... I'll hear it in my head every time I jerk off for the rest of my life."

It shouldn't have been possible to be more turned on, but the rush of desire his words inspired made me think I might come again if I just thought about them.

He stood and unbuckled his belt, and unzipped his pants. I held my breath as he pushed them and his boxers down. Holy shit, he was naked. I mean, I was naked, but *he* was naked, and outside of porn, I'd never seen a guy so...naked. It was literally the only word I could think of. And whatever Ian had meant about looking like a gory wreck was completely untrue. Sure, he wasn't super cut and muscular, and yeah, he had slight love handles, but he was far from unfuckable. And the whole dad bod thing was kind of cute.

I stood on legs that were still basically jelly and tentatively put my arms around his shoulders, bringing our bodies together, skin to skin, every bare inch against every bare inch for the first time. The length of his erection pushed against my stomach. His arms encircled me, and I leaned my cheek against his chest.

"Do you still want to do this?" he asked softly.

Yes. More than anything, I wanted to do this. "Yeah. I really do."

I turned around and pulled the duvet back. The slight bend of my waist made me seriously consider just leaning over and letting him fuck me from behind, but that seemed kind of advanced for a beginner.

Now, for the potentially embarrassing part. I slid onto the bed and looked up at him, hoping I didn't appear as nervous as I felt. "Look...I'm not sure if it's true that you bleed the first time, or... I mean, if you don't want your sheets messed up… The internet says no, that doesn't happen, but my friends in high school said that it does—"

"I wouldn't know," he said, brushing the backs of his knuckles down my cheek. "I've never been anyone's first. But I promise, I'm going to be careful. And the sheets are the last thing on my mind."

He retrieved the condom from the folds of the bedding and tore the wrapper open. I watched, fascinated, as he rolled it on.

"Aren't you supposed to put a drop of lube in there, so it feels better?" I asked, remembering something I'd read in Cosmo. "Do you have any lube?"

"I do, but the last thing I need is more stimulation. I'm worried about lasting long enough as it is," he said, opening his nightstand. He took out a black bottle with a pump top. "Probably better if we use some for you, just to make things easier."

He was worried about lasting long enough? Like, he was *that* turned on by me? My skin pricked all over with goose bumps. "How do you want me?"

He frowned, squirting a few drops of the lube into his palm. "I think that's up to you. Whatever you want."

"Okay." I shivered as I watched him slick the gel down his cock. My bottom lip trembled, and I didn't know why, but I felt like I might cry, despite how much I was anticipating this. "I think I want you on top."

Why couldn't I be sexy? Like, even for two seconds?

My total non-sexiness didn't seem like a deterrent, because Ian practically leapt onto the bed, between my legs. He kissed me, my mouth, my neck, the hollow of my throat and the tops of my breasts. All the while, the tip of him prodded against me, but never quite made it inside.

"Are you ready?" he whispered beside my ear.

I gripped his shoulders and lifted my head to whisper back, "Yes."

His hand moved between us to guide himself. *This is it.*

My toes curled against the sheets in tense anticipation. I'd imagined this in hundreds of different ways, tried to figure out how it would feel. I'd compared it to fingering myself, because it just made sense to me. But the head of his cock pushed against me, and I realized how wrong that comparison was. I was slick, the condom was slick, and the lack of friction made everything seem so fast. I stretched, and he was in. At least, a little. It didn't hurt, but I definitely felt full to capacity, and he was barely inside.

He looked up, and his expression flickered to panic as our eyes met, so I must have looked scared out of my mind. I kind of felt scared out of my mind. Out of control, at least.

"Are you all right? Do you want me to—" he asked, moving like he would pull out.

"No, keep going," I breathed.

He pushed deeper, and I spread my legs wider. He withdrew a little, and my muscles tensed.

"I hate to ask," he began, his voice pained. "But it feels like you're going to snap my cock off. Is there anything I can do to help you relax?"

"Oh! I'm sorry!" I laughed. I sounded like a crazy person. I took a deep breath and blew it out, closing my eyes. "This is just really exciting. And a little nerve wracking."

"Well, you're doing fine," he reassured me. He leaned down to kiss me, sliding deeper as my mouth opened under his.

I turned my head away to gasp, "Oh my god, Ian!" against his cheek. I wanted something from him, but my brain and my body were too confused to articulate what, exactly, I was looking for. He withdrew and stroked back in, gentle and slow. I wanted him to really be inside, so that our bodies were flush against each other. "You can go deeper. You're not hurting me."

He obliged me on the next stroke, filling me until he bumped my cervix, and I startled. He pulled back. "Too far?"

"No, it's perfect, I just… I'm surprised by how different this feels—" The pitch of my voice rose with the slow drag of his cock as he pulled back. I shifted under him. I didn't know what to do with my hands, so I tentatively laid one on his shoulder and the other on the small of his back. I pushed my face into the bend of his neck. His cologne smelled amazing. "Please fuck me. For real. Please."

"For real?" I heard the amusement in his voice. He reached to snag one of my legs and pull it up, around his waist, opening me wider as he moved.

I tipped my head back and rocked with the rhythm he set up, slow and steady. It felt good, but I still needed more sensation to take me all the way. "Um, do you mind if I…play with myself a little?"

"Fuck, no, I don't mind," he practically growled. "I want to feel you come."

I slipped my hand between us. The angle was different, and I definitely didn't have much wiggle room. Curiosity drove my fingers lower, to feel where his cock glided in and out of me. He groaned when I spread my fingers around him.

There wasn't a single thing about the night that I was going to forget. Not the feeling of his hands on me, not the way he smelled or how his chest hair felt scraping over my nipples. Not the panting sound of his breath or the flex of his hips between my legs, or the way his body seemed so much bigger, so much stronger and thrillingly intimidating when I was under him. My fingers slid over my clit, and it only took me a few seconds to reach the edge. My feet cramped, and I heard myself moaning, but all but one sense, tactile sensation, had faded into the background. I dug my nails into Ian's back and practically screamed as my orgasm washed through my body. My internal muscles seized on him in sharp pulses, and my limbs went weak. I clung to his shoulders, not exactly sobbing, but not exactly moaning, either. I was so overwhelmed, I blurted, "Oh my god, I'm actually having sex!"

"Ah, Doll, not for much longer, I'm afraid." He laughed, out of breath, and kissed me. Then, with an almost disappointed-sounding groan, he drove deep, his body jerking and trembling over me. His cock pulsed in me, and I realized with a shock that he'd just come, buried so deep in me I couldn't breathe.

After that, it was like all the strength had poured out of his body. He eased out gently and rolled off me, onto his back. Still breathing heavy, he caught my hand and brought it to his lips. "You all right, Doll?"

"Yeah." I blinked up at the sky through the window over our heads. "Yeah, I expected that I would be... I don't know. Weepy? That I would feel some profound sense of transition from one phase of my life to the next? But I don't."

"Fair enough. How do you feel?" He reached for something in the dark. Probably a tissue so he could take off the condom.

That supposition was confirmed when he flinched and hissed a second later. I covered my mouth to keep from giggling.

"I feel...tired. And really, really good. Can I have two orgasms every time we do it?" I rolled onto my stomach to lean up on my elbows beside him. He was so handsome I couldn't resist dropping a kiss on his cheek.

"God, minimum, I hope." He grimaced. "Maybe I'll last longer than five minutes next time."

"It's okay. I think probably a little bit of sex the first time is better than way too much sex." I reached between my legs. I was definitely puffy and a little bit sore. "But it didn't hurt at all."

"Thank God!" He put his hands over his face and mumbled through them, "That was my biggest fear, doing this."

"I know. Which is why I wasn't nervous." It was a lie but a harmless one. I would have been nervous no matter who

I'd done it with. With Ian, those nerves had been at a minimum.

"This may sound a bit creepy. You'll have to just forgive me for that," he began haltingly. "But thank you. I know you waited a long time, and I know how much this meant to you. So, thank you for letting me share it with you."

I leaned over to kiss him. "I love you. I know I didn't say it when you did, but I felt it, then. I just wanted it to be…special."

"You're special, Penny Parker." He cupped my jaw with his big hand. "And I love you, too."

* * * *

Sleeping naked next to someone, feeling all of their skin, their entire body pressed against yours, it was…sweaty. Really, super sweaty. I hoped Ian didn't notice how gross I was when he woke up. I tried to wipe some of my perspiration off on the sheet before he opened his eyes.

The alarm clock on the bedside table read ten-thirty in the morning. That was some serious sleeping in for me. My bladder was more than aware of it. I rolled out of bed, praying I wouldn't sneeze or cough or laugh or even just walk too fast. I kicked the bathroom door closed behind me and sat on the toilet, groaning in relief as I urinated. Dammit, that was another *Cosmo* tip I'd forgotten! I was supposed to have peed after sex, so I wouldn't get a bladder infection.

When I wiped, a little pink showed on the toilet paper, and my whole general area was sore. I guess any body part ached after you introduced it to a new exercise. I just hoped it would fade quickly so we could do it again.

I hurried back out to the bed, feeling pretty awesome about my nakedness. Nothing to be modest about, now. The thought put a little swagger in my step. And why not? I felt amazing. Like a big ashamed-of-my-virginity shaped weight had been magically lifted from my shoulders. I wanted to shout it from every rooftop in New York.

*Oh my god! Rosa!*

Ian was still snoring away—I was so glad I didn't snore, that would be mortifying—and snuck downstairs to get my phone. Walking around his bedroom naked was one thing, but walking around his apartment naked? I felt super exposed in the wide-open space, in front of all those damn windows. I ran on the balls of my feet to the sofa, where that soft white knitted throw was, and snatched it up.

A pair of jeans slid off the back of the couch.

"Are these the same…" I frowned, trying to wrap the throw around myself and get a better look at the pants. They were. They were the same jeans, he'd just re-hidden them.

Wow. Ian's life was a mess.

I slipped my feet into the pants and pulled them up. They were way too big for me. I cinched the belt to the tightest hole and rolled up the legs, then pulled the throw around me like a poncho and shuffled off to get my purse.

My phone's battery was almost dead, so when Rosa answered, I greeted her with, "I had sex last night!"

"I'm at the post office," she said, her voice a forced normal.

"Don't care. Put me on speakerphone, if you want. I will not care." I flicked my gaze upward and tiptoed away from the open section of ceiling. I would be fine with the post office hearing my squee, but Ian would tease me mercilessly.

"So, the parent test worked?" she asked.

I nodded, even though she wouldn't be able to see me. "He flipped out. He called them monsters."

"He did not!"

"He did! He basically called them the worst parents in the world, which, you know, they are. Oh, and by the way, that whole family curse thing? Was a total lie—"

"I knew that."

"*And*," I said, ignoring her, "we got fortune cookies, and mine said—"

"Skip to the dirty part. I'm almost at the front of the line," she ordered.

I took a deep breath. "We came back here, and I was like, 'I want tonight to be the night,' and he took me upstairs and basically had me accessing the Akashic records, I came so hard."

"Good job, Ian." I heard the smile in Rosa's voice. "Are you back home now? I want details."

"No, I'm at his place. He's still asleep, actually."

"Well, have a good time," she sing-songed.

"Oh please, we're not doing it again right now. I'm way too sore." But not too sore for more oral action. I might actually suggest that when he woke up. I could even go down on him. I could wake him up that way. And maybe I wasn't actually too—

"You're going to do it again," Rosa said flatly. "Welcome to the point of the relationship where all you do is fuck." Something muffled the mic on her phone, and I heard Rosa snap, "Then maybe you shouldn't listen to other people's conversations!" She came back on. "I have to go, I'm next in line. Do not think we're not celebrating. You only lose your virginity once."

"Thank god, because it was nerve wracking." The next time, I would squash my nerves and be a total pro. "Okay, go do the postal thing. I love you."

"I love you, too." She paused. "And I'm really glad you're happy."

I smiled to myself and hung up, then looked to the stairs. I could have gotten into Ian's fridge and started making some breakfast—he actually had the supplies to do it, this time—but the thought of getting back into his bed and curling up next to him was so much better. But when I got upstairs, he was already awake, his head resting on one arm stretched out on his pillow. He squinted at me as I stepped inside. "Are those my jeans?"

"Yeah, I found them." I tossed the throw across the end of the bed, standing in front of him topless. I held out my arms. "The Mickey Mouse look isn't as sexy as the Donald Duck look, huh?"

"Oh, no, I think it's sexier," he said, his eyes wide, as though the answer were bewilderingly obvious. "Your tits are out."

I laughed and folded my arms over my chest, suddenly self-conscious. *He had his dick in you last night. I think you're safe to be naked in front of him.*

"So…thanks, by the way. For making last night…" I shivered, remembering it, and he grinned at me.

"You're speechless and trembling. I get the picture." He pulled back the blankets. "Get back in here."

I shimmied out of his jeans and got into bed beside him, chewing my lower lip. "Don't take this the wrong way, but I don't want to have sex, right now."

"Feel it this morning?" he asked gently.

"Yeah." I rubbed my inner thighs. "I think I pulled a muscle, too."

"A nap is always good for that," he suggested, and I laughed.

"We just woke up!" I scooted up close to him. "But I'm fine with staying naked in bed all day. It's so relaxing."

"I'm loathe to get out of bed, but my contacts are glued to my fucking eyeballs. I want you to stay right here, and when I get back, we'll talk about breakfast." He leaned over to kiss me, and I didn't even mind his morning breath.

"Don't look at my sad, flat arse while I'm walking away," he ordered as he headed off.

Pff. I was totally going to look. "I love your sad, flat arse!" I called after him.

When the bathroom door closed, I snuggled down in the bed and held a pillow over my face as I squealed and rolled from side to side. I'd done it. I'd had sex with someone, and things hadn't fallen apart. He still respected me, he wasn't going to walk out and leave me heartbroken for life, he was still here, and happy to be.

God, my parents had really fucked me up, hadn't they?

A memory of last night's war crime of a dinner stopped me. The thing about Ian's siblings had been stuck in my mind, but I'd been too distracted to ask. I heard the toilet flush then the water running. I had to figure out how to ask him what was up with the two missing siblings. Were they estranged? Were they…were they dead?

*Maybe you shouldn't ask.* But my curiosity got the better of me. When he walked out of the bathroom, still totally, comfortably nude but for the thick-rimmed hipster glasses he'd replaced his contacts with—and holy cats, was that sexy—I sat up a little.

"I wanted to ask you about something you said at dinner last night," I began.

He grimaced and slid into the bed with me. "Yeah, that wasn't my finest hour. I'm sorry if I made things… Well, I'm sure I made things difficult for you down the road with your parents."

"You did, but I don't care about them." It wasn't a shock to realize it, but a shock to realize how little the statement mattered to me. "What I wanted to ask about was your family."

He paled slightly.

I went on. "You told me on our first date that you were one of nine children. And then last night you said—"

"One of seven. Yeah." He cleared his throat and did his looking-off-over-there thing that he always did when the discussion became uncomfortable for him. Now, though, I could tell it wasn't about nerves.

"So…if this is out of line, you don't have to answer. I was just wondering…why did you leave out the other two?"

He looked down and picked at the sheet absently. He didn't need to answer. I already understood.

"They died, didn't they?" I asked softly.

"Yeah." He cleared his throat, paused as though he would speak, then cleared his throat again. "I don't, uh. I don't generally talk about it."

"Oh. Sorry." Now I felt really bad, because I'd stirred up some horrible tragedy in his mind.

"No, it's fine. I don't like to tell people, but I should tell you." He took a deep breath and exhaled noisily, as though he were resigning himself to jump into an ice-cold pool. "My brother, Robby, and my sister, Cathy, were uh. They were murdered."

His sentence went up at the end, as though it were a question.

I gasped without thinking.

"Yeah," he responded, as though I'd said something. "It was... Cathy was going with this guy. A right arsehole. We never trusted him, not a one of us. But Cathy was Cathy, and she was going to do her own thing. So, she moved in with him—broke my mother's heart, that they were living in sin—and she got pregnant. And he started beating her. I mean, really, just... She would come over with black eyes and bruises all up and down her—"

He broke off and closed his eyes. I reached for him, but he tensed, so I drew my hand back.

"Anyway, he beat her so bad she lost the baby. Kicked her in the stomach hard enough that he ruptured, ah, I don't know. Something you don't want to rupture, I suppose. I was nineteen at the time. I didn't ask questions. The police were fucking useless. If they had—" He stopped. "I've gone over what *should* have happened enough."

I had to touch him. I couldn't stand to see him in pain.

"When Cathy got out of hospital, Mum said that was it, she was coming home. If the police weren't going to help, well, there were plenty of us to keep him away from her. We thought the prick was at work, so Robby went with her to collect her things, but the guy was waiting and he... He shot them. Both of them."

"Ian..."

"Ah, I shouldn't have burdened you with that," he said,

forcing a laugh, as though he'd done something silly, but not serious.

"It's not a burden." I thought of the picture he'd been drawing of his brother. "You went through something terrible. I can't even imagine it."

"I was at university at the time, but I'd come home when Cathy was in hospital. She was my twin, you see. And when you're a twin, you do, I know it sounds like an old wives' tale, but you do know." He sniffed. Oh god, he was tearing up. He reached behind his glasses with one finger to wipe at an eye. "I knew the minute she died. I was in a pub, having lunch, and I just got this feeling. It was like all the color in the world vanished. I got there before the police did, but there was no chance of saving either of them. He'd just… Her head was…"

"Don't, you don't have to tell me." I pulled him into my arms and held him. He squeezed me tight, his face in the crook of my shoulder and neck to hide the tears I knew were falling. I could tell from every hitch of his breath that he was crying, though his muscles were rigid from trying to hold back.

After a long moment, he lifted his head, sniffed, and said, "Well, now you know it. I'm sorry you do. And I'm sorry to ruin our morning—"

"Stop it. I asked." There was no way I was going to let him blame himself for sharing something so intimately painful.

"You're the second person I've told. Mostly, it's just family who knows. After it happened, I went to Glasgow to be closer to home for my mum, went for a more practical profession, and moved here as quick as I could." He rolled onto his back and stared at the ceiling, wiping his eyes. "Ah, here I am, blubbering like a fool when I should be making you breakfast or going on about how fantastic last night was."

"No, don't…" I stopped myself, so I could phrase it just

right. "Don't feel like you have to be happy all the time. Or that you have to protect me from who you are. I want to know all the stuff about you, good and bad and…fucking horrible."

"All the stuff?" he repeated, cracking a smile.

"All the stuff," I reaffirmed.

He rolled to his side and took my face in his hands. "And I want to know every fucking detail about you, Doll."

Yeah. I totally changed my mind about having sex, again.

## CHAPTER FOURTEEN

Being in love with Ian was like no relationship I'd ever had before. And that wasn't just limerence talking. We got along so well, it scared me. I seriously considered that I might be in that version of *The Matrix* where everything was too perfect, so the human mind rejected it. If we did run into situations that called for compromise, we came up with solutions that didn't require one of us to silently feel we were getting the short end of the bargain. If I stayed over at his place during the week, he stayed at mine on Friday, though I knew he didn't care for my bed. I didn't care for trying to be quiet while having sex, so I didn't mind if we spent a little more time at his apartment than mine.

Rosa had been totally right about this stage of a relationship. Ian and I couldn't get enough of each other, in the very best ways possible. He'd gone down on me for a full hour one night, savoring me slowly while I came again and again in orgasms like gentle waves. Once, we'd had sex in the backseat of his car, parked on a side street at two in the morning, because I'd mentioned it was an experience I'd never gotten to have, and that had bummed me out.

The car thing hadn't been as great as all the movies made it seem, but it had been great because I'd been with Ian.

He was so different from anyone I'd dated before. He didn't ask me to wear less makeup or not chew ice or sing along with the radio. There wasn't anything he did that annoyed me, either, which was a nice change from constantly biting my tongue about someone's whistling breathing or constant nose sniffing. I never felt like I had to be someone I wasn't when I was with him. I didn't doubt myself for a single moment when we were together. I didn't doubt us.

And I definitely didn't feel like I had to look perfect all

the time, which was good, because by November, my apartment was *freezing*. Our landlord paid for the heat, and he never turned it on until after Thanksgiving. So it was a comfort to know Ian would still want to fuck me later even though I was wearing a flannel nightshirt and wool socks under the blankets as I curled up next to him. We were watching the "Charlie's Mom Has Cancer" episode of *It's Always Sunny In Philadelphia*, with my head resting on Ian's chest. On the screen, Charlie flipped out at a Catholic mass over the amount of standing and sitting, and I laughed, "Oh my god, is there really that much standing up and sitting down?"

"More," Ian said, adding, "You should come, sometime." *What.*

I sat up. "You're kidding, right?"

"I…wasn't." He pushed himself up to sit taller against the headboard. "My faith is a very important part of my life, and I'd like to share that with you."

Had I hurt his feelings by laughing at the show? I guess I could see how he found it offensive, if he did. I wanted to apologize, but I was more hung up on the part where he wanted me to go to church.

Like…*church* church?

"I don't know… Ian, I'm not a…god person." *God person? Where do you think you are, Greek mythology?*

"I know," he said gently. "And I'm not asking you to be. I'm not under any delusion that you'll come to mass and suddenly feel so moved by the Holy Spirit that you want to be baptized on the spot. But if you wouldn't mind coming along once, just to see that part of my life, it would mean a lot to me."

I knew he cared about this. I just didn't know why. The idea of religion wasn't abhorrent to me, but I really didn't understand it. Signs, I could understand; you only had to believe that it was possible for coincidences to show you the truth about what you should do or what might happen in the future. Believing that a paternalistic God spent his days either ignoring or torturing the people on Earth, but cared enough about them to send his son down to get murdered, that was a much bigger stretch.

Knowing what I did about Ian, though, and what he'd suffered through over his siblings' deaths, it made sense to me that he might want a version of the world that had clear rules and a cosmic parent looking out for everyone, and everybody would see each other again in heaven.

And because of all of that, going with him to his place of worship made me even more nervous. "What if I do the wrong thing and embarrass you?"

"Are you going to take your top off?" he teased. "Start shouting obscenities?"

"Of course not." Maybe I was being a little silly. I looked down. "I have to admit, there's something…weird about it. It's really intimate, people praying around you."

"And that's why I want to share it with you. I don't expect you to understand or share in my beliefs. But I want you to know me." He shrugged. "Think about it. I'm not going to pressure you. If somewhere along the line you decide—"

"Do you want me to come on Sunday?" I blurted.

"If you'd like." His lips bent in a close-mouthed smile of gratitude. "You're coming over tomorrow night, aren't you?"

"Yeah. No. Should I do that, though? I mean, spend all night having sex with you then go to your church? It sounds…disrespectful." I chewed my lip, imagining how awkward it was going to be sitting in a church full of people I was sure knew we'd been getting totally dirty the night before.

Ian took my hands and kissed them, then held them in his lap. "I appreciate your concern. We can stick to oral tomorrow night, then."

I grabbed my pillow and smacked him with it. For a

supposedly mature adult, he could be a real dork sometimes.

We didn't keep Ian's "just oral" promise on Saturday night, but I wasn't going to break *my* promise. I got up with his alarm and went to get ready in his bathroom, which he graciously ceded to me most mornings. I showered and scrubbed extra hard, like there were going to be sin-detecting dogs at this place.

*Not "this place", Penny. Church.*

There had never been a time in my past that I'd had to actually face going to church. I'd gone to a bible camp a few times with a friend, but that had been more of a non-denominational sleep over. I'd been to weddings, and while god had been mentioned at those, they'd been barely religious. It was like hearing about god in the pledge of allegiance or something. Just a word.

But it wasn't just a word to Ian. It was a huge part of his life, one I couldn't ignore. I wanted to be with him, and that meant trying to learn some of this Catholic stuff, even if I had no intention of joining the club.

One of the things I hadn't figured out was how, exactly, I was meant to dress. I should have asked him. He wore suits every Sunday—I'd appreciated watching him get dressed in the mornings, from my vantage point in his warm, comfortable bed, just as much as I'd appreciated pulling his tie off and having my way with him when he'd gotten home later—so I'd taken a cue from that and chosen a navy, boat-necked dress with gray polka dots. I paired it with a gray cardigan and a thin red belt around both then ditched the belt. Something about red leather in a church seemed a little too rebellious for a guest.

I used my straightening iron to smooth my hair and curl under the ends, put on just a touch of makeup, and took a deep breath. Usually, I would still be in bed, waiting for Ian to leave so I could get up and go on my Sunday run and luxuriate in his amazing bathtub before he got home. Now I was worried I was dressed to offend his god.

So just another relaxing Sunday.

I checked my phone as I headed down the stairs. Ian had said we'd need to leave by nine-thirty. It was twenty-five after, and he was still in the bathroom. Diva. "Ian?"

"Yeah, Doll, on my way."

I leaned against the back of the couch, my black wool peacoat folded over my arms. Ian rounded the corner from the bathroom, rocking the funeral director look hard. It was actually starting to grow on me.

I pointed to my dress. "Is this conservative enough?"

"Yeah, it's fine," he said, as though he were bewildered I wouldn't realize it on my own. "I like your hair."

"Thanks." I touched it self-consciously. I liked it a lot better when it was messy and textured. "I thought since your sister would be there I should forgo the bedhead look. I didn't want her to think it was, you know…"

"Actual bedhead?"

My stomach roiled with nerves, but I tried to smile. "Yeah. That."

Having never been in a sexual relationship with someone before, I didn't know how to deal with meeting someone's family when the night before that someone had been fucking me from behind so hard the bed had rattled. Meeting that family in church? That only seemed ten times more wrong. But I'd promised Ian, and this was such a big part of his life. And I totally wasn't willing to skip Saturday night sex for the rest of our lives.

"You'll be fine. If it helps, she's not going to like you the first few times she meets you, anyway."

"That doesn't help." I sighed "I just want this to go well. I know this is important to you."

"It is. But what's most important to me is that you were willing to come along, even if it's just this once." Ian reached for my coat and helped me pull it on, then donned his suit jacket and long, gray trench coat.

Outside, a few bastard snowflakes blew down from the

dreary clouds.

"Oh, no. This is crazy. It can't snow yet," I objected, as though I had some power to stop the weather.

"You'll be in church today. Pray that it doesn't," he said. After a pause, he added, "I'm sorry. It wasn't a comment on your beliefs or trying to change them. I was just trying to be funny."

Wait, he thought he'd offended me? If he was as worried about that as I was about offending him, we were on a level playing field. I grinned. "Oh, I know. You were just failing to be funny."

St. Basil's was located in a tidy working-class neighborhood in Brooklyn, about a twenty-minute drive from Ian's apartment. There was a church closer, but St. Basil's was where Ian's nephew worked. If that's what it was called. I wondered if it was weird, having a family member wield the power of god's approval over you. Of course, I was still pretty murky on how that worked. Despite how much I enjoyed knowing random trivia about science stuff, I'd never really bothered to look into the whole religion thing. I had a feeling I was about to get a crash course.

I was so jumpy, even my skin tingled as we walked across the small, cracked parking lot toward the brick building. It looked exactly as I imagined a church should look, with a steeple on top and a tall, peaked roof and stained glass windows. We went up the front steps and through the wide open doors, into a vestibule with a checkered floor. People were greeting each other, hanging up their coats, standing around and blocking doors. It was far busier and noisier than I had expected.

Ian took my coat and hung it up on the long rack provided, which seemed like a pretty trusting thing to do. I mean, it was a church, sure, but if I wanted to steal coats, this would be the ideal venue. I followed Ian into the main part of the building, where the pews were, and it was comforting to see that it, too, looked just like I'd imagined from the movies. Actually, quite a lot like the church from that episode of *It's Always Sunny In Philadelphia* that had roped me into coming here to begin with.

I could have titled this day, "The Gang Makes Penny Do Something Extremely Uncomfortable."

"I feel really overdressed," I told Ian in a low voice.

"Don't feel that way. You look beautiful, and besides, my parents always insisted that you should dress well for mass, since you're in the presence of God. It's just respectful." If he'd meant for those words to reassure me, they did not. I was meeting his sister *and* his god?

This was insane. Panic clawed up my throat, and I smoothed my skirt down with clammy palms. "Okay, is there anything I have to do?"

Ian shook his head. "No, God knows you're not Catholic." He kept talking about god like he was a real person, and it was starting to freak me out. "You just have to come into the church, sit in the pew beside me, stand when we stand, sit when we sit, kneel if you'd like, and smile warmly at my sister."

*Oh, is that all, Ian?* I wanted to snap.

He went on, "Oh, and don't take communion. You can just stay in the pew when we go up."

"Go up?" I blinked in confusion. I hadn't read about that term when I'd googled Catholicism on my phone this morning.

"I promise I'll give you direction. Please, don't be nervous," he said, and I wanted to kick myself for being so uptight. Of course he wouldn't let me do anything to embarrass myself or him.

I followed Ian to a rack of glass votive holders. Some of the candles burned already. He dropped a twenty-dollar bill into a slot on the rack, then picked up a long wooden taper and started lighting candles.

"What's this for?" I whispered. Everyone in the seats

were mumbling prayers together, and I wasn't sure if things had started or what, but I didn't want to be rude.

He lit a final one, the fifth, as he said, "You light them to remember your loved ones who've passed on."

"Oh." I counted them off in my head. I knew his parents had died, and obviously two were for his brother and sister. The fifth I didn't know, but if he had another sad family secret, now was not the time to ask about it.

Ian crossed himself before we walked away. He seemed to do that a lot; when we walked in, he dipped his fingers in holy water and crossed himself, too, and when we got to an empty pew, he took a knee and crossed himself. Didn't his arms get tired?

He gestured for me to go ahead of him into the row. He sat beside me and asked, "I have to go bother Danny for absolution. Will you be all right on your own for a second?"

*What?* He was going to drop me in the middle of totally unfamiliar territory with a bunch of strangers—*chanting* strangers—and leave me alone? "Um. Maybe?" I looked around at all the parishioners on their knees, dangling beads over the pews in front of them. "I'm a little freaked out by all the chanting."

A guy at the front of the church bellowed, "The fifth glorious mystery: The coronation of the Blessed Virgin Mary, Queen of Heaven and Earth," and everyone started saying the Lord's Prayer in unison.

What was even happening?

"Ah. Yeah, I could see why that would be unsettling," Ian said guiltily as he scratched his neck and looked away. "It's just praying the rosary. Nothing scary. Sit tight a minute?"

"Oh, the rosary!" I said, a little too loudly, and smacked my forehead with the palm of my hand. I lowered my voice at the startled look from the woman in front of us. "Sorry. I should have known. I'm just a little nervous."

"Don't worry, you're doing fine," he said with a reassuring smile as he slid from the pew.

It would have been easy to be peeved at Ian for not adequately preparing me for this, but I wasn't. None of this was foreign to him, so he probably took it for granted that everyone knew what Catholic Church was like. I took a deep breath and reached for the thick, laminated paperback book in the rack bumping my knees. At first, I thought it was a bible, but upon further inspection, it was full of songs—a lot of songs—and various biblical passages. I thumbed through it. The whole production seemed to be outlined. Oh my gosh, it was a manual! Exactly what I needed to keep from embarrassing myself today.

"Cutting it close this week. I should be out there getting ready for the processional. You better not have many sins." I heard a voice say, and I looked around. Everyone else was looking around, too. It seemed to be coming from the speakers attached to the walls.

I frowned and flipped to the front of the book. It sure didn't sound like it could be a part of the script inside.

"I always have many sins."

Oh my gosh. That was Ian's voice. It was quieter than the other voice—Danny's, I realized with crashing dread—but unmistakably Ian.

"I don't have time for the full rigmarole today. Penny's waiting out there," Ian went on, and my face flushed. I heard a few chuckles in the back of the room, but mostly there was a lot of muttering as the conversation went on over the PA system.

"Penny! You brought her?" Danny said in surprise. *I thought Ian had told his family I was coming.*

"Things have been going really well. I thought it might be a good time. Did I mention things are going well?" Ian said, and I cringed. I really hoped he wasn't about to go into how well things were going.

*Oh my god, he was going back there for confession.*

I thought I might actually consider crossing myself, at that point.

"You're lucky Mom's not here," Danny said. "No, you're not lucky. You're going to hear about it when she finds out she missed the chance to meet the woman who's been stealing her baby brother away."

Oh, that was great. Ian hadn't been joking about Annie not liking me, apparently.

"She's not going to be here?" Ian asked, sounding pretty upset. "I told her I was bringing Penny. Where'd Annie run off to?"

"She and Dad are on the ladies' altar society marriage retreat to D.C. She must have forgotten to mention it. They're going to mass at the National Basilica today."

We had a *national* Basilica? What happened to separation of church and state?

Wait, no, I was focusing on the wrong thing. Why hadn't Annie told Ian she wouldn't be here? She really didn't want to meet me. My heart dropped. Ian's family was important to him. If they didn't like me, how could we hope to be together?

"Good for them. They deserve to get away."

A lady who'd been sitting at the front of the church sprinted up the aisle, an amused expression on her face. I assumed she was going to stop anymore of our personal business airing over the speakers for the whole congregation, some of whom were looking at me with interest. My cheeks were probably as red as a tomato.

"Uncle Ian," Oh, good, he'd used Ian's name, so *everyone* would know who they'd been talking about. "If you're serious about wanting Mom to meet this girl, you're going to have to bring her to the house. Do you have any idea how much I hear about this?"

"I can only imagine. I wanted to keep my relationship with Penny private while we got to know each other. This is a first step, and a pretty big one. She's not religious, at all, but she's here because she knows what this means to me. She's *the one*, Danny."

*The one.* Ian thought I was *The One.* Suddenly, his accidental public airing of our private business didn't seem that bad anymore. Neither did the fact that his sister clearly didn't want to meet me. I didn't know what that was about, but I didn't care, at the moment. *He thinks I'm The One.*

"I'm happy for you. But if she's the one, you've got to bring her around to meet Mom. She's ready to put your tackle in a mason jar over this girl."

There was a loud thump and crunch over the speakers, and a few people covered their ears.

"Oh no. Tell me that wasn't on," I heard Ian say, then, after a pause, Danny said, "Oh, fuck me."

Gasps echoed all around the room. I pressed my fingers to my forehead. So, cursing ran in the family. I filed that away for when Ian and I had kids.

"For Christ's sake, turn it off!" Ian shouted, eliciting more gasps. An old woman across the aisle crossed herself. I guess they really took the whole "don't take the Lord's name in vain" thing seriously.

The mic cut out then, and I sat, staring straight ahead, totally aware of the eyes on me and the murmurs of outrage from the parishioners. *Shoot me now.*

No. I wasn't going to be embarrassed. My true love had just declared me his true love in return. Yeah, it had been in the absolutely most inappropriate way conceivable, but it had happened. When he slunk into the pew to sit beside me, he whispered, "Sorry about that."

We didn't face each other but stared straight ahead at the altar.

I laughed. I couldn't help myself. I tried to hold it in with my hands, but it ended up sounding like I was spitting.

"I'm glad you found that funny," Ian said, a note of humor creeping into his voice. "Danny is going to get a lot of complaints today."

I giggled and whispered, "Well, tell your sister that if she puts your tackle in a mason jar, she's going to get a complaint."

* * * *

I will probably go to hell for even thinking it, but Ian was even sexy at church. Maybe even a little sexier. The suit was a big part of it, but most of it was how genuinely he believed. He wasn't just reciting words to say them, he truly believed them. Every now and then, he would cast a glance at me, and I would smile to reassure him that I wasn't about to flee the building. When Danny delivered his sermon—relating to the grim gospel reading about the earth passing away and nobody knowing when it would happen—it was obvious that Ian heard the words of his priest, not his nephew. And when Danny said the gospel was a metaphor not only for living your life free from sin but living your life to the fullest, Ian reached over and squeezed my hand.

After mass, Ian and I bolted. The whole "airing of our personal business over the church PA system" thing was too big an elephant to ignore in the church's tiny fellowship hall. Once we were in the car, pulling out of the parking lot, he said, "So…"

"If your plan with the microphone mix up was to make my first visit to your church even more awkward, congratulations." I drew a heart in the foggy glass of the passenger window.

"That bad?"

I looked over at him, and his jaw was tight, like he was clenching his teeth. I shouldn't have joked. "I'm just teasing. It wasn't terrible, at all. And I got some really, really good news out of your nephew's mistake."

He flushed red and laughed nervously. "Well, now that you know I'm spending my spare time doodling hearts around your name in my notebook, I'm not sure I can look you in the eye."

"It's not necessarily a bad thing to have the woman who loves you know how much you love her," I pointed out. "If you caught me talking about you without my knowledge, you would probably want to change your address."

He took a quick glance away from the road to smile at me. "It would be that bad, would it?"

"Yeah," I said, pleased with the still growing grin on his face. "I have a lot of fantasies about our future."

"So, you've picked out the names of our children, then? Planned our wedding?"

He'd poured out his heart without knowing I was listening, so I might as well share the depths of my new love feelings, to even the score. "Have I named our children? Are you kidding? I've seriously researched the benefits and risks of epidurals on pregnancy websites."

"Yikes," he laughed.

"Kinda makes 'she's the one' seem less embarrassing now, doesn't it?" I paused. "You like to read, right?"

"Aye, I do."

Ah, that occasional "aye" that hadn't been fully replaced by American speech patterns. I was a sucker for that. So much so, I almost forgot my original point. "Right. So. Okay, are you ever reading along, and something happens, something so earth-shattering for the characters that you can't believe they'll ever recover from it, so you skip ahead to make sure that everything turns out okay?"

"Chapter sixty-nine of *A Dance With Dragons*," he answered without hesitation.

"And when you saw that whatever was happening actually turned out okay, you still wanted to read the book, right? Knowing the ending at that point didn't ruin the rest of the chapters for you."

The corner of his mouth twitched. "Yeah, after I saw that everything in *A Dance With Dragons* turned out all right for Jon Snow in the end, I felt much better."

"Well, that's how I feel about us. No matter what happens between us between now and then, I know that at the end, we're together forever, and it takes the pressure off. That's what your nephew's bad judgment with AV equipment helped me realize today. So, don't worry about it." I waited for the rush of fear I would inevitably feel, having spilled all of that out. It never came. The pressure truly was off, because Ian wouldn't freak out to hear that.

He put his hand on my knee as we pulled up to a traffic light. "So, epidural or no epidural?"

"Oh, epidural all the way," I laughed. "But that's a little ways off."

"Agreed. Right now, we should be focusing all of our efforts on rehearsing the conception." He glanced in his rearview mirror to change lanes. "Would you care to do that, right now?"

"I think that's a fine idea." I walked my fingers up his thigh, thrilling at the way he visibly stirred beneath his trousers in anticipation of my touch.

Practice makes perfect, after all.

## CHAPTER FIFTEEN

It was too bad I wasn't religious. I could have used the power of prayer to help keep my hands off Ian as we drove back to his apartment. He'd stayed in the car when we'd stopped at my place for clothes, which was good, because if he hadn't, we wouldn't have left for a *while*. I wanted him so bad, I was already wet and could feel the silky glide between my thighs with every dazed step I took.

There was a high probability I hadn't even grabbed the stuff I needed in the morning; for all I knew, I'd dragged sweatpants out of the hamper instead of a skirt out of my closet.

But I was a good girl and exercised so much self-control that I deserved a gold star. I even almost made it up to his apartment in the elevator without jumping him.

Almost.

"Easy now," Ian said with a bark of laughter. "If you want to fuck in an elevator, I have a more private option upstairs."

"I know," I teased to cover up my frustration. "I just can't keep my hands off you. Don't complain, just go with it."

Even though I wanted to maul him with both hands, once we were inside, the windows distracted me. Ian had remarked more than once I was dating him for the view, but I couldn't understand how he'd become so used to just living in a place with clocks for windows. It was amazing! I took my coat off and rushed over to the one in the living room, like I always did, and peered out between the Roman numerals. "Wow, it's really snowing."

"Maybe you'll get snowed in," he said as he hung his coat in the closet in the entryway. He came over to join me. "We could have a 'Baby It's Cold Outside' situation on our hands."

Oh, that song was so gross. "I hope you don't drug my drink."

He frowned. "What do you mean?"

"That's a line from the song. She's like, 'hey, what's in this drink,' or something. That song is disturbing." I gazed out at the blowing flakes with a pang of homesickness. I remembered sitting at the kitchen table—I was never allowed in the dining room—eating my grilled cheese and tomato soup lunch as my nanny, Theresa, washed up the dishes, watching the snow fall. Though I'd been only six or seven at the time, I remembered thinking, *this is normal. This is how other kids live.* Later, I'd gone outside and tried to make a snowman, though there'd barely been enough to cover the grass, let alone make into a ball.

I looked at the man standing beside me, whom I planned on being with for the rest of my life. Or…his life. I didn't like thinking about that. But here we were, watching our very first snowfall together. I wanted it to feel as memorable and as real as that moment at my kitchen table, when I'd felt a sliver of normal. "You know what we should do?"

"Fly to Miami and escape the winter while we still can?"

I pulled a face. "I like the snow. I mean, not this early. But after Thanksgiving, with the lights on everything and the stores playing holiday music, I really dig the snow. I was going to say that we should grab a blanket, go up to the roof, and snuggle."

"In the snow?" he asked incredulously.

"Not in the snow. You have that little roof thing." I pointed up. "Come on, if it's too cold and you don't like it, we can always come back inside."

He was going to like it, though. Because I was going to make it worth his while.

"Coming inside is exactly what I wanted to do today," he said with raised eyebrows.

Even though we had regular sex—and some irregular sex, like when he'd had me bent over the kitchen counter earlier in the week—I still blushed at all of his dirty little insinuations. "Shut up."

"Fine," Ian said with heavy finality. "I'll go upstairs and freeze my bollocks off, all in the name of pleasing you." He even sighed for dramatic effect.

I rolled my eyes. "I promise I'll warm them back up for you."

We wrestled the fluffy, down-filled duvet from his bed into the elevator then rode up to the roof. The second the glass doors opened, I realized I was an idiot. It was way too freaking cold, and the weather, which had looked charming through the window, now had sinister intentions toward us. The snow wasn't drifting softly down like in a Christmas movie, but blustering sideways and scattering flakes all over the lovely covered seating area.

The furniture wore snuggly waterproof coats of its own. Ian leaned down to unzip the cover over the chaise longue. "This is insane."

I totally agreed. So, when the cushions of the chaise were clear, I belly flopped onto them, mummified in the duvet.

"Could I get in there?" Ian asked, pulling on a corner of the blanket.

I reluctantly gave up my sarcophagus of warmth to let him in. "It's way colder than I expected."

He leaned against the chaise's slanted back and helped me settle in, my legs between his, my head low on his chest. "I do think I mentioned the cold once or twice," he reminded me, playing with my hair.

I could lie on Ian like this for hours, or at least until his legs fell asleep and then he limped around dramatically to get the feeling back into them. Ian and I fit together, and the addition of his body made any couch or chair or bed ten times more comfortable than the factory standard.

"It'll get warm here soon," I said, pulling the duvet tighter around my shoulders.

"For you." He waved his arms up and down to

demonstrate how not-covered they were by the blanket. "I'm basically just wearing fluffy down trousers."

"Ooh, I didn't think about that." I tapped a fingernail against my front teeth as I considered our problem. I'd been looking forward to cuddling, as well as getting dirty, but he was right; he would freeze to death out here in just his shirt. I would have to speed things along. "You know what? I can just pull the blanket over my head—"

I didn't wait for an answer before wriggling down farther on the chaise and pushing the duvet up to replace the space where my body had been. "There, that's better, isn't it?" I called up to him.

"Not really, no." His reply came through the thick, muffling layer of down.

I opened his fly and slid my hand inside to grip him. "How about now?"

I curled my fingers around his shaft. He was half-erect already, as if he'd been envisioning this exact same outcome. "Well, that *is* a little better, now that you mention it."

There was something almost meditative about lazily gliding his foreskin up and down. I didn't have to think about anything except the measured pace of my hand and the way his chest rose and fell a little faster as I stroked him. I licked my lips and leaned closer, until I felt just the heat of his skin near my lips. I blew a long, soft breath across the tip of him. The vein along the underside of his shaft thrummed harder, which was thoroughly gratifying. I barely parted my lips to brush them against the head. His hips lifted up, and I laughed, my mouth still pressed to his cock.

Before I'd met Ian, there had been no possibility that one day I would be so carefree about sex that sucking dick on a Brooklyn roof wouldn't faze me. Sure, I wasn't entirely *un*fazed, and I was hidden from view by the thickest, warmest blanket in New York, but with Ian, I could act on all sorts of impulses that were once sexually out of my league, and I never once got the impression he would judge me for it.

I pulled his foreskin up to cover the head of his penis and ran my tongue all the way around, then pushed my tongue beneath that flexible skin. I'd read up on blow jobs online, and every website I'd looked at had suggested that particular move. They hadn't misled me; I took him into my mouth and heard him exclaim, "Jesus!"

Getting Ian to take the Lord's name in vain as a curse word wasn't that difficult in general conversation, but hearing him blaspheme during sex was somehow extra hot. Especially after church.

Did that make me a church pervert or something?

Rather than examine those implications, I took him into my mouth, all the way to the back of my throat, and triggered my gag reflex. Not enough to puke all over him—Sophie's vividly worded shower-blow-job-emesis story came disgustingly to mind—but enough that he would hear it. The first time it had happened, it had been an accident, but he'd made the most delighted sound when he'd heard it; I hadn't been able to help myself since. Plus, it made me drool a ridiculous amount, which he'd confessed to really enjoying, so I kept doing it.

Another great tip I'd gotten from the websites I'd visited was to go slowly and change it up, so you wouldn't hurt your neck. I took this good advice to heart, letting my hand do some of the work as I licked and sucked. I pressed my thighs together; the crotch of my panties was wet. I leaned on one elbow to tug them down halfway then let the natural shifting of positions wiggle me out of them altogether.

It occurred to me I could get Ian off with my mouth; he would make sure I had an orgasm, whether we had intercourse or not. But I really wanted to fuck him. I debated this for a while, until I settled on jumping to a finishing move and letting him decide how to proceed.

I rubbed my lips up and down the underside of his shaft.

The little vertical ridge right beneath the head was super-sensitive, and if I kept concentrating on that, he would have to stop me soon. He fumbled a hand beneath the blanket to touch the top of my head. "Why don't you come back up here before I embarrass myself?"

"Why should you be embarrassed?" I asked, but I toed my panties from my ankle and came up for air. The cold was surprisingly tolerable; giving head under a blanket for an extended period of time got you all sweaty. "You always say that. Trust me, I would be so pleased to make you come too soon."

I knew I'd gotten close before. I would break him, eventually.

"You'd be pleased? How would I fuck you?" He leaned up and steadied me with his hands on my ribs, just beneath my breasts, so I could straddle his lap. Then he got his shocked, blinky face on. It was one of my top five favorite Ian facial expressions. "You had panties on when we left the house, didn't you?"

What kind of pervert did he think I was? My jaw had just gotten too much of a workout to hang open the way it did. "Of course I did!"

I rummaged behind me for physical evidence and presented him with my satiny pink underwear. They went from my hand straight to his nose.

"Oh my god, that's so gross!" It didn't really bother me to see him sniff my panties; after all, he spent a lot of our time together with his face in my pussy. But I couldn't help my reaction. I may not have been totally clueless about sex before, but knowing about something and experiencing it have much different levels of shock value. The way he savored the scent of me jarred me into realizing how sexy he found me, and I was still kind of timid when it came to my own perception of myself as a sexual person.

"Not at all. You're one of my favorite smells." The low, serious tone of his voice made it clear that he was not joking, and I got a tingly thrill. I ground myself against the length of his erection. It would have been so easy to just shift and slide onto it.

His breath hitched. "We have to go back inside for that. I didn't come prepared."

*Well, we'd better go inside then,* I thought, and I was very proud of myself for how rational and even-headed it was.

I wasn't going to *do* that, if I could get Ian to go along with me, but I was impressed that I had enough non-horny brain cells to come up with a responsible solution.

"Oh, just this once? Just for a little bit?" I begged. It wasn't fair, I knew, to keep rubbing my pussy all over his cock as I asked, but my hips moved of their own volition. "Just to know what it feels like."

He made the pained face of a person who saw their future self doing something they should know better than to do. "Just as long as you're aware that this could have potentially unintended consequences up to and including—"

"I had health class, Ian." I rolled my eyes at him. We'd already done a risk analysis conversation about our sexual pasts. As for the likelihood of getting pregnant, the chances of that happening this one single time were like, ridiculous odds. Become-a-millionaire odds. Besides, "You could always just pull out."

"Well, here's hoping," he said, all the resolve he might have been able to muster leeching out of his voice.

He lifted me up before I could even move, and I reached between us to position our parts. It took a little wriggle to get him inside, and I sat back, sliding myself onto him fully. We both groaned.

Without the condom between us, I felt more of him. More heat, more texture, and definitely more stimulation as the ridges and veins rolled through me as I moved on him. I squeezed my eyes shut at the unbelievable difference. "*Fuck* condoms."

"Hey, they have their place. I've had some very good

times that wouldn't have been possible without them."

I was glad that he had, because he was passing a lot of that experience onto me. And obviously, if he hadn't been responsible in the past, I wouldn't want to have unprotected sex with him now. But I wasn't an idiot; I liked this enough that I was going to call my gyno first thing in the morning and look into hormonal birth control. I laughed at how easily I'd come to that decision, when it had been at the back of my mind for the past month. "Shut up and let me feel this."

Everything I did got a reaction out of him, whether he realized it or not. When I clenched around him, he stopped breathing. When I rocked fast on him, he dug his fingers into my thighs. When I went too slowly, he lifted up impatiently beneath me, as if he were threatening to take matters into his own hands, or cock, as it were. And I guess I went a little too slowly for him, because he grabbed the back of my neck and pulled me down. The position restricted my movement and made good on that implied threat, that he would drive us both if I wouldn't keep my hands on the wheel. He thrust into me fast as he held me captive in a dizzying kiss.

My skirt bunched up between us and scratched my belly. The top felt suddenly too tight, and the underwire in my bra chafed my perspiring skin. "Get my zipper."

"You'll freeze to death." He bit my earlobe playfully.

Shit, that was right. We were on a roof. And here I wanted to take my clothes off, when it was snowing all around us.

Snow would be really good for cooling off. I gasped, "I don't care. I'm burning up."

His hand fumbled at my back, then I heard the whiz of the zipper, and the dress became mercifully looser. I pulled it over my head and tossed it aside. A gust of wind caught it. Oh god, I hoped it wouldn't blow away! Ian and I both stared at it until it came a stop on the floor, and I heaved an inward sigh of relief as I unfastened my front-closure bra. Ian watched me reveal myself as though I were about to unveil a finely restored painting or present him with a culinary masterpiece. Then he pulled the duvet around me and started to thrust again, and I pushed down on him at the same tempo.

It felt better than before. It felt…well, extremely naughty, to be on the roof of a building, outside, in a city of millions of people, riding my fully clothed boyfriend while I was completely naked. It was even naughtier that I didn't care and that I was actually getting off on the idea. In fact, I was going to make myself come, and I didn't care a bit if anyone saw.

I reached between us and slid my middle finger over my clit. His cock put pressure exactly where I needed it. "That!" I shouted, hoping he took it as a compliment when I slapped my other palm against his chest. "Don't stop doing that!"

I was going to come. Right there, on the rooftop, in an icy wind that hopefully would muffle the sound of my cries, I was going to come. I leaned back, my muscles stretching and tightening as his cock pressed mercilessly against my g-spot. Ian edged me along with shallow thrusts and sharp moans of his own. I was close. My pussy fluttered around him, ready to clench and squeeze and—

With an agonized groan, he pulled out of me, still thrusting his cock between us. The full, slick length of him sawed over my clit for the space of a blink before the building pleasure exploded, sending shockwaves from the epicenter of my clit all the way to the tips of my fingers and toes. He grabbed my hips and kept me moving, extending the pleasure when I would have stopped. He jerked his shirt up, threw his head back, and groaned as he shot pearly ropes of semen over his stomach.

I couldn't hold myself up, anymore, and though I knew it was going to be a big, sticky mess, I flopped onto his chest anyway. "I know." I laughed. "I thought about it, but I'm too tired to stay up."

He managed to pull his shirt and undershirt over his head

without jostling me too much. If we stayed there much longer, I would fall asleep. I was never so comfortable as I was in his arms. I snuggled my face into his neck. "I can't believe we just did that on the roof."

"We're on the roof?"

I gave him a playful push. "By the way, that feels really good. Can we do that all the time?"

"If you don't mind using an alternate method of birth control."

Well, obviously. I wanted to have Ian's babies. I just wanted to have them *later*. "Okay, I'll look into it. And as soon as I have something, we're doing it this way every time."

"Can we change the venue to somewhere warmer next time?" he asked, and I remembered his earlier comment. He held his breath as I reached between our bodies to cup his balls.

"See? They didn't freeze off."

He slapped my butt, and I squealed. The temperature was swiftly becoming an issue, so we cleaned up with his shirt, grabbed my dress and panties, and hurried into the elevator. He snagged me into a cocoon of his body and the duvet, and I was powerless to do anything about it with my clothes folded over my arms.

"Do we still have any of that ice cream from the other night?" I asked.

"I think so."

I smiled at him and hit the button for the lowest level.

It was so nice to be warm, or at least, warming up. Ice cream was a silly idea, considering the fact that we'd just been fucking in the Arctic Circle, but I needed something sweet.

"Why is everything salted caramel all of a sudden?" Ian grumbled as he pulled the container from the freezer. "I just got used to everything being blueberry pomegranate acai."

"Brace yourself, peppermint is coming," I warned him

grimly. I'd been watching *Game of Thrones* in the hopes that I would understand his fascination with it. "Every October, like clockwork, pumpkin comes in. The day after Thanksgiving, everything is mint. Which is just about the most disgusting flavor I can think of."

"I rather like mint myself." He peeled back the lid of the carton.

"Oh, well, true love totally called off," I teased as I went for the spoons. I rounded the end of the counter so I could face him from the other side.

"Don't you want to go sit down?" he asked, nodding toward the dining area.

I shook my head. He hadn't come in me, but there was definitely a moisture situation going on. "Uh, no. I really don't feel like leaving a slime spot on your chairs."

"It's not slime," he said, almost sounding offended. "It's proof that you just had an incredible time, and I'd like to think I have a little something to do with that."

"Oh, you had a lot to do with that." I snatched the carton from him and took the first bite of ice cream. I moaned almost as loudly as I had when we were up on the roof. "You were so sexy today."

"I thought I looked like an undertaker," he said, trying to block my spoon as I went for a second bite.

"It wasn't that. It was seeing you at church, how much you really believe in all of it. That was sexy."

"Why is that sexy?"

"I don't know." I really didn't. I knew a lot of things. But I couldn't explain romantic attraction, even if I tried. I took another spoonful of ice cream. "Having faith in something makes you vulnerable. Vulnerability in a man is hot."

"Why does believing in something make a person vulnerable?" he asked with a slight frown.

"Because if you believe in something, you can be let down." Wow, I was a real ray of sunshine. "Like, okay, look at me and Brad. I thought we were really going to be together forever. I *believed* that would happen. And when it ended, I was destroyed. I made myself vulnerable to that hurt through my faith that everything would turn out all right."

Ugh, did Brad have to come up all the time? Still?

"But you just told me, not a full two hours ago, that you believe we'll turn out all right," he reminded me.

And he had a point. "Yeah, but we've had signs. The fortune cookies. They never lie." I paused, my brows and lips scrunching at the same time. "I supposed believing in superstitions is a form of faith. Maybe I really am setting myself up for disappointment down the road."

"Never, not with me," he reassured me. Like making that promise was so simple, he didn't even have to think about it. He scooped up a spoonful of ice cream, swallowed it, and said, "All humans are vulnerable, emotionally. We pretend we have control over it, but we truly don't."

It was so simple and weirdly defeatist, but in the most positive way possible. I laughed. "Well, let me believe, okay?"

Because looking into his eyes, I couldn't summon up a single doubt.

* * * *

"Ian Pratchett. Leave a message."

I groaned at Ian's voicemail message. When the tone sounded, I forced my voice to be chipper. "Hey there. I guess we're fated to keep missing each other. I'm going to bed early tonight. Just give me a call tomorrow. Love you."

"Missed connections day?" Rosa asked, slipping on her boots. She had a work party tonight. Everyone had work stuff going on, it seemed.

I sighed. "Yup. How pathetic am I? Be brutally honest?"

"Not pathetic," Rosa said, with a sympathetic smile and not a trace of sarcasm in her tone. "You're totally in love with him."

"I am," I agreed. "I just wish I could get him on the phone."

"You want me to bring you back anything?" She asked as she pulled on her coat.

I shook my head. "Nah, I won't be up. I think I'm going to call it an early night."

Work had been brutal lately as we rushed to finish up the New Year special edition. I hadn't even gotten home until seven. It was nine now, and I was already yawning.

After Rosa left, I tucked into bed and turned on the television. I didn't know why, but I'd had this weird, lonely feeling all day long. Hearing some voices would help, I hoped. I was yawning through a rerun of *Archer* when my phone rang. Even though it wasn't Ian's ringtone, I scrambled for it, thinking he could have been calling from work.

I saw the name on the screen and groaned. It was Amanda.

"Hello, Amanda," I said, trying to sound polite, but I was already pretty annoyed at her. This had been a pattern when she and Rosa had been dating before; if Amanda couldn't get an answer from Rosa, she started calling me, demanding to know where she was. She had this totally weird jealousy vibe about me, even though I'd assured her time and again that I wasn't into women, and even if I were, I wouldn't make a play for someone else's girlfriend.

"Hey, sweetie," she said, and I rolled my eyes. She was only that syrupy and nice if she wanted something. "How are you?"

"Really tired. About to go to bed. So, can I call you back another—"

"Oh, poo. Rosa said you might be able to do me a favor," she said, slightly wheedling.

There was a reason Rosa couldn't say no to Amanda. She had the perfect wheedle in her voice when she needed it.

"Okay, it really depends on the favor," I warned her.

"I forgot my carpal tunnel brace at your apartment. I put it on the floor next to the coffee table—"

I got out of bed and shuffled into the living room. There was the brace.

"—when we were eating, and now I'm at work, and I really, desperately need it. Do you think you could bring it to me?" she begged.

Amanda worked at a sushi place in midtown. "I don't know. That's kind of far away. What's in it for me?"

"A dragon roll?"

I considered.

"Come on, please, please, please. You're my favorite one of Rosa's friends," she added to butter me up.

Buttering was unnecessary; my mouth was already watering for a taste of eel.

"I'm the only one of Rosa's friends who'll talk to you," I reminded her. "Throw in a cup of miso, and I'm there."

"Deal. Thank you so much. You're a life saver."

I got dressed in the nearest available dirty clothes, grabbed the brace, and headed out. I didn't even know why I was helping her out. Amanda had cheated on Rosa, and after what had happened with Brad, I was starting to really rethink my stance on whether or not cheaters could be good people. But Rosa trusted her enough to start things up again romantically. It wasn't my business.

What *was* my business was that I missed Ian like crazy. Which was so stupid, because we spent so much time together. It wasn't like not seeing him or hearing from him for a day should be that unbearable. I was starting to get on my own nerves. I had to tone it down in a big way.

I reached the restaurant and asked for Amanda at the hostess station. In just a few minutes, I saw her bright red hair bopping across the floor. She kind of commanded all of the attention in a room.

"Thank you to Jupiter and back!" she gasped as soon as she was within hearing distance.

I held up the brace, and when she reached for it, I snatched it back. "Ah-ah. I believe we have a hostage trade situation going on here?"

She rolled her eyes. "Come on back."

I followed her through the crowded restaurant, to the bar, where she typed in an order for the dragon roll and miso soup. I handed her the brace, and she slipped it on.

"So, how's your night going?" I asked.

"Running off my feet. Had a lovely white woman suggest I try acupuncture." She rolled her eyes "I'm Vietnamese, not Chinese. And if I'm going to stick a needle anywhere in me to fix this, it better be attached to a syringe of morphine."

She buzzed off to grab another table, and I waited, drumming my fingers on the bar top. I took out my phone and checked to see if Ian had called. Nothing.

Then I heard him laugh. Okay, I had to be losing my mind, now, if I was hearing things.

I heard it again. And I spotted him across the restaurant.

With a gorgeous blond woman. And they were laughing.

My heart was going to puke.

They both stood, still chatting. Any second, they were going to start walking my way. The bar stool nearly toppled in the wake of my hasty exit. There was no way I was going to be humiliated in front of The Other Woman. I'd already done that once this year.

Oh god, what if *I* was the other woman? My tears burned my eyes as I stepped out into the blustery November night. Maybe that was why his sister didn't want to meet me, because I was his mistress. Maybe he wasn't divorced. He could have been feeding me a line this whole time.

Maybe I could ignore all this. I could go home, cry, and eat myself sick.

*Dammit!* Eating myself sick would be a lot easier to do with some actual food. I stood on the sidewalk, torn between wanting to run away before he saw me and wanting something to eat after the inevitable confrontation.

Sushi won out over heartache, especially since postponing the confrontation we were going to have would only make it worse. Might as well get it over with, like ripping off a Band-Aid. Then I could deal with the shock of the fact that, once again, a man who I'd thought was the love of my life was cheating on me.

*It's you*, a nasty little voice in my head sneered. It sounded a lot like my mother. *It had nothing to do with being a virgin. It was just you. You're not enough.*

I lifted my chin and strode confidently through the restaurant doors.

Ian was nearly to the door with his...whatever she was to him. God, she was even more perfect-looking up close. Her highlights were flawless. Her skin was the kind you had to buy from a dermatologist who had lasers and grinding tools. I was pretty sure her nails were her actual nails and not gels.

I was in a crumpled T-shirt, with unwashed hair.

And Ian didn't say, "Hi, Penny," or look happy to see me. Instead, the first words out of his mouth when he saw me were, "What are you doing here?"

*What are you doing here?* I silently screamed back at him. I forced myself to smile, as if nothing was amiss. "I dropped off a wrist brace. Rosa's girlfriend works here, and she left at the apartment. In return, I got dinner."

"Oh, the carpal tunnel waitress," the woman said with a laugh. "What a coincidence. Penny, was it? I'm Carrie Glynn."

Carrie... The name rang a bell. An alarm bell. "Glynn? As in Glynn resorts?" I was so stunned I actually shook her hand. Carrie Glynn was a hotelier with an empire that spanned continents. She was routinely listed among the worlds' richest women. I made thirty thousand dollars a year. There was no way I could outclass her.

"Guilty," she said with a smile, and her perfect teeth almost blinded me.

"This is my girlfriend, Penny," Ian said quickly, "whom I

was telling you about. Penny, Carrie is an old friend I worked with in the 80's."

"Ah." I nodded. I didn't say anything else, because I was perilously close to screaming, "I thought you were going out to do business, not old friends." And I didn't want to lose my cool in front of the woman I was increasingly suspicious of.

If the pause in our conversation was awkward, I didn't care one bit, though.

"Well," Carrie said. "I was just leaving. Ian, it was wonderful to see you again. Please, do give consideration to my offer. The sooner I have an answer, the better."

*What the fuck did you offer my boyfriend?* I seethed as he shook her hand. Then she was out the door, and he turned to me.

I took a deep breath and started counting to ten. And when I hit ten, I was absolutely going to let him have it.

# CHAPTER SIXTEEN

Ian stared at me as the storm front rolled in between us. Before he could ask, I ground out, "I'm counting to ten."

"Pardon?"

"I'm counting to ten," I explained, patient with fury, "before I run out of here. So, your 'old friend' doesn't see."

"Or, you could come home with me. I can give you a ride home, and you can tell me why you're so angry." The tone, the awful, patronizing tone... *Ugh!* I wasn't the one who'd just been caught lying. I wasn't the one who'd been on a date with another woman.

"You want me to tell you why I'm angry?" I titled my head, my lips pursing. "What if I canceled my plans with you for a 'work dinner', and it turned out to be with some hot billionaire I happened to be acquainted with?"

"I think Sophie would rip your hair out at the roots," he said.

Okay, he had me there. But why the fuck was Ian joking at a time like this?

"But there was no romancing going on tonight," he continued, still with that tone that suggested I was being needlessly worried.

That only made me more suspicious. "Oh please. You're an architect, Ian. You do office buildings. What, are you going to build Glynn world headquarters or something?"

I didn't need to make that sound as snarky as I had. But my heart felt mean, and at the very same time, it felt broken *and* reluctant to make Ian feel bad. It was an awful combination.

I saw his calm slipping a little at the implied insult. "No, I was planning on designing a hotel. Like I told you before. Can we either discuss this in my car, or at another time? Because I don't feel like having our first argument in the lobby of a restaurant."

"Well, I didn't feel like running into my boyfriend with a hotter, more age appropriate billionaire in the lobby of a restaurant, so maybe we don't all get what we want," I snapped and turned for the door.

"Aren't you supposed to drop off a brace?" he asked.

"I already did!" But he probably thought that was a lie. He'd seen me walk in and right back out. I bet he thought I'd stalked him to the restaurant or something.

*You're so pathetic*, I sniped at myself as I walked, head down, to Ian's car. He didn't say anything, but tension radiated from him. He was really mad. Why did he get to be mad, when he was the one who'd done something awful?

I shouldn't have agreed to the ride home. It would just give him time to lie to me. The smart thing would have been for me to walk away, and then just...

*Then just what? Ride it out until he dumped you?* It would have hurt worse, then, because I would live in constant fear of it. It was better to bring it up, now, and get this all over with, even though the thought of it made my chest hurt.

We got into the car, and he turned on the engine but didn't pull away from the curb.

"Are we going?" I asked.

"I don't want to fight and drive. Do I get a chance to explain here, or have you just decided that I'm stepping out on you?" he asked, and I felt a stab of shame.

"You don't have to talk to me like I'm a child, just because I'm angry," I managed through gritted teeth. "How do you think it looks, you calling me and leaving a voicemail saying we can't get together tonight because of work—which, by the way, I totally understand—and then, you're out with a woman, an 'old friend' who doesn't even work in your field, let alone at your firm?"

"I should have been more specific. It wasn't business within the firm. Carrie is looking for a team to design her next resort. And because she knows me—"

"How does she know you?" I demanded. Because I couldn't imagine a scenario in which my boyfriend would know a hotelier who was frequently called the world's richest MILF by the tabloids.

"She started in architecture. We worked together thirty years ago, and we've kept in touch on and off. It's nothing sinister, I assure you." He groaned in frustration and dragged a hand down his face. "And I really don't appreciate your condescension."

"When did I condescend?"

"'What, are you going to build Glynn world headquarters or something?'" Even without altering his accent, he repeated my inflection accurately.

I sucked so much sometimes. My anger deflated into exactly what I didn't want to feel, foolish and immature. "I'm sorry. That was really uncalled for. I just... I was intimidated. And shocked. When you said you had a work thing, I was envisioning you and several other people, not you and one stunning blond."

"I would have much rather been with one particular stunning blond this evening, but I had to meet a potential client, instead." He shook his head. "Have I ever done anything to indicate that you shouldn't trust me?"

He had me there. I slouched down, staring at my hands in my lap so I wouldn't have to look at him.

"I know that your last boyfriend did something horrible to you," Ian began, his voice softer. "And it's perfectly natural that you're suspicious. But I promise, there is no other woman on this planet that I want to be with more than you. I wouldn't risk what we have for something as stupid as a one-night stand with Carrie Glynn, or anyone else."

Tears threatened, and though I could hold those back by blinking, I had to sniff to keep watery snot from falling. I looked up, hoping to distract myself by looking out the windshield, but it was fogging fast. "Cheating is never about a one-night stand. It's a symptom of a bigger problem."

"That's a bit trite, isn't it? What have you been reading?"

He was too eager to joke about this, and that sent my distrust levels sky high once more. I glared at him. "I'm not a child, Ian. Don't treat me like one."

"I'm sorry. Now I'm on the one who's condescending," he apologized. "Go on. You said you were intimidated. Why?"

I couldn't keep up my anger. My despondency was too strong. "I just turned twenty-three a few weeks ago, Ian. I'm working at a job I got with a degree I didn't want in the first place, I have practically no money, no idea of what's going to happen in my future… I am the definition of not-having-your-shit-together. And you're so… I mean, you have your own firm, you've accomplished things, you're actually doing what you want to do—"

"No, I'm not," he interrupted. "I'm not doing what I wanted to do. I wanted to be an artist. I wanted to go 'round Paris sleeping under bridges and sketching beautiful, tragic women in cafes. I never wanted to be an architect. It was just something I happened to be good at."

"I forgot about that." How could I have forgotten about that?

"Well, sometimes, I do, as well. And believe me, that's almost worse than knowing that I'll never have that life. Forgetting your dream, that's a hell of a thing." His words hit me like a battering ram of truth. Forgetting your dream *was* a terrible thing. But not allowing yourself to have it in the first place…

"You're worried that I would want to be with Carrie Glynn? Why? Because she has money?" he went on.

"No." *Yes.* "I mean, the money does figure in. But it's more about the overall picture. The reason she has that money is because she's confident and accomplished and successful. Literally everything I'm not." I shrugged. There was no way I could articulate why seeing him with Carrie

Glynn had disturbed me so much. They had just...looked right.

"Exactly. She's everything you're not," he agreed. "Which is why I don't want her. I want you, Penny. Not the opposite of you."

I didn't know how to respond to that.

"You mentioned her age. Is that another thing..."

"Yeah." I nodded in vehement agreement. "Yeah, your age is intimidating, and it's something that I haven't brought up before because... I don't know. I'm afraid that I make you feel bad about being older than me. But you make me feel bad about being younger than you."

"Oh?" He sounded incredulous, which only made me more defensive.

"Yeah. You make these little comments all the time about how old you are in comparison to me. 'My knees used to be able to do that,' or 'humor an old man.' If I complain about something, you just brush it off with, 'imagine how you'll feel in thirty years.' Why would you want to be with me, if I make you so self-conscious and self-critical?" I stopped myself, because my voice became shrill. "It just made sense to me, when I saw you with her. Wouldn't you rather be with someone who doesn't make you feel like Methuselah?"

"I never said I felt like Methuselah, did I?" he asked. Then, he waved it away. "No, I know that's not the point. I— Penny, when I say those things, they're because *I'm* intimidated. You're so beautiful, and you have so much energy and optimism... I say those things because I feel dishonest if I don't remind you that you can do better."

And that was the problem. My boyfriend, for all that his age should have brought him wisdom, was a fucking idiot. "I don't want better. I want you."

He gazed at me expectantly.

*Ah.* Just like I wanted him exactly as he was, he was happy with me the way I was, too.

He laughed softly. "You're not out there looking for

someone better. I'm not, either."

I hadn't trusted him.

I should have trusted him.

I was the worst girlfriend in the world.

Wiping my tears, I insisted, "Just so you know, I didn't follow you here. I really did have to drop off Amanda's arm brace."

"I believe you. She was our waitress," he said evenly.

"I was just coming back in because I forgot the food she was bribing me with—" My brain made an instant connection. "Wait, was Carrie Glynn the woman who told her she should get acupuncture?"

"Yeah, why?"

That was going to make this whole thing a lot more bearable. I knew my jealousy and anger toward Carrie Glynn was unreasonable, but it made me feel better to know that she was embarrassing. I shook my head and smiled. "Nothing."

"Are we okay, now?" His voice was painfully tight and hopeful.

Could I be a bigger asshole? I turned to him. "We're okay. I'm embarrassed that I didn't trust you. But we're okay, as long as you can forgive me."

"I've forgiven people for worse." He leaned over the console to kiss me. The moment our lips met, it felt as though all the awfulness and tension of the fight simply melted away. Everything felt right, if not exactly as right as it would in an hour or two.

"All right," he said when he sat back. "I haven't been home yet, and I have to feed Ambrose. Do you want to come stay the night?"

"Ah. You know…" Oh, I wanted to. I really wanted to. But I'd already kind of crashed his evening plans, and I didn't want him to think I was hanging pathetically on so he couldn't hook up with his side piece later. I want him to believe that I was confident and unthreatened, now that we'd resolved our issue. As hard as it would be to turn him down… "I don't want you to think you have to—"

He put his hand on my arm. "Penny. Come home with me. Neither of us wants to be alone tonight."

"Sure." I had no willpower. Or maybe he was just irresistible.

We stopped by my apartment so I could get my stuff— was it pathetic that I already had kind of a bug-out bag ready to go in these situations?—then went back to his place. That awful cat was waiting for us, like a mom catching her teenager home after curfew. Ian fed it and had a slightly disturbing one-sided conversation with it as he did. Maybe it was a good thing I was spending so many nights over.

It was rare that Ian and I didn't have sex on a night together. I think we were just both too tired to even think about it. And even though make-up sex was supposed to be awesome, I just wanted make-up cuddling. I needed to touch his skin and get peacefully connected.

"I wish we hadn't fought," I mumbled against his shoulder as I lay snuggled at his side.

"It was inevitable. And it was our first. We should celebrate." Ian yawned. I felt guilty staying over during the week, because he was always so tired.

"Well, I'll pop the champagne." I closed my eyes, resolved to stop talking and get to sleep. Then, it occurred to me that I'd overlooked a pretty big detail in the middle of all our fighting. I sat up, blurting, "Oh my gosh! Ian, I'm such an asshole, I didn't even ask you about the project!"

He startled, his whole body going tense, then reluctantly relaxing again. "It's the Bahamas project I mentioned before. You could stop someone's heart doing that, you know?"

I ignored his dire prophecy. "The one you would have to go away for?" I chewed my lower lip. "Are you going to take it?"

"It looks as though I'll have to. It's…going to be a lot of

money." He winced slightly as he said it, like money was a bad thing. Or that I would think it was.

Had he even *met* me? I'd researched his probable salary before our second date. I'd been raised to worship the god of money as fervently as he'd been raised to worship Jesus.

"So? That's good, right? You'll get a lot of money for your firm?" The sheets slipped down. His eyes fell immediately to my tits. It was like they had some witchcraft power over him. I left them uncovered, just to take advantage of that.

"Yes. And I would take home a pretty nice bonus, as well." He paused, and something in his body language, or maybe it was the tone of his voice, made my stomach pole vault over my heart. "Enough that I would be…comfortable settling down. Putting money back for a child's college fund. Or two."

We *had* discussed our desire to have kids within the next couple of years. But now, that seemed so close. The excitement overwhelmed me. "Two is good."

"Yeah. How much do…" He stopped, frowning and making a sound that seemed like it could be associated with acid reflux. "Do you know how much weddings run these days?"

"Well, I mean, I guess it depends on where you're having it. In the Bahamas or…" I rocked my legs side to side in a nervous bounce. Was he proposing? Maybe not officially, but we were planning our future. It was…incredible.

"I suppose we would have to take that into account at the time." He leaned up, and I moved in for a kiss, smiling against his lips. We interrupted ourselves again and again with our goofy grins. Finally, he gave up, breaking away to say, "I think we should be clear, though, on how long a separation this would be."

I made a "tch" and sat up. "I was really hoping we wouldn't have to talk about that, but you're right. We need to be responsible."

"It's going to be over a year."

My heart plummeted. "Over a year? When would you leave?"

"July. And I'll likely stay there until they break ground in 2017."

I didn't trust my voice to speak, so I didn't.

"I know. I can't bear the thought of it, myself. But as we said before, you could always come visit."

Visit. Not come with him.

By July, we would have been together for almost a year, and he wouldn't want me to come along?

"Yeah." I chalked up the sadness I felt to how tired I was, and the fact that I'd already put myself through an emotional wringer already tonight. I forced a smile and said, "Pretty convenient honeymoon spot."

"It could be," he agreed, but my façade wasn't as good as I'd thought it was. "Ah, what's the matter, Doll?"

*You're going away for over a year, and you don't want to take me.* We'd only been going out for a few months. It was ridiculous to expect him to move me to another country with him. Maybe he couldn't. Although, he'd just said he was going to make a lot of money, and I had some meager savings. If he was fine talking about marriage and children but not fine with the idea of living with me when he *was* fine with being away from me...

"I'm just... really going to miss you." I settled back in beside him, silently willing him to offer to take me along.

He didn't.

Instead, he kissed the top of my head and pulled me close. "I'm going to miss you, too. Believe me, if anything could tempt me away from this job, it would be you."

But I wasn't enough. And I couldn't get that out of my head, even when the alarm sounded in the morning.

* * * *

The grossness of my fight with Ian seemed to evaporate

overnight, though I could tell he still felt terrible about it when he dropped me off at work.

"Oh, shit," I said as we pulled up. Sophie was already walking toward the building.

"I made you late again," Ian said grimly. "Do you want me to come in? Charm her? Beg forgiveness?"

"No, please do not 'charm' my boss. I think you've done enough of that." I rolled my eyes. Maybe I shouldn't say stuff like that, after our fight last night. But it was still weird knowing my boss had fucked my boyfriend.

I gave Ian a kiss that was way, way briefer than I would have liked and jumped out of the car. I managed to sprint to the door just as Sophie reached it, and I opened it for her.

"You're still late," she said with a knowing smile.

"I'm sorry." I'd been saying that a lot lately. "Ian and I got into this huge fight last night, and we—"

"Stayed up all night making up?" she finished for me as we crossed the lobby for the stairs.

"Not exactly. But we did make up." I followed her up the stairs.

"I'll level with you," she said over her shoulder. "I'm late, too. I'll cover for you, if you promise to play along."

"Deal."

We entered the office and nodded to the receptionist, a slender white girl named Bethany, with dark hair and a bad case of resting bitch face. But she was really, really nice. She gave us a big smile and a chipper "Good morning!" when we came in.

"You saw us earlier this morning, remember?" Sophie said with a pointed look.

Bethany nodded in understanding, making a silent "Oh" with her mouth.

When we got into the main office, Deja was leaning over a desk, talking to Matt, one of the graphic designers. Her dark hair was half-shaved, and the angular bob on the other side covered her face. I thought we might sneak past her undetected, but she looked up at Sophie and I and frowned. "Are you both late now? Is this catching?"

"I wish. The card machine was down at Fry's, so Penny had to come rescue me with petty cash." Sophie swung her purse off her shoulder and handed it to me without looking. "I'll pay it back."

"I will never understand how you're a billionaire and you never have cash on you," Deja said, totally buying the fib. Sophie winked at me as she walked past.

The rest of the day went pretty smoothly, considering it started out with a lie. It was around three when my cell rang. It was Ian, which was strange; he tried to avoid taking or making personal calls during the work day. I answered with a "Hello?"

"You're American."

"You noticed," I said, adjusting my phone on my shoulder. They should make cell phones thicker, so holding them like that didn't feel so awkward. "Hi, Ian."

"Hello, Doll," he said with a chuckle. "Do you know who else is American?"

"You are, even though you rarely admit it." I looked over my shoulder to make sure Sophie and Deja were both deep in their discussion of the next issue's layout.

"How dare you. I was going to say, my sister's husband is American. And since I assume you're not going to spend Thanksgiving with your lovely parents—"

I snorted.

"—maybe you'd like to come to Thanksgiving dinner at her house, with me?"

Spend American Thanksgiving with Scottish Catholics? My WASP parents and their Mayflower pride would recoil in horror. "I'd love to. But…"

"But?"

I sighed. "Your sister doesn't want to meet me. That was kind of obvious when she ran away to D.C. to avoid me."

"She didn't run away. And even if she did, this time, she

couldn't. Because I know where she lives, and that woman would never abandon a turkey." He tried for a laugh. "Look, I don't want to pressure you—"

"No, it's fine." I pressed my fingertips to my forehead. "I'm sorry. I don't know why I'm being a bitch about this."

"It because you're nervous You know that it's important to me that the two of you get along. But I swear, Penny, I am not going to kick you out of my life if you're not my sister's favorite person."

I ignored the fact that he hadn't argued with my use of the word "bitch". "Why do you assume it's going to go down that way, instead of the other way around?

He graciously overlooked my snippiness. "Because I know my sister, and I know that of the two of you, you're the one who's going into this wanting to get along."

"And your sister, she's not going to want to get along?" Nothing seemed more appealing to me than spending Thanksgiving with someone who'd decided to hate me before she'd even met me. At least my parents had reasons to dislike me, even if they were unfair.

"She's going to be cautious. I won't mince words about that," Ian replied.

"That sounds kind of mince-y to me." It still sounded like he was prepared to go into battle over me.

"I believe that my sister will like you. And she'll want to like you, as well. But she'll stay guarded. When she sees how much I love you, and how important you are to me, she'll back off." He didn't sound very sure of himself.

"If I don't get along…" My throat went dry, and I had to start over. "If I don't get along with your family, our relationship isn't doomed?"

"Did I get along with your parents?" he countered. "You'll get along just fine. If you don't, we'll live with it. But Annie doesn't decide my personal relationships for me."

This was important to Ian. That much was obvious. And I did want to see what kind of family he came from. I'd only met his nephew, and I didn't know what to make of him. If a swearing, snarky priest was any indication of the kind of people Ian came from, it was almost worth going, just for curiosity's sake.

"Okay," I agreed. "Is there anything I should bring?"

"No, don't. Annie will think you doubted that she could handle all the food, and she'll take it as an insult. I'll get a really nice wine and we can bring that," he said.

Great. His sister was apparently the type of person who took even simple gestures of kindness as slights. That would be fun to navigate.

I decided to look on the bright side. "We?" I giggled at the word, because just saying it filled me with sparkly excitement. "I like that sound of showing up places as a couple and only needing to bring one dish to pass."

"That's one of the benefits of serious, long-term relationships. That and health insurance."

"Do you need my health insurance?" He probably had that amazing no-copay kind that successful adults seemed to have.

"It's probably better than mine," he grumbled. "Well, we can compare our plans later. But you'll go with me on Thursday?"

"Yes," I said, and my heart squeezed. "I'll go anywhere, as long as it's with you."

Anywhere. Like a small island country, for example.

"Noted. Do you want to stay at my place on Wednesday night?"

*Noted? What's that supposed to mean?* I was torn between hope that it meant he would ask me to move with him and despair that he might be just dismissing me, hoping I would ignore it.

"No," I declined his invitation. "It's the biggest bar night of the year. I'm going out with a couple of friends. But I can meet you at your place on Thursday."

One night away from Ian wouldn't kill me, even if our

time together was precious, with him moving away. I needed to go out with my girls, and Kelly Sullivan knew the owner of a great place in the village.

"Fair enough. I'll find out what time we should be there, and I'll let you know tonight."

We said "I love you" and hung up. I cast another guilty glance at Sophie's office and opened up my pictures on my phone. I found a selfie Ian and I had taken in a movie theatre while we'd been waiting for the previews to start. God, he was so handsome. Even the lines by his eyes when he smiled and the silver in his hair. I thought about not seeing that face for eighteen months. Not curling up beside him on the couch or smelling him on my pillow after he left in the morning.

A lot could happen in eighteen months. He could meet someone else, someone prettier and more interesting. Someone his own age, who didn't make him feel old whenever she talked about her interests and her upbringing. Someone who wouldn't sit at home and pine for him, because she was more independent than I was.

That fear was the worst one. What if I did wait for Ian, and the waiting made me look needy or clingy or desperate? How long would it take for "I miss you" to sound like an all-inclusive guilt trip?

And what if, when he came back, things weren't the same? If in the intervening time, we both changed too much, and we didn't fit together like we did before?

He had to have his reasons for not wanting me to come with him. Maybe he did want me to come with him, but he thought I couldn't leave my life behind. And maybe he just didn't want me to come with him, because he didn't feel the same way about me that I felt about him.

I couldn't ask him. I didn't want to hear the wrong answer.

## CHAPTER SEVENTEEN

In hindsight, I should have stayed at Ian's apartment. The city was packed with people out for the parade. Getting a taxi was impossible, and the subway was packed. I was twenty minutes late and super apologetic as I rang the buzzer.

"I'm here!" I shouted through the intercom. "I'm sorry!"

"Meet me inside," Ian replied, and I couldn't tell if he was angry or not. I went through the doors and waited in the building lobby. Ian was downstairs within minutes, and when he saw me, he smiled hugely. So he couldn't have been that angry with me.

"You look beautiful!" he said, gesturing at my dress.

"Thanks." I'd had no idea how to dress to meet his sister. After what he'd said about not bringing any food in case I insulted her, I'd worried that dressing too informally would seem like I didn't care about impressing her, and that dressing too formally would seem like I was trying too hard. I'd settled on a brown plaid dress cut in a retro style, with a wide yellow sash around the waist. It was something I would wear to work, occasionally, though I hated the idea of going to a holiday "business casual".

Ian looked pretty damn great, himself. He'd ditched his funeral director Sunday clothes for a hunter green sweater and a pair of dark gray corduroy slacks. But then, I always thought he looked great, even in his undertaker gear.

"I'm so sorry I'm late," I started, and he shook his head.

"It's no big deal. Annie knows what a mess the city is on parade day. She'll just be thrilled that you weren't my overnight guest."

My already queasy stomach went queasier. "She has a problem with you having sex?"

"Only extramarital," he said, and alarm bells went off

like crazy in my head. Why had he chosen that word? And why would he make that joke when we'd recently had a big fight about me suspecting him of cheating?

"Okay, so, what level of physical contact am I allowed to have with you?" I asked, brushing my bad feelings aside as we walked to the car. "I mean, obviously I won't maul you in front of your family, but if your sister is so weird about you and sex, is she going to expect me to leave room for Jesus if I sit next to you?"

"Leaving room for Jesus only applies to dancing," he said, opening the car door for me.

I rolled my eyes and waited for him to walk around the car and slide into the driver's seat. While he buckled his seatbelt, I tried again. "You know, I want to be on my best behavior here and make a good impression."

"Just be yourself. You're not on trial," he said, and I knew it was supposed to be reassuring, but somehow it only made me more nervous.

Annie lived about twenty minutes away, in a blue-collar neighborhood with teensy, tidy houses and cracked sidewalks. Ian parked in front of one of the long, narrow homes, separated from its neighbors by such slender strips of grass they might as well have been connected.

"Ready?" Ian asked, and he reached over to squeeze my hand.

I felt like I was going to the dentist to have a tooth pulled.

I smoothed my skirt and touched my tousled bob as we walked to the door. I hoped I'd done a good enough job with the concealer that the dark circles under my eyes didn't give away the fact that I was pretty hung over from my pre-Thanksgiving partying the night before.

Ian didn't knock, he just pushed the door opened and called, "We're here!"

His nephew, Danny, was lounging on a sofa directly to the left of the door. The curtains over the wide front window were open, letting in the gray November light and causing a glare on the flat screen television positioned in front of a clearly out-of-commission fireplace. Danny sat up to greet us; it looked odd to see a priest in his black pants, short-sleeved black shirt, and Roman collar just laying around.

"Uncle Ian. Penny. Good to see you again." He cleared his throat, as though he were only just remembering the last time we'd seen each other.

"Nice to see you, too." I didn't know what I should do, so I hugged him. He seemed taken aback. Were you supposed to hug priests?

"Sorry," I said, stepping back. "I didn't get a lot of affection as a child. I don't know how to do family dinners."

"Nah, you're fine," Ian said, steering me toward the dining room. He'd carried the promised bottle of wine with him as we navigated around the La-Z-Boy near the archway that separated the two living spaces. The dining table was far too big for a family of three, so I assumed Annie hosted many of the holiday functions. A white lace tablecloth covered the top, and a centerpiece of fake autumn leaves and a hurricane shade over a battery operated pillar candle stood proudly in the center. On the walls, framed pictures showed people that just had to be related to Ian; they all shared the same black hair and green eyes. I spotted Ian in one photo. He was younger, his hair darker, without any gray. He stood with two other adults, one of whom bore a ridiculously striking resemblance to him, and a whole gaggle of kids.

I didn't have a chance to ask about it, because Ian took my hand and kept walking, marching us straight through the swinging door at the back of the room and into the tiny kitchen, which was currently occupied by a tiny, dark-haired woman and a huge guy whose buzz-cut and ruddy face made him resemble a gym teacher in a movie. A trickle of sweat ran down the side of his face as he pulled a pie from the oven.

"We're here," Ian said again, and the dark-haired woman wiped her hands on a kitchen towel.

She came toward us with a warm smile and hugged Ian hard. "I'd almost forgotten what you looked like."

"I thought you'd wait at least until after the blessing to start guilting me." When she released him, he put a hand at the small of my back to push me gently forward. "This is Penny."

"Ah, the infamous Penny," the gym teacher guy said with a bright smile. "We've heard a lot about you."

"This is my sister, Annie, and her husband, Bill," Ian said.

All the warmth faded from Annie's expression, though she still smiled. "How nice of you to come."

"How nice of you to have me," I said, suddenly wanting with every fiber of my being to not just make a good first impression but to make her like me. Her approval seemed to be of the utmost importance. "This will be a great chance to get to know you all."

"Well, not all of us," Annie corrected me, still with that insincere smile. "Don't forget, there are many of us across the pond. I hope you have a passport."

"Is there anything we can help with?" Ian inserted himself into the conversation smoothly.

"No, no, I've got it all under control. Why don't you go and visit with Danny and keep out of the way," Annie said, shooing us toward the door.

And that was it. First impression made, and I got the feeling I'd been found wanting.

As we passed through the dining room, I stopped Ian by the picture I'd noticed. "Are these more of your siblings? The ones I need a passport to meet?"

"Yeah, that's David," he said, pointing to the clone standing beside him in the photo. "And his wife, Brandy. She's from California. And those are their children—" Ian listed off the names of all seven children, and I didn't catch a single one. They all looked exactly the same, which didn't help.

"Big families," I said, a little stab of fear lancing through my heart. Ian had said only three or four, right?

"Well, you know. Catholic." He shrugged.

*What the...* I really hoped he didn't expect me to push out that many kids.

"Don't blame the Church," Danny said, coming up to stand beside us. "Nobody forced them to have that many."

The kitchen door swung open, and Bill emerged with a gleaming silver platter bearing a turkey that could have come out of a Norman Rockwell painting. It was clear from the spotless state of the house and the presentation of the bird that Annie took pride in her housekeeping. When she followed behind Bill with a bowl heaped with more mashed potatoes than five people could reasonably eat, I said, "Annie, the turkey looks amazing."

"Well, it didn't come out as brown as I would have liked," she said, exasperated.

Ian put a hand on my shoulder and gave a little squeeze. "Take the compliment, Annie."

As Annie and Bill turned back to the kitchen, I tried again. "Can I help bring anything to the table?"

"No, the kitchen is far too small for three people, you'd just be in the way," she replied, and in nearly the next breath, she ordered, "Danny, come help with this."

When they disappeared again, I turned to Ian and mouthed, "What the fuck?"

He put his arms around me and kissed my forehead. "Just let it go, for now. She'll thaw."

"None of that monkey business in my house," Bill joked said he came back with a plate of cranberry sauce. It was the kind from a can, cut into neat slices.

I liked Bill.

Annie came in with onions au gratin. By the time they'd brought out the bread, a green bean casserole, and several other dishes of the oh-god-I'll-have-to-run-off-all-those-carbs variety, I began to doubt that it would be just the five of us.

"Do you have other kids coming?" I asked Annie. There had to be at least four more people on the way, to justify this much dinner.

"No, Danny is our only child," she said tersely.

Ian coughed into his hand. "Everything looks great, Annie. You've really outdone yourself."

"Well, apparently, I've made too much," she said, then turned and stormed into the kitchen.

Ian cast an apologetic look to me. "I'll be right back."

I watched him go after Annie, just passing Danny, who emerged with a handful of serving spoons. He took one look at me and said, "Ah, just ignore her. She's set against liking anyone, after Gena."

"She really liked her, huh?" I asked, my throat sticking closed.

"Nah." Danny shook his head.

*Great.*

Bill came out and took the seat at the head of the table. He smiled at me and said, "I'm glad you could make it. Otherwise, we'd be eating these leftovers forever."

"I don't think Penny is going to be able to take care of all of this herself." Danny winked at me as he took a seat at the other end. He motioned to the two chairs on the side of the dining room with the window. "You and Uncle Ian can sit there."

I gave him a grateful look and sat. With every excruciating second, it became more and more clear what Annie and Ian were doing in the other room.

Danny leaned over. "If there's no shouting, that's a good sign."

"So, Penny. You work at a magazine?" Bill asked.

"I do," I said, eager to change the subject from Annie's dislike of me. "It's called *Mode*. It's a fashion magazine."

"So, you're interested in clothes, that kind of thing?"

"Um…not really?" My sentence went up at the end, a

question or an apology, I wasn't sure. "I'm an assistant. It's just kind of a job."

Something in the kitchen slammed.

"Excuse me," Bill said with forced cheerfulness as he stood and quickly exited.

I looked at Danny, and he puffed his cheeks out as he exhaled.

"So," he began. "I know you're not Catholic. Did you grow up in a church?"

I shook my head. "Not really. I don't have anything against your religion or Jesus or anything."

"I'm not here to judge you," he said with a laugh. "I'm just asking because according to my uncle, you two are pretty serious."

"Oh. Um." My face burned. Was I supposed to be talking about this with a priest?

Danny rolled his eyes, reached into his shirt, and pulled out his collar, slapping it on the table. "Better?"

I blinked at him.

"Uncle Ian told me you've been talking about marriage and family. And I have to know… Did he ask you about the Church?"

"Like…" I leaned in and lowered my voice. "Like convert?"

"If that's something you'd want, down the line. My main concern is that he's honest with you about how your children are raised—"

"Danny! Get away from my girlfriend!" Ian barked.

Danny sat up and grabbed his collar, sliding it back in the neck of his shirt.

Annie came back in and gave me a tight smile.

Bill followed behind and pulled his chair out as Annie sat across the corner from him. "Danny, you wanna bless this?" he asked.

"Sure, Dad." Danny pressed his fingertips to his forehead. "In the name of the father, and the son, and the holy spirit—"

I *felt* Annie's eyes on me as they all crossed themselves and I sat there like an idiot, not knowing what to do. Danny said a prayer about how lucky we were to have things to be thankful for. Or something like that. I wasn't listening so much as hoping there wouldn't be some response required, a response I wouldn't be able to supply.

"Thank you, Danny," Ian said, after they'd all crossed themselves again. He shook out his linen napkin and laid it over his lap.

"All right. Now that that's out of the way," Bill said, standing and lifting a battery-operated carving knife, "let's eat."

While Bill grappled with the turkey, Ian, Annie, and Danny passed dishes in a complex and dangerous ballet. A hot bowl handed off on one side of me, while the plate of wobbly cranberry sauce went by on the other. The only reason any food made it onto my plate was because Ian asked, "Potatoes?" or "Bread?" as things came our way, and I scrambled to grab spoonfuls.

Somehow, we all ended up with turkey and the trimmings, and wine in our glasses.

"So, Penny," Annie began, cutting into her turkey. "How long have you and Ian been together?"

"Since the end of August," I answered, counting backward in my mind. "So, three months, now?"

"Three whole months." Annie's voice slid up at the end of her sentence, hinting at a sarcastic, "Isn't that nice?" that didn't follow. "My brother tells me the two of you are quite serious. Talking about marriage already."

I gave him a sideways smile. "Have we?"

"Sure, earlier this week," he said, with a wink that made Annie's face turn stony.

"Is it official, then? Have you set a date?" Danny asked from his end of the table. "You need six months for counseling, at the very least."

"She has to come over, first," Bill said with a nod to his son.

"Come over?" The walls of the conversation were closing in around me.

"Convert," Annie supplied. "But they can't get married in the church, anyway, because of the divorce."

"No one is converting to anything," Ian snapped. "Leave her alone, for Christ's sake. That's a long way off. Neither of us have asked, and nobody has said yes."

There was nothing untrue about that statement. He hadn't proposed. I hadn't, either. No real commitments had been made between us. It was all still painfully hypothetical.

"Besides," Ian went on, his anger subdued. "We wouldn't even think about a wedding until I came back from Nassau."

Well. I guess that gave me the answer to question I hadn't even realized I wanted to ask. It wasn't that I expected Ian to set a date after three months, and dating for two years before getting married wasn't unusual. It was just that Ian had talked about it as though he were eager to get the whole marriage-and-family thing kicked off as soon as possible. Was he just downplaying it for his sister?

I valiantly made small talk for the rest of the meal. I learned that Bill had worked at a plant that made parts for cars and that Annie had been a homemaker, but now that Danny was grown, she worked part time at the church office. Danny had gone to Notre Dame on a scholarship and chose to pursue seminary after that.

I also heard some fascinating Ian stories, like his infamous Flock of Seagulls haircut he'd sported in college and his childhood penchant for peeing out of windows. By the end of the dinner, some of my panic had eased, and that was due in large part to Ian himself, and how he behaved toward me. His eyes barely left me throughout the entire meal. He flushed bright red from some of the anecdotes his sister shared, and he hooked his ankle around mine under the table.

Sure, I'd gotten emotional whiplash, but all of that aside, it seemed like it had been a pretty successful dinner.

"Well, I'll get to these dishes," Bill said, pushing back from the table.

"Nah, Dad, I've got them," Danny volunteered.

Bill waved a hand at him. "You don't get many days off. Go take a nap while you can. I've got the whole weekend."

"I can help," I offered, pushing my own chair back.

"And Ian and I can take out the garbage," Annie said. "Starting with that carcass."

The kitchen was a flurry of activity as Annie and Bill got out Tupperware, and Ian and I packaged up the leftovers. Plates were scraped and the "carcass" of the once movie-perfect turkey slid into its own bag. Bill ran water while Ian and Annie lugged the bags out the back door and down the steps.

Bill showed me where the dishrags were, though he wasn't happy about my participation in the chores. "You're a guest. You shouldn't have to do the washing up."

"The washing up," I said with a giggle. "That's so cute."

"You pick up those things from them," he said with a grin. "You'll see."

I smiled right back, but out of the corner of my eye I caught sight of white plastic. "They missed one."

"They'll be in, soon," Bill said placidly.

"I'll grab it." I wasn't trying to get out of doing dishes, but escaping the heat of the tiny kitchen for a second would be nice.

"Don't you need your coat?" Bill asked, but I was already headed to the door, trash bag in tow.

"The cold will be good for me," I said cheerfully. Then I backed out of the door into a cloud of what could only be cigarette smell.

"Ian?" I frowned and waved at the blue curls wafting through the air from where he and his sister stood. "You smoke?"

"No," he said guiltily, hiding the cigarette behind his back.

"Then is your coat on fire?" Was it weird to be mad at him over this? He was an adult, after all. But it seemed like it might have come up at one point or another, if he wasn't actively hiding it.

"He quit a long time ago." Annie reached behind him and snagged the cigarette, and he cursed and brought his knuckles to his mouth. "I'm a bad influence on him."

"You burned my fucking hand, is what you did." Ian pressed the backs of his fingers to the metal stair railing. "Sorry, Penny. I swear, this isn't a regular occurrence."

"No, don't worry. It's, um." I shook my head. "No, don't worry about it."

"Don't tell on me, would you?" Annie asked, motioning to the house. "I think I do a good job of hiding it."

"It must run in the family." I jerked my thumb over my shoulder. "I'm going to go back in."

"I'll be along in a minute." Ian scuffed the soles of his shoes on the pavement. "I'll need ice for my hand."

I hoped he didn't think I'd be getting that ice. He'd burned his hand being all deceptive and smoky. That was his injury to deal with. Then, I remembered, "Well, I have to put this trash away first, actually."

"No, let me," he said, stepping up to take the handles of the bag from my hand. "Consider it my penance."

I went back inside and hoped Bill wouldn't smell the smoke on me. "Okay, trash is taken care of."

"Ian and Annie out there having a cigarette?" Bill asked, wiping a glass dry.

I froze. "You know about that?"

"Oh, yeah. They think they're real sneaky. Annie hides her smokes in the ceramic frog at the bottom of the steps." He shrugged. "It gives them some private time."

"They seem really close," I observed, slowly invading Bill's personal space until he moved over and let me help by washing the dishes.

"Well, after what happened— Ian did tell you what happened, didn't he?" Bill asked.

I lowered my voice. "With Robbie and Cathy? Yeah."

"All the kids were real close after that. Not so much now that they're all split up all over the place. But get them together, and it's like they see each other every day, you know?" Bill spoke of the family with such affection, it made me long to be a part of it. "But being the only two over here, Annie and Ian are kind of the only family they've got."

They definitely behaved the way I assumed siblings would.

"Look," Bill said suddenly. "This isn't my place. But don't let Annie scare you off. She's just being protective, after the way things ended with Gena."

Considering how helpless Ian felt over what had happened to their siblings, I couldn't blame her for wanting to keep the rest of them safe from every kind of hurt possible. "I know. And I promise, I'm not out to hurt Ian. That's the last thing I would want to do."

"She's not worried about you hurting Ian. She's worried about him hurting you. Because of the cheating."

The puke feeling from earlier returned with such a vengeance that I clenched my back teeth before I could speak again. "Right. Because he cheated on Gena," I bluffed, hoping I was wrong.

Bill nodded as he rinsed the suds off the plate I handed him with numb fingers. "Annie's worried because she thinks once someone cheats, they're going to do it again, no matter what. But that's not always the case. Ian and Gena had real problems."

Ian and Penny had some real problems, too. He'd cheated on his wife? And he hadn't told me? Worse, he'd *lied* to me about it. "Yeah, the thing about how she didn't want to have kids."

Bill frowned. "Gena wanted kids. They went to a fertility

specialist and everything."

The air in the room became very thin. The blood drained from my face and my extremities, racing toward my suddenly pounding heart.

"Oh, gosh." Bill's face was ashen. "I said too much."

"No, it's fine. It's fine." I flinched at the sound of the back door opening.

"Bill, you look like you're going to pass out," Ian said with a laugh. "What did you do to him?"

I would not cry. I absolutely forbid myself from crying. I turned to Ian. "We were just talking about you and Gena."

Ian's eyes went wide. "No, no, no." He looked to Bill and Annie before his eyes flicked back to me. "Penny, it's not what it probably sounded like."

"I don't think this is the proper place to discuss this," I said, and I could have sworn it was my mother's voice coming out of my mouth. "Let's go talk about it in the car while you drive me home." I gave Annie and Bill truly grateful glances. If they hadn't welcomed me into their home, I wouldn't have found any of this out until it was too late.

I really owed them one.

"Thanks for inviting me today. It really was a lovely meal. I definitely got to know someone better." My voice cracked, and I turned for the door.

In the living room, Danny lay on the couch, watching an episode of some car show on the television. He sat up when I grabbed my coat off the rack by the door.

"You're going?" he asked, and though I felt terrible for not responding, I couldn't trust myself to speak.

I ran out to the car then stood stupidly on the sidewalk, because I didn't have the keys.

Ian was just a few moments behind me, pulling his coat on with an agitated curse.

*This isn't the place for this. This isn't the place for this*, I reminded myself. But I couldn't hold back. "Thank you for bringing me here. I got a much clearer picture of who you are."

"Penny, there is a perfectly reasonable explanation for this," he tried to assure me.

"You've been saying that a lot, lately." *But he did have a perfectly good reason last time.* At least, he'd said he had. His dinner with Carrie Glynn only seemed innocent without the knowledge that he was a liar and a cheat. Now that I knew…

"And you've been assuming the worst of me a lot, lately," he argued. "Get in the car. I don't want to have this fight on the sidewalk in front of my sister's house."

"Don't tell me what to do!" I shouted. I was so angry I didn't care who overheard us. "And don't try to be fucking reasonable about this. You cheated on your ex-wife!"

"I didn't cheat on Gena!" He started off shouting but quickly lowered his voice to that maddening calm tone again. "I told Annie that I cheated on Gena so she wouldn't know the real reason we got divorced."

"On what planet is that supposed to make sense to me, Ian? 'I didn't want my sister to know that my marriage broke up because of this totally not horrible reason, so I told her I was a complete asshole instead?'" Did he think I was an idiot?

"I know it sounds implausible—"

"Implausible?" I laughed, because it was that fucking ridiculous. "Ian, why should I trust you?"

"When have I lied to you before?" he demanded.

"You told me that Gena didn't want to have children. Bill says that the two of you saw a fertility doctor." I folded my arms over my chest, because it was cold and because I felt like I might need to hold my heart it. "You apparently smoke, that's out of left field—"

"I smoke an occasional cigarette, that doesn't make me a murderer!"

"But it does mean that there are some fairly simple things

about you that you haven't bothered to share with me. Do you think if you just don't tell me things, they don't count?" My throat stuck shut. I pressed my fingers to the sudden throbbing in my temple. "How do you really know Carrie Glynn?"

*Please, tell me I'm being paranoid. Tell me I'm too suspicious. Tell me something I can believe, so I can still love you.*

A muscle in his jaw shifted. "We used to work together. And we slept together a few times."

I gulped in air, the last desperate gasp as I sank into the reality of what this conversation really was.

We were breaking up.

"I would have told you—"

"And you and Gena. Did you try to have a baby?"

He looked away. That stupid look away that made it so he didn't have to commit to confronting reality. "We did see a fertility doctor. And we did try to have a baby, for over a year."

I squeezed my eyes shut. My tears went from hot to shockingly cold on my cheeks.

"Penny, I promise you, all of this… It seems indefensible. I know that it must look like I'm this…pathological liar, but I'm not."

Was there an explanation? Or would it just be more lies? "No. You cheated on your ex-wife, and you lied to me about it. You know what I just went through—"

"Oh, for fuck's sake, I am not Brad!" Ian shouted, finally losing his cool. "You were hurt, and I understand that, but I'm not going to be punished for something someone else did to you. If you need to work out your feelings about your last relationship, feel free to end this one!"

An hour ago, we'd been fine. And now, we were…

Oh god. We were over.

"Just take me home," I said. All the fight had gone out of me. I just wanted to get away from him, to retreat to my bed and stay there all weekend. Which sucked, because I'd been planning on spending the weekend in his bed. The thought crushed me. "No, wait. Take me to the nearest train."

For a guy with a passionate need to explain himself, Ian sure was silent on the drive to the nearest station. And I was glad. I didn't want this to be happening, but I would be an idiot if I let him lie to me, anymore.

As he pulled the car up to the curb, he finally spoke. "I don't want to break up, Penny."

"Well, you don't really get a say," I snapped. It was easier to be angry than sad.

"I was going to say," he began again with emphasis. "I don't want to break up. But I do wonder if you and I both needed more time to get over our last relationships."

*Why did you say that?* I wanted to punch myself. *If you'd just said you don't want to break up, either, maybe you'd still be together. Maybe this wouldn't be happening.*

"I do love you, Penny. But our timing is…" He stopped. "Maybe I go to Nassau, and when I get back…"

"When you get back, you won't have lied to me?" I didn't want to face it, but that was the truth. No amount of time was going to change my hurt. Ian had lied to me, he'd probably cheated on me with Carrie fucking Glynn, and now, he was going to move to the Bahamas for a year and a half and probably cheat on me there, too. There was no sense in setting up some stupid long-distance maybe and waiting around for him. "When you get back, I've spent two years waiting for you, without being with you, on the off chance that you'll be different?"

He didn't have an argument for that, and I didn't care to pursue one with him.

"I love you, too," I said, my voice breaking. "Or at least the parts of you that were real."

"Penny—" he began, but I pushed the door open and got out. I closed it behind me, silently praying, *Please follow me. Please stop me. Don't let me walk away from you.*

My feet and brain had better sense than my heart. I kept walking. I didn't need another liar. I didn't need another guy who would hurt me. I needed the man I'd been in love with this morning.

I'd never really had that man at all.

I heard the car's tires as he pulled away, and I stopped where I stood, my pulse pounding so hard in my throat that I thought it would choke me. I wanted to run after him, screaming and waving my arms and promising that I could just ignore the gigantic lie he'd been feeding me for months.

Instead, I got on the train.

## CHAPTER EIGHTEEN

"Okay, Bella Swan," Rosa said, plopping down beside me on my bed. "Time to get up."

"It's Saturday," I mumbled, still facing the wall.

"Yes, and you have been spending every Saturday in bed." She gave my butt a push. "Get up. The holidays are over. You've got to get past this before Valentine's day or you'll spiral even worse."

We'd been going through this every Saturday since mid-December. Rosa had been fine with it at first, and it hadn't affected my job performance…much. But even I had to admit that this whole weekend depressive thing wasn't healthy all these weeks later.

Health be damned. I still wanted to wallow, and January was a perfect wallow month. "Just leave me here. I'll die an old spinster, like the curse says."

"The curse is not—"

"I know the curse isn't real. But I feel like I willed it into being. Look what happened." I'd had the same conversation with myself over and over, trying to decide if it was a good thing I'd picked Ian for my first time if this was the outcome. It hurt bad. And I couldn't tell if it felt so much worse than my other breakups because I'd had sex with him or because he really was supposed to have been my true love.

No, he wasn't my true love. Because your true love didn't pretend to be someone he wasn't. Your true love didn't lie to you. I couldn't remember a single fairy tale where Prince Charming had cheated on his ex-wife.

"You have got to stop with this magical thinking bullshit. Do you really think this happened because you fucked him? People fuck and breakup all the time. That's not a sign. It's just something that happens." Rosa sounded annoyed at having to repeat her lines in this conversation yet again. "Don't you have that benefit tonight?"

"Yeah, for Mr. Elwood's charity." I rubbed my eyes. "I really don't feel like getting dressed up tonight."

"Normally, I would ask you if you absolutely had to go, but I don't really care." Rosa rubbed my back then plucked at my gnarly T-shirt. I'd slept in it and cried myself to sleep on most nights during the week. "Although staying home and doing laundry would probably be a great idea."

I pushed myself up and squinted at the time on my phone. It was almost two in the afternoon. I really did have to get up and start getting around. I would need a shower and to shave basically everything. My gown was black and strapless, so some light bronzing lotion on my shoulders wouldn't hurt, either. I needed to do my nails—there wouldn't be time to go to a salon—then put on makeup… Ugh. The whole process was exhausting. "No, I have to go."

"There's that enthusiasm for life you're known for," Rosa said dryly. "But you might meet someone. Some rich someone."

"I'm not I the mood for rich." I'd had rich. Or, at least, richer than I was, and about to get richer. "It didn't go well."

I would take a guy I would have to financially support for the rest of our lives, just as long as he wasn't a liar.

"Wow, your phone has been blowing up," Rosa said, reaching for it on the nightstand. "Are you answering it?"

"Just for work stuff." I said with a shrug.

"Is he still calling?" The way Rosa said it made it sound like Ian was stalking me, and he wasn't. He'd tried a few times before he'd given up. My voicemail had messages from him in it, but I hadn't listened to them. I'd been telling everyone my voicemail wasn't working.

"He hasn't called since before Christmas. Maybe he's already gone to the Bahamas." The thought hurt me more than it should have. He seemed farther away. Then again, if he wasn't in New York, there was no chance of running into him anywhere. Like at the benefit tonight.

"You haven't checked your voicemail since before Christmas?" Rosa's long curls rustled as she shook her head. "Penny…"

"I know." I took the phone from her hand. "Is there coffee?"

"It's two in the afternoon," she reminded me.

I gave her my best big, pleading look.

"Fine." She stood and headed to my door. "But only if you check your messages."

She was right. I had to do it, sometime. Besides, I didn't have to actually listen to the messages. I could wait until they started playing and hit the delete button. If I was fast enough, I never had to hear his voice.

My hand trembled. I couldn't ignore this forever. I knew it was going to suck, but I would have to just forge through. I hit the voicemail icon and entered my password.

"November thirtieth, three P.M.," the voice droned robotically. I wanted to hit delete, I really did. But another part of me whispered, *This is the last time you'll hear his voice*. Then, it was too late.

"Hey, Doll. It's me."

*Doll*. My face crumpled into an ugly cry at the word.

"I know you don't want to talk to me. But I'm hoping that you will, eventually. When you do, I'm here." There was a long pause, and I imagined him looking away, running his hand through his hair, unable to think of what to say next. "I love you. I hope we'll talk later."

I sat there, paralyzed for a moment, then hit delete. It was like cutting off a finger.

"December seventh, Two P.M." All the calls seemed to have come during work hours. Not at drunk o'clock at night.

"Hey, Doll. It's me."

I hiccuped back a sob.

"I was just hoping… Ah, I don't know what I was hoping. I love you."

The message ended, and I hit delete again. It wasn't any easier.

The next two messages were the same, just days apart, both of them beginning, "Hey, Doll. It's me," and ending with "I love you."

Then I got to the fifth message, the final time he'd called me, the day before Christmas Eve.

"Hi, Penny."

I covered my mouth to stifle the shocked wail that welled up painfully in my chest.

"This is the last call, I promise. You don't want to speak to me. But I had to let you know… I never lied about how much I loved you."

*Loved.* Past tense.

"You made me so happy. And you're worth so much more than you believe you are. Please, don't forget that."

That was where the message ended. No "I love you." No promise that if I wanted to talk, he would be there.

I'd thought we were over before, because I hadn't been speaking to him. I'd thought I was letting the relationship die. Instead, it had languished on life support, until Ian had been forced to pull the plug. Listening to these messages, I felt like we were actually, finally over.

Now that his offer had expired, all I wanted was to speak to him, to tell him how stupid I'd been.

I must have been crying louder than I thought, because Rosa knocked on my door, then barged right in. She sat beside me on my bed and pulled me into her arms, petting my head and soothing me like I was a child.

It was over. Ian and I were over. And I still loved him.

* * * *

The Elwood Rape Crisis Resource Center was a huge building on the Lower West Side. It used to be a bank before it had been remodeled into the hulking facility it was now. There were several floors for inpatient mental health services, as well as counseling offices and a temporary shelter for people who needed to escape abusive situations. There was also an education and conference center that took up most of the lower level. Sophie had given a tour to those of us who would be working the party, and she'd explained her husband's commitment to his cause.

He'd been all over the media lately, lauded for being open about being a survivor himself. I was impressed by how willing he was to talk about the frame of mind that had kept him from acknowledging his assault for decades and his belief that better education and a more open dialogue about rape would help victims seek help when they needed it.

He'd spent so much of his own money on the place, he'd gone from tenth richest British person to the thirteenth. When I'd first heard those figures, I'd thought, "Oh, boo hoo," but that had passed quickly when I'd realized exactly how much he'd been willing to part with. It was no small potatoes.

The gala ball tonight was to raise even more money, and from the looks of the crowd, they would get it. The brightly lit atrium was filled to capacity with people in black tie. I'd seen a large percentage of the faces around me in magazines and on television.

I was pretty sure I'd just been in the bathroom with Gillian Anderson. But it could have just been another inhumanly beautiful person.

Guests milled around the fountain, a bronze rectangle with water that flowed down both sides, and waiters wove around with trays of champagne. The stairs curving to the second floor in a long arch could have come out of a palace in a fantasy movie, the first step an impossibly wide circle, the rest growing smaller the higher they got, until they were normal stair size.

I wondered if Ian's firm had a hand in designing this place, but those stairs definitely didn't seem like his style.

A big-band-style orchestra played on a temporary stage,

and a dance floor had been laid over the marble tile. I stood at the edge, my gaze flicking over the crowd. I knew I looked super hot, because Rosa had helped me with my hair, which swept back from my forehead in stiff waves that wouldn't move in a hurricane but looked chic and sophisticated, as befitting someone who worked at the hippest digital fashion magazine on the internet. When I'd shown Sophie my tight, floor-length, strapless black velvet gown a week ago, she'd praised its retro look and loaned me a thick silver choker from her mother's collection of 1990's jewelry. It really went perfectly with the whole Sharon Stone look I had going on.

So, working my hotness? Not a problem. But even though there were some incredibly sexy men in the place tonight, and I'd had more than one approving nod from some of them, romance was the last thing on my mind. I still had a misery hangover from my earlier trip down breakup voicemail road.

Which was a shame, considering my cleavage was impressive enough to hide a cell phone. And it actually was; my job tonight was to mind Sophie's phone, and my boobs were the only place I could think of to put it.

*Okay, Penny. Time to snap out of your funk. You didn't get this dressed up to do nothing.* I squared my shoulders and prepared to find a dance partner. Maybe even an anonymous sex partner. That might also be fun.

Bad breakup, new Penny.

That's when I saw Ian. Standing across the room, a glass of champagne in his hand, decked out in a tuxedo that made him look like James motherfucking Bond.

I felt like I'd been shot. This was so unfair. Why now? Why when I'd just gotten my confidence up? Why on the very day I'd listened to the progression of his messages from "Hey, Doll, I *love* you," to "Hi Penny, I *loved* you?"

But, for as handsome as he looked, he also looked really miserable. *Good.*

A part of me hoped that he would pretend he hadn't seen me, and we wouldn't speak. Another part of me desperately wanted him to approach.

The former part was disappointed, as my feet moved without permission from my brain or heart. My first instinct was to run from the hurt I knew I was about to feel, but even in my wounded and heartbroken state, I knew that was ridiculous. So, rather than turn in the other direction, I met him on the other side of the dance floor.

He looked even better close up, where I could gaze into his gorgeous green eyes and remember the width of his shoulders. *Take me back. Please, take me back*, I wanted to say, but what came out was, "Ian, what are you doing here?"

*What do you think he's doing here? He's Neil's friend.* I don't know why I hadn't anticipated this.

Were Ian's eyes actually watering? "I came to get you."

Okay. There were definitely less alarming things to say to your ex-girlfriend.

"That turned out creepier than I intended." He ran a hand through his hair, ruffling it from it's perfectly combed state. "But I want you back. I want you to come with me to Nassau. We can get a nice apartment with a pool and ocean views. We can go on the fucking *House Hunters* show if you want. Be their token older man, younger woman couple who can't agree on anything—"

"Ian…" I interrupted him, but I didn't have anything to say. I just didn't want him to keep dangling that hope when I couldn't even believe if this was really happening.

"You said once that you believed whatever happens between us, we would be together in the end. I believe that, too. I was stupid. I was so fucking stupid to say what I did to you. And to not fight harder for you. But I want you."

I took a breath so deep and sudden I worried that Rosa's double-sided-tape trick would fail me.

"I know you don't believe me, but I never cheated on Gena. I wish I could make you understand why I would lie about it to Annie—"

"Don't." I didn't want to hear about this. Not when my brain and my heart were going head-to-head. Whatever was in his past was in his past. It was over and done with, and it couldn't hurt me. And though I had nothing but my trust in him to guarantee that he would be faithful, that trust was so strong, I wondered how it had ever faltered. I wiped a tear away from my eye with my thumb and cut him off. "Dance with me?"

He accepted my invitation with a quiet, "Of course."

The band was playing that old standard, "I Wanna Be Around", which was the most horribly inappropriate song to heal a breakup to, but I didn't care. The moment his arm encircled my waist and he pulled me against him, everything I'd felt for him roared back to life like a fire out of control, burning me up with fear and sadness and exhilarating joy. It was all too much, and I gripped his shoulder as we started to move, as though by physically holding him, I could keep him forever. "I don't want to do this, anymore, Ian. I don't want to be without you."

"And I don't want you to rush into coming back to me." He paused. "I do want you to come back to me. I would love it if you rushed. But I want to earn your trust."

I leaned my head on his chest to hide my tears. "We have so much time to worry about that. But the way I feel about you? It isn't going to go away because of a lie you told someone in your past," I promised. "This isn't going to be perfect. It might take a long time to get back to where we were. But it will be worth it. And for right now? I just want you."

"You have me, Doll. You've always had me."

Relief overwhelmed me. I lifted my head and asked, "What if I said no to leaving New York? What if I told you I wanted to stay here? That I wanted you to stay here?"

There was no question in my mind that I was going. But I wanted to know if this was conditional. If it was, I didn't know how I would feel.

"I would turn down the job," he answered without hesitation.

"Ian…" I shook my head. What a stupid, impetuous man I'd fallen for. "That would destroy your career."

"I know." He shrugged. "I want you more."

"More than—"

"More than a few million dollars, yeah."

Holy shit. I hadn't realized he was going to make *that* big a commission. And he was willing to turn it down to be with me?

All I'd ever heard, my entire life, was how much I cost. My private schooling, my braces, the amount of cereal I went through in a week. How little my job made. How important it was to find a rich man, a nice house. I'd never heard anyone say I was *worth* something.

"You're such an idiot," I blurted then laughed. "I'm not really going to ask you to turn down the job. Of course I'm going with you. Do you have any idea how much snorkeling I can do down there?"

"Oh, you…" he started, but he leaned down to kiss me, and that was all that mattered in the world. His arm around me tightened, and my mouth opened under his. We weren't dancing anymore, just standing there, lost in each other.

I was still technically at work, and I really couldn't be doing this. At least, not in front of all of these people.

But it wasn't like the first floor wasn't full of brand new, totally unoccupied conference rooms.

I pulled back and looked up at him, naughty bravery swelling inside me. "Come with me."

I dragged him off the floor, hoping we wouldn't look too conspicuous cutting through the crowd that was gathering at the base of the stairs. It was almost time for Mr. Elwood to thank everyone. I'd overheard him practicing his speech with Sophie shortly after we'd first arrived. We had some time.

Ian and I hurried past the coat chec,k and I pushed open one of the doors that closed off a hallway. It was dark inside, lit only by the red exit signs above us and at the far end.

"What is this?" Ian whispered as the door shut behind us.

I hoped they didn't lock. But that was a problem for future Penny.

"It's like a conference center thing," I whispered back. "Sophie gave us a tour the other day."

"So, what are we doing here?" he teased as we waded farther into the darkness. "Corporate espionage?"

"No." Wasn't it obvious? The nearest door was unlocked, and I pushed it open. "Looking for a place to fuck."

I grabbed his shirtfront and pulled him inside with me. I jerked my dress up to my waist and hopped up on the table. "I love you. And I'm so glad we're back together. And we've got plenty of stuff we still need to talk out, but I'm asking you, please, please fuck me."

Sure, there were other things that needed our attention. Like working out my trust issues and his need to lie to keep everyone happy. I didn't want to think about that until later, when my body wasn't so hungry for him.

I thought he would push my panties to the side and slip into me. Instead, he dropped to his knees, hooked my legs over his shoulders, grabbed the sides of my panties, and ripped them off.

*Oh my god.* "I can't believe you did that!"

I didn't even care that they were a favorite pair. I gushed at the desperate need in the gesture. "Please," I begged him, and his tongue swept over me, between my folds. I braced myself on one hand, so I could stay upright, but the other sank into Ian's hair, holding him tight to me. He sucked my clit into his mouth and started the flicking motion with his tongue that always pushed me over the edge.

It was a good thing there was a party going on outside, because I couldn't keep quiet. A mixture of desire and happiness and relief wrenched from my throat in moans and shouts. I pounded the table with my palm and jerked Ian's hair so hard I was sure I hurt him. I came with a long, loud wail, flashes of light behind my eyelids.

Ian lifted his head, gasping for air, and I almost came, again, just from the sound. It was less sexy when he said, "I don't have a condom. So does this work for now?"

No. Not even a little. And that wasn't the only thing that influenced my decision. I wanted my life to be with him. Everything had moved so fast already, did it really matter if we threw caution to the wind and let fate decide when our next big step came?

"I don't care." I slid off the table and stepped up close to him, reaching down to unzip his trousers. "Just fuck me. Whatever happens, happens, okay?"

He hesitated for a frozen second. He said, "Yeah, I'm okay with that."

My heart clenched. I actually kind of hoped I would get pregnant tonight. Not because I thought it would keep us together, but because I was so damn impatient to get the future we'd planned, then abandoned. Sure, it was unrealistic, hormone-fueled, and probably a terrible idea. But it would be some conception story.

He helped me onto the table, my already rumpled dress irrevocably creased where it was caught between us. He spread my thighs, then he was inside of me, all of him in one deep thrust. He pulled one of my legs to lock around his back, sinking deeper. But before we could even get going, it was all over for him. His fingers dug into my hips and he pounded into me, so hard it hurt, and I welcomed it. Every sensation grounded me in the reality that this was actually happening. We were *us,* again. I felt him jerk inside me, and the wet burst that came on the heels of his deep groan.

"I'm sorry," he said, slightly breathless. "I thought that would be…better."

I almost laughed at him and his sense of duty when it came to sex. He was still throbbing in me, spiking pleasure through me with every twitch of his cock, and he was apologizing? "No, it was…" I sighed to release some of the happy pressure in my chest. "This is perfect. You're with me, and we're perfect."

He pulled out with a pained noise, and a trickle of wetness followed. I thought of walking back out to the party bare beneath my dress, my thighs sticky with evidence of what we'd been doing in here, and I felt like the sexiest woman who'd ever lived.

*The party!* I was supposed to be out there, available if Sophie needed help remembering names or something. Ian helped me find my panties, and he kept them. Because he was nothing if not a total perv.

And I loved him. I loved him so much, I wanted to run around in circles, shouting about it. But, at the moment, I had my job to do. "I should get back out there. I'm technically on the clock, and this…"

Ian laughed at me as I struggled to free Sophie's phone from my sweaty cleavage. I would definitely use a sanitizing wipe on it before I returned it to her. I shrugged. "It's Sophie's. Ah, shit. I missed a call."

Ian took my hand and lifted it to his lips. "Go. We've got all the time in the world after tonight."

"Yeah." I looked down, a smile bending my lips. "We do."

"You go first. I'll follow behind," he suggested, but he didn't release me. He pulled me in for another kiss, which I happily accepted. A few seconds more couldn't hurt.

The phone rang again, and he stepped back. "Go."

I lifted my skirt up to better run in my heels. I could only imagine what I would look like when I emerged in the atrium. But it didn't matter. Nothing mattered but Ian and me, and all the changes we had ahead of us.

I couldn't wait to see what they were.

There are two sides to every story…

Read Ian's in

# FIRST TIME
## (Ian's Story)

By Abigail Barnette

**AVAILABLE NOW IN PAPERBACK AND EBOOK
FROM ONLINE RETAILERS**

**Also by Abigail Barnette**

THE BOSS
THE GIRLFRIEND
THE BRIDE
THE EX

BAD BOY, GOOD MAN


**By Jenny Trout**

CHOOSING YOU


**Coming soon**

**A new chapter of the internationally bestselling
Sophie Scaife series**

**THE BABY**

**November 2015**

**Abigail Barnette** is the pseudonym of **Jenny Trout,** an author, blogger, and funny person. Jenny made the *USA Today* bestseller list with her debut novel, *Blood Ties Book One: The Turning.* Her *American Vampire* was named one of the top ten horror novels of 2011 by *Booklist* Magazine Online. As Abigail Barnette, Jenny writes award-winning erotic romance, including the internationally bestselling *The Boss* series.

As a blogger, Jenny's work has appeared on *The Huffington Post*, and has been featured on television and radio, including *HuffPost Live, Good Morning America, The Steve Harvey Show*, and National Public Radio's *Here & Now*. Her work has earned mentions in *The New York Times* and *Entertainment Weekly.*

She is a proud Michigander, mother of two, and wife to the only person alive capable of spending extended periods of time with her without wanting to kill her.

28035207R00162

Made in the USA
Middletown, DE
30 December 2015